Tales of Hardooth 6

MORE TROUBLE, MORE ENEMIES

Dara J. Carr

Tales of Hardooth 6

MORE TROUBLE, MORE ENEMIES

Dara J. Carr

Harrison House Publishing

Tales of Hardooth 6: More Trouble, More Enemies
All Rights Reserved
Copyright © 2018 Dara J. Carr
Edited by Betty Powell and Linda S. Carr
Covr Artwork by Eric A. Carr

Harrison House Publishing
www.theharrisonhousepublishing.com
info@theharrisonhousepublising.com
ISBN: 978-0-9996147-3-0
Library of Congress Control Number: 2018957368
Harrison House Publishing and the "HH" logo are trademarks belonging to Harrison House Publishing.

PRINTED IN THE UNITED STATES OF AMERICA

This story is fictional. No actual person or event is depicted. Any similarity with any person, living or dead, or any event, is entirely coincidental and unintentional.

OTHER BOOKS BY

DARA J. CARR

The Semi-Dragon Tale

Revenge Cometh Forth

Here Are My Shorts (a collection of short stories)

Volunteer…Spy?

The Original Owlam

What New Things We Can Learn?

The Lies We Tell to Survive

Countless Enemies and Discoveries

Enemies From Beyond

MORE TROUBLE, MORE ENEMIES

1

The Command Staff did everything that they could to keep in touch with the Teams assigned to spying on the six enemies. Almost 1,100 enemy ships were headed to Hardooth with only one thing in mind – destroy all living things on Hardooth in order to make sure they get the guilty party. Seeing as how Hardooth was the only inhabited planet anywhere near that area, the guilty party had to be on that planet, in spite of the low technology.

Wymini was listening to the recordings from the conference by the enemies. She pounded her fist on the table. "I need someone in here…who can translate that *chokwad* Doolood language."

"It has been translated," said Jeejow. "What more do you need?"

"It's more complicated than the others. I can hear what's being said with the others and…actually figure out what they're saying. Those Dooloods….it just doesn't come through."

Bonarain shook her head sadly. "What do you not understand, Sir?"

Wymini played the recording: *"Thoo soom hooppooned wooth oos."*

Bonarain smiled, trying to hide that she was ready to laugh out loud. "The same happened with us, is what was said."

Wymini played it three more times. She sighed and played the next line. *"Oovoory shoop coolld oon thoot thooy woore oondoor oottoock, froom oossooloonts thoot thooy cooldn't soo… oon oonoo soottoong."*

Bonarain pursed her lips and sniffed. "Every ship called in that they were under attack, from assailants that they couldn't see…on any setting."

Wymini licked her lips as she listened to the recording again. "With you here…it is finally coming through…but…I still…am not getting it thoroughly." She played the next line. *"Whoovoor woos oottookoong…thooy hoov oo vooroo noostoo oond poowoorfool ploosmoo boom thoot…ooroodoocootoos booyoond oonoothoong thoot woo hoov oovoor oomoogoonooned…oor oosed oogoonst ooch oothoor."*

Bonarain was able to hide her laughter a little better than before. "Whoever was attacking…they have a very nasty and powerful plasma beam that…eradicates beyond anything that we have ever imagined…or used against each other."

"Okay," said Wymini. "Then later on, the fishies made another statement." She hit buttons until she came to that part. *"Thoo gloos boorroor wools. Thoo thoongs thoot took oon hoondrood fooftoo-soox goonoorootoons too boold, woor doostrooyood oon oone dooy."*

Bonarain nodded. "The glass barrier walls. The things that took one hundred fifty-six generations to build, were destroyed in one day."

Wymini then played the last line. "*Oot wool took oot loost fooftoo goonoorootoons too roopoor thoot doomooge.*"

Bonarain nodded again. "It'll take at least fifty generations to repair that damage."

Wymini nodded. "This all means that their lives depend on those barrier walls. If that is what it means."

"Yes, Sir," said Bonarain. "They built those massive barrier walls to keep the big sea monsters out. As long as they keep them out of the cities, they can thrive... building spaceships, firestorm weapons and computers. If the walls are gone, they have to hide in caves that are too small for the sea monsters to enter. They can't live like an advanced society...without the barrier walls. As long as they don't have them...they're not much of a threat to us."

Wymini looked up from the report. "What about the others? What is slowing any of *them* down?"

Master Officer, Skalix answered. "Four of them...we destroyed their home planets. The Choks, the Jowfoonda and the Zizzikinza...their home planets will be no good for any inhabitable race...for at least 200 years. The Iyka planet is...permanently dead. We hit it so hard that the residual energy will probably be hanging around for at least 500 years...and during that time, any and all creatures, plants, microorganisms...anything...will die...if they're not dead already. In 500 years, if anyone wants to inhabit that planet, they'll have to do the same thing we did and transplant all of that from another planet, including bacteria and…hope that it can flourish."

Wymini looked a little disgusted. "Why didn't we hit the Doolood with the firestorm weapons as well?"

"How?" Jeejow shrugged. "Remember that the main function is fire. How far would the firestorm burn…underwater? We have no idea. Taking out the big glass barriers was the best way to knock them down a few rungs on the ladder. There's not that much land on the Doolood planet, so a firestorm weapon wouldn't have caused that much crippling damage there. A natural enemy seemed to be far more damaging than the bombs."

Wymini nodded. "Now, the last problem: The Mufayton! What's being done about them?"

Jeejow shook his head. "We've assigned two Teams – 511 and 512 – to spy on the Mufayton…on their ships. It's rather difficult because they're telepaths as well. You can't control them the same way you can control others, plus we can't communicate with our Teams telepathically because the Mufaytons pick it up. Right now, they're attempting to find some landmark on the Mufayton home world…so we can give them some grief as well."

Wymini sighed. "Meanwhile, 1,081 of their conquering spaceships are headed this way to eradicate an enemy that they can't even identify."

Yim nodded his head with a smile. "Yes, 1081 ships that we are going to have to do some clever coordination, in order to hop every one of them into dimension #45. I wonder what will happen when they're all there. I wonder if they'll battle each other…or attempt to figure out how to get back."

Xadorm grunted. "What would you do?"

"We're not talking about you or I," said Yim with a grin. "We're talking about six arrogant, antagonistic and ambitious conquerors, who will be placed in a situation that they are totally unfamiliar with."

"I suggest we decide on what we do, once it all happens… and we survive the encounter…without being eradicated," said Wymini. "Right now, does anyone know where those…enemies are specifically located?"

"According to all of the reports that are coming back, the armadas are still massing in certain places," said Jeejow. "Once they have all armadas together, then the word will be given and they'll head this way."

"Okay," said Wymini. "So…where are they massing?"

"We still don't understand each and every one of the technical languages of these different peoples…especially the navigation terms," said Jeejow. "Once we can figure that out, we'll know where they are and we'll be able to figure out…where and when they start moving."

Wymini scowled. "Then let's get some of our computer geniuses aboard the ships that have already massed…and try to figure it out."

Several members of the spy Teams Jumped back to Hardooth and escorted the computer personnel to the appropriate armada. Within three days all of the information was coming back to Hardooth from everyone except the Mufayton armada. The Owlamites in the Mufayton armada had to be extremely careful about when or how they transmitted. They did transmit that half the armada was at one collection point, however, they did not know exactly where it was.

All five of the other races had at least 75% of their group assembled and according to what could be pulled out of their computers, once they were all together, it would take six days for them to get to Hardooth at maximum speed.

"That tells us a little bit of how much time we have to prepare for their arrival," said Wymini. "Can you imagine what #45 will look like with all of these *chokwads* floating around there…with no target anywhere in sight?"

"We have a new report from the spies," said Jeejow. "It seems that none of the enemies gave the information accurately. Between the six of them, they have devoted 1,081 ships to this attack. In reality, they collectively have held back some 1,211 other attack ships…not just from this attack, but from each other."

Yim snarled. "What kind of people are they? They'll attack and enslave without any scruples, but they befriend each other…yet lie to each other. I don't understand."

"That's part of this last report," said Jeejow. "They really don't like each other at all. They all want to conquer the other five, but they're all just too powerful. They'll attack a common foe…together, but that is where it ends. They all want to conquer the galaxy and be the supreme ruler over all of it. But they realize that the other ambitious conquerors all want the same thing and none of them wish to share being the primary ruler."

Xadorm scoffed. "So they just get together in a mass attack in order to assure that there is no *seventh* marauder in this galaxy…that they would have to compete with."

"How diplomatically hypocritical of them," said Inditam sarcastically.

Wymini hung her head. "The only way that we're going to stop them from harassing us…is to wipe out their power… completely. Until they've been subdued, this fighting will only go on…forever."

"In other words," said Marbing. "We have to crush all six. We have to make them mad enough to send the rest of their power against us…and we have to defeat both mass armadas."

Wymini just looked up and nodded.

"We can't afford to make any mistakes," said Skalix.

A call came in from Officer Grade 4, Azhazha. **"We've got a home planet landmark for the Mufayton**!"

Wymini sat there a little surprised. "Who is…Azhazha?"

Jeejow smiled. "That would be the Team Leader for the two Teams that are spying on the Mufayton for us."

"All right," said Wymini. "So why didn't she give us more details?"

"Remember," said Jeejow. "The Mufayton are telepathic as well. Our people can only send one little message telepathically and then keep quiet for a long time, otherwise the Mufayton will zero in on them and that could be disastrous…for our personnel."

Skalix scoffed. "All right, how do we get back with them?"

Jeejow shook his head. "Haven't you been reading any of the updates? We can send freely to them, because the Mufayton have a limited range on what they can pick up. Our people will get the message and then – only then – if it's important enough, they'll respond again. Azhazha reported a landmark on the Mufayton home planet, now what are we going to do about that?"

Wymini smiled. "Can Azhazha Jump here?"

"Of course," said Jeejow.

"Then have her do so."

Jeejow closed his eyes and sent a telepathic message for Azhazha to come to the Command Staff conference room. A few moments later, Poroth was ushering Azhazha into the conference room.

Wymini smiled. "So good of you to join us Officer, Azhazha. Now, what about the landmark for Mufayton?"

"Yes, Sir," said Azhazha. "It is a very unique structure on their home planet. We thought, now that we have an individual landmark, someone could go there and start mapping out their planet…just in case someone wants to…hurt them…or stop them…or do whatever you want to…on their home planet."

"Let's wait to see if we survive this attack that's been

planned first," said Wymini. "If we can't get away from those people…what difference does it make?"

Azhazha shrugged and smiled. "Yes, Sir." She ambled out of the conference room.

Jeejow sighed. "I've just received word that…the Choks are on their way." He looked down at the table. "According to what we're getting, they'll be here in two days."

"Start executing the plan," said Wymini quietly.

Team 7016 got the word and was ordered to contact Roodeeska in order to Jump to the flagship.

Bonarain took her position directly behind the Commander of the entire armada. She started getting into his head with the mind reading and mind control. She shook her head in disgust. "**They've committed 176 ships to this mission. They have 210 more in reserve. If the battling spaceships of the other five are destroyed, they're going to launch the 210 after the others. My, aren't we a trustworthy bunch**?"

Everyone in the conference room reacted in different ways to the attitude of the Choks.

Bonarain continued with the mind control as the Owlamites Jumped (in Spy) twenty of their people into each ship in the Chok armada. Each one of them was not a full sized labyrinth collection of pieces like the first one the Owlamites had encountered, however, each one did have several sections. She finally gained full control of the Chok Commander and gave him an order.

The Chok Commander hit a switch on the armrest of his chair. "This is High Fontoolok, Gajatinimondo. We'll be arriving at our waiting point in 39 *tok*-cycles. We have a target date and time to start the attack. Until then, all ships are ordered to maintain complete radio silence. We don't know enough, regarding this enemy, to be prattling on at each other about superfluous information. So keep quiet. We will attack at the appointed time, no matter what."

One of the other officers walked up in front of the Commander's chair. "High Fontoolok, what if we have to make course adjustments…or one of the other five foolish ones tries to contact us?"

"If any of the foolish ones try to contact us, we will worry about that…at that time. If we have to make course adjustments, then the other ships will follow us."

The other officer stood there with his mouth open for a few moments. He headed back to his position. "As the High Fontoolok commands."

Wymini closed her eyes. "**Officer Roodeeska, let me know when everyone is in place**."

"**Yes, Sir, it shouldn't be too long**."

Wymini waited patiently while the Jumps were being finished.

Soolchakan, Kiyalee and Chyning were walking around the Main Bridge, attempting to find anyone that was looking at the other ships in the armada. Since the radio silence had been ordered, someone just might try to keep track – just in case one of the ships malfunctioned and had to fall out of the formation.

Chyning found a Chok officer who was staring at a screen that currently only had one number on the display – 175. She signaled Kiyalee. Kiyalee came to Chyning's position and the two of them, through mind control, paralyzed the officer so that he would not be able to react any changes on his screen.

Roodeeska called back to Wymini. "**All Teams are in place and ready to execute the plan**."

Wymini nodded. "**The Team Leader on each ship will give the order of execution. I'm not going to try to control all of it from here**."

Kiyalee and Chyning watched as the number on the screen started dropping rapidly. The Chok was shocked and he tried to say or do something about it and could not understand why he could not move or talk. Once all of the hops had been accomplished and the entire armada was in Observation dimension, the number went back to a steady 175. The Chok officer was released from the paralysis and he gaped, open mouthed, at his screen. He sat there scratching his chest for several moments. He went back through and checked the figures. Yes, he had seen a fluctuation, however, all ships were accounted for. No ships were missing and all were still in formation. Kiyalee sent a thought through his head of the possibility of the armada flying through some anomalous magnetic area and that was what caused the fluctuation. He looked over to the Science section of the Bridge to see if they had observed anything out of the ordinary. None of them were reacting in any strange manner, so he was left to contemplate and still be baffled as to what had happened.

Roodeeska called back to Wymini. "**The Chok armada is now in Observation dimension. They're still on course and will be at their rendezvous spot in less than two days**."

Wymini smiled. "**Were there any alarms raised**?"

"**None, Sir**."

Wymini snickered. "One down, five to go."

Roodeeska turned to Soolchakan. "You're job here is finished. You may return to Hardooth…and await the next armada."

Soolchakan just grunted and Team 7016 vanished.

When Team 7016 arrived in their apartment, Chyning gave a grunt as well. "My how they love to honor us."

Bonarain huffed. "I'm going to honor myself straight to the bathtub."

"Good idea," said Soolchakan.

Kiyalee turned the computer on. "Here it is. That's the landmark that they said was on Mufayton." She looked at Chyning. "Should we try it?"

Chyning blew a raspberry. "I'm going to take a bath as well."

Kiyalee turned the computer off. "Looks like the Mufayton

will have to wait to get destroyed." She headed up to her bedroom.

Roodeeska called in. **"The Choks have reached their start point for the attack.**"

Wymini responded. **"Are they still unaware of the change?"**

"They're clueless," sent Roodeeska with a snicker.

"We've received word that the Iyka are on their way," sent Wymini. **"Go ahead and hop that whole bunch of Choks into #45. We need all the personnel rested so we can do the hop job on the Iyka as well. We don't know when the others will start our way, so go ahead and put them in Jahong's Death.**"

Roodeeska looked around the Main Bridge of the flagship. **"We've got our order. Hop this bunch into #45 and... then we get to observe them as they...panic or...commit suicide...or...whatever they do.**"

The mass hop from Observation to dimension #45 was done in a very short time. The alarms went off in all of the ships as the sensors could not find any form of a known star anywhere near them. All 176 ships were showing the same emergency code for a major error in the computer system. The error being that the computer had lost sight of the target star system and was requesting information on finding it again. The Choks were at even more of a loss than the computer, once they discovered that there was only one star, that any of them could see, anywhere in the current dimension they were in. None of them self-destructed. They all were digging deep into their computers attempting to find out what had happened. They were getting virtually nothing – as far as positive results.

To assure that the Choks did not find the mass parking of captured ships, the Owlamites had hopped the Chok armada to a position on the exact opposite side of the great star. This placed a major radioactive obstacle between the Choks and the captured ships, plus something around seventy (or more) light years between them.

Roodeeska and the other seven main spies were getting a good giggle over the frustration of the Choks. They were recording all kinds of passwords and codes for the Chok computer system.

Wymini called Team 7016. "**Where are you? We've been trying to reach you and you have failed to respond**."

Soolchakan shook his head in exasperation. He looked up to the clouds. He saw a big one and Jumped himself, with his fighter, to the top of that cloud. He looked for one that was even higher, found it and Jumped to that one. "**This is Officer, Soolchakan of Team 7016. At this time, we were not communicating telepathically because we're on the Mufayton home planet looking for targets. As you know, they're telepaths as well and they can pick us up in either Spy or Observation. We have to concentrate completely on receive and not send, otherwise we give ourselves away. Now, what else did you want to know** regarding this situation, Sir?""

Wymini clenched her teeth. "**The lyka are on their way here and we need you to help in the hop to Observation.**"

Soolchakan hung his head. "**Why? Isn't Officer, Xookooz and his Team capable of doing the job**?"

"**No one else is as capable as your Team. When you're there, things go much smoother.**"

"**Is it possible…just once…to try it…without us… Sir**?"

Wymini looked around the conference table.

"I think we should," said Xadorm with a shrug.

Wymini cocked her head to the side. "Should…what?"

"Try it…at least once, without Team 7016." He shrugged. "What if something were to happen to them? Would we just… give up? No, we'd continue on. I believe that he's right, and we should attempt it without them. If we foul it up…we can always have Officer, Bonarain teach some classes on how to do it…so that we DO all start understanding it and *not* have to depend on one Team…the same Team…all the time."

Wymini sat there pondering. She finally just shook her head. "I can't argue with that. If we're going to depend on one Team…for just about everything…what good are we to ourselves?" She sighed and closed her eyes. "**Officer, Xookooz…you're going to have to have to do the job without Team 7016. They're on another mission. Any objections**?"

Xookooz looked at his Team. "You heard what the boss said. We have to do this. We have to do it without Team 7016. This means that we have to perform…up to the standards set by Team 7016. Is everybody ready?"

"Let's do it," said Quipiama.

The Iyka had the same confusing readouts on their screens as the 197 ships were hopped into Observation. The numbers dropped and then suddenly were back up to the full formation of ships being there, heading for the target star system. They decided to do some trouble-shooting of their computer system in order to find why the anomaly had occurred. Instead they got even more confused because the frequency the galaxy was supposed to be giving off was incorrect. The computer specialists went deeper into the repair and programming in order to find out what the problem was and the Owlamites were delighted as they got more good information on how to get into, control and/or sabotage the Iyka computer system.

Xookooz was rather proud of himself and his Team. They had pulled it off without having to depend on Team 7016. Now all they had to do was wait until the Iyka armada reached the place where they were supposed to launch the attack from – and hop them into dimension #45.

Team 7016 reported to the Command Staff.

"These Mufayton…are some devious people," said Soolchakan. "They have a manufacturing plant where one firestorm weapon comes off of the assembly line every thirty-three heartbeats. They have a massive stockpile of those nasty weapons on their planet and in each spaceship of theirs. They like blowing the *h'oolyach* out of the planets that they conquer. This way, if the unfortunate souls they enslave do figure out some way of escaping…they have nothing to go back to. They are now… homeless wanderers. Of course, they completely gut the planet of all natural resources before they destroy it."

"They also like making the slaves feel even more helpless," said Bonarain. "They make them procreate quickly and then kill the first generation slaves. The second, third, fourth and beyond are all born as slaves and don't know any other lifestyle or language… except to serve the heartless masters."

Am-Sisa looked off and huffed. "So even if we were to figure out a way to free them…they'd have absolutely no idea what to do, where to go or how to take care of themselves. They'd die…without some master telling them what to do."

"I'm afraid so," said Bonarain bitterly.

Wymini nodded. "You say that they have several thousand of those firestorm weapons on their planet?"

Soolchakan cleared his throat. "I'd say closer to…several *hundred* thousand firestorm weapons…everywhere…on that planet."

Wymini nodded. "Give the physicists some landmarks and we'll blow the *h'oolyach* out of their planet. Then *they* won't have anywhere to go back to."

Nine days later, 12,000 nuclear bombs exploded on the

Mufayton home planet. There was no way of telling how long the planet would be a toxic ball of radioactive waste. None of the Owlamites cared either.

Wymini smiled as Hrombisk was ushered in. "I understand that you set off quite a few firestorm weapons."

"Yes, Sir," said Hrombisk. "The firestorms overlapped… in many areas. There's not one piece of any of the four continents that didn't get scorched. We set off a few in island areas as well. The entire planet and the environment is nothing but useless waste because of the residual energy."

"Did you save any of the weapons for us…in the vaults on Zhagool?"

Hrombisk snickered. "The vaults are full to bursting. All twelve are so full of firestorm weapons, we couldn't get another one in any of them if we wanted to."

"Did you bother counting how many were on the planet to begin with?"

Hrombisk grunted in disgust. "We started counting the bombs in the northeast quadrant of the planet. When we got to 170,000, we stopped. No, we did not count all of them in that quadrant. We just let most of them melt in the fires."

Yim leaned forward. "Did you deploy any of the banners… that told them to leave us alone?"

"What for," said Hrombisk? "After the bombs went off, nobody was alive who could send a message…anywhere."

Marbing frowned. "So what do we do with the banners?"

"We could put them in the Mufayton ships," said Inditam. "Tell them to leave us alone, or we'll blow up their ships just like we did their home planet."

"I don't think we want to do that," said Wymini. "If we do that…we might be confessing that it *was* us who did that *chogo* job on their home planet and…they might get just a little more adamant about attacking us…with everything they've got."

"So we tell them nothing," sighed Nantasa.

Wymini just shrugged and nodded.

The same tactics were used on all of the armadas as they got closer to Hardooth. Now there were 1,081 ships floating around lost, in dimension #45. They had no Command Staff to call and request guidance. They had no stars to guide them – except that one massive star in #45. All they had was the ability to keep track of all of the enemy ships in the dimension where they were currently located.

No one was ready to start the shooting match because no matter who started it, they were badly outnumbered. They were all under the impression that if they started the shooting - all five, of the others, would target the instigator. As a result, there was nothing they could do except float around, in their clique, feel angry at their enemies and feel sorry for themselves.

It was nearly a month before all six of the antagonists realized that the bell-shaped conference station was floating around there in #45 with them. It was decided that the top three personnel from each armada should go there for a meeting.

Wymini was listening in to hear all of the information that was happening in #45. When she heard about the bell she sat there pondering. **"How did that thing get there in dimension 45**?"

Soolchakan growled at himself. **"We, of Team 7016, decided that those** *bimyocks* **didn't need it anymore. So we hopped it to dimension 45…for safe keeping. We placed it…where they are…just for general principles**."

Wymini shook her head while Xadorm and Jeejow sat there laughing.

Wymini scowled at the two men. **"It looks to me as if they're going to make use of it**."

Soolchakan frowned. **"And what are they going to do…in or with it**?"

Wymini sat there thinking for several moments. **"Very good question. Make sure that you're there…to listen in on the meeting**."

The three women of Team 7016 glared at Soolchakan. He just shrugged. Team 7016 Jumped to the bell-shaped conference station to listen in when the high brass had their meeting. The wait was not very long.

Before all of the leaders were in the bell station, Wymini called again. **"As soon as all of the leaders have entered the station, hop that bell back to Home dimension**."

All of Team 7016 looked at each other somewhat baffled.

Soolchakan finally gave up trying to speculate. **"Any particular reason you want that done**?"

"Yes! It seems that since we destroyed the home planet of each and every one of them, just like the Teltermak, we have no idea where their new home base of operations is located. The leaders of those armadas should have some kind of a clue as to where it is. If we strand them on that bell, with no backup ship, they'll have to call home, wherever that is, to come rescue them. Once they're rescued, we can find out where the new home is for all of those *bimyocks*."

Soolchakan chuckled. **"Consider it done. When all six are in…off to Home we go."**

Chyning looked around with an evil grin. "Our Supreme Officer is getting crafty."

"She has to be that way," said Bonarain.

"I still think it took her too long to get there," said Chyning.

Soolchakan sighed. "I can hardly wait until we can get rid of all of those Jowfoonda. Then, we all get a brand new, totally updated fighter…for everybody. Think of how old the ones we've been using are getting to be. A new one will be nice."

Kiyalee scoffed. "Think of how old our 459 cannons are. We're still using them. Without the updates…what would we be using?"

"Bow and arrow," said Bonarain flatly.

The six flagships surrounded the bell space station and all started stretching umbilical hallways to the bell. Once in place, a contingency of three of each personnel moved to the bell. They all came in and took their places at the table. They all looked angrily and suspiciously at all of the others.

Bonarain looked around at some of the fancy uniforms and the shiny medals. She snickered. "They sure like to look flashy, don't they?"

Soolchakan grunted. "Who cares? In a moment all of that glitter will be meaningless…when they start panicking and pointing fingers."

Kiyalee looked through one of the umbilical tunnels to the Chok ship. "Should we close these things…or…what?"

"Nah!" said Chyning. "Let's just give them all a nasty surprise."

"I don't know," said Soolchakan. "We do want the *bimyocks* in the bell to survive. That was the entire purpose for allowing this meeting. Let them contact their own people and then we can find out where their new headquarters are…for all six. If these *bimyocks* don't survive…we got nuthin'."

"We'll have to bust em off at the other end," said Chyning. "We can't close this end. We can close the other end…and make it look like a bell that's been shot full of arrows."

Soolchakan turned to Toktaya. "Have you got enough personnel ready to close off the other ends of these tunnels?"

She had an evil grin. "They're already there…ready and

waiting."

Soolchakan nodded. "Okay, but remember, because of those triangle headed Mufayton, we can't do this telepathically… unless it's a one word command."

"I cleared that with some of the others before we came in here," said Toktaya. "When I give the word, the bell will be isolated. After it gets isolated…Team 7016, hop the thing back to Home."

Soolchakan snickered. "We're ready."

Toktaya took a deep breath and let it out slowly. "**Now**!"

An alarm went off in the bell and several loud bangs were heard. Toktaya and her contingency Jumped off of the bell back to their respective ships. Team 7016 hopped the bell back into Home dimension. All of the six races started checking all kinds of things on their keyboards.

The first one to speak was the Jowfoonda. "We…we're back where we belong! The frequency…is correct."

"Not quite," said the Iyka. "We're about seventy *solchim* from where the conference station is supposed to be."

"So what," said the Chok. "At least the star patterns are correct."

The Zizzikinza slammed his fists down. "What is going on here?"

"Woo'r hoom," said the Doolood.

"I know that we're home," said the Zizzikinza. "How did

our ships get to…there…and how did we…get back…here?"

"Who cares," said the Chok. "We're home…and we can call our own ships…from here and…maybe do some more searching. Then we can find out who is behind this horrifying incident."

Soolchakan got in his fighter and moved it outside the bell. **"The plan worked. All of them are contacting their new headquarters and…we should have some more ships here very soon. They can be followed and we'll find out where their new homes are**."

Wymini leaned back in her chair. "Call the physicists and tell them to get ready to blow the *h'oolyach* out of those *bimyocks*… again. Get hold of the ones who made those banners and have them make some new ones. Have it written on the banners: If you attack us again, next time, we will make sure that none of you survive."

Some new Teams were assigned to spy on the foreigners in Home dimension. The Teams that had been spying kept up with their mission in #45, doing everything possible to get all of the information they could glean from the enemies. The Owlamites were gaining all kinds of new knowledge (and equipment). They started taking all kinds of things off the 1,081 ships that had been captured and watching how the indigenous races repaired or replaced the lost equipment and parts.

The ones in #45 had no problem establishing the new chain of command, since the disappearance of the ranking personnel and the bell conference ship. Instead of griping about the fact that the bell had vanished, they got together and constructed a new conference ship.

The Owlamites found that all six of these races were definitely of one mind. They refused to sign any alliance with anyone. They each wanted to be the dominant species in the universe. The only reason they allowed the other five to exist was because they simply had not destroyed or forced them into complete acquiescence. If they could force the others into complete submission, they would and then they would force the newly enslaved to do the fighting for the controlling race. The only reason they had the conferences was because they were determined that there would not be any wars with any seventh race. Fighting against five enemies was enough for each one. A new adversary was totally intolerable.

Wymini and the rest of the Command Staff could do nothing but shake their heads in wonder and snicker because of the bigotry of the antagonists. If they were to put aside their prejudices and join together, they could probably control…everything.

The Chokchakchok were very angry about the fact that their home planet had been totally irradiated. They had to find a new planet, where they were in complete control, in order to establish a new home, until the radiation levels went back to tolerable levels. They chose a planet they had conquered and made the indigenous citizens do all of the building. There were a few debates in the Command Staff conference room as to whether or not the Owlamites should assist the enslaved race, however, the final decision was that they had enough headaches keeping the conquerors off of Hardooth. To be the watchdogs for the entire universe was just a bit too much to handle.

The Doolood were doing everything they could to try to build new barriers. They had to use their battle spaceships inside their atmosphere to chase off, or kill, the big sea monsters. It was going to be a long slow process, however, they had little choice, as far as survival. They wanted to reestablish their underwater cities that were safe from the giant sea monsters. Since there was no other planet they had found, so far, where the water was equal in high saline and alkali content, they were stuck with the water of their own home planet. They had to use that finite source in order to survive.

The Iyka planet had been the first one victimized by their own weaponry. They were having a real tough time finding any planet that had the proper kind of mud suitable for their eggs. It was not just the placement of the eggs in a nest, it was protecting the nest from any of the indigenous creatures of the planet that was a problem. Yes, it had been overkill when the attack had been accomplished, however, the Owlamites learned from that mistake and were only going to go to that extreme if someone became a real headache.

The Jowfoonda had quickly found a suitable planet to continue the survival of their species. The planet they chose did not have a very large population of sentient species on it. The Jowfoonda arrived and started exploiting the planet for land and minerals along with enslaving the small population of originals.

The Mufayton planet would be a toxic radioactive wasteland for untold generations. Since there was nothing on the planet that could survive the massive radioactive holocaust, nothing was left alive. If they were going to bring their home planet back, they would have to wait a long, long time and then make attempts at restoring anything that they had on their ships that was indigenous and then try moving other mammals, reptiles, birds, fish, crustaceans, mollusks and plants in.

The Zizzikinza also had to find a new temporary home. Seeing as how they did not take up much space, individually, they were able to find a suitable place rather quickly.

All six were waiting for a call from the mass movement against Ponsok Kon Yeffan Chood. They were hoping to hear that the inhabited planet was being chopped to pieces by all of the massed ships. When they got the call from the Conference Ship, they were appalled at what they were hearing. Instead of victory, it was catastrophe – along with 1,081 inexplicably missing ships, that planet was untouched by any attack.

Now what?

2

It took ten years for the six antagonists to come to the agreement to send another mass armada to Hardooth. They (finally) felt that they could not afford to show any sign of weakness to this unknown enemy, especially since there were six of them against… what…they were not sure.

By now, they all had increased the number of ships in their arsenal. The Owlamites saw that they could possibly be facing 1450 ships total.

The ships trapped in #45 had been voided of all indigenous races. The Owlamites figured they had everything they could glean from those personnel (who after reading their minds, knew they would never capitulate to any kind of an outworld alliance). Now, the Owlamites were just going to start scavenging and using any parts they could for their purposes. They did like the idea of using the ships against the ones who were going to be attacking, however, they did not have enough Owlamite personnel for that kind of endeavor. The only thing the Owlamites could do was wait for the mass armadas to come to them. Then take care of the massed ships using the same strategy that had worked so well the last time.

Wymini did not feel like reading another report. She leaned back in her chair and closed her eyes. "Give me a briefing...on something."

Skalix picked up one of his briefings. "It seems that the Axswain are having a bit of a problem. When we hit them in that final battle in the northwest gorge, it left only twelve of them still alive. Since then, they've tried to procreate back to a...much larger population. With only twelve from the original gene pool... and only four of them women...the generations that are coming along now...the eleventh since that battle...are little more than deformed, sterile idiots."

Wymini opened her eyes. "Do you know if the original twelve are still alive?"

"Oh, yes, Sir, they are." Skalix shook his head. "It appears that...like us...they have a much longer life span than...most of the other Elf races...either that or they got hold of some of those longevity potions made by the Teltermak."

Wymini closed her eyes and sniffed. "Anything else?"

"Yes, Sir," said Xadorm. "The Teltermak are able to procreate without the problem the Axswain are having. Their gene pool was much larger. We don't know if any of the original Teltermak are still alive, however, we're still hearing that they want to find us and enslave us. They still haven't stated why, but they are adamant that capturing us alive is one of the highest priorities they have. Right now, though, they don't have a clue as to where to find us. They're also having a problem on Satroco Isle...in that the island is too small for their population. They're about to start pushing people into the water, but no one will allow them to expand…because there is still the story going around that they're the ones who nearly killed the supply of *Tuzine*. As a result, no one will allow them to expand anywhere off of Satroco Isle."

Wymini sat there chuckling. "We've hurt them…beyond anything they can fight against…but they still want to enslave us. All these years and they're still a very vindictive and hard-headed bunch." She shook her head. "If they want us alive…why do they keep killing any of us that they find alone?" She looked around and received no response to her inquiry.

"There's also a report from…where Algothon used to be," said Yim. "Most people are wondering what happened there. There are those who consider it a holy place while others consider it an unholy place. Certain people who practice polytheism think that it was some kind of a judgment from one of their gods. They can't agree on whether it was something positive or negative. They just pay homage to the big dust pit and quibble over it…as to whether it is holy or unholy."

Wymini chuckled again. "People who practice polytheism…they've got some god that they worship, hiding behind every tree or rock. With the existence of the holy texts of the Great Maker, I still wonder why some believe in multiple gods."

"Some just cannot accept the holy texts or they listen to some false prophet…who has written their own rendition of the holy texts," said Nantasa.

Jeejow huffed. "Egomaniacs who forget who God is. They

think that they're a god according to their own decision. Then, somehow, they actually find people who are gullible enough to follow them."

Wymini nodded. "What's the reports on our…collective enemies? Have they decided how many ships to send after us… this time?"

Jeejow looked at his information. "So far, the number fluctuates between twelve hundred and fourteen hundred. Each one is holding something back. Usually their finest flag ship… with a task force."

Wymini smiled. "Send the word to the spies on the enemy ships. When the enemy armadas start heading this way, hop all of the enemy ships that are being held in reserve into…#45. Any leaders…that are not on any of the ships…they get hopped as well."

Jeejow looked apprehensive. "Into…#45?"

Wymini bit her lip. "It won't matter much. If they're not in this dimension - they can't harm us. If they get hopped…into #2…and that particular spot is…far away from any inhabitable planet…in the void of outer space...it still achieves what we want. Their leaders will be…indisposed. They'll be permanently out of our hair."

"We may have to get extra personnel out there…in order to perform that," said Marbing. "There have been some cultures… who are led by a committee rather than just one monarch or… prime minister."

Wymini placed her hands flat on the table. "We use... however many personnel it takes. If we, on the staff, have to be a part of this mess in order to achieve it...so be it. We end this... persistent headache. We weaken all six of them to the point they will no longer be a threat to us or anybody else...hopefully... forever." She leaned back in her chair. "Or at least...not for a long, long, long time."

Xadorm nodded his head. "If we destroy all six of them... that could only make room for...another."

Wymini scowled at him. "Must you be so pessimistic? If that happens...we'll take the fork in the road that leads the way to our survival. That is also a reason why we'll never abandon our guardian beacons."

Xadorm smiled. "If you want me to think of something positive...I think of all of the new and updated fighter ships the Jowfoonda have unwillingly supplied us with. We have well over 18,000 updated fighters and if they come at us again...we should have nearly 40,000. All of them will be very new. We will be a most...formidable force."

"We'll be ready to take on...anything," said Inditam.

Wymini smiled. "Let's hope so. Remember how many we've lost...just when we thought that we were so...invincible." She smoothed her hair back. "Remember that I am the tenth *Voice of Power* and...just how the other nine died."

"We have another report here," said Am-Sisa. "According to this one...we can bypass any personnel on the Mufayton ships... and set off their self-destruct system."

Yim frowned. "How could we possibly do that? Don't you think that once the countdown starts…they just might do…something about it?"

"That's the beauty of it," said Am-Sisa. "Our people start the countdown in one of the Auxiliary Bridges. It has a silent count. No one on the Main Bridge will know about it…until it blows the *h'oolyach* out of them. Then, of course, it's too late."

"I thought that we wanted to keep these ships for new technology and spare parts," said Skalix. "What good does it do to blow them up?"

Wymini snickered. "We have almost eleven hundred that we're ransacking for parts and other goodies. When they attack again, we'll get…probably another twelve hundred…or more. Turning one or two lead ships into…debris…isn't going to be very much of a loss."

Skalix still looked perplexed, however he shrugged in acceptance. "One or two *dozen* won't make that much difference…I guess."

Wymini frowned. "Have they been able to do it on any of the other enemy ships?"

Am-Sisa scoffed. "According to Tula, it's impossible on the Chok ships. Those mazes have so many fail safes programs on those flying labyrinths that…we might blow up one or two sections…but…they already have contingencies for losing part of a ship…and immediately assigning a new Main Bridge…complete with a Command Team."

Wymini shook her head. "That's pretty good planning for a bunch of giant walking hairballs. We have to remember that they are not stupid…just because they appear to be." She stretched her arms out and yawned. "Is there anything else…from our personnel on those captured ships?"

"Yes," said Jeejow. "Those Doolood ships…when you drain the water out…it takes a long time to get all of the mold and fungus out of there. They found the best method of killing all of that…wet muck…is to open all hatches and let the thing sit in the middle of the desert on the Desert planet for about a month."

Xadorm looked a little sick. "Don't they have to clean the dead stuff out afterwards anyway?"

"Yes," said Jeejow. "The easy part there is…once it's totally dead by complete dehydration…you don't have to worry about it growing back and it is so dried up that all you have to do is peel it off of the wall."

"I thought that the Iyka ships stunk as well," said Inditam. "How did they get around that?"

Jeejow smiled. "That one is a lot simpler. Just hose out the muck with clean water. Fortunately there's no residue…or residual smell…in that case."

Wymini smiled. "And we still have almost eleven hundred ships that we scavenge from and utilize in whatever manner we desire. All we're waiting for now…is for those *chokwads* to come up with the intestinal fortitude to attack us…and then we'll have over twice as much to play with."

Marbing snickered. "Leaving all of it in #45 helps a lot as well. We still haven't seen anything or anybody…other than what we've dumped in that dimension."

Almost one year later, the call came in that there were 1,365 ships headed their way. Between the six antagonists they held back only 85 of their ships.

Skalix sighed. "Shall we start the plan going now?"

Wymini shook her head sadly. "I guess so. I'm getting tired of this, but…all of these *bimyocks* keep on trying to turn us into their toys. Let's go."

It required almost two days to get everyone into position. They now had ten Owlamites on every ship in the attack armadas and the 85 ships that were held back. 14,500 Owlamites spread all over the place in another situation where their dimension hopping capability was going to be used in order to protect themselves from enslavement.

When Wymini gave the order, all 1,450 enemy ships were hopped into Observation. They were still headed for Hardooth, however, they did not know that their weaponry would be useless. The 85 that were still back at their home planet could not pick up any chatter from the planet, however, they were concentrating on the communications from the armadas.

It was not until two days later that the 85 realized that there was something amiss when they could not contact anyone on the ground. They sent shuttle craft to land and find out what the problem was only to realize that they were now unable to contact, touch, or hear anything other than their home ship or the armadas. Once all six races realized that they were in trouble that was when the higher ranking individuals, in each race, were now jettisoned into other dimensions by the Owlamites. The chain of command in each group was being severely compromised as all of the top officers systematically disappeared. The only hope that the ones who still remained had was to finish the mission and hope that all problems would be solved.

The 85 that had stayed behind now had no choice but to join the six armadas heading for Hardooth. They had no place they could land or communicate with other than that bunch. They also had no way of resupplying their ships. They were all in it completely. No one holding back unless they were not on any of the attack ships at all.

When the joint armadas arrived at Hardooth, they mercilessly opened fire on the planet and, much to their consternation, saw nothing happening. Power beams and bombs were causing no damage at all. The indigenous citizens were going about their business and not even noticing all of the barrage of mass weapons that were hitting them.

When the 85 joined the 1,365 and saw that things had really gone wrong for them, they decided to have another conference at the bell.

Wymini got the message about the bell conference station. She tried to think for a few moments. The armadas were here and she wanted to keep them close. If they all headed away to the bell, they would have upset a part of the Owlam plan. "Where is that silly bell?"

Jeejow shrugged. "It's where they last put the thing."

Wymini clenched her teeth. "Can someone get the thing… and Jump it here?"

"I suppose," said Jeejow. "Who did you have in mind?"

"Who is not busy right now?"

Yim smiled. "Us."

Wymini shook her head. "NO! We need to stay here and coordinate." She snarled. "Find Team 7016. Get them to do the Jump on that station."

Jeejow cleared his throat. "In which dimension do you wish it to be located?"

"Go ahead and let them have it in Observation. That way, they can have a conference and still not know what's going on."

At that time they were contacted, Team 7016 was located on the Main Bridge of one of the Jowfoonda ships. Soolchakan and Bonarain just looked at each other and sighed. Kiyalee rolled her eyes and shook her head in disgust. Chyning pulled out her pulse pistol. There was a Jowfoonda maintenance man working under one of the consoles on the Bridge. She hopped the business end of her pistol into Observation and blew his brains out. It took several moments for any of the other Jowfoonda noticed that he was dead. Team 7016 had already Jumped to the bell station before the Jowfoonda could start an investigation in regards to the very mysterious death.

Team 7016 was sitting in some of the chairs in the conference room.

Kiyalee yawned. "What's the plan?"

Soolchakan looked around bored. "We hop it to Ghost. Once we've done that, we can Jump it back to Hardooth and not worry about joining with any of those enemy ships in Observation. When we're sure that we're not going to join with any of those ships…we hop the *chokwad* thing to Observation…and let those *bimyocks* play with their toy."

Bonarain sighed. "Whenever you're ready…let's do it."

They hopped the bell ship to Ghost. Soolchakan gave the order to Jump. The bell station was now located inside the aft section of one of the Iyka ships.

Chyning smiled. "Ghost was a good choice."

Soolchakan nodded.

As soon as the Iyka ship moved away, they hopped the bell into Observation. The reaction was immediate. Almost all of the enemy ships stopped moving anywhere. One ship from each armada came to the bell station.

Bonarain shook her head. "Now we get to listen in on more of their frustrations."

"I'd like to see *them* frustrated rather than us," said Chyning.

Kiyalee stared at Chyning wide-eyed. "You said something intelligent!" She looked at Bonarain. "She said something intelligent!" She shook her head. "Amazing!"

Chyning stuck her tongue out at Kiyalee.

Soolchakan pointed at Chyning. "*That's* the Chyning that we all know and love."

"Just remember," said Bonarain. "When the Mufayton get in here…don't mentally send anything to anybody."

The representatives started coming into the bell. Once they were all there, they started complaining, bellyaching, comparing notes and trying to figure out what had happened. For five days they talked and solved nothing because none of them knew what had happened or how and could explain nothing.

After the fifth day of the talks going around in aimless circles, Wymini called out. **"I've had enough. Send all of these *bimyocks* into #45. There's no more reason for us to listen to any of their *h'oolyach*. Just hop them and then let's start some more scavenging**."

No one in the bell space station was saying anything. They were all too flabbergasted to even think. All of the ships were disappearing and they had no idea why. Then the bell was hopped to #45. Now they saw all of their ships and they were even more confused. They were not confused for long because they were jettisoned from the bell without any warning or ceremony. Now they were nothing but floating debris.

The remaining Chokchakchok survivors that were not on the spaceships were all located on one planet. A planet they had plundered and now needed in order to survive because of the attack on their home world. Once the indigenous citizens of the planet found that the Choks no longer had any of their nasty weapons from the sky backing them, there was a global revolution against the Choks. The fight lasted for over three years and when it was over, the Choks numbered around 5,000,000 and all of them were on only one of the nine continents of the planet. There was only one continent smaller than the one where the Choks now had to call home (without any of their technological toys). They had to constantly remain vigilant to attacks from the originals. They had almost no time to build anything new there because of an extreme lack of supplies, raw minerals along with very few of their engineers and technicians. They finally realized they were no longer an empire of space traveling conquerors.

Without their spaceships to protect them, the Doolood found the reconstruction of the glass barriers was going to be an incredibly slow process. The sounds of connecting the pieces together seemed to attract the sea monsters they feared the most. They had no access to any of their equipment that was designed to move the big pieces of the wall. All of that was out there in open water. They were going to have to build a minor wall tunnel to the location of their construction equipment before they could use any of it. They figured that by the time they got there, they were going to have to dig all kinds of coral and clinging mollusks off of the equipment before they could even test it. Most of the good mud, where they preferred to lay their eggs, was also out there in the unprotected sea area. Any eggs that had been there when the wall disappeared were probably gone by now because of that wretched egg eating eel that caused them no end of grief. They realized that it was going to be a very long time before they were any kind of a force in the universe again.

The Iyka found themselves on a planet that was not very suitable for their taste or survival. They had made some emergency moves to get their people to this planet as a temporary substitute. Since they had lost all of their spaceships they were stranded. There were only a few places in the equatorial regions where they could place their eggs and have any hope of successful hatchings. The indigenous race found out about the egg hatcheries and the Iyka had to defend them constantly. Survival and procreation became a daily battle for the remnants of the Iyka on a strange planet that hated them totally. Like the others, if they survived, it would be a very long time before they were space traveling conquerors again.

The Jowfoonda were in even greater trouble on their temporary planet. Once the originals saw that there were no more spaceships causing them grief, they attacked with great zeal against the invaders. The Jowfoonda fought back with just as much zeal because they had nothing else they could do and nowhere else they could go. After almost three years of constant fighting, the originals found a rare weed that grew naturally on their planet that was deadly poisonous to the Jowfoonda. With this new found knowledge, they began growing and harvesting the weed in great abundance. In less than a year, the Jowfoonda became totally extinct as a species and would not be any trouble to anyone ever again.

The remaining Mufayton numbered less than 100,000. The only reason they were able to survive on their new home planet was because they were able to read the minds of the originals. Though they could outsmart them and outmaneuver them the Mufayton had no chance of taking over and controlling the originals. The Mufayton were outnumbered more than 65,000 to 1. Any hope of controlling and conquering, in view of those odds, was totally impossible. They might be able to control about 500,000, however, that control would end if even more came into the picture. Seeing as how they were stuck here until, who knows how long, they did not dare build and use any nuclear devices. The only way they could survive was to evade and avoid…and hide. They saw very little in their future as far as going back to being a space travelling conqueror.

The only way that the Zizzikinza could survive on their new planet was to slither into openings and slits that the indigenous race could not fit into. They had to hide in caverns and any other underground area they could find. They had to find a way to dig to each of the clusters of their people in order to unite and attempt to figure out a way out of the mess they were in. They had a very large labyrinth of tunnels going all over one of the continents on their new home planet. They were able to get together as one unit, however, they could not expand anywhere because the originals were always on the lookout for them and were getting to be pretty good shots at any Zizzy that was unfortunate enough to be seen outside of the tunnels and caverns.

Six races who had, at one time, conquered and pillaged all over the galaxy in different star systems were now lowered to being stuck on one planet each...or dead (as far as the Owlamites were aware). Each of the surviving races wondered if they would ever be able to return to their former glory. It did not appear they would be able to achieve that in their lifetimes. They were going to have to be patient and start rebuilding – in totally hostile areas – and hope that someday, far into the future, their children could once again escape to another planet and start marauding again.

Wymini sniffed. "This is what our spies are reporting... about all six of those *bimyocks*?"

Jeejow smiled. "If we ever get attacked again...it won't be any of these *chogos*. They haven't got anything to attack us with and won't for a very long time."

"There was one satisfaction...with knowing who was out there," said Yim. "At least when they showed up, we know, from the shape of their ships, who it was. Now, if someone else attacks... we won't have a clue who they are or what their capabilities are."

"We've still been able to do a pretty good job of surviving," said Marbing. "Yes, we've lost a lot of our people...but we're still here...and we learn each time. I think that we can handle...just about anything that anyone throws at us."

"I hope you're right," said Wymini. "When I think of how many we've lost...and so far, the doctors haven't figured out any way for us to…procreate…each loss is…just totally incalculable and irreplaceable."

"So we have to remain vigilant in watching," said Xadorm. "That's the main secret to our survival. Our tactics haven't changed that much. They still work."

Inditam huffed. "For how long? All of us…are somewhere between 1640 and 1700 years old. How long are we capable of living? We have no idea. The only ones who have died, died in battle."

"No one looks as if they're getting any older," said Nantasa. "We all still look…as if we're about thirty years old. Do you see any of us that look…old?"

Most of them shook their heads.

"So we don't know how long we can live," said Am-Sisa. "If we live to be 10,000 years old…I'd still rather live all of that fighting for freedom rather than capitulating to some arrogant race of *bimyocks*."

Yim started digging through some of the reports. "How are we doing on scavenging from all of those spaceships?"

"We're about 80% done with it," said Jeejow. "After four years, that's pretty good, I'd say."

Xadorm looked a little apprehensive. "Do you still want us to slam a few more of the skeletal remains into the back side of Niygool?"

"Of course," said Wymini. "We spread a little of the local dirt on some of them so that any outsider will think they've been there longer than they actually have. Why?"

Xadorm huffed. "I still think that the material that makes up the hull of those ships could come in handy…as replacement parts."

"That's why we've only slammed seven of the hulks into Niygool," said Nantasa. "We still have over 2,500 ships that we can utilize and get parts off of them. I don't see why the loss of seven should bother you."

"I still think that we should preserve everything," said Xadorm. "I don't like wasting anything. We have an enormous advantage over others in the fact that we can hide anything and everything in good old #45 and…so far, we don't know of anyone else who has ever been there…unless we sent them there. We can put it all there and not worry about anyone fooling with it."

Jeejow scoffed. "Unless someone else finally figures out a way to get there through technology. Then we'd have a big problem trying to preserve any of our…captured possessions."

Yim snickered. "One of the really nice things about that last attack by the Jowfoonda, every one of us has our very own private fighter craft…with several thousand to spare. We really don't have to worry about any of that…for a long, long time."

"True," said Nantasa. "However we may still find uses for some of those larger landing craft that we obtained as well. We just haven't figured out what to do with them."

"We'll take that fork in the road when we get there," said Wymini.

3

261 years later, in the 279th year of the tenure of Wymini, the people who were watching the skies around their star system, saw a formation of ten spaceships entering the system. Each ship was a straight pointed cylinder that was over 2 kilotaja in length and .7 kilotaja in diameter. About half way down the length of the ships there were two large square wing like appendages on the sides. In the rear it appeared as if they had an upper tail fin. Each one of these wings or fins stuck out .5 kilotaja from the body of each of the craft.

The alarm went out and all Owlamites immediately hopped to Spy. No one wanted to be the next one whose name ended up on any wall of memory for the dead. Each one of them sat in there fighter craft, waiting for the word from Wymini as to what tactic was going to be done.

Wymini went to her fighter. "**Exactly where are these new *bimyocks* at this time**?"

The call was answered by Officer Grade 6, Omasasa of Team 505. "**Right now, all of those *bimyocks* are orbiting Bri. They're…shining some kind of beams down on the planet. I think they're doing an inventory on the mineral content of Bri…just like everyone else has done**."

Wymini snarled out loud. "**Great! That means that the only way we'll get rid of them is total destruction. All Owlamites…prepare to perform another extinction… on an unknown invader**." She sighed in frustration. "**Team 7016…I'm afraid that we need your expertise in being on the point for this discovery of the new strangers**."

Soolchakan could feel the disgusted looks on the faces of his Teammates, even though he could not see them in their fighters. "**Sorry! Let's get out there and…discover**."

"**Onward to Bri**," sent Kiyalee in a caustic manner.

"**I know my job**," sent Chyning sardonically.

"**So Jump to Bri**," sent Bonarain.

Team 7016 made the Jump and were momentarily distracted by what they were seeing. All of the stranger ships were putting on an incredible light show. There were different colored beams, emanating from the underside of each ship, and were moving all over the surface of Bri as the unknowns did their inventorying survey of minerals.

"**They all look the same**," sent Soolchakan. "**I can't tell which one is marked as the lead ship. I'll just pick one…and the three of you…follow me**." He shook his head, aimed the nose of his fighter directly at the closest one and slowly headed for the target ship. "**The only thing that we can be certain of…it is NOT one of those six headaches…that gave us so many headaches**."

Soolchakan and Bonarain flew into the bow of the ship.

Kiyalee headed for the stern. Chyning flew into the middle.

They found the Main Bridge very quickly. Everything about it said Bridge, the way that it was arranged. There were two seats in the middle that were occupied by two people who had all kinds of colorful and superfluous decorations on their clothing. On both sides there were several computer work stations where operators were feverishly working on…something. In the front, high and centered was a large view screen that showed the surface of Bri and all kinds of symbols as the inhabitants of the ship were inventorying the mineral wealth of the big planet. Directly below the view screen were two work stations. Bonarain was able to get some quick translations and found that the station on the left was navigation and the one on the right was the primary weapons station.

Soolchakan looked around in confusion as he saw that there were two distinct differences in the people on the ship. Some of them were in shiny gold, silver or coppery clothing. Others were in dingy rags. The ones with the shiny clothing were making a habit of beating, slapping, kicking, yelling at and otherwise abusing the ones in rags. He checked on Bonarain to see if she had noticed this difference in the people. She was sitting behind the two fancy clad people in the middle and was concentrating on reading their minds. He decided to wait until she was finished before asking her what her thoughts on the differences were.

Chyning broke in. **"Have you taken a look at…any of their work consoles? They have…rows of keys…26 rows…that are 40 keys long. That would mean…that they have…1,040 symbols…in their alphabet, punctuation** and numbers. That's ridiculous!'"

Soolchakan looked at one of the keyboards and was astounded at all of those keys – and at the way that the alien had his fingers flying all over the keys.

He closed his eyes and tapped his fingers against his forehead. He needed to get back to concentrating on what they needed to find out first. He aimed his biosensor at the alien he had been looking at and turned it on.

Specimen is very similar to Heyyah in all internal bodily systems. 7.1 taja in height. Male reproductive system. Skin is light gray with some randomly scattered blotches of dark red. Biped, walks upright, seven fingers with opposable thumb on each hand. Very little hair anywhere on the body that is mostly umber in color.

Soolchakan looked at the information closely. He turned the biosensor to one of the ones in rags and turned it on again to see if the slaves were any different.

Specimen is very similar to Heyyah in all internal bodily systems. 6.9 taja in height. Male reproductive system. Skin is light gray with some randomly scattered blotches of dark red. Biped, walks upright, seven fingers with opposable thumb. Very little hair anywhere on the body that is mostly umber in color. This specimen has numerous contusions, abrasions and other injuries that show continuous abuse against the person. Appears to be suffering from malnutrition.

Soolchakan shook his head. **"It seems that they enslave their own. I wonder what the difference is…as** to who is the master and who is the slave."

"**I found the engine room**," sent Kiyalee. "**These** *bimyocks* **love repetition. They got four light speed engines and ten conventional engines. It appears that... they could survive on one light speed engine and... maybe only two conventional. Either they love overkill or redundancy...or a lot of backups.**"

"**The third choice sounds most likely**," sent Soolchakan.

"**They sure love beating the** *h'oolyach* **out of their slaves**," sent Chyning. "**I think this one...dressed in copper, just killed one of the ones in rags.**"

Bonarain finally came out of her trance. "**We're not on the flagship. I can show you which one it is though. Should we go to that one?**"

Soolchakan felt a little confused. "**Do you think it's important?**"

"**I think we'd find out a few more important things about these** *doovofts* **If we do.**"

Soolchakan sighed. "**Okay, Team 7016, let's meet outside of** *this* **ship...and go to the main one...lead on Officer, Bonarain...or should I say...less than great one.**"

She scowled at him as she flew her fighter to three different ships before she slowed and got ready to enter the ship she wanted.

Soolchakan could not tell any difference between the ships.

"**What is so special about this one**?"

"**Look at it**," sent Bonarain. "**On the sides…the numbers are outlined in gold**."

Kiyalee chuckled. "**Those are numbers? Are you sure**?"

"**As was pointed out earlier, their keyboards have over 1,000 keys**," sent Bonarain in an admonishing manner. "**These** *bimyocks* **have twenty different numbers in their counting. They have ninety-four different types of punctuation…three of which I have no idea what they're used for. The rest is upper case, middle case and lower case letters. Each one of the keys on those keyboards has three different letters, numbers or punctuation**."

Chyning scoffed. "**Oh this is gonna be a real joy**," she sent sarcastically.

Soolchakan felt a little overwhelmed with the information. "**All right, we're entering the flagship. What, exactly, do we need in this ship that we couldn't find in the other ships**?"

Now it was Bonarain's turn to be sarcastic. "**The Tolod and the Gyvbufu of the ruling Vagehymin party. Any more stupid questions**?"

Soolchakan, Kiyalee and Chyning all sat in their fighters with their mouths hanging open. They all decided that it was time to keep quiet until they had been given some of the special translation information from Bonarain.

All four of them entered the Main Bridge. This one was more lavish than any Bridge they had ever seen. There were six seats, in the center, that were literally heavily padded, golden thrones. Each one had a footrest in front. Each footrest had gold legs and heavy padding on the top.

The two thrones in the middle had backs that were much taller than the outer thrones. Sitting on the middle thrones were a male and a female that were dressed in gold colored clothing and adorned (ostentatiously) with numerous jewels, necklaces, bracelets, earrings and anklets. The female was currently getting her feet washed by two females in rags.

The outer thrones on the left had a male and a female who were dressed in silvery clothing and covered with expensive jewelry. The two sitting in the thrones on the right were dressed almost the same as the ones on the left.

Bonarain shook her head in disgust. "There you go. The ones in the middle are the top members of the ruling Vagehymin party. He is the Tolod, she is the Gyvbufu. They rule with an iron fist, a steel boot and a nasty whip. Standing behind the two middle thrones is the current ship's Commander. He is the Atogo. If the Vagehymin party loses out, in the next election, to one of the other political parties...he is executed and the new ruling party puts their own...doormat...in command of the armada." She grunted in disgust. "The *bimyocks* on the right are the representatives of the Afzylovabi party. He is the Boliluwy and she is the Jufamy. On the left are the representatives of the Gaholvib party. He is the Vofyhonah and she is the Byfoli. The ones, in rags, who are washing the feet and serving the food are of the Lujetfyvoh and

Jonlyan parties." She parked her fighter and got out. "These hypocrites have…what they call…a democratic vote, every five…of their years. If the Lujetfyvoh or Jonlyan party win any election…they're punished, in horrible ways, for misusing their votes. Only the Vagehymin, the Afzylovabi or Gaholvib party can be in charge…according to the rulings of those three parties. And they say that *all* are equal. The three ruling parties are also very adamant about claiming how benevolent and altruistic they are as well."

Chyning scoffed. "Well why can't the members of the… two low-life parties just switch affiliation and raise their status?"

Bonarain sighed. "You are *born* into your party. You can't switch…under penalty of death…*especially* the Lujetfyvoh or Jonlyan."

Soolchakan spat on the floor. "And thus the three main ruling parties maintain their *absolute* rule…and still have the monumental audacity to call it fair."

Kiyalee chuckled a little nervously. "What do these *bimyocks* call themselves…as a race I mean?"

Bonarain gave her a disgusted look. "They DON'T! They go by political party affiliation and nothing more. For a Vagehymin to admit that they're the same species as any Jonlyan would be…to admit that they actually *are* equal." She sighed. "There's nothing in any of their minds that states a species. All they go by is political party."

Chyning blew a raspberry. "What a mess."

"The two bottom parties…are stuck," said Kiyalee sadly. "I sure wouldn't want to have any children…and then raise them in that kind of an environment. I couldn't even think of it."

"Let's wait until we've read some of their history and archives before we judge them," said Soolchakan. "There may be more here…than we're seeing in just this first little bit."

Kiyalee sniffed. "Why don't we just hop this bunch into dimension 45 and let them rot?"

Soolchakan did a mental communication with the Command Staff. They agreed with hopping the flagship into #45 and checking the reaction of this bunch. Team 7016 hopped the ship and watched to see what would happen. The results were a total shock.

Bonarain looked rather startled. "Oops! I think…we underestimated this bunch."

Soolchakan looked skeptical. "Why?"

The color left Bonarain's face. "They're… communicating…with the other ships in…Home dimension."

Soolchakan's jaw dropped. "WHAT? But…how? That's not possible…is it?"

"They're doing it," said Bonarain with a shrug.

Soolchakan closed his eyes. **"Supreme Officer, Wymini, I think we need to send all of the ships into 45 and then…send all of the personnel into…198 (Desert) without any of their technological toys."**

Wymini came back. "**What are they doing? Are they trying to get back to Home dimension...using their... toys?**"

Bonarain broke in. "**YES! They're analyzing... apparently from both sides and they're trying to get back.**"

Wymini tried to sound calm. "**Are they showing any signs of succeeding?**"

"**They're firing up all four of their light speed engines...in order to come up with enough power to do the job,**" send Bonarain desperately.

Wymini made a general call. "**Is anyone else in the vicinity of the new invaders?**"

A call came back. "**This is Officer Grade 3, Dendia of Team 1779. We're very close to one of the foreign ships.**"

"**Good,**" sent Wymini. "**Get inside the closest one to you and hop it into 92 (Stink)...inside the planet's atmosphere, so that they all get a snoot-full of that gas. Maybe that'll give them something to worry about.**" Wymini growled to herself. "**Is anyone else out there?**"

"**This is Officer Grade 3, Chi-Amka of Team 2212. What do you want us to do?**"

"**Pick another ship and hop it into 15 (Bugs)... again on the planet so that they have their ship crawling with vermin. We have to watch their reactions...and**

see if there's any panic…or concern." Wymini looked at the Staff. "Did any of you ever dream of anything like this happening?"

"We have no way of knowing the capabilities of any alien that lives out there…until they show up here…and expose their talents," said Jeejow looking very worried.

Wymini shook her head. "This is horrible. If they're capable of hopping…"

"Then we take their toys away," said Xadorm. "Just like he said. Hop them into 198 (Desert) without any of their techno toys."

Wymini shook her head. "That doesn't seem like such a bad idea now." She thought for a few moments. "**We need more than one individual who can understand these *doovofts*. I know that it can be taxing…but…we need to know**."

Bonarain looked at Soolchakan. "Can be taxing? HAH! It IS taxing."

Soolchakan shook his head. "What can we do?"

Bonarain looked around angrily. "Let's get back to our home. If I'm going to be mentally trashed until tomorrow, at least I'll be in my own bed."

The four of them Jumped back to their apartment. The three followed Bonarain into her bedroom. She hopped her bed into Spy. She force fed the information to Soolchakan, then to Kiyalee, then to Chyning. She staggered to her bed and fell down.

"I think I'm getting used to it," muttered Bonarain. "I'm… not really out of it, but, I'm…not really…" She laid her head down on the pillow and in a few moments she was asleep.

Soolchakan turned to the other two women. "If for no one else, we have to defend our Teammate. Right now, she's helpless. We have to keep those *bimyocks* away from here and away from killing or taking this planet and turning everyone into slaves…or dead meat."

The three of them hopped back to the alien ship in #45 and found there were two Teams that had already been looking around the ship.

"I'm Officer Grade 3, Endinga of Team 257. I'm one of the computer Teams. Is there anything that you can tell me about this…unholy horror of a keyboard?"

Soolchakan looked at one of the keyboards and shook his head. "Only what she said before: Twenty numbers and thousands of letters. It could take years to get used to this overly complicated mess."

The other Team leader seemed a little disgusted. "I'm Officer Grade 4, Oona, of Team 2495. I'm one of the physicist Teams. We need Officer, Kiyalee and Officer, Chyning to go help the other Teams with the other two captured ships.

Soolchakan shrugged. "Kiyalee, go to the one in Stink. Chyning, you get Bugs."

Chyning clenched her teeth. "Why do I get Bugs?"

"Because Kiyalee would be puking her guts out in either

one. At least in Stink, she has an excuse. In Bugs, you can at least hold your lunch."

Kiyalee gave him a disgusted look. She closed the visor on her helmet and hopped her and her fighter to Stink. Chyning sighed as she closed her visor. She then hopped, with her fighter, to Bugs.

"All right, they're in the other ships," said Soolchakan. "Now, what do you need here?"

"We need to know how to get into their computers," said Endinga. "How much of it do you know?"

He looked at her as if she were crazy. "I know that it exists," he said caustically. "We haven't had enough time to do anything with their computers and you want a full detailed description… NOW?"

Oona broke in. "If you can't give any good briefing on the computers, at this time, is there a way to stop them from… opening some kind of dimension…portal or opening…back to Home dimension?"

He sighed. "They fired up all four of the light speed engines in order to attempt the crossover. Apparently it takes a lot of power to do it. My best guess is…break the light speed engines and…that should deprive them of the energy they need."

Oona looked around a little concerned. "Can you do it?"

Soolchakan took his fighter to the engine room, with Oona in tow. He saw the four big multicolored cylinders as they made their noises and flashed all kinds of undulating colors. He pulled his pulse pistol out, hopped the barrel into 45, aimed at the top of one of the cylinders, fired a short burst and watched the pandemonium as a cloud of vapor came spraying out of the breach. He aimed at a second cylinder and breached it as well. He then translated some of the comments for Oona.

"They're reporting a breach in the core and a coolant leak on number 2 and 3. They're shutting down all four of the light speed engines and requesting that multi-dimensional opening be done by the ships in whatever that word is or our Home dimension. The ship's Commander has agreed and is making the call for help to the ships in…Home."

"We can't let them go back," said Oona.

Soolchakan shook his head in disgust. "**Kiyalee, Chyning…we have to disable the light speed engines in all of these ships. Otherwise, they'll all be hopping all over the place uncontrollably**."

Kiyalee answered. "**I kinda guessed that myself**."

Chyning came back with her normal vitriol. "**What gave you your first clue on that one**?"

"**Finish damaging the ships where you are and let's get back to Home and mess the other seven ships up**," sent Soolchakan. He hopped back to Home in his fighter and headed for one of the other ships surrounding Bri. He flew into the engine area and saw Kiyalee shooting the frames of the engines in this one already. He took off for the next ship to damage it. 'I kinda figured that we might cross paths,' he thought. 'No problem, there's only seven of these things still in Home.'

Once all ten ships were disabled, they now had the pleasure of watching how the aliens handled themselves in the crisis. It did not take the aliens a long time to determine they had been sabotaged. They reported to all of the ship Commanders that all of the light speed engines had been damaged by a plasma burn from some kind of unknown alien power weapon. They started going through some films, taken in the engine rooms, to determine all of the who, what, when, where, how and possibly why – especially since they had been able to repair one breached frame and it was immediately breached again.

Soolchakan was on the Main Bridge as the Science section was attempting to find the saboteurs. They were running the film through several different types of filters that made the picture on the screen turn all kinds of weird colors. They would run it through one filter and play the part where the breach occurred. If they saw no anomalies they would change to another filter and run through it again.

Finally they found it. Soolchakan, Endinga and Oona watched in horror as the view screen changed to different shades of blue. There, very clearly, stood Soolchakan with his pulse pistol. He aimed at the top of the light speed cylinders, fired and the breach occurred.

One of the aliens got on a communication device. "We found it! Dimension filter number 22683! There are intruders aboard and they're sabotaging our equipment."

A reply came back through a speaker. "If they can be seen on 22683, start protocol 5466 and eradicate them…immediately!"

Oona looked scared. "What's protocol 5466?"

Soolchakan looked at her incredulously. "Like I care? I don't care! All I know is that they can see us and I don't like it. We need to get out of here until we can figure out how to do this... safely."

Wymini immediately ordered all Owlamites back to the gorge. According to what had been translated so far, all of the other light speed engines would require at least two days to be fixed. Meanwhile they had to figure out what protocol 5466 was and how it would affect any Owlamite...and the entire star system.

Wymini shook her head. "They can see us? They can see us in...Spy dimension? How is that possible?"

Nantasa scoffed. "How are they able to communicate from one dimension to another...with their electronic toys?"

Xadorm cleared his throat. "Apparently, those filters... that can see through dimensional barriers...are also able to send electronic messages through as well."

Wymini nodded. "Until we have something more assured, that's as good an explanation as any. What are they doing in... trying to track us?"

Jeejow looked at a report. "According to the last personnel to Jump off of those ships, they were all putting some kind of strange goggles on. My best guess is that those goggles have the same filtering capability."

Skalix looked around apprehensively. "They can see us in

Spy…have we tried to look around their ships in…Observation?"

"That wouldn't do us much good," said Am-Sisa. "We can't hear anything in Observation."

"We'd at least know whether or not they can see us…in Observation," said Skalix. "Any advantage that we have…or can find, we should use it."

Wymini hung her head. "Send one of the physicists back to one of the ships. Send that individual in Observation and see if anything happens."

Marbing cleared his throat. "What if that…individual… gets noticed immediately?"

Wymini gave him a nasty look. "Then GET OUT… immediately!"

Hrombisk got the message to send one of his physicists. He sat there shaking his head. He did not like the idea of delegating something like that without trying it out himself – at first. He remembered that the flagship was in #45. He got in his fighter and hopped to #45. He saw the big cylindrical ship and headed for it. He hopped to Observation as he got closer. He entered the lavish Main Bridge of the ship and parked his fighter. He got out and walked around, making all kinds of obscene gestures directly into the eyepieces of those strange looking goggles. None of the aliens reacted. He nodded. **"None of the aliens has reacted to me at all. I think it is possible that they have not…because I have not done anything to them…in Observation. We know that they can see us in Spy…so I think it best that we hold Observation for just that: Observation."**

Wymini looked around the table. "Any other suggestions?"

"Yes," said Inditam. "Get in there in Observation and hop the whole batch into #45. Do some quick hopping into Spy, in order to make sure that they don't get their light speed engines fixed…and then maybe go ahead and hop them all into Desert, and as stated before, hop them in there without any of their techno stuff."

Wymini nodded. "Any alterations to that…that any of you can think of?"

"Yes," said Yim. "Let's put a few of them in that Doolood aquarium and do some mind reading on them. Maybe a dozen or so…of the technicians."

"I like that," said Wymini. "That will also give Officer, Bonarain some more opportunity to dig deeper…along with the rest of us."

Xadorm smiled at Wymini. "How many Teams do you suggest we use in this mass hopping?"

"One Team hopped that flagship into 45," said Wymini thoughtfully. "That tells me that…we're all getting more adept at hopping large objects. Let's make sure that Teams, other than 7016, can do the same."

"Nine Teams then," said Xadorm.

"Let's use the physicists," said Inditam. "We have ten Teams of physicists. Let them prove themselves."

"Call them up and do it," said Wymini.

The Command Staff was pleased when the physicists proved themselves capable of hopping the other ships into #45 using only four personnel per ship. That was ample proof that all of the Owlamites should be able to do a feat like that – if they did have enough practice at hopping large objects.

Now the big test of moving the personnel on the ships. There were just over 4,000 aliens on each ship and trying to match each of the political groups with their sect was a daunting challenge seeing as how they, for the most part, dressed alike. The Owlamites finally decided that the quibbling factions would just have to learn to get along with each other and hop all of them to the same place – with the exception of thirty technicians who would end up trapped in the big Doolood aquarium.

They waited until almost all of the light speed engines had been repaired and they started hopping the engine room technicians into Desert first, along with certain navigators and science personnel. They did not give the science section enough time to start running through all of the filters to find out what was happening to their personnel.

The Owlamites were rather disgusted with the fact that as soon as personnel were hopped to Desert, the three ruling parties immediately began punishing the two slave parties for… who knows what? The Owlamites saw just how benevolent and altruistic the three ruling parties actually were. In a very short time the desert was littered with numerous dead bodies…dressed in rags. The killing stopped when the three ruling factions realized that they would not have any servants if they killed all of them. The ruling factions would have to perform any and all menial tasks themselves. That thought was just so utterly humiliating, they stopped the killings.

Wymini was tapping her fingers on the table. "What's the report on those bigot *bimyocks* in Desert?"

Skalix scratched his chin. "We're still feeding them… some fruits and vegetables. Those…ruling class…give the other two just enough to survive. A lot of the lower two are dropping dead from heat stroke. We can't figure out a way to get them out of there without major upheaval because the upper three have made sure that the lower two have virtually no education. All they've been educated to do…is serve."

Marbing snarled. "How does anyone do that? How can you enslave an entire group and…keep them there?"

"Propaganda, absolute control and brutality," said Am-Sisa in a droll manner.

"Fine," said Wymini. "There's nothing we can do for them. We can't start a revolution for other people." She sighed. "Now, what about those planets? It has been over 250 years. How are the planets doing?"

Inditam smiled. "Chokchakchok has a lot of plant, fish, bird and animal life in island areas that weren't hit by the firestorm weapons. A lot of them are coming back. A lot of birds are migrating and are now nesting in areas where…there are virtually no predators…other than other breeds of birds. The residual energy has died down to a point where…if the Choks still had their technology...they might be able to go back and...start rebuilding their empire again...from their home."

Wymini smiled. "Do we want to allow them to do that?"

Everyone in the room looked around chuckling.

Wymini leaned back. "Next?"

"Doolood," said Am-Sisa. "Those fish have been very busy building new walls. They've reestablished two cities. The cities are not the manufacturing cities, but now they're safe in those cities where they can procreate and make more of their special glass. So far they haven't started on any weaponry or space ships."

Wymini nodded. "How big are those cities?"

"They're nothing like the ones they originally had...when we first found them. Those cities were huge. The two that they have now are only about 200 kilotaja in diameter. The ones they had before were ten times that size. Now, they're just building glass."

Wymini shook her head. "Next?"

Marbing scoffed. "Iyka is still just a dead planet. All of the land is brown with nothing growing on it and all of the water is just there, with no life of any type in it...not even fungus. Nothing has changed since the initial blasts."

Wymini frowned. "What about that resort area? Didn't that place survive?"

Marbing shook his head. "Everything that was there

was made of wood. After all this time, most of the wood has completely rotted away. There's very little sign that anything lavish ever existed there."

Wymini sighed. "The Jowfoonda planet?"

"The lower life forms are coming back in the isolated areas," said Nantasa. "Since the Jowfoonda don't exist anymore, there's no reason to worry about them coming back to remake their empire. The planet may come back, but they sure won't."

Wymini shook her head. "Did we actually do all that damage? DON'T ANSWER THAT! Who's next?"

"The Mufayton planet is coming back," said Xadorm. "The Mufaytons are not. They're still stuck hiding on that other planet. If someone does go to the original Mufayton planet, they might claim it, but they're not going to conquer anything or anybody... or be able to use it."

Wymini leaned back. "The Zizzikinza?"

Yim shook his head. "They're not in the same condition as the Mufayton. The planet is coming back, but the Zizzys are still having to live in hiding."

"So we clobbered six races of conquerors and...now we get another one that could cause us some more headaches," said Wymini. She scoffed. "We still don't know what to call them because they only go by political affiliation. What kind of...bigots do that?"

"Autocratic type, control freaks," said Jeejow.

"One of the things that we need to do is figure out how

they're able to talk into different dimensions," said Xadorm.

Nantasa chuckled at the thought. "What if we do figure it out?"

"Then we can shut it off and keep the spaceships," said Xadorm. "If we don't find the way to shut it off, they might just come with a new armada and go try to retrieve them."

"Okay," said Wymini with a shrug. "Get the computer people on that project."

Eight years later, there was finally a breakthrough on the incredibly complicated alphabet they found in that huge keyboard. There were actually only 32 letters, 10 numbers and 33 punctuation marks. The other several thousand symbols were only there to muddy the waters. A message was typed up and then color coded. After setting the color, they would type a random number of letters in among all of the characters that made up the message. Once that was done, all characters were then changed to one color. If you did not know the color coding by the typist, you could never figure out the actual message by getting rid of all of the excess nonsense. Now they were able to decode thousands of documents and find out a lot of secrets that those people did not want anyone to know.

Ten years later, another cylindrical ship entered the star system of Hardooth. It came in calling out to the ten ships that were sitting in #45 with only Owlamites on board. It was actually a blessing for the computer personnel because once the call was received by the ships, they were able to isolate the program that was receiving the call. They were then able to disable it completely and the ten ships were lost forever to the political bigots.

Wymini gave the order that this eleventh ship was to be slammed into Niygool. Just in case some other members of that race happened to come along all they would find of any of their ships was wreckage.

The lone ship gave away more secrets than the political bigots would have ever wanted anyone to have. Because of the hailing being performed by the lone ship, it gave the Owlamites the ability to find even more things in the archives of the ten ships than they had ever had before. It gave them pictures from the home planet of, what the Command Staff had decided to call, Vagens. The word Vagehymin seemed a little too complicated, so it was shortened for convenience. Now they had some landmarks on the Vagen home planet and now they had to decide if they were going to turn it into a radioactive wasteland as well.

Wymini looked around the table. "A decision has to be made. Do we attack these people the same way we did the others...or do we just keep destroying their ships?"

"I don't think we should be so eager to destroy," said Jeejow. "I suggest that we go ahead and survey their home planet for...targets. Once we've identified all targets, we use that banner system...first. We warn them with the banners. We tell them that if they don't stop coming...to our home, we will destroy theirs. The fact that we can get the banners into high security areas, without them seeing or catching us doing it...maybe they'll get the hint and leave us alone."

"If we don't use any of their coding system, they might get the hint," said Xadorm. "We spell it out, in their language that we understand their codes and computer systems and that we can go to their home planet any time we want to…and destroy them."

Wymini frowned. "Does anyone disagree with that tactic?"

No one disagreed.

Wymini nodded. "Send a reconnaissance Team to the Vagen planet and find all of the targets. That'll tell us how many banners we need to make."

Team 7016 was contacted immediately.

Soolchakan turned to Kiyalee. "Are the fighters powered up and supplied and ready to go?"

Kiyalee scoffed impatiently. "When are they *not* ready?"

"Team 7016, it's time to be honored again and do our duty," said Soolchakan.

Chyning just grunted in disgust.

They put on their suits, got in their ships and Jumped to the landmark given to them by the Command Staff. They divided the planet into four quadrants and spent the next month going all over their part of the planet looking for anything of military significance.

When they arrived back on Hardooth, Team 7016 was a little surprised by some new information that the Command Staff had obtained. Another Vagen ship had entered the system while the recon was being done. This ship had the normal five political factions on board, in their normal positions. This ship also had slaves of different races on board as well. One group of those slaves just happened to be member of the Chokchakchok race. The only difference here was that none of the Choks were wearing any of those fancy sashes. The findings of the investigation of these Choks concluded they had not been a part of that giant combined task force that was coming to attack Hardooth. They had been in charge of a colonized (or enslaved) planet. The Vagens had showed up and conquered that planet out from under the Choks and were now using the former masters as slaves.

Soolchakan looked at the report in wonder. "They say that…they can't find anything in the minds of any of those Chok slaves that…indicates they were part of that big attack force."

"So they were bossing around some people on another planet," said Bonarain. "They were not added to the attack force, because of their job. Once the attack force was…captured…and rendered useless…those Choks had no space ships to defend their position."

Kiyalee giggled. "The mighty Choks were taken prisoner and enslaved…by a force they couldn't deal with."

Chyning shook her head. "That means that we had something to do with turning the conqueror…into the conquered. My, how life can…lead to such changes."

"I wonder if there are any more Jowfoonda out there… in the same position," said Bonarain. "All of them that we knew of…are dead."

"It does make one wonder," said Soolchakan. "I like the idea of turning the slaver into a slave...but that means that slavers still exist. It would be nice if we could end that blight...completely...everywhere."

"We can't control the entire infinity of space," said Bonarain. "Let's just try keeping control of our area...and stay out of the slave issue."

Wymini looked at the reconnaissance report from Vagen. She dropped the pad on the table and hung her head. "I don't think I like the idea of contaminating another planet...for who knows how long."

Xadorm shook his head. "This society is incredible. 3,516 military targets...on their home planet. They build everything... everywhere. Seems like a bit of overkill to me."

"I don't think so," said Jeejow. "It is...a system of making sure that no one can hurt them with one attack. When you build the components of your spaceships in forty different plants, all the same components, it is impossible for one attack to cripple that part of your manufacturing line...unless you hit all forty at the same time."

"That means that we have to manufacture...3,516 banners...in order to scare them off," said Nantasa. "All we have so far is 473. We're going to need to put more Teams on making banners...if we're going to get this warning done...in less than five years."

Wymini smiled. "Then that's what we're going to have to do. Send out the orders and let's get those things made. 3,000 Teams should be able to put out one banner each...shouldn't they?"

"That's an awful lot of fabric...and thread," said Am-Sisa.

"I'm sure that the Vagens would be able to supply a huge portion of that material," said Inditam with a leering grin. "Of course, once we finish all of the banners anything that's left over... we could use for our own personal desires. We did do the same thing with the city of Algothon...why not the Vagens?"

"We need to send a lot of personnel to the Vagen home planet for...collection," said Skalix.

"Let's quit wasting time talking about it and do it," said Wymini.

Team 7016 had to go back, with all of the physicist Teams, in order to find enough fabric for the banners. After finding twelve plants, with enough fabric, they unleashed several thousand Owlam Teams on the plants and completely gutted the supply of fabric and thread from all of the plants.

The Vagens who were assigned to investigate the mass thefts instantly went to the security films. They started running the films through all of their filters and were finally able to see the Owlamites purloining all of the materials. The Team that was still there (in Observation) spying on the Vagens reported back to Wymini about the filters.

Wymini called an immediate meeting of the Staff. She

stood at the end of the table instead of sitting in her chair. "I want the plant that manufactures those filters put out of commission... NOW! I don't care how many Teams it takes to find it...or them...just get to work finding those plants and...get rid of that headache."

Marbing shook his head. "Their spaceships! They already have those filters. They have the filters in goggles. Do you realize how great a task this is? We have to find all of their ships... throughout their entire domain...and...it's a massive undertaking."

Wymini leaned towards Marbing with her teeth clenched. "Then the sooner we start, the sooner it'll get done."

Marbing sighed. "Yes, Sir...that's very true."

Yim smiled. "May I make a suggestion?"

Wymini turned to him. "As long as it's relevant."

"Yes, Sir," said Yim. "Before we start...just ransacking... anywhere and everywhere, I suggest that we first find out where all of the things are...then strike at all of them at one time. If we hit one place...then another, then another, then another...they'll see the pattern and then they'll put extra security on all of it. They've been able to find us with those filters...after the fact. Take ALL of their filters...in one swoop...and now they have nothing to use... to look for us, as well as no plant to build more."

Wymini smiled. "That sounds like a good task for you... keeping track of all of that." She stood tall. "Call out to all personnel...find the filters but don't steal them yet. Report the locations of all these filters to Master Officer, Yim. Once we're satisfied that we've found them all...STRIKE!"

Jeejow sighed. "Look for filters...in between making banners?"

Wymini flopped down in her chair with a disgusted look on her face. "Unfortunately...yes."

4

For two years the Owlamites dug through everything that they could find on the Vagens. They used the archives on the captured ships and they snuck in to the areas on the Vagen home planet to get all of the information they could find.

Wymini pursed her lips. "All right...what do you suggest now? We have exactly 65,882 targets...as far as the location of those rotten filters. There are less than 25,000 of us Owlamites to do the job. Where do you suggest we start...without being caught stealing the filters?"

"We do it one ship or office at a time," said Skalix. "One thing to remember – if we completely gut the supply of filters in one office, or ship...they won't have any filters to find us...in that office or ship. We strike as quickly as possible and as thoroughly as possible. That will mean that each ship or office will have to call out to another ship or office...to assist. Hopefully by the time someone calls out...we're already grabbing, or finished grabbing, the filters on the ship...or office, that they call...and now they don't know whom to call in order to resupply their filters."

"The primary target should be the manufacturing plant where they make the lousy things," said Xadorm. "If we don't take that out, they'll be able to replenish the home planet in less than five days. That plant is putting out over 50,000 of that particular filter per day."

Am-Sisa frowned. "How and why are they able to do it that fast?"

"Because that's the one filter that has been used to see us," said Jeejow. "Since they figured that out, they've increased production on that one specific filter by five hundred percent."

Wymini nodded. "Start with their home planet…mainly the manufacturing plant. As soon as we've hit all of the targets on the planet…then we branch out to the spaceships. It'll take, according to our physicists, at least eight days for the nearest spaceship to get back to the home planet and perform some kind or resupply." She sighed. "We must sabotage the *h'oolyach* out of that manufacturing plant. We can't afford to give them any time to find us or even be able to look for us."

Yim shook his head. "According to the number of targets on the home planet, we'll probably have to go all out, with every Owlamite we've got…including ourselves…in order to gut the supply on the home planet. Anything less than all out…we could be in trouble."

Inditam chuckled. "Uh…Sir…what about the banners? Do we unfurl the banners…at the same time we blow the *h'oolyach* out of their manufacturing plant…or do we wait until after we've purloined all of the filters?"

"We start putting the banners out…as soon as we start the destruction," said Wymini. "That should hit them the hardest… seeing all of their filters disappear and getting a great big warning at the same time. Tell them that we're not going to go down without a monster of a fight and that we want to be left alone."

Skalix snickered. "Who wants to be the one who blows up the area of the plant where they make those filters?"

"I think I'll do that," said Wymini. "It has been some time since I was really involved in any action and...since we all have to be a part of it...I think I'll be the one who drops the hand-held bomb on it."

"Uh...NO!" said Skalix. "If you use a hand-held...it will take at least four hundred of them to do the job. The area of the plant where the filter is made...I think that we need to use the larger conventional bombs. According to Hrombisk...it'll take at least three large conventional bombs to destroy that part of the plant."

"I didn't realize that it was that spread out," said Wymini. "I guess I'll need some help with that sabotage." She sighed. "We'll hit the plant...when everyone has gone home for the night and...the fewer casualties...the better."

Skalix hung his head and groaned. "Unfortunately...as was stated before...they've increased production by five hundred percent. They're working around the clock on that one filter. It doesn't matter when we hit it, there'll be a full crew working at the time." He looked up. "The number of casualties will probably be somewhere between 600 and 700...depending on the exact placement of the bombs."

Wymini stared into space for a few moments. "Make a new banner. On this banner we state: Next time we use one of the..." She frowned. "What did *they* call the firestorm weapon?"

"A nuclear bomb," said Xadorm.

"Yes," said Wymini. "Next time we use a nuclear bomb on the plant. If you persist in attacking us and our star system… we will explode at least 200 nuclear bombs on your home planet." She looked around the table. "I don't think we'll have to use that many…or I hope that we won't have to use any. We'll still make the threat."

Jeejow cleared his throat. "What if they don't listen? What if they continue to give us trouble?"

"If we make a threat and they don't listen…" Wymini hung her head. "We'll have to carry through with the threat…or they'll never believe us…on any subject again. If we carry out our threat…then they'll have to believe us."

Marbing nodded. "So either they leave us alone…or die."

Nantasa looked up. "So when do we begin?"

Wymini looked off to the side sadly. "As soon as we can get five bombs in place in that manufacturing plant."

Nantasa looked shocked. "He said that it would take three bombs."

"He said that it would take at *least* three bombs," said Wymini emphatically! "I don't want minimal damage. I want it to be *done*! I want to leave no doubt in their minds that we mean what we say…and we're willing to back it up…with their total destruction." She leaned back in her chair. "Somebody call Hrombisk and tell him to get the bombs in place."

"In which dimension?" said Skalix.

"We haven't done anything to them in good old 108 (Observation)," said Wymini. "Put the bombs there…until we're ready to detonate them. We'll put timers on them and then… hop them to Home…with about three heartbeats left on the timer. Then…boom."

Skalix looked somewhat nervous. "Who are the ones… who will hop the bombs…once their activated?"

Wymini looked at him soberly. "Me…my Team members, Poroth, Afa-Im and Choychata…the fifth will be…Hrombisk. One of Hrombisk's Team members will unfurl the banner…in an area outside of the blast. That way they'll see it and be warned. It's up to them to heed the warning."

Skalix picked up his pad. "Are there any other instructions… other than what you've given so far?"

"Yes," said Wymini. "I was just thinking. After all this time…we still seem to not have enough of those 459 cannons to go around. Why not?"

"There's no one with the technical skill to manufacture new ones," said Xadorm. "If we were to ask someone else to make the parts - they'd surely ask why. What do we say then?"

Wymini nodded. "What about the 456 cannons?"

"There's a good supply of those," said Jeejow. "They have been kept up, but not used very much because of the devastating power of the 459."

Wymini smiled. "As soon as this project is over, let's start a mass upgrading of the 456 cannons. We may not be able to make them as nasty as any 459, however, I'm sure that we can make them nastier than what they're capable of at this time. Look at how the 459 has been improved with just some new wiring…and a lot more power behind it. If we're going to scare the *piddleeyanks* out of any enemy…we have to have the fire power that's necessary to do it. Since we don't have enough 459 cannons to go around… upgrade the 456 cannons and start mounting them in the same manner as the 459."

"We'll need a lot more platinum wires," said Inditam. "That *is* one thing that we do know how to manufacture."

Wymini gave her a big smile. "Yes, and we know exactly where we can find a bunch of that platinum, don't we?" She stood up. "Contact the appropriate Teams on the manufacturing of wire and the upgrading of the 456 cannons. Then, let's get to work on these…Vagens."

Andatam of Team 1150 and Seequeta of Team 1151 visited Kiyalee.

Andatam nervously twiddled her thumbs as she tried to consider all alternatives. "How much wire do you think we'll need…for all of the 456 cannons?"

Kiyalee shrugged. "As soon as this *h'oolyach* with the Vagens is over…just start making as much wire as you can. We've had a few of the 459 cannons malfunction and we've had to repair them. We still have a sufficient supply of platinum wire from the first time you made it…but that was only with the supply of 459 cannons in mind. Now that we have to upgrade *all* of the 456…

well, I don't know how much we're gonna need."

Seequeta nodded. "We may have to go back to Bri and get more. That's okay though. As Wymini said…there's plenty of platinum there."

Soolchakan nodded. "For now…we've all got to get ready to go bully the Vagens and let them know that *we* won't be bullied. Let's hope this campaign won't take long and we can all get back and have some fun…rebuilding a few thousand of the 456 cannons."

Andatam nodded. "See you on the Vagen home world." With that she vanished.

Seequeta just smiled, waved goodbye and vanished.

Kiyalee shook her head. "I've got to get all of the computer repair people together and…look at all of the specifications, diagrams, schematics and other whatnot on those 456 cannons." She shook her head and sighed. "Oh what fun," she said sarcastically.

Soolchakan just grunted.

"Let's get our suits on and join everybody on Vagen," said Bonarain.

"Yeah," said Chyning. "Go do what we've been doing best for over 1,900 years: Theft…and destruction."

The Command Staff were all in attendance when they arrived at the main manufacturing plant for the filters.

Wymini snarled at what she saw. "This is gonna be tougher than we thought. Look at all of the guards around the building perimeter…wearing those *chokwad* goggles and…what kind of pulse rifle is that?"

Xadorm scratched his chin. "I suggest that we do a one-on-one. Get enough people here so that we can hit all of the guards at the same time. We grab their goggles and we grab those rifles. We get the goggles and rifles back to Hardooth and blow the plant up."

Inditam shook her head. "How many of those guards are there?"

Wymini scoffed. "Who cares? Just keep calling in Teams until we see that we have the necessary one-on-one. Then we strike. Don't call on the Teams that are already supposed to be here, because of the bombs and the banners."

Skalix, Yim and Xadorm started calling in Teams. Jeejow was giving instructions to the personnel as they arrived.

Wymini just stood there watching. "I wish we didn't have to do this."

"As long as there is the existence of arrogant and ambitious conquerors, it'll be necessary," said Marbing sadly.

"It'd still be nice if we could have had almost 2,000 years of peace…instead of having to fight off all of those others," said Inditam.

"Let's just hope that the future will be better," said Nantasa.

"We've always had hope," said Am-Sisa. "I'd like to have

results."

Fifty-two Teams were called in for the mass theft. Each Team member was assigned a specific guard and they each stayed with that one waiting for the order to grab both goggles and rifle.

Wymini looked up at the security cameras around the building. "I wonder…if they can run filters over whatever is being filmed and…then find us in Observation."

Skalix clenched his teeth. "You're right. They could be watching us…and not realizing it until they run the film through another set of filters. Then…we could very probably lose Observation as a hiding place."

"Get the computer people here," snarled Wymini. "Everything is on hold until we find out where the film…or hard drive…or any kind of technology that they're using to film us. We've got to keep at least one hiding place…seeing as how *one* is all that we have left at our disposal…regarding this bunch."

Sankiki and Tula were called in along with all of their Teams to find out anything that they could. After two days of searching through the computer systems in the building and tracing wires they reported.

"Not a problem," said Sankiki. "A closed circuit system and it is all here in this building. They don't want to bother anyone else with their problems, so they have everything here. The only thing that is required is for there to be another command of execution. This one will be first. When the order is given, my Team members will pour some rather nasty acid on the three hard drives. Once the acid starts eating those hard drives and before they can react, the second command is given and…Boom! The plant is destroyed and they have no evidence of who did it or how, because the acid will have destroyed a vast amount of the information initially. Once the bombs go off, the acid catches fire and it is double trouble for the hard drives."

Wymini had a wan smile. "Step one: Destroy the hard drives. Step two: Grab 506 guns and goggles. Step three: Unfurl the banners and then…Boom!" She sighed. "Is everybody in place?" She turned to Hrombisk. "Since the bombs require the timers, I guess you and you're Team will need to give the orders."

Hrombisk nodded. "I understand. We can set the timers for anything that we want in order to get the steps in the proper order."

"At least we're in Observation," said Nantasa. "We can see the bombs go off but we don't have to listen to them."

"Thank the Great Maker for that," said Am-Sisa.

"It's your show," said Wymini to Hrombisk.

Hrombisk inhaled hard and let it out. "**Start the timers**!"

Five of the physicists hit their switches.

Hrombisk looked at his chronometer and nodded his head a few times as he counted. "**Pour the acid**!"

Sankiki's Team members hopped the bottles into Home and poured the acid on the hard drives. The Vagens who were in the security room heard the sizzling immediately and thought that it was a fire. They hit the fire alarm and ran for some extinguishers in order to put it out…while the fumes were burning their eyes and lungs.

Hrombisk bit his lower lip. **"Grab the guns and goggles**!"

506 Vagens were now shocked and confused as rifles and goggles disappeared from their heads and hands. They were already excited and agitated over the fire alarm going off, now they had been robbed. Some of them panicked and ran.

Hrombisk kept on staring at his chronometer. **"Unfurl the banners**!"

Four large banners, placed in areas that should be relatively safe from the blast, were hopped to Home and unfurled.

"Hop the bombs and Jump out of there!"

The five bombs were hopped into Home and all Owlamites Jumped out of the building. Two heartbeats later the bombs went off and they were able to observe the fiery blast from the safety (and silence) of Observation dimension. The bombs turned out to be stronger than they thought or the building was not as sturdy as they thought. When the bombs went off, it was a very short time before the entire structure completely collapsed into a pile of flaming rubble. Over half of the confused perimeter guards were crushed by falling walls, burned to death or killed by flying debris. The survivors were the ones who had taken off running (the swiftest and away from the building) at the first sign of trouble in the area.

Am-Sisa swallowed hard. "I think we made a mess," she said with a concerned look on her face.

Xadorm hung his head. "I don't think that anyone...who saw the banners...is still alive. We blew up the building...but none of the Vagens know why...or how."

Wymini shook her head in disgust. "Get a few more banners here...and put them outside...of the destruction."

Nantasa nodded. "Not a problem, Sir."

An Owlam woman appeared directly in front of them. "Sir, there's some emergency response vehicles on the way here. It looks like they have goggles as well."

Skalix nodded. "Thank you, Officer, Beeskeen." He looked off in the direction she had pointed. He turned back to Wymini. "Do you want to stay or go?"

"Since we're in Observation, I don't see a problem right now," said Wymini. "Let's wait until the banners arrive. After we're sure that they've seen them...then we'll depart."

Skalix nodded. "Heading for the next target?"

Wymini simply nodded as she stared at the flaming rubble.

As rapidly as they could, all of the Owlamites were involved in the task of obtaining all of those goggles and destroying any technical data on them. As soon as they got word of any of the things cropping up somewhere else they reacted with full force in depriving the Vagens the use of the filters in their computers or being able to use any of the special goggles.

After another year of hopping and Jumping around the

Vagens, the Owlamites had acquired over 25,000,000 goggles, 900,000 of those strange pulse rifles, corrupted countless computers where the data was stored on the goggles and filters and, of course, wreaked all kinds of havoc on the Vagen computers on the ships that used computer technology turning their attention to computer repair instead of manufacturing filters to look through the dimensional barriers into Spy.

There was a huge population of Vagens that were very upset over all of the losses that had occurred in that time span.

Wymini looked over the reports. "There's nothing here… but anger on their part. Those Vagens don't want to negotiate anything at all."

Skalix scoffed. "Usually, after getting your posterior scorched as many times as we've burned them, *somebody* is willing to attempt some peace talks. All of the spies are reporting in that…the more equipment of theirs that we destroy – the more determined they are to find out who is doing it…conquer and enslave this enemy and use their capabilities to assist the master race in conquest of the entire cosmos."

Wymini shook her head. "How can anyone be so hard-headed?"

"They're nothing but narrow minded, control-freak, politicians," said Jeejow. "The only thing they want is *control*. Their ideology is: I am right, you are wrong. If you disagree with me, then I have to kill you or enslave you. They go for total control of every aspect of the lives of the people…for the entertainment and comfort of the elitists in charge. High positioned politicians with huge government and huge control."

Xadorm dropped his pad on the table. "I command – you conform! That's all that they want. Totally the type of control that's one step away from monarchy or oligarchy."

"And they try to sell themselves as benevolent and altruistic," said Inditam. "Greedy blood-suckers is all they are."

Yim held his hands up. "I'm receiving a telepathic communication from…one of the spy Teams under my command… and *urgent* message!" He closed his eyes and concentrated.

The rest of the Staff sat there quietly while Yim was receiving the message.

Finally Yim opened his eyes. "The Vagens are doing it. They've built a new spaceship. This one has six light speed engines and therefore almost unlimited power. When they use all six of them together, they can create…what they call a dimension shifting vortex. It's an opening into another dimension. They won't need the goggles. They're going to go into Spy dimension, in force, and search us out there.

"I thought that each ship, with four light speed engines, could hop through the dimensional barriers," said Wymini.

"They can," said Yim, "However, once they've gone through they have to shut down their light speed engines for almost half a day. It takes a great deal of energy and those things get very hot. This would be one super space ship that could open a doorway and let…maybe hundreds of ships through. That would be the only one that would then have to shut down for a while."

Wymini snarled. "Where's Hrombisk? Get him here and…let's figure out a way to stop them…completely…even if we have to do another…1,200 bomb firestorm attack on their home planet."

Hrombisk showed up with three other Team leaders from the Teams of physicists. He listened intently to all that had been discovered about the new Vagen capability of dimension shifting through technology. The Staff was desperate to find some kind of powerful weapon that could be used to combat this new threat.

Officer Grade 4, Itchami of Team 435 sat there snickering. "You don't need anything spectacular," she said. "All you need is one little hand-held bomb."

Wymini leaned forward. "Explain yourself."

Itchami smiled. "These light speed engines…are very powerful. They are also extremely dangerous. They all have an electromagnetic barrier around them. If that barrier ever fails… it is absolutely necessary to shut the thing down immediately… no matter what you're doing. If you don't, the results are…total annihilation."

Xadorm looked horrified. "One little hand-held…could destroy something that powerful?"

"Yes, Sir," said Itchami merrily. "That's why they have eight different types of redundant, electromagnetic barriers around those things. If one barrier fails, they still have seven. If two fail…they still have six. If another one fails…they perform a precautionary shut down until they have all of the systems back on line. They fully recognize how dangerous a cascading, cataclysmic explosion could be."

Skalix shook his head. "And we can cause that kind of explosion…in the light speed engines…with one lousy hand-held?"

Itchami nodded. "One lousy hand-held, inside all eight barriers and…there is no containment in the cosmos that could protect them from the resulting explosion."

"Good," said Wymini. "Our spies tell us that there's a place out there where the Vagens are experimenting with this…dimensional shift thing. We're going to go there and foul their experiment. We're going to go there and watch it happen. Then we're going to watch the thing get blown up…with one hand-held bomb."

"The light will be too bright," said Itchami. "You'll have to cover your eyes during the initial blast…or your eyes will end up broiled…and blind. Observation might protect us from the noise and the blast but…the intense light is a completely different thing."

Wymini sighed. "All right, so we cover our eyes during the initial blast. Fine!" She turned to Yim. "Get your spies to collectively Jump us to the experiment sight so we can do some damage to their experiment."

After all of the coordination was accomplished, the entire

Command Staff and several of the physicists were present at the Vagen experiment site. They were, of course, watching from Observation.

Toktaya from Team 500 was the one giving the oration on what was about to occur. "**They've brought the big ship out here. That fatter one is the one that's going to open up the pathway to the other dimensions. As you can see they have other ships scattered behind it and those are the ones that're going to be going in and out of the dimensional rift once it is opened up.**"

Wymini looked at the other ships that were randomly parked in space behind the main ship. "**How many are there**?"

"**There are fifty ships out there behind the experimental ship**," sent Toktaya. "**They're just sitting there waiting for the opening to be created. Once done, they all go through and come back in singles and groups. This way they know that it works both ways and there's only one ship that ends up spending its energy. The main thing here is to find out how long that ship can maintain the opening before it overheats.**"

Xadorm pondered for a moment. "**Officer, Toktaya… weren't you spying on someone else…for us**?"

"**Yes Sir, I was spying on the Jowfoonda. Now that they're extinct, we don't need anyone watching their graves.**"

Xadorm cleared his throat. "**Good point**."

Wymini chuckled over Xadorm's embarrassment. "**What are we watching for here**?"

"**The fat lead ship. The entire front end of it will start lighting up. About two kilotaja ahead of it, you'll see what looks like a big circle...like water going down the drain through the center. It'll be sparkling all around and through it. The other ships will slowly go through the center of it and disappear.**"

Inditam frowned. "**What do you mean – disappear? Why can't we see them**?"

"**Because we're in Observation and they're in Spy.**"

'Enough of the superfluous questions,' thought Wymini. "**When is the best time to drop the hand-held on the big fat ship**?"

"**That will be when the other ships start moving towards the drain. The fat ship will be right in the middle of doing their deed and won't be able to shut their light speed engines down fast enough. The fireball created by the explosion will light up everything around here and if you look into the fireball...you *will* be blinded. Anything in close proximity to the fat ship should be damaged...or destroyed. Actually, we don't know to what extent they'll be damaged...but that is partially what this observing is for.**"

Wymini cocked her head while thinking. "**Okay, Itchami, who is going to drop the hand-held**?"

"That'll be Officer, Shibashasha from my Team. She'll drop it after I give her the signal."

"This is Shibashasha! When she gives me the signal, I'm going to activate the hand-held. Just before it blows, I'm going to drop it in Home right next to the light speed engines and Jump back to Hardooth. I don't wanna be anywhere near this thing when it goes off...no matter what!"

"That's fine," sent Wymini. "We'll all know that when she gives the signal it'll be just a couple of heartbeats before the whole sky lights up. We're ready."

"They're starting it up," sent Itchami. "Get ready."

All of the Owlamites watched as the entire pointed nose of the big ship lit up with a very colorful display. It would have probably been rather attractive if it were not for the fact that this was a weapon. A cone of light shot out of the nose. At a certain point the light stopped and a strange, and very massive, whirlpool appeared in the area, some two kilotaja away from the ship. It sparkled as the strange lines started spinning faster. The faster it turned the more sparkling there was in the big circle. Four ships started moving towards the whirlpool. All the other ships started moving up to get in line.

"Now," sent Itchami.

"It's activated...and I'm gone," sent Shibashasha.

All of the Owlamites bowed their heads, clenched their eyes shut and placed a hand over their eyes. The sudden brightness was so intense that it almost seemed as if their eyes were open and there was no hand in front of their face. The brightness remained for several heartbeats and then just as suddenly it was dark again.

Wymini still had her eyes shut. "**Is it safe yet**?"

"**Yes, Sir**," sent Itchami. "**But you're not going to believe what you see**."

Wymini opened her eyes and looked around where the enemy ships had been floating in space. She saw several oddly misshapen…things…that were glowing a strange orange. "**What is that…those…uh…what am I looking at**?"

"**That is the remnants of the enemy ships that were caught in the blast area**," sent Itchami. "**I believe they were superheated by the blast and partially melted. I don't think that anyone…on any of those ships is still alive. The heat would have been…oh so horrible. They were all cooked…in the blink of an eye…before they even realized what happened**."

Wymini blinked several times trying to comprehend the overall situation. "**Did any of the…enemy…make it into… the other dimension**?"

"**I'll check**," sent Itchami. A few moments went by. "**Strangely enough, one of the ships did make it…alive… and is now calling for help. There is another one in Spy that got cooked as well**."

Am-Sisa was a little surprised. "**How could the blast have cooked one of the ships in Spy? It didn't have any** effect on us...except to nearly blind us. How did that ship get...destroyed?"

"Apparently it was just transitioning and...the ship got cooked before it got there and the opening was closed...after it got...cooked," sent Itchami. "Of course that's just a guess."

Wymini chuckled. "For lack of any other explanation, I'll accept that one. I'm confused as to why...there was no lasting firestorm...that came out of that explosion."

Itchami had to hold back her disgust as a result of the stupid question. "A fire needs three things to keep burning. You need heat, fuel and oxygen. In the void of space, there is no oxygen. The fires burned out as soon as they used up all of the power of the blast. No oxygen – no lasting fire...just a big shock wave that seems to have died out."

"Makes sense," sent Wymini feeling rather stupid for asking the question.

Xadorm shook his head. "What do you suggest that we do now?"

Wymini shrugged. "Go back home and wait for any new intelligence data from our spies. What else is there? Unless maybe you'd like to inspect the burnt remains of the...melted ships in this vicinity."

Xadorm chuckled. "No, I think home is a good place to be right now...and wait for the next target where we have to do an all-out attack."

Wymini sighed. "**Right! Keep sending our people out to claim all of the goggles and pulse rifles…if any still exist**."

5

Kiyalee was given fifty of the Vagen pulse rifles. She sat there looking at them for a long time rather worried. If they were anything like the Owlamite pulse weapons, they had multi-stage triggers, which would kill the user if you did not do the steps in the correct order. She had not seen the things fired and had no idea what their capability was.

She looked over the entire outer portion of the rifle before finally conjuring up the courage to open one of the panels on the gun. She found nothing but wiring and a few electronic components. She was going to have to test each one of the components to determine exactly what it was in relation to electronic components she was familiar with. For two days she pondered the weapon while the rest of her Team brought food to her and let her just sit there worrying.

"I need a schematic of some kind," said Kiyalee anxiously. "Without it…I've got nothing. I don't know where to start or what to look for." She scoffed. "All that time looking for these things and…fouling up their computer systems…and now…I'm supposed to figure it out…on my own. *H'oolyach*!"

Soolchakan sighed. "Have you tried firing one of them?"

She shook her head. "I don't even know how to turn it on,

let alone fire it. Without a schematic…or an instructional manual. I'm *stuck*…going nowhere!"

Bonarain cleared her throat. "I'm going to request that some of the computer people work on it. See if they can find something in the Vagen archives or…maintenance manuals or somewhere…find something."

"Maintenance manuals," said Soolchakan nodding. "That has to be it. They've gotta have something that tells *them* how to fix or fire the stupid things."

Bonarain sent a mental communication to Jeejow, asking for the use of some computer personnel. Since the rifles had become an important issue, it was only fair that someone assist in finding out what they could about these "special" weapons. Jeejow responded that he would inform Wymini and see if they could help. Before Bonarain could get disgusted with what she thought was an evasion, two women were at the door asking if they could enter the apartment of Team 7016. Officer Grade 7, An-Soyma of Team 257 and Officer Grade 7, Bantasang of Team 258 were allowed to enter. They informed Team 7016 that they were computer operators and that they were to give any and all assistance that Team 7016 needed with the rifles.

"I need a schematic on these rifles," said Kiyalee. "Without it…I can't even start."

The two visitors went to two of the consoles that were in the big public room of the apartment. They both logged in and started searching through technical manuals that had been captured earlier.

After nearly half a day searching, An-Soyma just shook her head. "These things are *very* special. There's nothing...*nothing* at all in these manuals. We may have to find something new...on their home planet in order to understand this new-fangled gadget."

"I agree," said Bantasang shaking her head. "Either they're so new or so secret that there was nothing on them in the stuff we got from the other ships."

Soolchakan picked up one of the rifles and looked it over. "There's got to be something somewhere that can give us information on it. They didn't just...invent this thing that quickly. No one does that. Not with a technical pulse weapon. You test it over and over and over until you perfect it. Then you tell the appropriate people how to use it."

Kiyalee scoffed. "I know that we allowed all of those Vagens in the desert to starve to death. We still have about forty of their technicians in the aquarium. Maybe we can do some mind-reading on those *bimyocks* and get something from them...that'll give us some kind of clue."

Bantasang looked horrified. "Why did we let them starve?"

"They were too much trouble," said Chyning. "Do you have any idea how much food we had to take to them on a daily basis? They weren't worth it."

"Once we found all of their top technicians and engineers, we had no need for any self-serving, ambitious politicians...or lackeys," said Bonarain. "All that a politician does is manipulate, fabricate, control and spin...and if things don't go their way, they have a temper tantrum and blame everyone else for their failures.

The lackeys…almost as worthless as a politician. They're obedient, but totally ignorant. The people who build and repair… they're worth keeping."

Chyning scoffed. "Will they let us near the prisoners?"

"This is important," said Bonarain through her teeth. "They want us to figure these things out. Any step that we have to take to find out anything that we can about them…they'll let us do it. They have to, otherwise they assigned this task to Kiyalee for *nothing*!"

"You have 34 technicians to go through," said Inditam. "Read the minds of any or all and find out what you want. I hope they can give you something…even if it is involuntary."

"Thank you, Sir," said Soolchakan. He turned back to his Team. "Okay, we pull them out one at a time. We delve into their mind…collectively. We find out if they know anything about the pulse rifles. If they do know, we separate them from the rest. If they don't know…we put them back in the box."

An-Soyma looked at Soolchakan with skepticism. "Why are we needed for this mass mind reading? You're better at it than we are."

He gave her a disgusted glare. "You know what you're asking for. I'm just assisting in filtering out some of the superfluous *chogo*. You and Kiyalee have to go for the *real* good technological stuff."

"Sounds good to me," said Bantasang merrily.

Chyning stood there leaning against the glass. "Where do we start?"

Soolchakan turned to Kiyalee. "Pick one."

Kiyalee sighed. "Let's start on the left end…and move right."

Someone off to their right hollered. "HOLD ON THERE!"

The six of them were startled as they looked at who was yelling at them.

Soolchakan was a little indignant. "Who are you?"

The man came up to them. "I'm Officer Leader, Zoolkog. I'm the one in charge of taking care of the prisoners."

Soolchakan now felt a little foolish. "Sir…uh…were you informed as to why we're here?"

"Yes, I was," said Zoolkog. "Before you try, what I'm sure you were going to try, you're going to need some help."

Bonarain smiled. "What did you think we were going to do…Sir?"

"Read their minds and control them," said Zoolkog with a patronizing look.

Now Bonarain was the one who was embarrassed. "Uh… Sir…how did you know that?"

Zoolkog smiled. "Because that's the only reason that anyone comes here. No one has come here just to gaze at their irritated faces and make funny faces back at them. They come here to try to get information by reading their minds and controlling what they think by asking them questions that make them think of the answer."

Soolchakan sighed. "We're no different than that. Is there something that you have as a suggestion…before we start?"

"Absolutely," said Zoolkog. "It seems that they've become used to seeing us take control of them. Now, every time we do, they try to stop us by going to the person who appears to be under control and slap the *h'oolyach* out of that person…until we release control. So…now that we know this, we have to call other Teams in to assist in the mind control. All 34 have to be controlled, simultaneously, or else whatever you're trying to find out will be severely interrupted. We must do a mass mind control."

Soolchakan nodded. "All right, Sir. Who are the Teams that are going to assist in this mass mind control?"

Zoolkog smiled. "It goes by rank…of the Teams that requested to be here during the next mass control time." He looked at his pad. "Since there's already six of you…it'll include my Team and six other Teams. Teams 1396, 1488, 1787, 1959, 2030 and 2127."

"Hold on," said An-Soyma. "I'm on Team 257! We should get precedence over all of those Teams."

Zoolkog smiled. "Only if your Team Leader put in the request. Was that request entered in my messages?"

An-Soyma looked off to the side, partially disgusted partially embarrassed. "If you don't have it…Endinga didn't request it."

Zoolkog turned to his Team members who had quietly entered the area. "Emakti, go over there and put the banners up for the first six Teams on the request list. Inform them that we're going to do a full mass control of the prisoners and their presence is needed."

Emakti smiled, nodded and spun around heading for the Jump in area. It did not take long for the area to fill up with the necessary 34 Owlamites to perform the mass control mind manipulation of the Vagen prisoners.

He turned back to An-Soyma. "One of the stipulations of getting yourself on this list is that you have to do some practice on the mind control. There are three of the *bimyocks* in that room who are very strong willed. If you don't completely overwhelm them…you don't control them at all."

Bonarain looked through the glass. "Which three are they?"

Zoolkog started looking them over. "One of them is the tall one with the very long dark hair in the back. The second one is the one with the torn silver vest in front. The third is the short fat one off to the right." He sighed. "If no one is here that can individually control any of those three…we'll have to call in reinforcements."

Bantasang smirked. "And whom would that be?"

"Team 777 said that they want a second shot at doing some controlling," said Zoolkog. "Right now, they're number one on the list for a second chance."

"Well let's get to it," said Soolchakan impatiently. "We're wasting time talking about it when we need to start getting as much information as possible on that *chokwad* pulse rifle."

Zoolkog passed out assignments as to who should control which one of the prisoners. The prisoners started looking a little agitated as each one was pointed at by Zoolkog. Once all of the prisoners had been assigned a controller Zoolkog let out a deep breath and then sniffed.

"Is everybody ready?" Zoolkog looked for nods from everybody. "Here we go…NOW!"

Most of the prisoners were now standing there with a dull look on their face. The three that had been pointed out were shaking their heads trying to fight off the control. The tall dark-haired one started looking around and started slapping the ones near him.

Zoolkog scowled. "Who had him? You're losing him!"

"I'll get him back," said Officer Grade 5, Eensang. "Don't worry!"

"We're losing more," said Zoolkog. "Now I've lost mine." He snarled. "Vooskani, go call Team 777. This isn't working."

Everybody let go of their victim. Vooskani went to the Jump in point and came back moments later with Team 777.

Zoolkog smiled at the newcomers. "Officer, Soonkono, do you remember that hard-headed one that I told you about?"

Soonkono nodded with a smile.

"He did it again," said Zoolkog with a shrug.

Soonkono snickered. "No cooperation at all I see."

"No," said Zoolkog with a shrug. "We're going to have to double up on him and the other two, just to make sure."

Soonkono looked at the one in question while nodding. "Let's do it."

It took almost half of the day, however, they were able to isolate three of the Vagens who knew about the super-secret weapon. Zoolkog got those three out of the aquarium and had them trussed up with enough chains, to the point where they could barely walk.

Chyning snickered. "Is all of that hardware necessary?"

Zoolkog nodded. "According to Wymini...yes."

Chyning scoffed. "It's going to take a while to get them back to the apartment."

"Unless we Jump them," said Kiyalee.

Chyning gave her a dirty look. "Let An-Soyma and Bantasang do that. It's your project, not mine."

Team 7016 along with the two computer personnel and the three prisoners did the Jump to apartment 12-562. Now they were ready to see if they could figure out what these weapons really were.

The three prisoners fought as best they could to not give up any information, however, being hit with the constant bombardment of mind control it was a lost cause for them. They finally gave up what little they knew about the rifles and Bantasang was able to find a well hidden technical manual on the weapon in the archives of the original Vagen ships that had been captured.

Kiyalee now had the information that she needed to look this special weapon over completely. She read some of the technical data and it did not make sense to her. She looked it over thoroughly and finally just huffed in frustration.

Bonarain knew how impatient Kiyalee could be so she tried to assist in reading the manuals. "What is it you're having so much trouble reading?"

"It just doesn't make sense," complained Kiyalee. "Maybe…I'm not getting the translation right. I don't know. It just…isn't coming through."

Bonarain nodded. "Let me read it. I'll send it to you while I'm reading and maybe it'll come through a lot more clearly." She read it to herself and sent the translation mentally. She stumbled over a lot of the technical jargon, however, she did her best to send it as clearly as possible. When she finished the first page she looked up at Kiyalee apprehensively.

Kiyalee shook her head. "That's what I got as well…but it still doesn't make sense." She picked up one of the rifles. "Right here, you hit this button to turn it on. Once the blue light comes on, it's ready." She pulled the trigger and waved the business end of the gun around in a figure eight pattern. "Okay…nothing's happening. What good is it?" She pointed at the illustration of the rifle. "Plus…look at that. The tip of the barrel has some kind of… cluster…of wiring on it. Do you see that wiring on the tip of this barrel…I don't."

Soolchakan cleared his throat to get her attention. "Didn't it say something about wearing those goggles when you're using this thing? Does anyone have any of the goggles here…now?" He looked at the information on the screen. "It also tells you to make sure of your target in the *zone*. What does it mean by *zone*? Since they pulled this out to use against us in Spy dimension…is it possible that the word *zone*…is a synonym of dimension?"

"That sounds silly," said Bantasang. "How could two words like that be so close in another language?"

"I don't know," said Chyning. "Remember the Chok language? The words 'home' and 'murder'…sound so much alike. They're both three syllable words in the Chok language and the accent that you put on the second or third syllable makes a tremendous difference in what you're saying or meaning."

An-Soyma opened her eyes. "My Team Leader, Endinga is requesting a set of goggles right now. If you're supposed to be using the goggles when you use the gun…maybe that's why you can't see any reaction of any type. Endinga said that she was bringing some goggles here…as soon as she can get some."

Chyning giggled. "Not to mention the fact that there's nothing in this room that is located in Spy dimension. Do we have anything in the apartment that's located in Spy dimension… anything at all?"

Bonarain looked up in shock. "MY TRUCK!" She looked at Kiyalee in horror. "What direction were you aiming that thing… when you pulled the trigger? If you aimed it at the garage…what happened to my truck?"

Bantasang scoffed. "Why would you put your truck in Spy dimension?"

"So you can fit more vehicles in there," said Soolchakan.

Bantasang stilled looked skeptical. "Like how many?"

Chyning admonished her in a whiny voice. "If you put two trucks in Home, one in Spy, one in Observation and one in Ghost, you can put an entire motor pool in there."

An-Soyma chuckled a little. "Oh my! That sounds… useful."

Meanwhile Bonarain was running to the garage. She pulled the door open and vanished. She reappeared a moment later. "MY TRUCK…IS…DEMOLISHED!" She looked back in the garage. "You ripped my truck to shreds…with that thing." She put her hands on top of her head. "My truck is in shambles." She glared at Kiyalee angrily. "You owe me a new truck!"

Kiyalee hopped to Spy dimension and looked, in anguish, at the wreckage of Bonarain's truck. When she had been holding the trigger down, the pulse ray or whatever it used had been thoroughly dissecting the truck. The beam had gone right through the walls of the apartment in Home and destroyed anything in the path that was in Spy. She hopped to Home and saw that the big 161, along with Soolchakan's red truck were still intact. She hopped to

Observation and saw that her yellow truck was intact. She hopped to Ghost and saw Chyning's green truck was undamaged. She hopped back to Spy.

Soolchakan pointed at the rifle in Kiyalee's hand. "Look at the tip of the barrel. You said that you couldn't see any wire cluster…in Home. Now that we're all in Spy…I can see the wire cluster that was in the illustration."

Bonarain had a look of horror on her face. "That means… that the Vagens…using their technology…can do a partial hop… just like we can." She looked at Kiyalee. "They've figured out a way…to do what we do…naturally…with technology."

Soolchakan sighed and shook his head. "There's something that the Command Staff needs to know about…now!"

Kiyalee held the Vagen pulse rifle up. "Sirs, what you see is a very strange weapon. It has been modified by the Vagens so that they can come after us in Spy dimension." She looked at the gun. "Now, Sirs, if you would put those special goggles on, I'm sure that you're in for a surprise."

They all put the goggles on and every one of them did get a surprise. Most of them pulled the goggles away and then put them back on several times while staring at the alien rifle.

Wymini was the first to speak. "What is that…on the tip of the barrel?"

"It has something to do with aiming," said Kiyalee. "I haven't been able to go through the entire manual yet, but somehow, through technology, the Vagens can hop the tip of this pulse rifle into Spy, while the rest of it is in Home. They can then…shoot a very deadly pulse beam into Spy…and kill us…if we're hiding in Spy…at that time. The goggles allow them to see us so that they can…aim true and do their dirty deed."

"We need to get in their archives and find out how many dimensions *they* are aware of," said Skalix.

"Already done, Sir," said Bantasang. "All of the stuff that I can find on 'other dimensions' shows that they've found nineteen different dimensions…and are trying to figure out a way to start conquering in all of them."

"That is an incredibly ambitious plan," said Xadorm. "Can you even comprehend how big their military would have to be…in order to accomplish the enslavement of one galaxy in one dimension…let alone two or three…or nineteen dimensions?"

Nantasa scoffed. "And the entire time, they're convincing themselves about how benevolent and altruistic they are with their autocratic, control-freak agenda."

"Right," said Inditam. "We enslave you to teach you how nice we are. Now, fetch and carry or I'll kill you. Such nice people…HAH!"

"Because they are *so* superior as a race," said Jeejow mockingly.

Marbing shook his head. "What kind of people are they? They even enslave some of their own…because of political differences…and then claim that those others are a different race…

even though there's no physical or genetic difference between them. I can't even comprehend where that goes."

Yim pulled his pad up. "Have you been reading some of the propaganda in their archives? According to them, it is not just their destiny to enslave this and all other dimensions to their whim…it is their solemn duty to bring everyone to *their* way of thinking…whether they like it or not. Bow and serve…or die."

"And with this technology, where they can do partial dimension hops…they feel like nothing can stop them," said Am-Sisa.

Wymini sighed in disgust. "What do we know about their overall power?"

"They have five different classes of attack ships," said Xadorm. "They also are still looking at the experimentation of using one ship to open that…dimension vortex…so that other ships can crossover without having to stop and replenish their power."

"We did put a *big* strain on that one when we blew up their prototype," said Jeejow with a grin. "The spies are reporting that they're back in the laboratories trying to figure out what went wrong. They're trying to recreate the same circumstance in order to correct the flaw. If they can't correct the flaw, they're going to have to scrap the whole idea."

"Right," said Wymini. "Now, about those five different classes of ships…how many are there of each one?"

Xadorm nodded and hit some keys on his console. "Class

1 is not very big or brutal. If they find an inhabited planet where there is a sentient race…who is just discovering how to make fire and the wheel…they use the Class 1. A Class 2 goes after a planet that is just getting into metallurgy and a weapon like the bow and arrow. Class 3 is for a planet where they are just starting to understand technology. Class 4 is for a planet that has technology but no outer space capability."

Wymini scoffed. "And Class 5 is for someone who is in outer space."

"Yes," said Xadorm.

Nantasa snarled. "Do we have to guess which Class is coming after us?"

Suddenly there was a disturbance outside of the conference room. One of Wymini's Team members, Officer Grade 7, Afa-Im was pushed backwards into the conference room, followed by Officer Grade 4, Toktaya.

Toktaya looked around angrily. "I'm sorry for this intrusion…Sirs, but…this is news that…is incredible and very important."

Wymini clasped her hands under her chin and smiled. "It had better be important." She dropped her hands to her lap and scowled. "*Very important!*" She looked at Afa-Im and smiled. "That will be all."

Afa-Im nodded and turned to leave, however, she did give Toktaya a very nasty snarl before departing.

Wymini leaned forward, placed her right elbow on the table

and rested her chin in her right hand. "Okay, what's so flaming important?"

Toktaya nodded. "The Vagens, Sir…they're not from Home dimension. They're from dimension 85…what we used to call *Heea 1*. There were some things that…just didn't make sense to me whenever I Jumped to their home planet. Now, I know why it was so taxing, or tiring, to make that Jump…we weren't just Jumping to a different planet…we were also hopping to a different *dimension*."

Xadorm hung his head. "So those *bimyocks* are already, well in, the middle of trying to conquer more than one galaxy…or dimension."

Nantasa scoffed. "No wonder they can make a rifle that can exist in two different dimensions at the same time."

Wymini was now sitting upright. "How many dimensions are they aware of?"

Toktaya pulled a paper out of her shirt pocket and looked down at it. "They know of 1, 13, 19, 22, 51, 53, 73, 79, 85, 94, 99, 128, 136, 145, 156, 160, 184, 202 and 205…but they didn't discover them in that order. Did you want that…the order that is?"

"No, that's not necessary at this time," said Wymini. "The order that *they* discovered them in…completely unimportant. They have our Home dimension and Spy." She suddenly looked as if she had been slapped. "Hold on! We introduced them to 45 (Jahong's Death) and 198 (Desert). Have they added those to their list?"

"No, Sir," said Toktaya. "When we introduced them to 45, WE hopped them there. They were *not* introduced through their own technology so they had no idea where they were or how they got there. When we tossed them into 198, we did so without allowing them to take any of their technology…so they were even more ignorant of that one. Besides that…all of the ones that were thrown into 45 are either dead…or stranded in our aquarium. There's no way that they have contacted their home planet and given them all of the necessary information about 45…or 198."

Wymini sat there thinking with her teeth clenched. "When we blew up their factory…for making the goggles…was that on their home planet…in 85?"

"Yes, Sir," said Toktaya with a smile. "All of that damage was on their home planet in dimension 85."

"They're not indigenous to this dimension," said Xadorm. "I don't think that we should respect their intrusion on us. I think we should rip them apart in their own home. I'm of the idea to have another 1,200 or 12,000 firestorm bomb attack on a home planet…of an enemy…especially this one."

Wymini sighed. "First things first! I want some spies… in all of the dimensions they've…polluted. I want to find out how much power they have in each one. Then…we'll blow the *h'oolyach* out of their home…and any other stronghold that they have in those other dimensions. If we don't demolish all of their strongholds…we might be wasting our time with just their home planet."

Soolchakan looked a little down. "I thought that our

information was important," he muttered in a glum manner.

"It is," whispered Bonarain. "Coupled with what Toktaya just said, it *is* very important. Both of them complement each other."

Soolchakan nodded in agreement. "Put that way…it does sound better."

Over the next four years, 2,200 Owlamite Teams were wandering through the eighteen dimensions (not worrying about Spy dimension) for any star systems they could find where the Vagens were overwhelming the originals with their political bigotry.

In their home dimension of #85, they were in complete control of fifteen populated star systems and were battling for three others. The second dimension they had found was #145. Populations were not that common in the area they had covered so far and they were only in control of 4. In #184 they had eleven systems and were battling for one more. In #22 they had six systems and were fighting for three more. In #51 they had nine systems and were battling for two more. In #205, there was a tremendous area of nothing. They had to wander far and wide to find six systems they controlled.

Dimension #13 (which had originally been called Soolchakan 7) made Team 7016 a little mad. The Vagens had taken over a very hot planet that had an atmosphere with no liquids of any type. They had somehow created two large oceans on the planet. This made it very extremely humid, however, there was a colony of Vagens existing on that planet. There were nine other systems that the Vagens controlled in this one and one that was being fought over.

#79 had originally been called Shogoot's Search. It had the acid water planet in the system. There were no inhabitable planets in that star system so the Vagens had branched out to eight others that they were controlling.

#160 was a treasure trove for the Vagens. They had conquered twenty-three systems and were currently winning the battle in seven others. #19 was one of the dimensions where the Owlamites had been able to see a nebula. There were now ten systems under Vagen control and two others under contention. #136 was another one with very little to fight over. There were only two inhabited systems that were under Vagen control. There were nine others where they had some work going on, however, those systems had no inhabitable planets. #94 had twelve systems under control and three being fought over. #128 had seven under control and four being fought over. #156 had nine under control and three being fought over. #73 had thirteen under control and four being fought over. #99 had six under control and five being fought over. #202 (which was originally called Soolchakan 14) had seven under control and 3 being fought over.

Finally in Home dimension or #1, the Vagens had control over five star systems and were now engaged in the frustration and confusion over the Owlamites Holgotho system.

Wymini looked at the figures shaking her head. "These *chokwads* have full control of 163 star systems in 18 dimensions and…they are currently involved in conflicts over 42 others…as well as ours." She looked up with horror on her face. "They are currently fighting on 42 different fronts. How much firepower do these monsters have at their disposal?"

"It's worse than you think," said Jeejow. "I've been looking at some of this and…I found that while they are currently fighting on the 42 fronts that you were referring to…it also appears that they have to constantly patrol the areas that they have control of because there are some who want to fight back to free themselves or else take property from the Vagens."

"That'd mean that they're fighting in hundreds of fronts," said Skalix.

"Our spies got into some of the really classified computers on their home planet," said Inditam. "They found that the Vagens currently have a fleet of 3,229 space ships which are in the attack category. They have only 167 ships that are in the cargo transport or passenger transport category."

Marbing shook his head. "3,229 plus 167. They've probably gutted the mineral content of over a thousand planets like Bri. The spies also report that there are also 657 new spaceships currently under construction. That'll put them over 4,000…in a very short time…operating in nineteen dimensions."

Xadorm scoffed. "Maybe we should have kept a few thousand of the firestorm weapons that the Mufayton were manufacturing. We could sure use them right now."

"No," said Wymini. "The Vagens have a few thousand of their own. All we have to do is start setting them off inside their attack ships and…pretty soon we'll make a massive dent in their armada. Of course, if you remember, all it took was one little hand-held bomb to destroy that prototype and fifty other ships in one shot. Maybe we can do the same thing again…to all of them."

"I think that we should figure out some way to completely kick them back into their own dimension," said Am-Sisa. "If we don't push them back in there…they might still try conquering… even though we knock them back to their pre-space travel era."

Xadorm gave a pained look. "What you're saying…is to kill all Vagens…that are in any dimension outside of 85."

"Yes, I am," said Am-Sisa adamantly.

"I agree," said Nantasa. "Destroy all of their assets outside of 85 and they just might think again about being the superior race of multiple dimensions and star systems."

"Hold on," said Jeejow. "Why don't we attack their home planet? If we attack there…they just might start recalling ships from other dimensions to come back and defend the home. If not…we'll learn a few things about their character."

Yim scoffed. "Character? What character? They enslave their own…and then go out and try to conquer all. The only character they have is ambitious snobbery."

"That might be true," said Jeejow. "Either way, if they do or do not defend the home, that might give us a clue as to what our next move is."

"I agree," said Wymini. "Hit them at home…hard. Watch their reaction and then go from there." She leaned forward smiling. "Let's get four of our Jowfoonda battleships out of number 45 and fire them up. We're going to pay a nasty visit to the Vagen home world. As I recall, we can get a lot more damage out of a 459 when we power it through a light speed engine. We don't need a firestorm weapon…just eight of the 459 cannons."

"We hope that's all we'll need," said Skalix.

"Don't be so pessimistic," said Nantasa.

"I'm still hoping for the best," said Skalix. "But we should prepare for the worst."

"Good point, as usual," sighed Wymini.

6

Eight days later, they were ready with four of the Jowfoonda ships. The tricky part was going to be Jumping all four of them to the Vagen home world without being detected. Jumping in Observation from #1 to #85 was not an easy maneuver. It was made even more difficult when Jumping a full sized outer space battleship.

The Jumps were accomplished successfully, in spite of their reservations, and they were there around the Vagen home world with the Jowfoonda spaceships (in Observation).

Skalix looked at Wymini nervously. "We're running a tremendous risk here. If we hop these ships into Spy dimension, we're exposed to these Vagens. They could open fire on us and… we really don't know the total capability of their weapons yet."

Wymini glared back at him. "Do you think I'm having fun here? I know it's a risk. But all things concerned…we either defeat them totally or we surrender totally. Which do you prefer?"

Skalix looked at the other members of the Command Staff for some kind of support. He saw nothing in their faces that led him to believe that he could depend on them in a debate against this attack.

Wymini took several deep breaths. She leaned her head

back and closed her eyes. "**All Owlamites in the attack force…prepare yourselves. All four ships are in place… each with two 459 cannons. The cannons are warmed up and ready. When I give the signal, the ones who are supposed to hop the ships to dimension 85, do so without hesitation. The ones on the cannons will open fire. You will maintain fire for five heartbeats. After five heartbeats, you are to Jump back to the dimension 45 parking lot and wait for further instructions. There are four Officer Leaders, with their Teams, who will observe what happens in the attack and will report any significant things that occur on the planet as a result of the attack. Are there any questions**?"

Soolchakan looked through the telescopic sights that he had been issued for this attack. He was looking down on the planet from outer space and saw a large city with four rather large buildings in a square. He decided that this would be his first target. He would take out all four buildings in a quick circular pattern. He wondered just how small the movements would be with the cannon in order to take them out and then have time to do some larger sweeps with the cannon. Now was a good time for experimentation.

Bonarain was on the same ship as Soolchakan and she was on the other cannon. There were two of the cannons on each ship and Team 7016 was assigned to handle the cannons on this ship. Kiyalee was behind Soolchakan with an extra power pack (for some unknown reason since the attack was only going to be five heartbeats). Chyning was behind Bonarain. She had no idea where Soolchakan was aiming, however, there had been no instructions on specific targeting. Apparently the Command Staff was only concerned with an initial flash attack with massive damage and worry about any specific targets later.

Wymini sat there listening for any questions. After counting to ten – twice – she nodded. "**NOW!**"

The ships were hopped to #85.

Soolchakan had his sights centered on the northeast building. When he pulled the trigger, he saw the lower floors of the tall building blow out and the building started to topple to the side towards the northwest building. He moved the cannon slightly to make an attempt at the southeast building and found his beam ripping a path through the city and then the countryside and striking at least 40 kilotaja southeast of the primary target. At this height, even the slightest move made an incredible difference as to where the beam would hit on the planet's surface.

Bonarain rapidly drew a big circle and then a square. She did not see Soolchakan's beam in her sights, so she figured that he was aiming somewhere else (especially since he was on the other side of the ship). His beam would have been easy to spot because the area that they were firing at was in early evening planet time. She wondered what the beams looked like coming from the ship that was on the nighttime side of the planet. She wondered if the ones on those cannons could even see a definite target.

"**HOLD!**"

With that, the attack was over and the four ships were hopped to #45. The four Teams that were assigned to inspect the damage stayed in Observation and started slowly losing some altitude in order to get a good look at the aftermath of the attack.

As they were going down they suddenly observed numerous small craft launching from the surface and coming up to where the four ships had been located as they assaulted the planet. They stopped their descent in order to see what was going to happen up there 225 kilotaja above the surface. The Vagen ships started a circular search pattern and the Owlamites saw lights on the noses of the small ships that were changing color and intensity.

One of the four Officer Leaders, Bybisi, sent a message to the other three. **"Maybe we should be listening to their minds and find out what they're doing and how."**

The other three Officer Leaders sent back that they agreed. The four Teams mingled with the Vagen ships and started reading minds. What they found was that these small ships had the same kind of filters that the bigger ones had and they were looking for the attackers in other dimensions. They had been able to triangulate on the precise origin of the beams from the surface of the planet and now had these small, but very deadly, fighter ships looking for the attackers. There was a lot of frustration and aggravation in the minds of the Vagens because they could not find anything in regards to the attackers – in any of the nineteen dimensions they knew of. By the time they finally gave up in their search, the planet had taken one half of a revolution in its daily turn. They reported back that whoever the attacker was – these people were even craftier than anyone else they had ever experienced before.

When the Vagens gave up their search, the Owlamites had to Jump back to Hardooth in order to get a resupply of oxygen for each one of their small fighter ships. They then Jumped back to the Vagen planet to look for damage.

Bybisi sent out to all of the other observers. "**Do you think we'll get our job done this time**?"

"**I really hope so**," sent Officer Leader, Chazand. She shook her head as she neared the surface. "**It won't be hard to find the damage…from what I'm seeing. It appears that it was extensive…even viewing it from only ten kilotaja above the surface.**"

"**I think that someone opened up a sleeping volcano**," sent Officer Leader, Yoganay. "**I've already see some lava flowing in an area north of the volcano and it looks like the population is evacuating, in a completely panicked manner, right now. There's going to be some extensive property damage from that lava flow. It appears that at least three towns are being overwhelmed. Would you believe that there are actually some looters who are trying to get anything they can and…many have been run over by magma**?"

"**I guess that we're going to have to measure just how deep the pulse beams cut into the planet's crust**," sent Bybisi.

"**If we opened up a volcano…I think we cut deep**," sent Officer Leader, Yiba. "**That would be a very deep cut.**"

"**It all depends on how soon that volcano was gonna erupt anyway**," sent Bybisi.

"**This is Officer Grade 4, Toktaya. Can I get my**

Teams back on the planet to find out what their High Command is doing…in any area that isn't being overrun by lava?"

"**Yes**," sent Bybisi. "**Any time you're ready, go back and find out what you can. As a matter of fact, take a few more Teams in there to find out all you can.**"

Twelve days later, all of the spies and observers were in the Command conference room ready to tell their tales.

"The 459 pulse beams cut furrows…over ninety kilotaja deep into the surface of the planet…in most cases," said Bybisi. "The Vagens were originally talking about filling in the furrows but…they're now saying that the things are just too deep…plus some of them have actually widened since the attack and…we don't know why. They can't find that much dirt or rocks or gravel anywhere. There were three of the furrows where…they connected with the ocean and…filled in rapidly with sea water. Now, they're just talking about building bridges across the chasms."

"That seems odd," said Xadorm. "They've gutted the mineral content of a thousand planets in order to build their fleet… and yet they won't go back to those ravaged planets for *dirt, rocks and gravel*. I wonder why."

Bybisi shrugged. "I can't make those decisions for them, Sir. I'm just going with what we heard."

Wymini scoffed. "We're not worried about *dirt*! Are the Vagens recalling any of their battleships from other dimensions?"

"Not at this time," said Toktaya. "We may need to hit them again…even harder. They don't seem to be too scared from this attack. Confused – yes. Scared and defensive – not even close."

Jeejow shook his head. "Their home planet is attacked… and they don't seem to care. What is it gonna take to scare them?"

"Several more attacks that are even more destructive," said Yim. "We got their attention. Now…we have to hurt them… badly, in order to make them more defensive and recall some of the ships to dimension 85."

Wymini nodded. "I'm afraid you're right." She hung her head. "Set up another attack. Ten ships this time. Mount four 459 cannons on each. Let's see if that scares them into recalling some of their military."

"We can do something else," said Inditam. "If we mount some 456 cannons on those ships as well…say eight or more…we can use them to ward off any of those small defensive fighters that were sent up by the Vagens. Attack the planet and destroy some of their defenses…hopefully that gets their attention."

Wymini nodded. "Do it. Twelve 456 cannons on each one."

The second attack with ten ships caused massive damage to the planet and some cities. The Vagens lost over a third of their planetary defense forces in attempting to fight the marauders. They recalled twenty-one battleships from 1, 99 and 202.

Wymini threw the report down. "Twenty-one! That's all?

They don't seem to care about their own home planet the way the Choks or the Zizzikinza did, do they?"

"I think that we're going to have to use some firestorm weapons," said Skalix. "If that doesn't get their attention...I don't know what will."

"I'm confused about these firestorm weapons," said Marbing. "Why aren't they creating new races on the planets that we attacked...like they did here?"

Nantasa looked at Marbing as if he were crazy. "It has been...1,920 years since the Algothon attack and...just NOW... you're wondering about that?" She looked off to the side and scoffed.

Marbing glared at her. "I've been wondering about it for a long, long time. I just...never voiced it before."

"I wondered about it as well...and I asked," said Wymini. "According to our physicists...the only thing that they can think of is...either our planet has some peculiarity about it...or the peculiar thing was the Algothon weapons. This planet suffered something unique from that mass attack. It could be either reason. We don't have any more Algothon firestorm weapons so until something, like what happened to us, happens somewhere else...we are in the dark as to which reason it was that new races were formed...as a result of the attack."

Am-Sisa shook her head. "How many firestorm weapons are we talking about...as far as the attack on Vagen?"

"Hit the Capital city...with three of them," said Wymini.

"That should get somebody's attention."

"*That*…is not a clear target," said Bybisi.

All of the Command Staff looked up at her confused.

"There are at least twelve cities that could be capitals, or *the* Capital," said Bybisi. "It all depends on which faction is in charge at the time. It is also possible that eleven of them are capitals of… provinces. If we blast one city…they have the capability to move all of the decision making…to one of the other cities. Again…it all depends on who is in charge."

"Twelve cities," said Wymini flatly. "Then I guess we'll need to use thirty-six firestorm weapons…won't we?"

"We hit them all," muttered Jeejow. "That *should* make a mess."

Inditam sighed. "What about the banners?"

Wymini looked around the table. "They're ready…aren't they?"

"Yes," said Nantasa flatly.

"Then make sure they get there and are in a place to be seen," said Wymini. "Now get everything ready."

"One thing," said Xadorm. "Should we destroy some of the bigger ships as well? If you want to bring in some of the big battleships from other dimensions…shouldn't we deplete the ones that are already there?"

Wymini sighed. "I guess you're right. We're also going to need a few more observers for the…before and after. Call Officer

Leader, Iquanza and let her know that she's the new…on site Commander. Get a total of twelve Teams that'll do the observation and inspection. Once they're in place, the Officer Leaders will do the observing while their Team members each take out a larger ship."

"I think the extra destruction will be necessary," said Marbing. "Especially since they have added to their fleet. They now have 3,452 attack ships and 670 more under construction." He shook his head. "They've stepped up production considerably."

Wymini scoffed. "Wouldn't you?"

Wymini looked at the Command Staff. "What's the report?"

Skalix stretched. "Each one of the firestorm weapons is being placed in an area where the one who starts the…" He looked a little confused. "…critical mass…or mess, or whatever, has a chance to get out of there after hopping the thing into dimension 85. We're going to try to make them all blow…at approximately the same time. They're trying to make sure that each bomb is placed in an abandoned building or one with little or no personnel. That way, no one'll see it and have any chance to raise an alarm of any type."

Wymini nodded. "Just make sure that everybody gets out of there before anything happens. I don't want to hear that someone waited until the final moment…just for some silly thrills and giggles. I want everybody out…IN TIME!" She sighed. "Where are the banners?"

"The banners are going to be placed 85 kilotaja from the center of each blast," said Nantasa. "There will be four banners... for each one. We're going to place them as close as we can to north, south, east and west of each blast."

Wymini frowned. "Why can't we place them exactly north...or south of each blast?"

"Roads," said Xadorm. "They don't all have a road that conveniently goes due north of each city. Some go northwest... others northeast."

Wymini nodded and waved her hand at him. "That's fine." She bit her lip. "Will thirty-six firestorm weapons do...as much lasting damage to the planet...as we did with some of those others?"

"No," said Jeejow. "According to Hrombisk, The immediate area will be affected for 70 to 80 years...but the planet won't suffer that badly...especially as badly as a planet where we blew up over 200 weapons at the same time."

Wymini nodded. "Let's hope that we don't have to teach them another lesson."

There were several statements and words of agreement from all personnel in the room.

Wymini cleared her throat. "Master Officer, Skalix...as soon as everyone is ready, I want you to be the one to give the order of execution. I'm tired of...sending one word...that causes the deaths of...I don't know how many souls."

Skalix nodded stoically. "Yes, Sir."

The bombs were in place and the Owlamites were ready. Skalix gave the order and numerous things were ready to go kaboom. All thirty-six nuclear devices were armed and headed for critical mass. Above the planet, there were twenty-four large, class 5 battleships that had a hand-held bomb placed next to the light speed engines (out of sight of anyone in the engineering section). There was a large ship building hangar in outer space where several hand-held bombs were going to be used to blow a wall out and cause rapid decompression in several areas of the complex.

Thirty-six nuclear bombs went off, laying waste to the twelve capital cities. Twenty-four battleships blew up when their light speed engines were breached. When the outer space construction hangar was compromised, five partially built ships were demolished as debris coming out of the breaches causing the fatal damage to the partially constructed ships. The banners were unfurled in their designated areas.

All of the participants in the attack had Jumped back to Hardooth. Now, Officer Leader, Iquanza gave the order for all of the personnel left behind to start watching the reaction and check out just how much damage had been done on the planet's surface and in outer space.

The Vagens on the home planet were at a complete loss because all of the leaders (in the currently elected party) had been blown up in the attack. They had to recall 106 of their battleships to the area for defenses as well as getting some high ranking personnel (who were currently on those ships) at home who had enough rank to make big decisions.

There was an extremely large amount of anger and consternation over the discovery of the banners. Who were these interlopers that dared to set foot on the hallowed soil of the home planet, let alone attack it and give insulting warnings to the greatest sentient race in all of the 19 known dimensions?

Wymini threw the report down angrily. "Here we go again! Another bunch of *bimyocks* who think that they're so superior to everyone else who has the capability of abstract thinking." She shook her head. "Will it ever end?"

Xadorm hung his head. "Not as long as there is one individual who has the megalomaniacal ambition to control others…completely against their will."

"They're already making noises that they believe it was us," said Jeejow. "According to the report, they're saying that the attacker had to come from a star system where they just arrived. Ours is one of three that they have just discovered."

Wymini started checking a few things on her computer. "Where's that list of the dimensions that they're currently infecting?"

Marbing frowned. "I've got it here…uh…what did you have in mind?"

Wymini glared at him. "What three dimensions are on the list…of the new star systems?"

"There is us in dimension 1," said Marbing. He looked through the information. "There is another one in dimension 94.

The third is in dimension 19. We are the primary one on the list because we've shown the capability of being in more than one dimension."

Wymini looked angry but thoughtful. "Other than those three dimensions, which one are they...rather busy...hitting others hard?"

Am-Sisa was looking at her information. "It appears that they're rather busy in dimension 73...why?"

Wymini looked sternly around the table as she talked. "Hit them...HARD...in dimension 73. Let's go all out to destroy anything that we find in dimension 73."

Yim closed his eyes and groaned. "And what if they start harassing us even harder in the process?"

"We'll put up a good front," said Wymini. "But we *will* still destroy anything that they have in dimension 73. Anything and everything is an immediate target...to be destroyed as soon as possible. Turn as much of their attention to 73 as we can. Whenever and wherever we find them...total destruction."

Nantasa cleared her throat. "Do we keep on...showing them some banners?"

Wymini smiled. "Good idea...yes...absolutely. That'll keep them confused."

"We might also want to hit them hard in dimension 136 as well," said Inditam. "It seems that they have huge mining operations in nine star systems in that dimension. That's where they're getting a lot of their raw materials...for construction of their space ships."

"That's another good idea," said Wymini. "Find that Officer, Eeleeg that kept destroying all of the Teltermak tunnels. Not very much difference in a tunnel and a mine. Destroy those mines internally and we won't have to worry about very many new ships being built."

"That's a huge operation," said Xadorm. "We have just over 24,800 Owlamites to work with…including ourselves. That's gonna keep a lot of us *very* busy…for who knows how long."

Wymini's shoulders sagged as if she were tired. "The whole point of it…is our survival. We have a right to live free. We either fight…or we are in servitude…to a despotic autocracy… who even abuse their own."

"So we start passing out assignments," said Inditam.

"Exactly," said Wymini. "Pass out the assignments…and if there aren't enough people…we go in as well."

Team 7016 was sitting in the middle of outer space in #73.

"**This is ridiculous**," grumbled Chyning. "**We're 33 light years from the nearest star system and…we have to look for Vagen ships in, what…seventeen different star systems in this dimension**?"

"**I agree**," sent Kiyalee. "**How are we supposed to find…anything anywhere in this dimension…without some kind of guide**?"

Bonarain smiled. "**What do you have to say to that, oh wonderful Team Leader**?"

He shook his head. "**Actually we do have something to go by. We just started at the wrong place. What we're going to do is hop to dimension 85. We then Jump to the Vagen home world…and then hop back to dimension 73. Whatever star systems they're vexing… have to be somewhere close to their system…in the other dimensions. Think of the Stink dimension. That's a planet, in another dimension…that is occupying the same space as Hardooth…in the other dimension. They might have the same situation among the Vagens**."

Bonarain sighed. "**As dumb as that sounds…it actually makes some sense. Lead on oh semi-great one**."

Soolchakan snarled to himself. 'I get enough of that *h'oolyach* from Chyning. Now it's coming from Bonarain as well…again.'

They hopped to #85, Jumped to the Vagen home world and quickly hopped to #73. According to their instruments, they were only two light years from the nearest star system. The Jumps were now going to be a little hazardous because they had no landmark to go to. All they could do was picture the stars a little differently in their heads and hope that there was nothing in their way when they Jumped again. Soolchakan determined that the safest way to do that was in #207 (Ghost). Once they arrive in the star system, the decision was to hop to Observation.

It took fifteen Jumps to get close enough to the star system where they could make out something other than more distant stars. The sixteenth Jump took them right into the heart of the system and they were able to find an inhabited planet that was being ravaged by the Vagens. They found the system, somewhat by trial and error, however they did find it. Soolchakan was pleased that the women were able to follow his lead in the Jumps. "**That worked rather well**," he sent. "**This proves that we can do it without too many problems.**"

Bonarain scoffed. "**What are you talking about? I didn't landmark on any kind of 'let's get closer to that star'. I landmarked on your fighter. Wherever you Jumped to…I made sure that you were still alive before I made the Jump.**"

"**I did the same thing**," sent Kiyalee.

"**I was landmarking on Bonarain's fighter**," sent Chyning.

Now Soolchakan wanted to backhand all three of them. He had taken all of the risk and they just went along for the ride. He fought hard to keep from sending them all a nasty remark. "**We're here…let's go investigate this planet and…knock a few of the Vagens out of existence.**"

Chyning snickered. "**Should we landmark something on the planet while we're here?**"

"**If you haven't done that already…you're several steps behind us**," sent Bonarain.

Now Chyning wanted to backhand somebody. "**I don't recognize those ships…that the Vagens are using.**"

"**That's because you didn't look them up in your computer, dearie…like you never do,**" sent Bonarain in an admonishing tone. "**If you had used your computer information, you'd have realized that they are Class 3 Battleships. The Vagens use those when they find a planet with a pre-technology society. Check your messages!**"

Now Chyning wanted to backhand somebody – again - hard.

"**I see four of the ships on this side of the planet,**" sent Soolchakan. "**Bonarain and Chyning, you two go west around the planet. Kiyalee and I will go east around the planet. We'll check and see if we find any more of those ship here.**"

When the two pairs met on the other side of the planet they compared notes. They now knew that there were a total of ten Vagen ships involved in the harassment of this planet.

Bonarain was puzzled. "**Ten ships seems a little bit too much for a planet that hasn't discovered electricity. I wonder why…ten.**"

Soolchakan sighed. "**Do you want to study the planet or just harass the Vagens?**"

Chyning scoffed. "**Do the studying on your own time. Right now, I wanna clobber these *doovofts*. Then**

get back home and take a bath."

"**Let's clobber and go**," sent Kiyalee. "**I need a bath as well**."

Bonarain flew up to the nearest enemy vessel. "**How do you want to do this? Do we slice them up with the 459**?"

Soolchakan looked at the supply box at his right. "**No… let's just drop a hand-held in the core of one of their light speed engines, watch them make a big glow…and go home. A bath sounds good right now**."

Before the Vagens had a clue what was going on, they were now minus ten Class 3 Battleships and Team 7016 was back in the gorge getting ready for some necessary hygiene and a meal.

Team 7016 had reported to the Command Staff the results of their raid. They also sent some photographs on a few landmarks on the unnamed planet they had partially rescued. There were thousands of (rather surprised) Vagens who were on the planet at the time of the raid who found themselves with nothing but several small shuttlecraft. The shuttles had a very limited range so until the Vagen High Command could get some more Battleships to the area, the ones on the planet were trapped.

Of the thirteen star systems in dimension #73 the Vagens had secured – they were now down to twelve secured and five they were fighting for. Once the Owlamite Command Staff read the report from Team 7016, other Teams were dispatched in the same manner and two days later the Vagens had zero star systems that were secure in #73 and they were minus 108 more Battleships of all classes. They also had over 12,000,000 Vagens stranded on the different planets.

Officer Leader, Iquanza, who was in charge of the twelve Teams spying on the Vagen home world, was sending back all kinds of reports on some very confused, irritated and rather worried Vagens.

The Vagens were debating all kinds of possibilities for the future of #73. Should they rescue all of the stranded Vagens, retreat and abandon? Should they go on an all-out attack on the planets in #73 in order to remove this embarrassing blemish on their record of conquering? Should they find out who the main aggressor was and try to work out a peaceful solution (which they would turn to their advantage - later)? Was this just a diversion from someone else because they had not suffered losses like this until they found that nineteenth dimension? That last choice did worry the Owlamites. The Vagens were in disarray in regards to the horrible setbacks in #73, however, they still were able to think clearly enough to know and understand the possibility of a diversion by another race that was capable of traveling through other dimensions.

While the Vagens went round in circles on their debates, the Owlamites were able to sit back and wait for the final decision – whatever it turned out to be.

Meanwhile Team 7016 was able to sit and do some leisurely resting.

"I've been wondering," said Kiyalee. "How is it possible…that when we're in another dimension…we hop to Spy or Observation or…Ghost…and we're still observing that other dimension? Aren't those dimensions…one of their own dimension?"

"Now you're really getting into something that the physicists should be contemplating," said Bonarain. "I've been wondering the same thing and…it gives me headaches just thinking of all the possibilities."

"Maybe it has something to do with some kind of independence of those dimensions," said Soolchakan. "Maybe… somehow they're all hooked together…or some kind of half-way thingy to another dimension."

Bonarain snickered. "See what I mean? Anyone can come up with a theory as to why we can Spy or Observe from dimension 1 or dimension 73…but until we understand quantum physics a lot better…all guesswork."

Chyning scratched her rear end and sniffed. "Should we ask Hrombisk?"

"I don't think so," said Soolchakan. "If you do…and he has figured it out…he just might show you some mathematical equation, that covers that entire wall, and you don't understand any of it…and he sits there and smiles and says that he has shown you the solution."

Kiyalee chuckled. "And he says: See how simple it is?"

Chyning looked at her empty glass. "I need some more of

that fruit juice."

"There's another pitcher of it in the refrigerator," said Bonarain.

The next day, Kiyalee walked into the dining room. She had a strange look on her face. She saw the other three having a meal. "I did it."

Bonarain looked at the other two and shrugged. "You did…what…dearie?"

"I went to Hrombisk…and asked him…why…are we able to…go to dimension 73 and still go to…Spy and still be…in 73?"

Soolchakan smirked. "Did he answer your question?"

Kiyalee sighed. "No. Officer, Disdasi did. She…showed me some…equation. It was nineteen pages long." She flopped down on a chair. "I've never felt so dumb in my entire life. All I could understand on…*any* of those pages…was the plus and minus signs. They have…symbols…that…I have no idea what they're used for. NINETEEN PAGES OF THAT *H'OOLYACH*!"

"You still know how to rebuild the engine on your big old 161 truck," said Bonarain. "Can any of those brainiacs do that?"

Kiyalee gave Bonarain a dirty look. "I don't wanna know."

Wymini did not like the fact that the Vagens had even contemplated the attack as a diversion. "We have to…divert again." She looked back at the report and snarled. "We have to attack them in a different dimension…and cause more massive damage…again."

Jeejow smiled. "May I suggest, *again*, dimension 136?"

Wymini looked up dully. "Why that one?"

"Because according to the reports, they have nine systems, that are uninhabited, where they have massive mining operations going on. They're gutting the mineral supply of those systems for raw materials to build more of their Battleships."

Wymini leaned back in her chair and stared at the ceiling. "Good choice."

Xadorm nodded. "We attack the mining operations with, firestorm weapons and the raw minerals will have that residual energy on them…for a good 70 years. They won't be able to restart the mining operations for several decades as a result."

Wymini looked gravely at Xadorm. "I hate using those things…but…anything that we can do…to cripple any of their operations…is a plus for our survival." She looked off to the side. "Nine of their mining operations…closed down…for at least seven decades." She sighed. "Sounds good. Let's do it."

Inditam looked horrified. "Do we have enough of those nasty things…to do that?"

"We can always steal what we want from the Vagens," said Yim. "We've done it before…we can do it again."

"We certainly can," said Wymini. "And we will. Start setting it up. I want it done…as soon as possible. Those monsters are already contaminating nineteen dimensions. Let's keep them from polluting a twentieth…or more."

Eleven days later, the nine planetary mining operations ceased to exist. So did 3,500,000 Vagens and 151 cargo ships.

The plan backfired. The Vagens were now completely convinced that the problems came from the one star system in the nineteenth dimension they discovered they had not conquered yet. They decided to do an all-out offensive on that rogue system.

It ended up being a seven year war – which the Owlamites won. The Vagens had 3,320 Battleships in the five classes. After seven years they had none. They lost all of their cargo and passenger ships as well. The ship construction sites were destroyed as well. At the end of the war the Vagens had just over two billion of their people left and only on their own planet where they had once had forty-two billion scattered throughout nineteen dimensions.

Wymini sat at the conference table shaking her head. "I hope that we never have to come up against anyone like that again. We miraculously didn't suffer any casualties of our own but…they could have done…incredible damage."

"They did do incredible damage," said Jeejow. "All of those messes…in all of those dimensions. That was…horrible."

7

Skalix looked at the new report. "What are we going to do with over fourteen hundred Vagen Battleships?"

"We'll use them for our purposes," said Wymini smugly. "We can always take parts from one to repair another, like we did with the Jowfoonda and Chok ships, and they're all relatively new ships. With all of the redundant power drives that those ships have, we won't need to build any new ones of our own…for quite some time."

"I hope that we won't need them…in any capacity," said Inditam. "I'm getting rather tired of war."

"We all are," muttered Xadorm. "We haven't started any of them…really…but we've finished all of them."

Jeejow nodded. "Let's all pray for…a long, long, long peace. We can still get to know all of the functions of our newly acquired battle armada…but learn it in peace."

303 years later an unknown and unseen enemy struck again. Once again the Owlamites were thrown into turmoil because no one could contact Supreme Officer, Wymini. Once again, a new command was going to have to be established – as soon as they could figure out who this new aggressor was.

Skalix was the next in line after Wymini and no one could contact him. The next one on the list was Jeejow. He was contacted and he started making decisions immediately. Everyone was to go to Spy dimension - again. Stay there until they could find out anything. Since Team 7016 was the most adept at learning new languages of any invaders, their primary duty was to find some – or any of the invaders and start the ball rolling.

Jeejow also did a quick roll call of all of the Command Staff. He had seen how the Staff had been almost completely destroyed by invaders in the past. He needed to know who was left and how many personnel would have to be replaced…quickly. He knew that Wymini and Skalix were gone. He went down the list by rank. He was able to contact Yim, Xadorm, Nantasa and Marbing. Am-Sisa did not respond. Inditam did respond. He knew that he was the new Supreme Officer and he was going to have to replace the missing members of the Staff. This was not a relief because it still meant that there were several who were dead.

He went down the list of personnel in each Team, starting with Wymini. Poroth and Choychata both responded. Team 37 led by Skalix – no one responded. Team 50 led by Am-Sisa – no one responded.

He checked the list for the next three Officers in the chain of Command. Officer Leader, Onga reported that her Team was intact. Officer Leader, Zoolkog reported that he had lost all three of his Team members and they would have to be replaced. Officer Leader, Tadesha reported that her Team was intact.

The new Command Staff was Supreme Officer, Jeejow. Master Officer, Nantasa was now the Sector 1 Commander. Senior

Officer, Onga was now the Sector 1 Vice Commander. Master Officer, Yim did not change his status as Sector 2 Commander. The new Sector 2 Vice Commander was Senior Officer, Zoolkog. Master Officer, Xadorm was still the Sector 3 Commander. The new Sector 3 Vice Commander was Senior Officer, Tadesha. Marbing was promoted to Master Officer and was now the Sector 4 Commander. Intidam was still the Sector 4 Vice Commander. Jeejow also made sure that they knew the order of their rank: Jeejow, Yim, Xadorm, Nantasa, Marbing, Inditam, Onga, Zoolkog and finally Tadesha. He ordered all of the Command Staff, and their Teams, to one of the Vagen ships in dimension #45.

Jeejow made a general call out to all Owlamites everywhere: **"Does anyone have a clue as to who attacked us…and from where? There doesn't seem to be anything on any computer monitor except we've been attacked and there are several Owlamites that are missing. Please report any information that you have**."

There were several responses from different Owlamites that there were some kind of strangers clanking through the halls of the gorge, however, no one could see them. There were numerous Owlamites who had been killed in their apartments *in the gorge*. No one could see the enemy. They could hear them stomping around in rooms and hallways. They were completely invisible, and other than their clanking footsteps, totally undetectable.

Bonarain was in Spy dimension, however, she was actively seeking out an alien mind…somewhere in the hallway of the gorge. She could hear all kinds of stomping around with no bodies making the noise.

She saw the door to apartment 12-561 open. No one lived there. Team 7015 lived in 12-560 and 7016 lived in 12-562. No one was standing at the door and no one entered. She still heard somebody clomping around. It sounded as if the soles of their shoes were metallic. The sounds of the footsteps neared the front door of her apartment. She looked around desperately attempting to find anything of these strange invisible aliens.

The door to the apartment used by 7016 opened. Bonarain looked inside and saw the rest of her Team standing there (in Spy) with pulse rifles ready. They looked back at her with confusion in their eyes.

Bonarain looked at her Team bewildered. "I can hear them…but I can't see them. I have no idea what's going on." She took a couple of steps and was standing in the center of the doorway.

All four of them could hear the clanking of footsteps as someone was going around the room. Then they realized that there were at least two of the strangers. Someone was headed to the kitchen and someone was going up the stairs to the second floor. Then they realized there was a third. Someone opened a door to one of the first floor bathrooms. Then the door to the other bathroom was opened. Whoever had opened the doors realized that no one was in there and decided to look elsewhere in the apartment.

Soolchakan went to the kitchen door to see if he could find out…anything.

The one that had checked out the bathrooms was now

headed for the garage. Kiyalee got a little hot under the collar as she realized that this intruder would possibly see one of the trucks that she had so painstakingly kept in good running condition over the years. She was not going to tolerate any sabotage of her work. She headed for the garage to do…she was not certain what she was going to do.

Chyning was looking up at the roof. "Whoever went upstairs…had better keep his…or maybe her hands off of my stuff." She Jumped to the second floor.

Bonarain was still standing in the doorway shaking her head because she was not sure what to do. Was this another one of those races, like the Teltermak, where you could not read their minds? Invisible and unreadable minds. This was terrifying.

Soolchakan was in Spy so he did not have to open the door to look in the kitchen. He put his face through the door to see… anything. He could hear someone clanking around and he saw a few of the utensils and bowls being moved on a counter as the intruder examined items in the kitchen. He still could not see the intruder. He strained his eyes to see any kind of anomalous movement or distortion or outline of any kind. It seemed impossible to him that these people could be so totally invisible. The clanking came back towards the door. For a very fleeting moment, something passed through Soolchakan, opened the door and departed the kitchen. Soolchakan yelped in surprise. He was also surprised because he could now read the mind of the alien intruder. He could read him but not understand him. He turned around staring, round-eyed at Bonarain. "I got him!"

Bonarain looked confused. "You got…what?"

He smiled with delight. "He…he walked through me… and…for a moment…I saw him. Now…since I saw him…I can read his mind. It looks like…we have to be able to see someone… or touch them…in order to read their minds."

Bonarain looked pleasantly surprised now. "Okay…uh… what's he thinking?"

Soolchakan growled. "I don't know. I can't understand him. It's all just jibber-jabber to me. You're the translator!"

At that moment Kiyalee, who was still standing in the doorway to the garage, let out a yelp. "I can see one…now…in my mind. He came back out of the garage and…I can read his… untranslatable mind."

Bonarain clenched her teeth. "Where are they?"

Soolchakan pointed at the doorway. "Stay there! They have to go back out that way! When they go out…you'll get them as they leave."

Chyning appeared in the room. "I…got him! I can read his mind! He was going through all of the rooms up there…and…I was standing in the doorway of…my room and…all of a sudden he went…*through me*! Now I can…read his…gibberish."

Bonarain squawked in anger with her teeth clenched. She stood in the doorway with her legs spread out, knees bent and her arms out, looking as if she were ready to pounce on some… thing. If anyone went through that doorway, she was going to make sure that she touched him…her…it…somehow. She heard more clanking in the public hallway behind her. Someone was going by to go check the other rooms that were further down the hall. There were five more apartments (unoccupied) beyond the apartment where 7016 lived. Whoever was doing this was being totally methodical about searching all of the apartments…in the gorge.

"I think mine is headed towards you," said Soolchakan.

Chyning was still looking up. "I think mine is headed to the third floor. I can't understand what he's thinking…but I can see…something…through his eyes."

"Mine is heading up the stairs…to look around there as well," said Kiyalee. "He didn't find anything in the garage that interested him." She looked back at her truck. "*Bimyock!*"

Suddenly Bonarain gasped and looked totally shocked. "HE DID! He walked through the door! I got him! He…he's going away from me!" She turned out into the public hallway and headed towards the five unoccupied apartments with her eyes squinted as if she were concentrating hard on staying in his mind. "I got you…you *bimyock!*" She put her fingers to her temples. "I may have to follow you…but…I got you."

Soolchakan sighed. "**Master Officer, Jeejow, this is Officer, Soolchakan. I think we've finally found these *doovofts*. Officer, Bonarain is trying to read their minds and get some translation going on**."

Jeejow gave out a slight grunt of relief. "**Who are they? Where did they come from? How many are there? How are they hiding**?"

"Sir! One question at a time! We *just* found them! Officer, Bonarain has just started the...language translation. We'll get what we can as fast as we can... and keep you informed."

Jeejow looked at the Command Staff. "We desperately need that Officer, Bonarain to...teach *all* of us how to do that... translation stuff."

"We tried in the past," said Nantasa sadly. "None of us was able to comprehend any of it."

"There's got to be some kind of imagery to it," said Yim.

"Right," said Jeejow. "For the moment...let's just... standby and see what she gets. This is...very frustrating...being attacked...by someone that you can't see...and until now...none of us could read...or even find their minds."

The one that Bonarain was reading was going to 12-564. She followed while she was reading him and getting a translation. He was Brinop, a Vandin 5 in the Tashkafa Invasion and Capture Force. Vandin 5 meant that he was enlisted (E-5). The job of his unit was to go through this entire structure in the gorge, finding any sentient creature and either capture or kill them. If they did not surrender immediately they were to be forced to surrender or exterminated.

He, along with his colleagues, were finding this area in the gorge to be very frustrating. It was obvious that most of the apartments were inhabited, however, they were having a terrible time trying to find anyone who would surrender. Every time they had found someone, those long-eared freaks had stood up. They were supposed to follow orders and go to their knees. None of the ones found here had listened so they had to be executed for their insolence. Instant obedience or death.

Brinop realized quickly that 12-564 was unoccupied because of all of the dust that was on a table. He ordered his two subordinates, Vandin 3 (E-3), Potchcoot and Vandin 2 (E-2), Voy, to continue to the next assigned apartment. They moved out and headed to 12-566. Apparently there was another team of Tashkafas that was ransacking the odd numbered apartments.

She tried to pick up any images from his mind as to what they looked like and how they could see each other. She got some very confusing pictures from his memory and could not tell if it was his home or some place that he had assisted in conquering or…could be anything. She continued reading him, going for every tidbit of information she could glean from him.

After finding that apartment 12-566 was vacant, Brinop stopped and waited. He was looking around at the other personnel with him – who were all waiting for someone else to come to this end of the hallway. They did not have to wait very long.

Bonarain heard someone else come clanking down the hallway to her current location. She saw the rest of her Team coming to where she was standing. She also saw Officer Grade 7, Lessyita of Team 6996 coming towards her in tears.

"They murdered everyone on Team 6997," cried Lessyita. "Where are they? I'm gonna get someone for this."

"Just hold on," said Bonarain. "I'm trying to read them… and you're not helping."

"Why can't I read them…or see them?"

"You have to touch them first. One of them has to walk through you…or you walk through them."

Lessyita looked around frantically. She started waving her arms. She took two steps forward and gasped. "I…found one!" She snarled. "Did you have anything to do with murdering Team 6997?" She clenched her teeth and eyes and started concentrating. "He is one of them," she cried. "He murdered my cousin… Ninyinti! He killed her…for no reason."

Bonarain was surprised. "Can you understand him?"

"I can see the image…in his mind…of shooting her down…with some kind of pulse weapon." She pulled a hand-held bomb out of her vest. "This is for Ninyinti you *melafathan fovok!*" She activated the bomb, counted to three and moved her hand forward. Her hand disappeared momentarily and she pulled her hand back without the bomb.

A moment later they all heard a gargled cry of pain. A man in some kind of shiny, full body metallic armor became visible and he fell forward to the floor with a loud clanging as he landed. The suit had a large globe like center where the torso was. There was a smaller globe like helmet on top with a slit in the front for being able to see out of the suit. The arms and legs were covered with the same armor, however, there were joints at the shoulders, elbows, wrists, hips, knees and ankles that allowed movement.

Brinop called out on some kind of communication device in the suit. "We have a shell-suit malfunction. Man down!"

Bonarain heard several clanks as if several of the intruders had performed some kind of hop.

Brinop called out again. "Tezzet, Tonkoton, it appears that Vandin 3, Ooskoson has had a rather bad suit malfunction."

Bonarain searched his mind for the definition of Tezzet. She found that a Tezzet was on O-6. He was equivalent to an Officer Grade 2. 'Good,' she thought. 'A high ranking officer. Maybe now I'll find out something a little bit more than...*search out and kill.*' She sighed. 'Now, if I could only see the *bimyock.*'

The downed man was kicked by the officer. Other than being jarred by the kick he did not move. The officer who kicked him became visible. "Vandin 3, Ooskoson! Get up!" He kicked the downed man again. When he saw no response, he tapped on his left arm with his right index finger. A small panel opened up on the arm. Tonkoton pulled a wire out, knelt down and plugged it into a small port on the side of the downed man's helmet. "Vandin 3, Ooskoson, can you hear me?" He moved his head several times as if trying to hear something. He then slowly unplugged his wire, stood up and put the wire away. "He's dead!" He turned and looked both ways up and down the long hallway. "Is this area secured?"

"Yes, Tezzet," said Brinop.

Tonkoton removed his helmet. "What happened...before he...fell?"

Five more Tashkafa became visible and removed their helmets. They all had very hairy heads except for the face. The hair was mostly black or dark brown. The skin on their faces was pasty white. They had large bulbous eyes and appeared to have no eyelids. Their noses were rather flat. They all had their mouths wide open, showing upper and lower rows of gray teeth.

"There was no warning, Tezzet," said Brinop. "He…just fell…and we didn't know why. There was nothing out of the ordinary…until he fell."

The rest of Lessyita's Team 6996 came walking carefully down the hall. Officer Grade 5, Sezazi, Officer Grade 6, Inikimti and Officer Grade 6, Broj.

Tonkoton pulled something out of his helmet and talked into it. "This is Tezzet, Tonkoton. I have a…body…of one of our personnel. We don't know how or why he is dead. I need rapid transport from this area to the morgue. We need to find out what killed him." He placed his hand up against his right ear and listened. He shook his head and cleared his throat. "All of you… move him out to the nearest balcony. One of our shuttles will take him back to the ship and…find out what killed him."

Bonarain was listening and translating for everyone in the immediate area.

Soolchakan decided that it was time to contact Jeejow. **"Sir, we've just had a rather revealing episode here…in the hallway on the level 12. It has given us some insight to these people…and their uniforms**."

Jeejow smirked as he looked around the table. "They've got uniforms…how odd," he said sarcastically. **"What difference does it make? One of their people was killed and you think that this death reveals something? I need relevant** information."

Soolchakan growled in frustration. **"Sir, you don't understand. Officer, Lessyita placed the hand-held bomb inside his suit of armor and…."**

"It killed him! So what?" Jeejow snarled. "He still doesn't understand the meaning of the word *relevant*."

Sezazi huffed. **"Sir! The hand-held bomb killed the man. It did NOT hurt the uniform."**

Now all of the Command Staff were sitting there looking at each other wide-eyed in total confusion.

"Explain what you mean," sent Jeejow. **"And this time…I'll keep my thoughts to myself…and listen without interrupting."**

"Thank you, Sir," sent Soolchakan. **"The bomb went off inside this…weird suit of armor. The blast of the bomb was completely contained *inside* the suit. It was so completely contained…when the thing went off…we didn't hear any boom. We just watched him drop. It was also so completely contained…the Tashkafa don't even know what killed him. They're going to transport him to their ship to have him examined by a doctor and find out what killed him."**

"That's an amazing suit of armor," said Xadorm. "If it can keep a blast like that contained…inside…it could also protect them from any blast…outside."

"Invulnerable and invisible," said Jeejow. "That's quite a

piece of useful equipment to have in your possession." He put his fist up against his mouth and did some quick thinking. He looked up smiling. "**When they transport the body…stay with it. Stay with that body at all costs**."

By now, Teams 6999 and 7001 had gathered with 6996 and 7016. All of them were looking confused or shocked by that last order.

Soolchakan shook his head. "**What good is that gonna do, Sir**?"

Jeejow chuckled. "**They're going to take the body to their ship. We don't even know where the** *chokwad* **thing is. We've been looking all over the place with every piece of technology that we have and we still don't have a clue where they are. Once you're aboard their ship, landmark something and…then we'll be able to get aboard at least one of them…depending on how many there are of…them**."

Now Soolchakan was smiling. "**Yes, Sir. Very good plan. How many of us do you want to go on this mission**?"

"**Whoever is there…all of you**!"

Soolchakan shrugged. "**Yes, Sir. That is currently… Teams 6996, 6999, 7001 and 7016. As soon as they start the transport…we're on our way**."

Bonarain huffed. "There's no way that I'm gonna be able to give all of you the information that you need. There's gonna be a bunch of you…wandering around that ship and you won't be able to understand a thing."

Soolchakan smiled helplessly. "Maybe if you give it a little slower…it won't hit you as hard and…maybe you'll be able to send it to…more?"

Bonarain gave him a dirty look. "You're first."

They put their foreheads together.

"Slow and easy," he said.

She sighed and sent the Tashkafa language – slower. She pulled back away from him and was a little surprised by the fact that she did not feel as tired as she had before. He was staring at her in shock.

She backed up a little more. "What's the matter?"

He shook his head. "All this time…I always looked at… what you sent me…and not how you did it. Now…you gave it to me slowly and…I saw how."

She shrugged. "So?"

"So…you were *compacting* it…and I never saw the imagery…until now."

She was now the one with a shocked look. "Imagery?"

He closed his eyes and sent it back to her. He opened his eyes. "Do you see what I mean?"

She stood there dumbfounded. "I…was…cramming it together…and…that's what knocked me silly. All I had to do was…send it…a little slower and…" She looked off to the side. "Oh *H'OOLYACH*!" She grunted in disgust. "All I had to do was send it slower."

Sezazi smiled. "Would you like to try it on all of us…in the slower manner?"

Bonarain took a deep breath. She closed her eyes and started sending it to all of the Owlamites in the immediate area. She finished and opened her eyes. She stood there shaking her head. "All that time…and that's all that I had to really do."

Broj waved his hand. "Uh…excuse me…but the Tashkafa are moving the body. Shouldn't we be following?"

"Let's go," said Sezazi.

The body was dragged out to the balcony of apartment 12-566. The Tashkafa personnel started looking around for something. The Owlamites could not tell what they were looking for or where…until they saw a very strange sight.

Directly in the middle of the air, a large panel slid up revealing the interior of some kind of vehicle. A plank extended from the bottom of the opening to the edge of the balcony. While the Tashkafa were moving the body onto the plank, the Owlamites were all running along the plank into the…vehicle. They all got inside and watched as the body was moved inside. There was a brief discussion between the crew and Brinop. They closed the door and the shuttlecraft started moving up at a rather rapid rate.

Soolchakan and Sezazi squeezed into the cockpit to see what they could find. They were shocked. As soon as the shuttlecraft broke free of the atmosphere, they saw over 100 large spacecraft parked around Hardooth.

"This ain't no minor invasion force," said Sezazi.

Soolchakan just shook his head. "Why don't you go ahead and tell Jeejow? You're the ranking one anyway."

Sezazi snarled at him. "Coward!" She shook her head. **"Supreme Officer, Jeejow, this is Officer Grade 5, Sezazi of Team 6996. We're in the Tashkafa shuttle and… apparently they have some kind of filter in front of them…in their front windows…and they can see their own ships. There are probably hundreds of them…from what I can see. They're invisible to us…but not to each other."**

Jeejow wanted to gag. **"They could have thousands of their troops that're landing on Hardooth. They're taking over and killing millions. This is not going to be a short term situation."**

The shuttlecraft pulled into a bay on one of the big ships. There were some personnel standing by with a large cargo truck that was designed to carry one of their own when they were inside their protective armor.

Each one of the Tashkafa were completely covered with dark hair. They stood about seven and a half taja in height. Their faces and the palms of their hands were the only places on their bodies that were not covered with the thick hair. They were much like the Choks in that they wore no clothing other than some sashes. The sashes were different colors and had all kinds of symbols on them. Even though she had taught them to understand the language, Bonarain seemed to be the only one who could read the symbols and tell them what each one meant. She had to do another sending to teach all of the present Owlamites all of the information that they needed in this little trip.

They had been ordered to follow the body, so they did. They were all present in the morgue when the doctor opened the shell armor and was shocked at the charred and demolished body that he found inside the suit.

The doctor looked at the mess inside the shell and shook his head. "This is impossible! The only way that this could have happened…is if someone were able to introduce an explosive… *inside*…the shell-armor." He looked at his colleagues. "I don't see any other way that this could have happened."

"You're not right," said another man as he walked up to view the remains. "What you're saying *is* impossible. No one could have possibly introduced an explosive into the suit… without punching a hole in it. What we're looking at here is…a cataclysmic failure of the suit itself."

The doctor sighed. "But…Vykonik (O-7), Jojokit…there's no evidence that the suit malfunctioned. There's some foreign debris…or shrapnel that is inside the suit. The injuries to the body show…blast damage from a small device…that had to be inside the suit. Any cataclysmic failure of the suit…would *not* cause this kind of damage."

Jojokit scoffed. "You medical personnel...you don't understand certain types of technology so you put the blame on certain things that are impossible." He got directly in the face of the doctor. "It is impossible to place any foreign device inside the suit. It was the suit that malfunctioned and that is final."

The doctor calmly but angrily responded. "I will find all of the foreign debris that is in the body. I will give it to your precious technological freaks and let them piece it back together, you can have it analyzed and then try to tell me that it is a part of the suit that malfunctioned."

Jojokit laughed. "The challenge is on! Go ahead! Find your...foreign debris. Once it is pieced back together, you'll see that it was a part of the suit that caused this mess."

The doctor shook his head. "Don't you remember what those talking fish said? They said that once they got to *this* star system...everything went completely *spipwot*! They were never able to determine how the people of this planet were able to do it, but, this planet was the downfall of the talking fish and several other powerful races in this sector."

Jojokit walked away. "You put too much faith in the words of a talking fish. Those fish extended themselves too far and tried to blame their shortcomings on someone else. We have attacked this planet and so far we've only lost *one* member of our military..." He turned back around and glared at the doctor. "...and the only reason that we lost him was because of a malfunction in OUR equipment." He walked away shaking his head and laughing.

The doctor huffed. He looked at his colleagues. "Prepare

to start removing all of the shrapnel from the body. We're going to give all of it to those technocrats and let them find where the debris came from. I still don't believe that it came from the inside of the suit."

The other personnel in the room started assisting in sifting through the destroyed organic material looking for any foreign object that was not part of a body. Kiyalee was the first one in the corner puking her guts out. A few others joined her in losing their lunch as well.

Soolchakan snarled. "**Supreme Officer, Jeejow, this is Officer, Soolchakan. Can you hear me**?"

Jeejow came back immediately. "**Yes, I can. What do you have to report about the enemy ship**?"

"**Nothing yet, Sir, because you told us to stay with the body. We're still here watching a…rather gruesome autopsy and…we're not making any headway into the ship itself**."

Jeejow sat there speechless.

"You have to be careful how you word your orders," said Xadorm. "You told them to stay with the body *at all costs*. You are now the *Voice of Power* and with that…they will obey any order…exactly as you gave it."

Jeejow hung his head and his shoulders sagged. He looked up and scoffed. "You're exactly correct." He sighed. "**Since you are now on the ship…that was what I wanted. You can now go explore the ship and find out anything you**

can about these intruders. I would appreciate it if you
would leave one person in the medical area…to keep us
informed on what they find in the autopsy."

Soolchakan turned to Kiyalee. "Go look for the engines."
He did not have to tell her twice. He turned to the other Team
Leaders. "Who should be the one to stay?"

Officer Grade 5, Nosiska of Team 6999 (who was looking
a little sickly) turned to the male member of her Team. "Pimbot,
you seem to be the only one who isn't turning some shade of
green…or even purple…while observing this…procedure. You're
the one to stay. Also, once they've got all of that…debris…out of
the body…stay with that."

Pimbot smiled. "Not a problem, Sir."

Soolchakan signaled to Bonarain. "Let's go find the Main
Bridge."

Officer Grade 5, Ijamaki of Team 7001 was a little irate.
"Why are you the ones to explore the Bridge?"

He sighed as he gave her a dirty look. "Because we've
done this many times before and…no matter what…Officer,
Bonarain is still the expert in determining languages and other
idiosyncrasies of aliens."

Ijamaki bit her lip. "Okay, you win that round." She turned
to her Team. "Okay, Team, let's start in the bow and explore all
the way to the stern. Find out anything you can and map this
chokwad ship out. Be as thorough as possible, but still try to do it
as quickly as possible."

Sezazi looked at her Team. "Let's do the same. Don't worry if you hit an area that someone else has already been to, we're trying to find out what we can as quickly as we can. Total layout of the ship and what these people are like."

Chyning walked up to Soolchakan. "What should I do?"

He snickered and whispered to her. "Do what you do best. Look around and find something interesting…and steal it."

She giggled as she walked away. "Love to."

He turned to Bonarain. "Let's go find the headache center."

She nodded and smiled as the two of them headed out of the morgue.

Since they had no landmarks on the ship they had to explore thoroughly before finding the Main Bridge. On the way to the Bridge, they heard numerous conversations about how those "other" races had said that this star system was so dangerous. Someone had already talked about the "talking fish" so maybe there was a hint about the Zizzys, the Choks and even the Mufayton. They were definitely going to check into that possibility when they found the Bridge.

They also heard a few mental communications between some of the other Owlamites on the ship. They found the main Galley, they found the Brig, they found the Engineering section, they found the Science section, they found the Supply section, they found Security, they found the fighter and shuttle Hangar and they found the Weapons supply area. Each one drawing their own little map of the ship as they wandered through.

Finally they found the Main Bridge. They looked at the view screen and saw that this ship was flying over South Chilamte (big surprise). Sitting in the big chair was another one of the hairy beasts with fancy markings on his shiny golden sash.

"That one is a Beerforda," said Bonarain. "That's equivalent to an Officer Leader."

"What I'm more concerned about…" Soolchakan was looking out a porthole. "…that out there." He pointed. "In here… you can see their other ships. There are hundreds out there…just from what I can see here. I haven't looked out the other side but…I doubt if it is any different." He shook his head. "These people came to stay."

Bonarain grunted. "I'm hearing more about the "other" races that they're talking about. It definitely sounds like some Choks, Doolood and Zizzys. I haven't heard anything about the Mufayton though."

Soolchakan chuckled. "If you couldn't read minds, would you want to be around someone who could? If they did find some Mufaytons, they probably killed them all. The thing I'm wondering about…as well…I haven't heard anything about the Iyka or the Vagens either."

She looked thoughtful for a moment. "You're right. I haven't either. I wonder…no I don't. I don't care about those lizard people or those dimension jumpers."

He nodded. "Those peoples are all retro. This bunch…is here…now. This is what we need to worry about. We need to find out more about this bunch and how to get them out of our hair."

"Once we get some information here…we'll get the computer people up here and let them start having fun." She grunted in disgust. "Over 2,200 years and I finally find out now…I was cramming the language stuff in your head too fast. That STINKS!"

He chuckled. "No matter how old you get…you can still learn something new as well."

Chyning called in mentally. **"Hey Teammates! I got something that I wanna steal off of this ship."**

Soolchakan rolled his eyes. **"Just exactly what is that?"**

"How about one of their shuttlecraft?"

Bonarain frowned. **"Why would you want to take one of those? We don't need any shuttlecraft. We can Jump!"**

"We can Jump," sent Chyning facetiously. **"But we can't see these *doovofts*…without the front screen of the shuttlecraft. There is some kind of filter on the front screen and…I can see all of the people on the hangar bay area that are invisible…through the front window… without turning anything on."**

Soolchakan and Bonarain stopped what they were doing on the Bridge and looked at each other.

"THAT…could be extremely useful," said Soolchakan.

Bonarain just stood there nodding with her mouth hanging open and a slight grin.

Pimbot called in from the morgue. **"These *doovofts* have finished picking all of the shrapnel out of the body. They have a wonderful computer system that has already pieced the puzzle together. They've decided that there was some kind of explosive device that was introduced – by method unknown – and that some foreigner murdered one of their citizens."**

Xadorm scoffed. "Foreigner…HAH! Those *bimyocks* are the foreigners."

Jeejow thought for a few moments. **"How soon could we start destroying those enemy ships that are surrounding Hardooth?"**

"Now," sent Kiyalee. **"All we have to do is drop a hand-held bomb into the light speed thingy. A few heartbeats later…BOOM! The problem though is that we can't see the other *fovok* things without the screen from the front of one of their shuttlecrafts. Until we figure that out…we have a hard time finding them to destroy them."**

Marbing cleared his throat. **"Can you see the invisible ships…while sitting in one of the Tashkafa fighters?"**

Chyning looked towards the fighters. **"I don't know. I'll have to check."**

"**Who is sending this? I was just having a conversation with Officer Kiyalee**," sent Jeejow.

Chyning huffed. "**Kiyalee is in the Engineering section. I – Officer, Chyning – am sitting in the Hangar bay for the fighters and shuttlecraft. I'm the one who would be checking the front windows of these craft**."

"**Please do so**," sent Jeejow. He looked at the Staff and shrugged.

Chyning looked back at a group of the Tashkafa who were in the armor suits. Whatever they were doing they were taking their time doing it. They were connecting hoses of some sort to the armor and just standing there watching some kind of monitor. Then they would unplug. She quickly scurried over to a fighter. Before getting in the fighter, she looked back at the armor suited ones. All she could see, while outside of the shuttle, were hoses that were hanging in midair. She got into the fighter and looked towards the hoses…and smiled.

"**Yes, Sir, the fighters do have the same kind of screen**," sent Chyning. "**They've installed the same filter in all of their glass**."

Jeejow shook his fist and smiled in joy. "Yes!" He snickered. "**What I want done, is to steal one shuttlecraft and one fighter…for the moment. Take them to the gorge….**"

"**We can't take them to the gorge**," sent Officer Leader, Iquanza. "**Those *bimyocks* are making themselves at home in the gorge**."

Jeejow growled. "**These monsters somehow found the gorge…and are the reason that we're all running from our own homes…again! All of the Tashkafa in the gorge…start hopping all of them to dimension 45. There is still plenty of room for them to float around there. If you have control of a Tashkafa shuttlecraft or fighter, take the thing to one of the vacant apartments in the gorge. Make sure that the ship that you take is in Spy.**"

"**Sir, you can't Jump it through Spy to the gorge,**" sent Iquanza. "**There's a bunch of us here in the gorge, in Spy, and we're hopping the Tashkafa into dimension 45. She'll have to go to Observation.**"

Jeejow sighed. "**Officer, Chyning, go to Observation to Jump the Tashkafa ship into the gorge.**"

"**I can do the hop and Jump,**" sent Chyning. "**But I need some kind of diversion so that none of the Tashkafa sec the ship disappear here in the Hangar. I need help doing that.**"

Jeejow nodded. "**I'm sure that your Teammates could do something to assist in this kind of diversion.**"

Chyning giggled. "**Team 7016, it's time to get to the Hangar bay, which I believe is deck number 17 on this big bucket, and let's work out a diversion.**"

Soolchakan called to Jeejow. "**Sir, Officer, Bonarain and myself…we're on the Main Bridge. We're getting some valuable intelligence information right now.**

Kiyalee is in Engineering and can create some nasty havoc in there…if needed. Is it possible for Team 7001 to create the diversion?"

Jeejow rolled his eyes. **"Team 7001, proceed to the Hangar bay and do…something to distract the Tashkafa…for Officer, Chyning."**

"This is Officer Grade 5, Ijamaki of Team 7001. What part of deck 17 are we supposed to go to?"

Chyning shook her head. **"ALL of deck 17 is the Hangar bay. All of it from bow to stern. Just get to deck 17…near the stern and you'll find me."**

"Thank you," sent Ijamaki. **"We're on our way."**

"Call me when you're there, Officer, Ijamaki," sent Jeejow.

"Yes, Sir!"

The Command Staff sat there fidgeting while they waited for the next call from Ijamaki. They did not know how big the ship was nor did they know where Team 7001 had been when they were called so they had no idea how long it was going to take. None of them were sure what to say at the moment so they all just kept quiet.

"Officer, Chyning, this is Ijamaki. We're on deck 17. We're a little turned around here. Which way is aft?"

"I see you," sent Chyning. **"Head to your left."**

All four of them started running to the aft of the ship. They saw Chyning waving at them.

Jeejow looked up as if he had been slapped. "**Team 7001 - STOP!**"

They all stopped running and looked at each other a little confused.

"**Sir, why did you want us to stop...before we reach her?**"

Jeejow collected his thoughts. "**Officer, Chyning, are you in the very rear of the bay?**"

Chyning shrugged. "**Yes, Sir, I am.**"

"**Good**," sent Jeejow. "**The diversion has to be somewhere up front...away from Chyning. You don't want to be standing directly beside her when you do the diversion.**"

"**Excellent point**," sent Ijamaki. She turned to her Team. "Anybody got any ideas about how to...divert their attention?"

Officer Grade 6, Bondox grinned as he pulled a hand-held bomb out of his vest. "I think that this'll do very nicely."

Ijamaki nodded in agreement. "**Officer, Chyning, are you ready?**"

"**Anytime you are!**"

Ijamaki shrugged. "Bondox, activate it...and toss it... away from Chyning."

He grinned. He walked over to the side where no one was

milling around or doing any chores in the area. He activated the bomb, counted to four, hopped it to Home, tossed it away and covered his ears. The blast occurred almost immediately. The desired results were exactly as they had hoped. The attention of everyone in the Hangar was now on the strange blast and cloud of fiery smoke in the center of the Hangar. All of them were wondering exactly what had blown up.

As soon as she saw the flames of the blast, Chyning hopped the ship she was in to Observation. She then Jumped it into the main room of apartment 12-567. She got out to look over the dimensions of the ship to see just how cramped it was in the room.

Jeejow was getting impatient seeing as how he had not received an update on anything. **"What's going on? Do we have a Tashkafa fighter in one of the apartments yet**?"

Chyning looked up a little disgruntled. **"No, Sir, we have a Tashkafa shuttlecraft in the main room of apartment 12-567. I decided to get a shuttle first**."

Jeejow was momentarily taken aback. **"Why…a shuttlecraft? Why not a fighter**?"

"Because I had to see if the *chokwad* thing would fit," sent Chyning! **"The fighter is not a problem. We can fit four of them in each garage. I had to check and see if a shuttlecraft would fit anywhere in the apartment**."

Jeejow glanced at some of the faces of the Command Staff and shrugged. **"Well…does it…fit**?"

"Yes, Sir, but barely."

Jeejow cocked his head to the side. "At least that did prove something." He sniffed. **"Officer, Ijamaki...what was the reaction on the Tashkafa ship?"**

"Well, Sir...there were a couple of...reactions. When the bomb went off...an alarm also went off. There were several of the Tashkafa people who went up to the smoke with...what appears to be some kind of fire extinguisher. There were two of them who were hurt in the blast. They're being attended to. The big problem is...that as soon as they shut the fire alarm off, they realized that another alarm was screaming. A light and an alarm located in the parking spot of the ship that Officer Chyning swiped."

Nantasa threw her hands up in disgust. "Wonderful! If we're going to take any more of their ships, fighter or shuttle... we're going to have to plan ahead."

"Then let's start planning," said Xadorm.

"I agree," said Jeejow.

8

The Team members of Jeejow had the melancholy task of performing a new roll call to see how many Owlamites had been lost in the last attack. While the roll call was going on, the Command Staff was planning on how to obtain a large amount of the Tashkafa fighters and shuttlecraft, without stirring up too much attention. The theft by Chyning had caused a big enough stir on the ship she had taken it from. The information was travelling throughout the entire task force that was surrounding Hardooth. The information was given by twenty Doolood who happened to be imprisoned on one of the Tashkafa ships. The Doolood told of how, according to the history texts, this specific star system had been the downfall of the Doolood Empire.

Another thing that was bothering the Tashkafa was the fact that they were not getting any more reports from those hidden apartments in that great gorge on that southern continent. There were a few more personnel dispatched to that area to find out what was going on and they were not reporting in either. So far this situation had not raised any great alarm. It was more frustration than alarm…at first.

The roll call was finished. 158 Teams were completely wiped out. 54 Teams lost one or more of their members. In looking at the partial Teams, they discovered that Team 4737 had lost the male member, Joogoto, of their Team. The three women were now assigned to Zoolkog's Team 55 so the newly promoted Senior Officer would have a complete Team. They also started reassigning personnel to try to make all complete Teams. When they finished, they only had one Team that was not the regular four. Team 4255 had five members – 2 men and 3 women.

The funeral pyres burned brightly – in Spy dimension. 722 Owlamites were now dead and after the fires were out, their ashes were spread around the original city of Owlam – in Home dimension. The number of living Owlamites has been whittled down to 24,142.

A plan was decided upon that would cause the Tashkafa all kinds of grief. Start stealing the helmets from them, because it was found that the same glass that was in the windshield of the Tashkafa shuttlecraft was also in the visor or the Tashkafa helmets. If you were wearing one of those helmets you could see the ones who were invisible. Then it was later decided to steal the entire suit. That way they could utilize it in the same manner as the Tashkafa except for the fact that any Owlamite would be in Spy instead of Home and they marked them so that the Owlamites would not be throwing each other into #45 (of course, if one of the Owlamites were thrown into #45, in the suit, they could always Jump back to Home). They were not sure if they wanted those suits because they were very awkward to walk in and the metal shoes gave your position away completely.

Bonarain finally found the flagship, by reading the minds of each ship Commander. It was while she was reading that mind, she discovered that the Tashkafa were getting ready to set up a mining operation on Bri and gut the mineral supply from that planet.

Several Owlamites were dispatched to Bri where they had a different plan in mind for the Tashkafa personnel there. The Owlamite hopped the Tashkafa into Spy, and partially pushed them into a boulder or the wall of a tunnel or cave, then hopped them back to Home. After twenty-two of these strange deaths occurred, the Task Force Commander dispatched an inspection team to Bri to see if this silly rumor was true. After three of the twelve inspectors died in the same weird manner, the Tashkafa decided to put off the mining expedition until they could fully understand, and/or try to stop, this bizarre phenomenon on that big planet.

Bonarain and the rest of Team 7016 were permanently assigned to harass the flagship. While Bonarain kept on collecting intelligence data from the Commander, Soolchakan wandered around the Main Bridge, sabotaging different work stations by disconnecting a circuit or burning one or making a circuit disappear altogether. Kiyalee was in the Engineering section giving all of the personnel there all kinds of headaches as nuts, bolts and rivets were suddenly coming out or off and ending up on the floor, causing several severe malfunctions. Chyning was having all kinds of fun…anywhere on the ship, just sabotaging anything that her devious little heart desired. One time Chyning blew up an oven in the galley…quite by accident. She was still deliriously happy about the results of crossing three different circuits and watching several of the Tashkafa get electrocuted.

It was finally determined that there were 368 Tashkafa

ships surrounding Hardooth. The flagship was currently stationed over Aerisau. The plan for the Tashkafa was to send their personnel down to the planet to start rounding up and enslaving the indigenous inhabitants and exploit the planet for everything the Tashkafa wanted. For some strange reason, most of the shuttlecraft seemed to be developing all kinds of odd problems and they were no longer able to send a sufficient number of soldiers to the planet at any one time.

The trick of placing an activated hand-held bomb inside a suit was done several more times – just to mess with the Tashkafa. They kept on finding foreign shrapnel, however, they could not confirm anything about how it had occurred. Since the Tashkafa were certain that no foreigner could possible infiltrate their ships it was the big guess that someone aboard the Tashkafa ships was putting a weapon in the armor shell to sabotage the entire mission for some insane reason. The only problem was proving how (and where the unfamiliar explosive came from). The trick was discontinued after a certain Owlamite got vindictive and changed the plan.

Officer Grade 3, Vintoyta of Team 667 was in a part of Monokland where the Tashkafa were causing numerous problems. She had one of the Tashkafa helmets on in order to see the intruders. When she saw a fresh group of the marauders enter a village, she called her Team to come to her. She had a flag they had landmarked on and she planted it on the roof of one of the rather mundane areas of the village. Her three Teammates showed up with a supply of hand-held bombs.

"Fizzakaya, I need you to head north," said Vintoyta. "Check and see if there are any more of those *bimyocks* headed this way. If there are, let us know. Baskaton and Hishsing, I need you two to start knocking off the ones who are in the town."

Hishsing looked around. "Got any idea of numbers...or locations?"

"I counted fifteen," said Vintoyta. "There could be more. They're spreading out and hauling everyone into the main square. The town isn't that big so...it shouldn't take them long...as long as they're alive. Once they're dead...the village will be free again."

Baskaton nodded his head. "Do you want us to kill them in the square...or when and where ever we find them?"

Vintoyta shrugged. "When you find one...kill it. No point in putting on one big show, in the village square, for the regulars. Just get rid of them when you find them."

Fizzakaya headed out north while the rest of the Team started a search and destroy mission on the enemy.

Baskaton found three of the Tashkafa in a small classroom that was obviously some kind of primary school. All of the children were very young and were being terrorized by the intruders. One little girl was picked up by a Tashkafa and while holding her upside down, by one leg, she was screaming at the top of her lungs while he was – Baskaton was very shocked at seeing this – getting intimately personal with the Heyyah child. Baskaton decided to read his mind and see what he was thinking.

'This is a nice specimen,' thought Vandin 4 (E-4),

Chochshimp. 'I'm going to enjoy taking one of these to my bed and sexually exploring it.'

Baskaton was totally repulsed at this thought. The girl could not possibly be more than six years old. He pulled out a hand-held, activated it, counted to three and shoved the bomb into the mouth of the Tashkafa instead of the torso area of the uniform. "Let's see how you enjoy that, you *melafathan fovok*!"

A moment later the bomb went off – before Chochshimp even had a chance to start choking on the obstruction in his mouth. It went off in the helmet instead of the torso area. There had been a few of the bombs that had loosened the connections between the torso and the legs or arms when they went off – in the torso portion of the armor shell. This, however, had the full blast inside the helmet and when it went off it blew the helmet portion (along with the head of Chochshimp) completely off of the body shell. The helmet did some ricocheting around the room before it lost momentum. The little girl was dropped and the rest of the suit became fully visible and the headless remains of Chochshimp fell down on the floor.

The other two Tashkafa in the room immediately opened a panel on the left arm of their uniform and hit several buttons under the panel area. Then they both vacated the room.

Vintoyta was about to activate a bomb and drop it in the suit of one of the Tashkafa when she suddenly turned from the twenty or so prisoners he had in the village square. He opened a the panel on his left arm and hit a few buttons and the four Tashkafa in this area started moving away from the people, heading for the northern area where they had entered the village. She started reading his mind to see what was going on.

"This is Vandin 8 (E-8) Hokontoko. Abandon the mission. Send the playback of what you saw to Second Mizhasak (O-10) Pipkitto. Let's get out of here! Get out while we're still alive."

Vintoyta was rather surprised. **"What happened? What is a Second Mizhasak? Why are they leaving?"**

Bonarain was the one who answered. **"The Second Mizhasak is the one who is in command of this task force. His rank is equivalent to a Master Officer. He's receiving some...playback from some cameras that they've installed in the suits. WHEN DID THEY INSTALL CAMERAS? These *bimyocks* are getting very sneaky! They're running the playback and...WHO PUT A HAND-HELD IN THE HELMET? You blew his...head...and helmet off! Now they're saying that...the sabotage IS happening on the planet."**

Jeejow interrupted. **"I'd like to know who did this as well! Who put the bomb in the helmet?"**

Baskaton cringed. **"Sir...I did it. Officer Grade 6, Baskaton of Team 667. When that *fovok* picked up that little Heyyah girl and...thought about how he was going to...sexually molest her...I...just couldn't help myself. I felt...he had to have some...special punishment."**

Jeejow rolled his eyes. **"I'm not fond of any child molester either. Remember though, we have to keep our emotions in check. If you had put the bomb inside the body area...it would still have achieved the desired** results."

Baskaton hung his head. "**Yes, Sir**."

"**It's done**," sent Bonarain. "**Nothing we can do about it now. We'll just have to watch their reaction to it**."

Chyning sent a personal message to her Team. "**Kiyalee is chucking up again. That playback went through Engineering and...she saw it. It might be funny if it weren't so gruesome. Oops! They showed it again... and she's blowing chunks again**."

Soolchakan growled. "**Get her out of there! As long as they keep showing it...keep her in some other part of the ship**."

Chyning did not respond. She was laughing too hard. She did help Kiyalee out of the Engineering section to a hallway where no one was watching any playbacks.

Then the Command Staff came up with a plan for stealing all of the 80 fighters and 20 shuttlecraft off of one Tashkafa ships, without the flagship knowing what had happened. They would have 100 Owlamites in the cockpit of each ship. At the command of execution, all 100 ships would be hopped to Observation and then Jumped to specifically assigned vacant apartments in the gorge. Before the Tashkafa on that ship could report the mass theft, a hand-held would be thrown into one of the light speed cylinders. The resulting explosion would leave the other Tashkafa ship with a mystery, however, they would not know about the theft of all of the smaller ships. They prepared for the mass theft.

It was determined from the first theft of the shuttlecraft that they would not fit in any garage. They were too wide. They decided to place one in the main room, two on the third floor and two on the fourth floor of a vacant apartment. They could put four fighters in the garage along with two on the second floor in the bedroom areas, two more on the third floor and two on the fourth floor. Since they were going to be in Spy dimension, they did not have to worry about the columns that were helping hold up the ceilings.

Jeejow sighed. "I said I want everyone off of the ships that surround the one we're going to blow up. I remember what happened before…when we blew up that one Vagen ship. The fireball was…so intense that it melted all of the ships around it."

Nantasa shook her head. "Do you really think that something like that could happen here…on a smaller ship?"

"It could easily happen," said Tadesha. "Just because this ship only has two light speed engines, instead of six, doesn't mean that it won't happen."

"It's good to be cautious," said Inditam.

Nantasa raised her hands in surrender and said nothing.

"I'm curious," said Onga. "How does one little hand-held bomb…blow up an entire ship that size. It just doesn't make sense that something so small could be so destructive."

"It has to do with what is inside that light speed cylinder," said Xadorm. "There is a chain reaction that goes on in there. It is a very delicate and absolutely precise mixture and if it is ever upset rapidly…the results are an enormous and catastrophic reaction. When one of the hand-held bombs goes off inside the cylinder, the mix for the chain reaction is thrown so far off that… you have a firestorm weapon. A weapon like that, going off inside a spaceship…total annihilation."

Onga nodded. "Okay. I've always wondered what happened…and no one ever explained it to me…in simple terms like that."

Jeejow looked around. "Can we get back to the subject at hand?" He glanced around again smiling. "Thank you. All Teams on ships that are over South Chilamte need to get off of them before the explosion. I don't want us killing any of our own. Our enemies are doing too good a job of that."

"Let them know when to Jump, Sir," said Xadorm.

Jeejow turned to his Aides. "Let me know when everyone is in position and is ready to make the Jumps."

Yilla, Toyzamia and Meekaha started calling to all of the personnel that were involved.

When all three of them turned to Jeejow and nodded he closed his eyes. "**All personnel who are on the surrounding ships… Jump to your homes NOW! All personnel on the target ship in the fighters and shuttlecraft, hop the things to Observation…NOW! Jump all target craft to the gorge, NOW! Drop the bomb…NOW**!"

Officer Leader, Iquanza called in. "**We just saw a massive bright light in the sky that was there for only about three heartbeats and then went out. I wonder what the local Heyyah are thinking about it.**"

Jeejow snickered. "**Irrelevant at the moment but thank you. What I need right now is a report on what happened to any surrounding ships.**"

Bonarain called in from the flagship. "**There are all kinds of initial reports coming in from ships that weren't damaged. It appears that there were at least six other ships that sustained damage. They're going to have to send someone to those ships because no one on the damaged ships is responding.**"

Jeejow nodded. "**Let me know when they have a complete report on the damage.**" He grunted a little in approval. "It looks as if it was definitely necessary to get our people out of the ships. If six others were damaged...some of our people could have been...possibly hurt...or killed...in the process."

Xadorm nodded his head. "It was most definitely a good call, Sir."

Three days later Bonarain called in. "**Supreme Officer, Jeejow, this is Bonarain. Can you hear me?**"

Jeejow sat up with a start. "**Yes, Officer, Bonarain. What kind of report do we have?**"

"The two closest ships were cooked and melted. 100% fatalities on both ships…from heat. The other four ships in the vicinity suffered massive heat damage from the blast. All four have been declared totally unserviceable. They're going to be scrapped. The Tashkafa are going to crash them into one of the gas giants…probably Chabayo. There are 75% to 85% fatalities on the four ships, due to heat and radiation. The survivors…might not be on the survivor list much longer. They all suffered horrible burns in the heat plus many of them are suffering from radiation poisoning."

Jeejow sniffed. "Seven enemy ships destroyed. Massive fatalities for the Tashkafa as a result."

Xadorm nodded. "That still leaves 361 enemy ships…not to mention the fact that they're still trying to investigate a way to exploit the minerals on Bri."

Jeejow hung his head. He looked up from under his eyebrows without moving his head. "How many of the 361 are orbiting Bri?"

Marbing looked at his report. "Ten, Sir."

Jeejow now brought his head up. "Our next target… singular or plural…the ships orbiting Bri. I want them to be *terrified* of that planet. That planet is in our system and I don't like the idea of outsiders coming in and stealing what should rightfully be ours."

Since Bri was a much larger planet, all ten ships had to be attacked, one at a time. They were all too far away from each other to affect any others.

Another ship orbiting Hardooth was attacked in the same manner and Second Mizhasak, Pipkitto was getting very perturbed over the fact that there was so much carelessness in his task force.

The Owlamites now had the shuttlecraft and fighters from twelve different Tashkafa ships. They were going to have to start storing them in #45 because they decided that storing all of those shuttlecraft and fighters in the gorge was getting a bit excessive.

While the Owlamites were able to keep most of their technology intact (not to mention the fact that they were improving on what they had by stealing from the Tashkafa), the Tashkafa had been causing no end to destruction and grief of the technology of other races all over Hardooth. The one place they did not mess with was the Turgon Wall. They, for the most part, just observed what was going on and agreed with the place being a super international prison. They were even considering bringing prisoners from other planets to be punished by having to fight for their lives against the Turgons.

After one year of stealing fighters and shuttlecraft and blowing up Tashkafa ships the count was now down to 44 enemy ships still in the air above Hardooth. Second Mizhasak, Pipkitto had called for reinforcements because of the situation when they were down to 90. The Tashkafa High Command finally agreed to send in 150 more ships to aid in the frustrating stalemate of taking over this planet and star system.

When the reinforcements arrived, there was a new

Commander in the task force. Pipkitto was relieved of command because of his ineffectiveness. Second Mizhasak, Inngonnthook became the new task force Commander.

After listening to the two high ranking officers talking, Bonarain sent a message to Jeejow. "**These *bimyocks* are going to try a new tactic, Sir. They're going to try some peace talks…with the faction that is causing them so much grief.**"

Jeejow looked with some surprise at the members of the Command Staff. "**Are they really serious about talking peace**?"

"**Not a chance, Sir. It's just a stall tactic so they can figure out which faction it is that is causing the grief. They have some super firestorm weapons aboard a ship that's waiting just beyond Denhahbon. As soon as they find out where you are…BOOM! Then they'll figure that they've eliminated the biggest problem and take over the planet.**"

Xadorm shook his head. "We should take out all of them… right now."

"No," said Tadesha. "Why don't we have some fun with them? Let them talk for a while…and then they'll have something that's even more confusing to send back to their home base. I mean…we still haven't been able to figure out where their home planet is. If *we* can stall for time to find out…maybe we can use this stall tactic against them."

Jeejow thought for a few moments. "**Does anyone**

remember where that silly conference bell is? I mean the one where the Doolood and Choks and Iyka and all of that met. Do we have it at our disposal?"

Soolchakan shrugged. "I remember where both of them are. They had their original and then the ones stuck in dimension 45 built a new one. Which one do you want?"

Jeejow smiled. "Get the new one. Can you place it out of their sight…on the back side of Niygool?"

Soolchakan huffed. "Sir, I can place it, in Spy, on the back side of that task force Commander's pants."

Jeejow chuckled. "No. Just place it, in Spy, on the back side of Niygool. Meanwhile, some or all of you computer people…get into their computers and find us a picture, somewhere, that we can landmark a spot on their home world."

Soolchakan shook his head. "We'll leave Bonarain here to listen to the two top *bimyocks*. Kiyalee, Chyning and I will go get the bell ship."

They Jumped to the location of the new bell in #45. They all grimaced at the smell inside the ship. The ambient air had not been circulating and it was very stale. There appeared to be all kinds of strange looking muck floating around in the Doolood water as well. They turned all of the equipment on and now air and water began circulating and the smell began improving very quickly. They then Jumped it to the back side of Niygool and then hopped it to Spy.

Soolchakan called back to Jeejow. **"The bell is on the back side of Niygool and the air is being circulated at this time. All of the equipment is turned on and working. It is at your disposal…for whatever reason you want it… now, Sir."**

"Thank you," sent Jeejow. "Nantasa, Yim, Xadorm, Marbing, you and your Teams…go get aboard the bell. Get ready to do some fancy Jumping in that contraption."

Xadorm frowned. "What have you got in mind?"

Jeejow chuckled. "The only way that you can find someone who is talking to you on some wavelength communication device…is to triangulate on their location. I imagine that they'll try that. So…while we're talking to them…we'll keep Jumping that bell to all kinds of places…all over the system. They'll go absolutely crazy trying to find us…when we keep moving…even if we move it to the back side of the Commander's pants."

Xadorm shook his head and grunted. "Other than the back side of his pants, where should we start?"

Jeejow got an evil grin on his face. "Place it in one of the remnants of the three cities that's on the west side of the Turgon Wall. That'll give those *doovofts* something to think about… before the first Jump…back to Niygool."

Onga looked puzzled. "Can we talk to them…from the bell?"

"It's set up for outer space communications," said Jeejow with a shrug. "I don't see why not." He turned to his Team.

"Toyzamia, why don't you go to the bell and start checking on the communications? See if you can hear some of the back and forth communications between the Tashkafa ships."

Toyzamia grinned. "Yes, Sir." She stood up and vanished. A few moments later she sent back. **"The system works fine. All I had to do was turn a dial until I found their frequency."**

"Wonderful," sent Jeejow! **"Officer, Bonarain...have they said when they're going to start this subterfuge?"**

"Sir, it could happen at any time. They're still working out some of the vocabulary in order to make it sound...friendly."

"How uncivilized of them. They're beginning to sound like the Vagens," sent Jeejow sarcastically.

"Yes," said Marbing. "Everything sounds politically motivated."

"Yes," said Zoolkog. "A big fat lie, a double-meaning lie or spin fabrication."

Xadorm Jumped to the bell ship. **"Where do we start?"**

The others were Jumped there as well.

"The city of Turgon itself," said Marbing with a grin.

"That sounds like as good a place as any," said Nantasa.

They Jumped the bell to Turgon. There were a few windows they could look out. They saw that the city was nothing but crumbling ruins. After 2,200 years there was nothing inside the wall that looked like it could be usable. The center of the city was still nothing but charred remnants of buildings and rubble.

"I'm glad we destroyed the Algothons," said Marbing bitterly.

Bonarain called in. **"They're getting ready to start their transmission. They're going to try to sound nice and sweet. They're hoping they can fool all of us into submission."**

Xadorm sniffed. "Let's get ready."

Jeejow and his Team Jumped into the bell. He sighed. "We await their transmission."

The transmission finally started after a rather long wait. *"This is Second Mizhasak, Inngonnthook of the Tashkafa Empire calling the inhabitants of the planet...who have been giving us a very rough time."*

Jeejow leaned back in his chair and put his feet up on the table. "Let's let them sweat for a while. I'll answer them...sooner or later."

Toyzamia handed the other members of the Command Staff a list of where they should go on each Jump.

The message was sent out four more times before Jeejow answered. He picked up the microphone and keyed it. "This is Jeejow. Drey Sssorg of the Owlam. What do you sniveling dung heaps want?"

Inngonnthook smiled. "It's finally working," he whispered to Pipkitto. *"It's good to hear from you...Jeejow. On behalf of the*

Tashkafa Empire, we would like to invite you to join us...as allies in our quest. We're trying to bring order to the universe and we only make alliances with the most powerful races that we come in contact with. We now realize that you are very powerful and we'd like to talk to you...face to face to discuss this alliance."

Jeejow fought hard to keep from laughing. "Why should we even think of discussing it with you?"

"**They found you**," sent Bonarain.

"**Move us**," sent Jeejow.

Yim and his Team made the first Jump. They moved the bell ship from Turgon to Algothon.

Inngonnthook looked at the Gunners. "Did you fire on them?"

The Gunner looked back half panicked. "They...they're not there anymore. We had a lock on them...and suddenly...no target. They...moved...somehow...or that *hoofquat* triangulation didn't work."

"FIND THEM!" Inngonnthook snarled. He calmed himself as he picked the microphone back up. "*There is always room for discussion. We can talk of this alliance and you can join us in a glorious quest to unify the universe...under one flag.*" He let off the microphone. "Now find them," he whispered harshly!

Jeejow chuckled. "We don't like talking to conquerors. We like crushing them. We've crushed several before you. Talk to the Doolood. Talk to the Iyka. Talk to the Chokchakchok. Talk to the Zizzikinza. Talk to the Jowfoonda...oh you can't talk to them.

We exterminated them…entirely."

"**They found you**," sent Bonarain.

"**Move**," sent Jeejow. He continued. "Talk to the Mufayton. Talk to the Vagens…oh you can't talk to them either. We stomped them into the dust as well."

The Gunner snarled. "What is this *figowit*? They suddenly appeared on a different continent…now…they're not even on the planet. The transmission is coming from…the smaller moon that's orbiting this planet."

"**They found you on Niygool**," sent Bonarain.

"**Next move**," sent Jeejow.

The Gunner growled in frustration. "Now…there's nothing on that moon…except the ancient wreckage that we saw earlier." He leaned back in his seat scratching his head.

Jeejow sat there snickering while waiting for the next statement from the Tashkafa.

Inngonnthook calmed himself before talking into the microphone. *"We're not conquerors, Sir. We are more…people who bring everything together…for the greater good of all. Come…sit down at a table with us…and you'll see. We're not really that bad."*

Jeejow shook his head back and forth in a haughty manner. "I'm sorry, Sir, but we haven't really seen how you could possibly be good."

The Gunner stood up and screamed.

Pipkitto snarled at the Gunner. "What is the matter with you?"

The Gunner looked at Inngonnthook in terror. "That… Drey Sssorg…he's transmitting…from OUR CARGO BAY 2, Sir! He's inside our ship!"

"**Move**," sent Jeejow.

Inngonnthook dropped the microphone. He stared in disbelief at the radio personnel who were doing the triangulating. They all nodded in agreement at the location just given. He slammed his fist down on the ship public address system. "SECURITY! Go to cargo bay 2…and look for any…foreign things in there."

Jeejow keyed his microphone. "So far, you've managed to kill almost two million inhabitants of my planet. 722 of them were my people. Why should I trust you?"

The radio personnel looked up. "They're orbiting that… big mineral planet."

The Gunner threw his arms up in exasperation. "None of our guns can reach that far."

"**They're dispatching one of their ships to go to light speed and intercept you, Sir**," sent Bonarain.

Jeejow shook his head. "**Somebody get on that ship and blow it up**."

"**This is Officer Grade 4, Oolsing of Team 2999. We're currently aboard the ship that is moving towards you. We'll hit it with a hand-held, Sir**." She ordered her Team off the ship and dumped a hand-held bomb herself and

Jumped. The ship blew up immediately after her Jump.

Jeejow got on the radio. "Oops! Did we have an accident?"

"Sir, this Officer, Sankiki of Team 254. We finally found something in their computers...that we can landmark on their planet. We also found out that they call their home world Konntong."

Jeejow jumped up and growled in triumph. He sat back down grinning. He calmed himself before keying the microphone. "You just saw what can happen to your ships. We can do it to any ship at any time. If you persist in this *bimyock* discussion of mendacity, in regards to your intentions, we will destroy every one of the ships that is polluting our star system. We will also go to Konntong and set off...oh say...250 nuclear weapons...on your home planet. How fierce are you going to be then?" He looked at Xadorm. "**Move**."

Inngonnthook was in agony. He had been sent here to turn the blunders of Pipkitto into something positive for the Tashkafa Empire. He was currently finding that he had no choice but to turn and run. He had been fighting for the title of First Mizhasak and now a defeat like this would probably get him demoted. He pondered several different things in his mind as he considered what he was going to say next. What he was going to say to the crew and to this headache named Jeejow.

"They're getting ready to call that ship that's orbiting Denhahbon. They want it to come in and deploy all thirty of their super firestorm weapons," sent Bonarain.

Jeejow nodded. "**Who is aboard the ship orbiting**

Denhahbon?"

"This is Officer Grade 4, Abra of Team 1007. We've already found the super weapons. I can fit all thirty on one small tabletop. For a weapon that powerful...they're awfully compact."

Jeejow shook his head. "Take the *chokwad* things to one of the vaults on Zhagool. I heard that those vaults are full to bursting but...if those things are that small... they should fit."

"Yes, Sir," sent Abra. "Consider it done."

Jeejow keyed his microphone. "Second Mizhasak, Inngonnthook...I suggest you get in contact with that ship that is far out there. The one with the super weapons. Ask them how many super weapons are currently on board that ship."

Inngonnthook looked at his microphone in terror. He turned to the communications officer. "Get them on...a secure line."

"Already on it, Sir." The officer punched a few buttons on his panel and spoke softly into his microphone. He looked back after a few moments. "Sir...Tezzet, Ilchpok reports...that...all thirty weapons...have vanished."

Inngonnthook went limp in the command chair. He sat there like that for several moments. He raised his head and looked around the Main Bridge at all of the personnel. He pushed himself up out of the chair. "Second Mizhasak, Pipkitto...take over. I'm going to my quarters." He walked slowly out of the room.

He trudged to his quarters. After drinking some of his favorite liquor…he committed suicide.

The Bridge Medical Officer turned to Pipkitto. "Sir…the life signs of Second Mizhasak, Inngonnthook…have ceased."

Pipkitto simply nodded. "All ships…recall all personnel on the planet and…retreat from this star system. Rendezvous at Summit Siskooson…as soon as possible."

Jeejow watched as all 193 ships departed the system.

Xadorm looked up sadly. "You don't actually believe that they're gone for good do you?"

Jeejow dropped the microphone on the table. "No I don't. Not for one fleeting heartbeat." He sighed. "Recall all personnel on those ships. We'll wait until they return. Then we'll blow the *h'oolyach* out of all of them."

9

It was 33 years later the Tashkafa tried to come back with 1,427 ships to overwhelm the pesky star system that had cost them so much. They along with their home planet were blown almost into oblivion. It would be over 300 years before they would become any kind of power again...permanently without the use of their home planet...and they decided to stay completely away from one specific star system...until they could figure out how to overcome (or even find) this unseen enemy.

102 years later, the spies were scouting the home planet of the Iyka in order to see if the planet was coming back or if anyone was trying to make it come back. They witnessed a tremendous battle within the star system between two factions they were unfamiliar with. The battle raged on for three days in different parts of the system. Over 800 ships were blown up and turned into nothing but wreckage floating around in the sky. When it was over, the side that was victorious, limped away with only five ships. Four of those were damaged and had to be escorted by the one that was intact. There was no battle of any type over the Chokchakchok home planet or any of the others.

211 years later another conqueror came to the Hardooth star system to take over. This one was nowhere near as impressive as the Vagens or the Tashkafa. Before they could even get close to the planet Hardooth, 84 of their 85 attack ships were crashed into the gas giants. The last one was crashed into the back side of Niygool. The Owlamites never really knew who they were and did not really care. They simply wished that all enemies were this unimpressive. Even their technology was not worth saving.

The Owlamites did some more exploring of their own planet. After the attack by the Tashkafa, technology had suffered greatly throughout the entire planet. The only types of computers that were operational were old style. They were a total retrograde style that the Owlamites laughed at. Large and bulky and they seemed to require a great deal of preventative maintenance. They knew they did not have that much to fear from any other races on Hardooth. At least not now. Even the Teltermak were having problems with their technology. They had lost most of their technology because of the Tashkafa and were now just trying to survive. The Axswain had become a race of inbred idiots and would never pose a real problem again…hopefully.

The Turgon Wall was a little different. After nearly 2600 years of the beasts attempting to climb the walls in different areas, the wall was starting to crumble. Jeejow ordered the seven construction Teams to the Turgon Wall to see if they could reinforce the wall – without anyone knowing about it. The construction Teams made a suggestion and it was followed. Some

2,000 Owlamites were at the wall (secretly) making the wall as strong as the walls in the gorge. The undertaking took three years, however, the wall was now standing firm, stronger than it had ever been before. The personnel in charge of the wall were a totally mystified at this miraculous occurrence, however, they did not complain.

Jeejow celebrated 350 years as the *Voice of Power* after the wall was reinforced. He had been the *Voice of Power* longer than Nagasoom, Plothok, Neenatha, Jahong, Nakalak, Holla and Wilfadge combined. He thought about the 548 years of Hadathoo, the 781 years of Till and the 696 years of Wymini. He wondered just how long he would survive this burden that was involuntarily and enigmatically dumped in his lap…or brain.

He reminded all of the Owlamites that most of them had been Watchers. The ones at the Owlam wall who watched their monitors for any enemy coming at them. "The longer we keep a vigilant watch, the less chance of any more Owlamites being killed by any enemy." The rest of the Owlamite survivors had been medical personnel and farmers.

All of the Owlamites were wondering about their longevity. On Jeejow's 350th anniversary, it was also noted that it was 2,580 years since the Algothon attack. The youngest Owlamite that survived had been just over 20 years old. They were all now over 2,600 years old and none of them looked older than 30. The great question: Just how long would or could they live? None of them had the answer. Not the doctors and not the physicists who tried to explain the longevity with some of their obscene fifteen page mathematical equations…that reached no logical conclusion regarding the possibilities of their total life span.

251 years later, just after the 600th anniversary of the administration of Jeejow, the watchers saw another set of twenty ships coming in.

Officer Grade 6, Foosena one of the Aides of Master Officer, Yim had been training with Bonarain attempting to learn her ways of quick translation from the mind-reading of strangers. Foosena wanted to attempt to use this skill before Bonarain was called upon to perform her magic once more. She Jumped her fighter to a place near the poison ice planet of Afkoth where the strangers had been seen. She sighted the armada almost immediately and used every bit of power in the fighter to catch up with them and enter their ship in Spy dimension.

She started describing the ships. "**The ships are all flat and circular. They're about five kilotaja in diameter and half a kilotaja in depth. They have four square… appendages…sticking out of the discs…northeast, northwest, southeast and southwest. They're all a flat gray color with a few lights randomly spotting the edges**."

She entered the ship and looked around at all of the inhabitants. "**They're terrapins**," she sent in shock. "**They're great big ugly, green and gray terrapins, walking on two legs and acting like they're intelligent. They have the same kind of face that…our unintelligent terrapins had…on Hardooth**."

Jeejow shook his head. "**If they're flying those ships… they probably are intelligent. Can you tell us anything else about them**?"

Foosena landed her ship inside the big ship. She got out and started wandering among the inhabitants.

She felt a little bit of a mean streak go through her and she pushed one of them onto his back…just to see if he was as helpless as some of the terrapins that she had seen on Hardooth. When he fell, several others, of his ilk, started laughing at him. Their laugh sounded like the honking of certain types of birds that she remembered hearing as they migrated around the planet. No one helped him get back up as he rolled back and forth helplessly. He finally let out a growl and started punching a specific spot on his chest. After the third hit, two doors opened up in the body area of the terrapin shell part. He got up out of the shell and stood up. He looked around growling at the others while they continued honking at him. He reached down for the discarded turtle shell, stood it up on end, put his arms through the arm holes and picked it up. He gave his comrades a few more growls and then hit something and the two front doors closed.

Foosena scoffed. "**They're not terrapins! Sir, they have a uniform something like the Tashkafa had…only this terrapin like shell…just covers the torso. Their arms, legs and face…look like a terrapin…but the body…looks Heyyah**."

Yim nodded as he looked around the conference table. "Interesting. They wear a big shell…as part of their uniform… that can leave them helpless."

Jeejow chuckled. "They seem to be their own enemy with something like that." He cleared his throat. "**Officer, Foosena…what about reading their minds and getting their language**?"

"**Yes, Sir, I'm going to attempt that…right now**." She went through all of the rituals of clearing her mind and concentrating on one individual. She worked his mind as best she could, however, she was only picking up one or two words at a time.

Jeejow sat there twiddling his thumbs. "**Officer, Foosena, we need to know your status. They've passed the orbit of Afkoth and are on their way to Bri. We need an update**."

"**Yes, Sir…I…I'm trying, I…uh…Sir…I…OH H'OOLYACH! Call Officer, Bonarain. I'm just not fast enough**." She dropped to her knees pouting.

Nantasa waved a hand to get attention. "Sir, before we send Officer, Bonarain, one of my Team members, Officer Grade 5, Lonosena, has been working on the translation. Can I send her first?"

Jeejow sighed. "Make it quick…but make sure that Officer, Bonarain is standing by."

Nantasa signaled Lonosena who smiled, saluted and vanished.

Lonosena Jumped to her fighter. She hopped in the cockpit, hopped the fighter to Spy, closed the canopy, fired the engine up and Jumped her ship to Afkoth. She saw the armada quickly pulling away from her. She Jumped her fighter up to the lead ship while pushing the fighter for all of the speed that it could muster. She pulled inside the lead ship. She saw Foosena sitting on her knees, grimacing while she was staring intensely at one specific terrapin. Lonosena picked one of the crewmen and started working on reading his mind and translating.

Jeejow sat in the conference room rapping a knuckle on the table as he counted. He counted to 50 and looked up at Yim. He then counted another 50 and looked up at Nantasa. "Do we have anything yet?"

Nantasa hung her head. "Call Officer, Bonarain."

Jeejow nodded. "**Officer, Bonarain, it's now your turn to get this mess under control**."

Bonarain sat there disgusted. "**Yes, Sir, Team 7016 is on the way**." She sent a private message to her Team. "**Why can't anyone else get it**?"

Chyning put her hands to her throat, stuck out her tongue and crossed her eyes.

Soolchakan just chuckled. "**Come on, let's get out there**."

All four of them were already in their fighters with canopy down, engine started and ready to go. They all Jumped to Afkoth, got their bearings on the armada and made two more Jumps to catch up and infiltrate the lead ship.

"**I know**," send Kiyalee. "**Find the engines**."

Chyning snickered. **"I get to find anything that I can mess with…or steal**."

"Be careful," sent Soolchakan. **"There're already two of our personnel with fighters here already. We don't want to crash into them**."

Bonarain looked a little shocked but realized that he was correct. She slowed her movement around the ship.

They found the Main Bridge, where there were two fighters parked in the back of the room. They parked their fighters near the other two, got out and started exploring. Soolchakan was checking work stations while Bonarain started the mind reading.

Lonosena was sitting on a desk swinging her legs back and forth. Foosena was still concentrating on the same alien.

Soolchakan went back to his fighter, turned the scanners on and did a bio-sensor search of the closest alien. The readout started giving information: Creature appears to be a reptile/ Heyyah cross breed. 8.6 taja in height. Male reproductive organs. Biped with five short stubby fingers and opposable thumb on hands with long sharp claws between 3.4 and 3.7 decitaja in length. Skin is mostly green and gray with occasional stripes that are red and yellow. Legs are only 19% of body height. Currently wearing a large circular piece of body armor that has numerous multifunctional circuits inside designed to take care of all bodily functions. Normal respiratory, circulatory and nervous system.

Soolchakan nodded as he read the information. "I wonder if they lay eggs or have live birth." He looked around to see if any of them appeared to be female. He could not distinguish any gender on any of them so he shrugged that off, turned off the bio-sensor and got out of the fighter.

He wanted to tell Lonosena to get to work…doing something. She was a Grade 5 as well and he did not know if he outranked her or not. She was a member of Nantasa's Team so he decided to let it go.

Bonarain walked up behind Foosena who was still trying to get the translation done. Bonarain sighed and sent the information to Foosena who jumped as if she had been slapped.

Foosena turned around smiling. "I got it!" Then she saw Bonarain, closed her eyes lost her smile and huffed. "You…gave it to me…didn't you?" Her shoulders sagged.

"You were already trying to get it, so you were in the proper frame of mind to accept it," said Bonarain with a friendly smile. "I just helped give you a boost. You were getting it, but… we don't have time to fool around."

Foosena nodded sadly. "I was…getting it…slowly but I was getting it."

"Just a little more practice," said Bonarain with that friendly smile and a pat on the shoulder. She turned, went to Soolchakan and started feeding him the translation. After she had given all of it to him, she looked for the Ship Commander.

Soolchakan started checking all of the work stations to see what each one was doing.

Lonosena folded her arms and scoffed. "Are you gonna give me the information?"

Bonarain looked indignant. "Are you gonna get off of your butt, quit lollygagging and help?"

Lonosena flushed. She hopped off of the desk and walked over to Bonarain scowling. "Give me the information!"

"Calm down. You're too agitated to accept it."

Lonosena bared her teeth for a moment. She closed her mouth and eyes and took several deep breaths. She opened her eyes and stood there quietly with a blank stare.

Bonarain fed her the information and then went back to looking for the Commander.

Soolchakan chuckled as he went from station to station. "I don't think that we're going to have a hard time finding a landmark for their home planet. Every one of these *bimyocks* has a photograph of their home above their work station."

Jeejow was again losing patience. "**Can we get some information here? At least…can you tell us what they call themselves**?"

Bonarain cleared her throat. "**Sir…are you ready? They call themselves - Cookrot**!"

All of the Command Staff sat there with their mouths hanging open.

Jeejow closed his eyes. "**Cook…ROT**?"

Bonarain sighed. "**Yes, Sir. Cookrot**."

"Oh my," said Nantasa. "Some words…just…oh what can I say?"

"Nothing," said Xadorm. "It probably means something entirely different in their language."

"I certainly hope so," said Inditam.

Jeejow shook his head. "**Can someone give us a clue...as to what their motive is in coming to our star system?**"

"**It is definitely a mission of conquering**," sent Soolchakan. "**Their long range sensors have already picked up the mineral wealth of Bri and their drooling over who is going to claim which part of the planet in order to make the most money for their own individual and selfish desires. This little armada is a reconnaissance mission...checking for how many planets are occupied and ripe for smashing, conquering, mining and enslaving.**"

Jeejow hung his head. "**Can you slow them down?**"

"**Sure...uh...yes, Sir**," sent Kiyalee. "**They have regular light speed engines. One little micro-fracture or loose rivet...or bolt and they have to shut it down for repairs.**"

Jeejow nodded. "**Shut em down.**"

Kiyalee reached down and hopped one of the rivets into Ghost. She pulled it out of the hole and laid it down on the deck. The alarms went off almost immediately and everyone in the Engineering section scrambled to their monitors to try to find out what had happened. Once they had performed an emergency shutdown, Kiyalee then smacked the outer cylinder with a tool she found in the area. She smiled as she looked at the fresh crack.

"That'll keep them busy for a while," she snickered.

When the lead ship slowed and stopped, all of the other ships stopped as well. They surrounded the lead ship in a defensive posture. They aimed all of their guns outward as if to protect the damaged ship while repairs were accomplished. There was a lot of chatter back and forth between the ships as to how long it would take and did they need any assistance.

Jeejow smiled. "**While they're stopped, I want at least five Teams on each ship. Let's hop all of them into Ghost. If they do decide to come here to Hardooth, we hop nineteen into dimension 45. The last one we'll talk with them…by way of a hopping bell ship. If they persist in the ideology of attempting to conquer us… we'll take it out on their home planet. Any questions**?"

There were none.

"**Good**," sent Jeejow. He looked at the Command Staff. "Start assigning Teams and have them get out there…as quickly as possible."

The Cookrots quickly repaired the damage that Kiyalee had inflicted on them. They fired up their engines and headed for Bri. Bonarain heard them making all kinds of noises, as they got closer, about their sensors finding more needed minerals on the next planet in the system. She rolled her eyes as she heard all the things she had heard before. Bri was a blessing of mineral content. It was also a curse because everybody wanted to be the ones who owned all of that massive mineral wealth.

Soolchakan watched as they broke formation and started looking over each part of Bri. **"Sir, the Cookrots are going to be here for a while. They're doing a full inventory of Bri."**

Jeejow huffed. **"All right. Let's get in the bell now and…start the communications. The sooner the better."**

Onga took her place in the bell. "Why do we have to get this thing ready to Jump this thing all over the place again? Do you actually think that they'll try to find us and kill us that quickly?"

"I don't know if they will or not," said Jeejow. "The best thing that we can do is prepare for the worst possible scenario. That way…if it happens…we're already one step ahead of them and that gives us an advantage."

Onga sighed and shrugged. "Makes sense."

"Turn the transmitter on," said Jeejow.

Toyzamia hit the switch. "We're ready to broadcast, Sir."

Jeejow keyed the microphone. "To the Cookrot people who have come into our star system…we ask you…what is your intention?"

Officer Leader, Iquanza snickered as she watched the Cookrot reaction to the sudden and surprise communication. **"Sir, they're receiving your message. They don't understand it. They're tweaking their international translator now. Try again."**

Jeejow shook his head and keyed the microphone again. "This is Drey Sssorg, Jeejow of the Owlamite people. Citizens of the planet Hardooth. Again, I ask the people of Cookrot, who have come into our star system…what are your intentions?"

The Commander of the armada listened to the translation and responded. "*I am Tolomosh, Undabagen. I am the Commander of the Forward Force. We are here to claim this star system in the name of the Cookrot Empire. Whoever you are…your rank is not important. The only people that can have rank are the Cookrot people. You will prepare to surrender your planet to us…any defiance will be dealt with harshly.*"

Jeejow sat there confused. "**Which is his rank and which is his name**?"

Bonarain responded. "**His rank is Tolomosh, which is equal to an Officer Grade 1, and his name is Undabagen, Sir**."

Jeejow had to think fast. "**What is their rank called… that is equal to my rank of Supreme Officer**?"

Bonarain huffed. 'NOW he has to ask this *h'oolyach,*' she thought. "**They don't have a rank equal to yours. The highest rank they have is the Superior Dymosh…who is equal to a Master Officer**."

Jeejow keyed the microphone. "As I said, I am the Drey Sssorg. I do have rank and it is more important to us than any rank of yours. My rank is higher than your Superior Dymosh, so you need to speak to me with some form of respect."

Undabagen laughed. *"There is no one higher than a Superior Dymosh in the military. The only one who is higher than a Superior Dymosh is the Inshondomik Tyntwomo! You are no Inshondomik. You are soon to be a slave!"*

Jeejow scoffed. **"What is a...whatever he said**?"

Bonarain huffed as she went through the vocabulary. **"The Inshondomik. That means King. If he's going to continue to be belligerent...pronounce it: Enshondok**."

Jeejow shook his head. **"Okay, Inshondomik means King. So what does enshondok mean**?"

Bonarain snickered. **"Phlegm**!"

Jeejow looked at the Command Staff. "Phlegm! How rude." He chuckled.

"It's appropriate," said Xadorm. "If *he* continues to be rude."

"I'll think about it," said Jeejow. He keyed the microphone again. "We have outlawed slavery in our society. Therefore you will not be able to do that to anybody on our planet. The penalty for attempting to enslave someone is death."

Iquanza broke in. **"This *bimyock* is just buying time. He doesn't care what you have to say. His people are trying to triangulate on you. They've got some special weapon that will be launched to track and destroy you**."

Jeejow looked at Yim. "Jump!" He keyed the microphone again. "I don't know what this enshondok Tyntwomo of yours is but I don't think that he could possibly be as rude as you are being."

Undabagen turned to his weapons officer. "Why haven't you launched?"

The man looked up. "Great One, they…moved…somehow and…we had to relocate them again."

Undabagen stood up. "So they moved a couple of *shkiken*! Tell me Skonmosh (O-4), Voovikto, why does that require the special tactics of a new spotting?"

"No, Great One," said Voovikto. "They…were about 23,000 *shkiken* closer to the star than we are. Now…they… somehow moved…over 18,000 *shkiken* further away from the star than we are. The other ships have confirmed the location."

Undabagen grinned. "A teleportation device…that can send them…over 40,000 *shkiken*…in a single *tyk*! I can hardly wait to get my claws on that technology." He sat back down. "Lock on to their signal and launch. Let the Death Torpedo find them. That's what the thing was designed to do." He keyed his microphone. "*The proper pronunciation is IN-shon-DO-mik. Learn to pronounce it properly! You will be using it quite a lot… for the rest of your worthless life. We're going to need a few billion slaves to mine the ore on this big planet. Pronounce it well and correct and we'll allow you to live…as a slave.*"

Jeejow shook his head in disgust. "Look here, Toolmush Undumboogun, if you persist in this stupidity, we will have to destroy you and your home planet." "**Do we know where this h'oolyach lives**?"

Soolchakan sighed. "**I'll check on it, Sir. I'll get back with you shortly**."

Undabagen looked at Voovikto. "Did you launch?"

"Absolutely, Great One. It will follow them…until it destroys them."

"**Jump somewhere**," sent Iquanza. "**They launched that thing and it appears that it has some kind of a tracker in it…that can follow you just about anywhere**."

It was Nantasa's turn to Jump the bell ship. She and her Team executed the move.

Voovikto looked up at the Commander. "Great One… that…ship has…moved again."

Undabagen calmly turned to Voovikto. "Where is it," he asked caustically?

"Great One…it is on the other side of the planet…that we're orbiting."

Iquanza looked at the Cookrot monitors. "**That torpedo has changed direction. I suggest you vacate your current location**."

Xadorm did not wait for anything from Jeejow. It was his Team's turn to Jump the ship. They did.

Iquanza looked at the monitor and saw the rocket change direction again. "**Where are you**?"

Xadorm answered. "**We're currently orbiting Dilhazass. That should give that rocket a rather long** trip before it gets near us again."

Undabagen saw the change of direction. "What happened? Where are they?"

Voovikto hit a few keys on his console. "Great One…they have…teleported…and they…are orbiting one of the gas giants in the seventh orbit."

One of the other officers stood up. "Great One, that is a teleportation leap of over 3,500,000 *shkiken*."

Undabagen started slapping his claws against the arm rests on his chair. "Oh, how I want this technology."

Kiyalee broke in. "**Sir, I found some of the information on this death torpedo. Seeing as how you've Jumped to Dilhazass, the torpedo has shut off its engine. It is now going on momentum. It'll turn on the engine and make any final adjustments when it gets closer…in about four days. It'll hunt you down until it strikes. The only way to stop it is to make it run out of fuel.**"

Jeejow threw his arms up in exasperation. "**Got any suggestions on how we do that**?"

"**Yes, Sir. Make another Jump to Denhahbon. That'll require a change of direction…a turn of over 80 degrees. It'll have to turn the engine on for that. After it has you marked there, make another Jump…oh say to Ragath. That'll make another turn of over 85 degrees.**"

Jeejow pondered for a few moments. "**How is that going to help in the long run**?"

"It only has enough fuel to make four or five major adjustments. If you make it do five or six...it'll run out of fuel very quickly. Then we can grab it and...drop it in the gravitational pull of...Rogoth."

Jeejow sat there nodding his head. "Whose turn is it?"

"My turn," said Marbing. "On to Denhahbon we go."

Voovikto groaned. "Great One...it is...as if they know the capability of the torpedo. They've made another...teleport... to the outer planet. The torpedo has made the adjustment. If they make one more...major move...it *will* run out of fuel."

Undabagen shook his head grinning. "Oh...how I really *want* this technology."

Jeejow pondered. "How much time do I have before that fool thing gets to my current location?"

Kiyalee giggled. "They launched it from Bri. Right now, you're orbiting Denhahbon. It'll take at least six days...at its current speed before it gets to you...on momentum alone."

Jeejow leaned back in his chair. "We're going to make two more Jumps. When that thing runs out of fuel, someone go catch it and get it out of our star system. I don't want those *doovofts* retrieving it and trying to use it again."

Kiyalee sighed. "I'm the one who is going to have to catch it. I'm the only one who has actually seen the silly thing. I'm the only one who can landmark on it. Where do you suggest I take it?"

Chyning broke in. "**Why don't you take it to the Iyka planet? Nothing lives there. If it blows up on that planet...it won't hurt anything.**"

Jeejow had a horrible thought. "**How many of those things are in this current armada?**"

"**They started with six on each ship,**" sent Kiyalee.

Marbing groaned. "That's 119 of those wretched things left."

Jeejow growled. "**All personnel who are on the Cookrot ships...find the torpedoes and...get rid of them. I don't want to have to play a game of runaway from 119 more of those things.**"

Kiyalee broke in. "**Sir, you don't have to worry that much about the rocket. It's the warhead that's the problem. Unload the warhead and it can't do any real damage...to anything.**"

Jeejow snarled and smoothed his hair back. "**All right! Get rid of the warheads! Do something! Disarm this bunch of *bimyocks*!**"

"**I'll get ready to chase the flying one now,**" sent Kiyalee. "**All the rest of you...the torpedoes are currently stored in...what the Cookrot call...weapon storage area 14. When you pull the stuff out of the warhead...don't let the green vial and the yellow vial touch. If they touch... big boom. One person take the yellow vials and one**" person take the green vials. Alone, they're inert. It's only when they mix that you get the big problem."

"Fine," sent Jeejow. "Dump all of the green vials in Ragath and all of the yellow vials in Rogoth. That way… we know that they'll never mix and we won't have to worry about them." He blew out his breath in relief. "Now… Jump us back to Bri so that the silly thing has to make another… major adjustment. After *it* has made that adjustment…bring us back to Denhahbon." "All of you who are collecting the vials…let me know when all of them are collected. That way, the Cookrot won't know about the theft until after it is over and all of their bang stuff is sinking into Ragath and Rogoth." He drummed his fingers on the table. "Officer, Kiyalee, are you ready to chase that *bimyock* thing down yet?"

"Yes, Sir. As soon as you run it out of fuel."

Jeejow snickered. "Has it made the last adjustment?"

"Yes, Sir."

"Let's go to…oh…Makatindi," said Jeejow. "That sounds good."

Kiyalee laughed. "All of the Cookrot are…rather angry. Their little death torpedo just sputtered out. That head *bimyock* ordered someone to go get it and prepare another torpedo for launch. I can get to it long before they can. You won't have to worry about the next one."

Soolchakan suddenly broke into the conversation. "Sir,

I've been to the Cookrot home world. I don't think that these *bimyocks* are going to quit…until we've hurt them…worse than what we did to the Choks or Zizzys. These are some very determined and nasty people."

Jeejow sighed and leaned his head back. "Do we still have some of our 459 cannons…mounted on the noses of some of those ships…when we tried routing power from the light speed engines through them?"

"Absolutely," said Yim. "No one came up with a reason to dismantle all of them."

Jeejow gritted his teeth. "**Officer, Soolchakan! Take one of the Tashkafa shuttlecraft. Get eight other Teams on that shuttlecraft and Jump them to the Cookrot home world. After they have landmarked, the eight Teams will go to dimension 45, get two of the spaceships that have four 459 cannons mounted to their nose. Those ships will be Jumped to the Cookrot home world. All eight cannons will be aimed at the Cookrot capitol city. All eight cannons will be enhanced by the light speed engines. All eight cannons will commence firing at the same time. Four of them will then start plowing trenches to the north and four will plow trenches to the south. We will cause massive damage to their planet and then maybe they'll listen.**"

When Undabagen found out that all of the death torpedoes had been disarmed he threw a monumentally royal snit-fit where he had twenty-five different crew members executed for not performing proper security of their weaponry. Once he calmed down, he radioed back to the home world that he was going against an enemy that had the capability of teleportation and that he would need all kinds of assistance in taking this adversary and gaining control of their technology.

Officer Leader, Vooglon of Team 57 was put in command of the attack on the Cookrot home world. He decided that since Soolchakan had been the one to do the first quick exploration of this strange world, that Team 7016 should be involved in the attack. Chyning was rather irritated on being "honored" again, however, she quit griping when she was assigned as one of the gunners that would be firing a 459 cannon.

The two ships were in place hovering some 40 kilotaja over the capitol city (in Spy) of the Cookrot home planet. Vooglon (and Team 7016) were on the ship that was assigned to sweep north.

Vooglon looked down on the capitol city. "Don't any of these Cookrot believe in 90 degree angles? Every building down there…is round. There is no originality in their architecture anywhere."

One of his Aides, Officer Grade 5, Ona-Nee just shrugged. "We don't know anything about their culture. Maybe it's been like this for…over 2,850 years."

He chuckled. "You mean a little bit longer than we've been Owlam Elf?"

Another member of Vooglon's Team, Officer Grade 6, Eeteeha called out. "All personnel are in position, Sir. We're ready to attack on your command."

Vooglon nodded. "**Everybody pay attention. You people on the 456 cannons, be sure to watch out on our flanks, forward and behind us. We haven't seen any planetary defense network, but that doesn't mean that there isn't one. They could come at us from any direction**." He whispered to Ona-Nee. "Has anyone seen anything yet…of planetary defenses?"

Ona-Nee shrugged and shook her head. "Maybe they think that they're so tough that no one would dare have the audacity or courage to attack their home planet."

He grunted. "*That*…is nothing but puerile insolence. No one is that tough…not even us." He cleared his throat.

Soolchakan was wondering what would happen when Kiyalee pulled the trigger. Rarely had she pulled the trigger on any weapon and usually it ended up bad. This time, the computer people had locked the 459 cannons into place. All four, on this ship, would be firing at the exact same spot. The ship was going to be moved north so that the concentrated fire of four cannons would always be together and not randomly tearing up the countryside. The four cannons on the southern ship were set up the same. The only cannons that were independent were all of the 456 cannons who were just waiting to see if anyone tried to attack the Owlam positions.

Vooglon took a deep breath. "**Remember that if you see lava start shooting up through the cracks…we've broken completely through the crust of the planet. The** crust is usually about 160 kilotaja deep and…we're still not sure of the overall destructive capability of the 459." He bit his lip. "Are there any questions from any of you?"

Chyning snarled. "CAN WE START THIS MESS?!"

Soolchakan and Bonarain sat there snickering.

Vooglon sighed in disgust. "All personnel on the 459 cannons…hop your barrels into Home dimension… commence firing…NOW!"

Soolchakan pulled the trigger. He watched as four beams rained destruction down on the capitol. Even from this height he could see a few large buildings start exploding. Then he saw an orange glow start coming up and getting bigger. They were already through the crust and there was lava coming up, right in the middle of the capitol.

The ship started moving north.

Bonarain looked, almost horrified, that lava was coming up already. They had broken the crust and soon, the capitol city would be nothing but a giant puddle of molten lava.

Kiyalee was staring wide-eyed as the beam went from her cannon to join with the three other beams. She knew that people were being cooked to death down there, however, since she was this far up, she did not have to actually see any of the horrible burns that would be the result and therefore she did not feel nauseous.

Chyning sat there grinning. Finally! The act was being accomplished.

They held the triggers down on the cannons. They did not

have to worry about the power packs on any of the cannons because the power was coming directly from the light speed engines.

The area where they were seeing lava was getting wider even as the ship moved further north. None of them had even thought of destruction that would have been so tremendous. More and more orange was spewing from the line that was being cut by the cannons.

Chyning laughed as she shook her head. "**I wonder how deep this is going. If we hit the center of their planet…I wonder what'll come up then**."

Bonarain scoffed. "**If that does happen, it'll be a global catastrophe that they might not be able to come back from**."

The ship continued north as did the destruction. They cut through several other cities and towns as they moved north, demolishing everything in the path of the quadruple beams of devastation.

"**I've got to shut down**," sent Kiyalee. "**My cannon is getting awful hot. The temperature gage is getting unsafe**."

Soolchakan checked his gage. "**Go ahead and shut down. We've still got three of them going strong**."

The ship continued north and the beams were no longer hitting land. They were shooting into the ocean and the turbulence in the water was incredible as massive geysers of steam came up from the triple beam. They continued north to a polar ice cap and saw ice being instantaneously turned into vapor.

Vooglon had been looking off to the side. Even though he knew that this was necessary and had been ordered by the *Voice of Power*, he was still disgusted with the amount of destruction. He looked back and nearly screamed. "**HOLD YOUR FIRE! STOP SHOOTING! CEASE FIRE**!"

Soolchakan was a little surprised at the order. They still had a little bit more north to go before the beams would not be hitting the planet. Then he saw what had happened.

Bonarain let off of her trigger about the same time as the others. She looked at the 459 to see if it had a problem. Then she looked back at the planet and gasped.

Chyning sat there looking down at the planet with her mouth hanging wide open.

Kiyalee just threw up.

Vooglon called back to Jeejow. "**Uh…Sir…uh…we… did as you…told us to do…uh…Sir…we…uh…I don't know how to tell you this**."

Jeejow snarled with his teeth clenched. "**Quit stammering and COMMUNICATE**!"

Vooglon continued with his faltering thoughts and could not compose an understandable or complete sentence.

Finally Chyning broke in. "**Supreme Officer, Jeejow… we just cut the whole *chokwad* planet in half**!"

Jeejow had a glass of water in his hand and it now fell

and shattered on the floor. He looked at the Command Staff dumbfounded. His body appeared to be totally catatonic. He cleared his throat several times trying to think of…anything. "**Could you please repeat that last statement**?"

Vooglon finally found his wits. "**Sir, as she said…we cut the entire planet in half. Sir…I didn't realize that these cannons were that…powerful. The two halves of the planet…are separating from each other and…there are trillions of…*things*…coming up off of the surface… because obviously…there is no more…gravity…or any atmosphere and…oh my**."

Xadorm had his hand against his forehead. "Sir, I don't think we need to try any more upgrades on the 459 cannons. I think…they're quite destructive enough."

Jeejow shook his head staring off into space in shock. "We cut…a…PLANET…in half. An entire…PLANET!"

One of the people on the 456 cannons called out. "**We have some incoming enemy ships coming at us**!"

Vooglon scoffed. "**Hop all of our equipment into Spy. I think we've done enough damage…for one day. Let those…enemy ships…get a good long look at… what happened here. I'm sure that they'll be able to contact their ships…near Hardooth…and tell them what happened**."

Soolchakan sat there a little bewildered. "**Now that everything is in Spy…what do we do now**?"

Vooglon leaned back in the Command Chair. "**Teams! Jump these two ships back to Hardooth…and then hop them back to dimension 45**."

Jeejow thought for a few moments. He shook his head and sighed. He picked up the microphone and keyed it. "Tolomosh, Undabagen! Your home planet has just been destroyed. It was destroyed because you did not listen to us and leave quietly. If you persist in any hostilities against us or persist in trying to remove any of our mineral wealth…we will be forced to destroy you and every member of your race as well. Leave now…while you are still alive."

Undabagen called for the long range transmitters and receivers to be turned on and find out anything he could about the home planet. The horror was confirmed by ships that were in the vicinity. The planet was gone and nothing that had been down there on the planet had survived.

10

Undabagen read all of the information and listened to all of the chatter that was going on back at – what used to be – the home planet. He picked up the microphone. *"I...along with every other member of the Cookrot race...declare a...Blood Curse...against you and your race...slave Jeejow. From now on...no Cookrot will rest...or stop attacking...until every member of your slave race is dead. Within...a year...we will have over 100,000 attack ships coming here...and we will destroy every part of your system. We will not stop until this Holy Compensation is complete. We will never contact you again. We will only urinate on your remains... before we burn them and erase any and all memory of you rancid parasites."*

Xadorm scoffed. "Holy Compensation? What kind of *h'oolyach* is that?"

Before anyone could comment back to Xadorm, Bonarain broke in. **"Sir, I wouldn't worry about his threat. They don't have 100,000 attack ships. They have 1,632... total ships. Of those ships, only 954 are attack ships. The thing we have to worry about is...all of the attack ships, that are not here, still have twenty of those death torpedoes on them. They're ready to launch all of them against us...if necessary...for holy compensation."**

Xadorm did some quick mathematics and hung his head. "18,680 of those wretched torpedoes." He looked up and sighed. "Oh…*h'oolyach!*"

Jeejow sat there with his eyes closed. "**Officer, Kiyalee… do you still have the torpedo…the one that is out of fuel**?"

Kiyalee was still a little queasy after seeing that planet destroyed. "**Yes, Sir, I didn't have a chance to disarm it… so I…have it…strapped to the side of my fighter.**"

Jeejow nodded. "**I'd like to see…the destructive capability of that thing. Someone suggested taking it to the Iyka home world. I think that that is an excellent target…to test it. Can you do that for us**?"

"**Yes, Sir. I think we can figure out a way to test it there.**"

"**Thank you.**" Jeejow shook his head sadly. "I want to see what the capability of this…*special* weapon is…especially if we currently have over 18,000 of the nasty things headed our way."

Team 7016 Jumped to the Iyka home world. It still appeared the same as before. There was nothing green anywhere on any of the continents. Everything on land was different shades of brown. The oceans were still blue, however, there was nothing in them that was living. The planet was still dead…other than some weather patterns.

Kiyalee looked down at the planet. "**Where should I drop it?**"

Soolchakan scoffed. "**Pick a continent. I don't think that we'd see any form of noticeable reaction if you hit the ocean...especially deep water.**"

Chyning looked at the rocket still strapped to the side of Kiyalee's fighter. "**Are we sure that *chogo* thing could possibly be that dangerous? It's only nine taja in length and...it's less than one taja in circumference. How could something that small...be that dangerous?**"

"**That's what we're here to find out,**" sent Bonarain. "**We won't know anything until...we see the chemical reaction between the green stuff and the yellow stuff.**"

Chyning shook her head. "**How are we gonna test this...thing? Are we gonna launch it or...what?**"

Soolchakan took a deep breath and let it out slowly. "**The three of us are going to back off from the planet. I want to be...800 kilotaja from the planet when that thing goes off. We all put our sensors on...to monitor the entire thing. I'll put my camera on magnification setting 1. Bonarain, you set yours for 10. Chyning, you set yours for 25. Kiyalee, yours will be set on 50. Go inside the atmosphere with that thing...drop it...as centrally as you can, on the biggest continent down there.**"

Kiyalee frowned. "**It doesn't have any fuel for propulsion. How do I...control it?**"

"**You aim your fighter, nose down towards the ground. Then you just unstrap the thing and let gravity do the rest. From what I understand, all it takes is the two vials being broken and the two chemicals mixing that causes something…really nasty. After you drop it…Jump back here to where we are…and watch…with your camera on**."

Kiyalee landmarked herself between Bonarain and Chyning. She hit the throttle and headed into the atmosphere. Once she got down to a certain level where she could safely Jump out before the rocket hit the ground, she hit the quick release latches on the straps. The fins on the rocket kept it going, nose down. She Jumped out to where the rest of the Team was waiting and made sure that her camera was on. "**Any time now**."

Soolchakan nodded. "**Just in case…it's anything like a firestorm weapon…close your eyes…once we see something…start. We can always look at the film later and see…what we missed**."

Chyning scoffed. "**Do you really think that it could possibly be that…big**?"

Soolchakan snarled. "**I DON'T KNOW WHAT TO EXPECT. I just…don't want anyone of us hurt…or blinded. I want to get out of this unharmed**."

Chyning shrugged. "**Okay**."

As soon as they noticed a bright disturbance near the center of the target continent, the three women clenched their eyes shut. Soolchakan put his hands in front of his eyes and squinted to protect himself from any form of a bright light. The light was rather bright for a few moments, however, it was nothing like a firestorm weapon going off. He slowly spread his fingers and peered through them.

"**I think we're safe now...from any blinding by a fireball. The initial blast is over and....**" He stopped sending and sat there with his mouth hanging open as he watched a wave of some type spread out from the central location and cover the entire continent...and beyond.

The three women were equally horrified and awed at what they saw.

Chyning was the first to send. "**Did that...just happen?**"

"**It's not over yet,**" sent Bonarain. "**Look at the... ocean...to the east of the continent. What's happening there?**"

"**I think it made...a hole,**" sent Soolchakan. "**The water is...rushing in...to fill the hole.**"

Kiyalee was flabbergasted. "**A...hole...that...BIG?**"

Chyning swallowed hard. "**And there could be...18,000 of those things...headed to Hardooth?**"

"**We need to get back to Hardooth...and let... everyone know about this,**" sent Soolchakan.

"**It's not finished,**" sent Bonarain. "**There's still... something going on down there. We haven't seen all of it.**"

Soolchakan clenched his teeth. **"Okay, so you stick around and watch it until everything calms down. We'll go back and show…what we've got to everyone. If there is something…significant…that happens later, you can bring that information when you come back."**

"Do you mind if I stay as well…until it's entirely over," asked Kiyalee?

Soolchakan licked his lips. **"No. I don't mind. Chyning…do you want to stay as well**?"

"No. I've seen enough of this…spectacle. I'm going home with you."

Soolchakan showed his film to the Command Staff. Chyning then showed hers with the different magnification.

Jeejow sat there looking somewhat scared. "This is what you saw…and you didn't stick around to…see the aftermath."

"Sir, Officers, Bonarain and Kiyalee are still there… watching the dust settle. They should have some more recording for you…when they return."

Jeejow nodded. He turned to the medical personnel. "What were you saying about the toxins?"

Doctor Kazkim of Medical Team 221 shrugged. "What I'm seeing in his scans say that…there is some kind of residual poison that is released when these things go off. From the looks of the film, anyone caught in the…wave of destruction…will die from blunt force blast trauma or a shattering earthquake. The people who are on the outside of the…wave area…will now have to put up with these toxins." He shook his head. "We've seen that we are immune to any and all bacteria and virus that has come along in the last 2,800 years. We don't have a problem with that residual energy…called radiation. Toxins? We're not sure about that. The only way to know…if we can be killed by these toxins… somebody has to go there and…breathe deep. If they die…we can be killed by poison. If they don't die…we're immune. I hesitate to ask anyone to volunteer for anything…that could possibly kill them."

Jeejow turned to the physicist. "Officer Leader, Hrombisk. What have you got to say about this…event?"

Hrombisk looked at his hands for a few moments. "It is definitely a tremendously violent chemical reaction. I was given one of the yellow vials and one of my associates was given a green vial. We've tried to identify what is in them…but we are physicists, not chemists. The doctors can't identify it…chemically…either. All we can do is look at the results and…If just two of those things hit this planet…we're doomed…or at least the planet is. We'd definitely have to move somewhere else…if those things hit Hardooth."

Jeejow looked solemn. "When Officer, Bonarain gets back…we're going to see if she can tell us a little more about this…holy compensation. If those *bimyocks* are determined to this cause…where no Cookrot citizen will rest…as long as we are alive…we have a huge problem on our hands."

"None of this would have happened if we hadn't attacked their home planet," said Nantasa angrily.

"Don't fool yourself," said Zoolkog. "They would've made that silly declaration no matter what…because we refused to surrender. We simply made them pay a huge price…before they did it to us."

Marbing scoffed. "So how do we prepare for over 18,000 of those things?"

"For one thing," said Jeejow. "We use everything at our disposal to determine where those ships are and then make sure that they can't use those things against us."

"Where are the twenty ships that are here?" Onga looked around confused. "Are they still skulking around in Ghost… trying to figure out what's going on?"

"Of course," said Yim. "We put them in Ghost, they can still see our star system, they can still move towards Hardooth, but none of them can hurt us…unless we go into Ghost as well." He chuckled. "They're orbiting Hardooth now. They've fired a few pulse cannons at us and can't understand why nothing is happening. They're also frustrated over the fact that they can't communicate with any of their other ships outside of Ghost."

Tadesha frowned. "Were they able to communicate with other ships…of their ilk…and inform them that we were the ones who…did a chop job on their home planet?"

"They were able to communicate that we did it," said Jeejow. "Whether or not the others of their race believe it…I don't know."

Xadorm thought on it for a moment. "If they are…as

conceited as the Vagens are then…they may not believe it. They couldn't possibly believe that an inferior race could have hurt them…at all."

"Don't fool yourself," said Inditam. "How could this bunch here have known about it…when they were so far from the actual occurrence? The others have to put some credibility to the story…especially since the others can't find them now."

Jeejow clenched his fists on the table. "Maybe, maybe, maybe, MAYBE! The only thing that we can do is…prepare. Worst case scenario. If even…just 10% believe it…that means that we will have 18,000 of those things headed our way. What we saw one of those things do to…the Iyka planet…what would 20 or more do to this planet?"

"So get ready for anything," said Xadorm. "They could attack us from any direction…at any time."

Bonarain and Kiyalee came back nine days later. It had taken that long for all of the dust to settle and for them to get a good unobstructed view of the target area.

The entire Command Staff was somewhat mesmerized by the spectacle – and the aftermath.

Bonarain pulled up a picture of the "before the bomb hit" on the planet. "As you can see here, Sirs, the continent was not flat. Here in this southern area and especially here in the western area it was very mountainous and rugged. According to what we knew about the planet originally, this western area had three of the tallest mountain peaks on the entire planet." She changed to a different picture. "Now…they've been completely flattened by that wave of destruction. The wave, as you can see, also created a large crater. Unfortunately you can't see the crater, as a whole, because when the wave went out into the ocean on the eastern side of the continent, the ocean water then rushed in…to the deeper basin of the crater created by the wave."

Jeejow pointed at a portion of the screen. "So all of this semi-circle is the north, west and south parts of the crater. The eastern portion…would be out here in this part of the ocean."

"Yes, Sir," said Bonarain. "We measured the crater from north to south, because it was impossible to do it east to west. The crater has a diameter of 19,644 kilotaja. The edges of the crater are 120 kilotaja above sea level. The mountain range that used to be here in the west, the highest peak was 151 kilotaja high, so the wave shoved everything out of the center. The central part of the crater, which used to be land that was all above sea level, is now 90 kilotaja below sea level. No matter how you look at it, this thing could end all life on any planet…with just one of them."

"I'm sure glad that they don't have any more manufacturing plants for that weapon," said Marbing.

Tadesha frowned at him. "What makes you think that they're not making more?"

Marbing scoffed. "According to what my Team found in some of the computer archives of the Cookrot. There was one plant where they made the rocket, one plant where they made the green stuff and one plant where they made the yellow stuff. All three plants were on the Cookrot home planet."

"That makes sense," said Zoolkog. "If you have a weapon that dangerous, you don't want it to be manufactured anywhere else that someone could get their hands on it. You keep it all in one place."

Nantasa scoffed. "Haven't they heard the saying about keeping all of your wealth in one pot? Someone steals that one pot and you're broke."

Yim chuckled. "Who could have foreseen their planet getting cut in half?"

"FOCUS PEOPLE!" Jeejow looked around sternly. "Right now, you're talking philosophy. We need to get back to the subject that…those *wathoot fovoks* have over 18,000 of those weapons that are *still intact*! That is not a philosophy that is a reality that we have to contend with."

All of the Staff sat there silently, some looking a little guilty, waiting for the next order.

Jeejow turned to Marbing. "Where did you get one of their computers…with archives?"

Marbing smiled. "Well, Sir, they are stuck in Ghost, so… my Team went to one of the ships and pulled the whole thing out… and they weren't able to do a thing to stop us."

Jeejow sniffed. "Did it ever occur to you to turn the thing over to Sankiki and her Teams or Tula and her Teams of computer repair and programmers?"

Marbing flushed and cleared his throat. "Uh…no, Sir.

But…we can show them how we took the thing and…we can get another system off of another ship…for them."

Jeejow snorted. "Well don't just sit here wasting my time talking about it, contact Sankiki and Tula and get to it."

Marbing stood up. "Yes, Sir." He signaled to his Team members. All four of them vanished.

Jeejow looked around wide-eyed. "Any other surprises about how we can take other things from those *doovofts*?"

Inditam smiled. "I haven't taken anything, but, I have an idea about how we might be able to get something…and use it against them."

Jeejow leaned closer to her smiling. "And that is…?"

"I remember when we first came across these Cookrots. Officer, Soolchakan said that it would be no problem landmarking their planet because every one of them has a picture in his work station of…home." She smiled as she started looking at the other personnel. "I was on one of the ships, snooping around for myself. They have a room on each ship that shows photographs of all of the current ship commanders…throughout the entire fleet. If we landmark on their faces…we just might be able to…get to their ships and…steal those *chogo* death torpedoes."

Jeejow leaned back. "That…can be risky. Is there something…in the legend of each picture…that tells whether they are dead or alive?"

"Sir, there was one section for the deceased, one section for retired and one section for current commanders," she said merrily.

Jeejow folded his arms. "Of all the things." He clicked his tongue. "Our main weapon against them…may turn out to be…their own vanity."

"What a shame," chuckled Xadorm sarcastically.

Jeejow nodded. "Let's see what we can find. There are 934 more of those ships out there, with over 18,000 of those death rockets. The sooner we can take them all out, the better…the rockets that is."

"I've got an idea where we start," said Xadorm.

There were numerous Owlamites now on board the twenty Cookrot ships collecting passwords and learning all kinds of new things about these snobbish people. They were able to get what they wanted by hopping the computers into Home while they left the Cookrots in Ghost. The Cookrots were swinging their fists and doing everything they could to stop the Owlamites, however, they could not even touch any Owlamite because of the dimension shift between Ghost and Home.

Each ship seemed to be having some trouble with the chain of command. Usually, there was a Commander and an Executive Officer who was second in command. On the Cookrot ships, there were five who were designated as Executive Officers and not one of them was sure which one was the ranking officer. The Commander was supposed to decide, on a daily basis, which one was the current second in command. Without the Commander on the ship it was nothing but turmoil and indecision.

The Owlamite Command Staff was currently standing by the big Doolood aquarium looking in at the Commanders of all of the twenty Cookrot ships. All twenty of the Cookrots were standing there trying to look defiant. In reading their minds, they found that the Cookrot Commanders were all baffled as to how they had gone to bed in the room on their ships and then awakened in this strange (funny smelling) room.

Jeejow saw the consternation on the faces of the Cookrots as they were holding their noses. "Haven't we been able to get that moldy smell out there yet?"

"No, Sir," said Zoolkog. "For some reason, that high alkali Doolood water has a very powerful and long lasting residual smell to it. We've tried to air it out, but, because this area is so humid… it just hasn't dried up completely."

"Oh, well," said Xadorm sardonically. "I find it hard to feel sorry for that bunch."

There was a lot of snickering among the Owlamites.

Jeejow sighed. "So…whom do we have here?"

Toyzamia looked at her list. "The three with the big gold stripe on their terrapin-shell uniform are the three Tolomosh. Undabagen, Squabok and Jijbokkok. The ones with the three silver stripes are the Fethmosh."

Inditam frowned. "What's a Fethmosh?"

"Fethmosh is equal to an Officer Grade 2," said Toyzamia. "According to the rank structure of these ships, there are twelve of the Fethmosh. Yooyooklob, Hishik, Diyd, Ooshoopos,

Chanjoo, Ongkwat, Zodz, Breebikon, Didlosk, Churj, Idziot and Handanikon. The last group of five are the Shillmosh. Shillmosh is marked with two silver stripes and is equal to an Officer Grade 3. They are Woobwum, Sysser, Myodzip, Tapotisk and Yik."

Jeejow acted like he was cleaning his ears out with his pinky fingers. "I don't care who they are…I wanted to know what they are…and why they are here."

"Oh." Toyzamia flushed and had a bit of a guilty smile. "These are the twenty ship Commanders…from the armada that we have in Ghost. They are here…in case you wanted to dig through their minds. They are also here because as long as we have them off of their ships…the next five on each ship don't have a clue who is the next ranking one. There is something in their command structure…they have five executive officers, on each ship. The Commander promotes and demotes as he sees fit. He can do this on a daily basis. If he is not on the ship and one of the five decides to take command, in his absence, and when he comes back, he disagrees with which one could take command as the second officer…he can be executed for insubordination. Right now, on all twenty ships, there is no assigned Commander. Each one has five very scared high ranking officers who can't make a decision without the permission of the assigned Commander of the ship…unless they are absolutely certain that their current Commander is dead. As long as these *bimyocks* are here…no intelligent decision will be made on any of those ships."

Marbing shook his head while giggling. "What an idiotic mess!"

"And it's of their own making," said Onga.

Jeejow got on the microphone and tried speaking to the Cookrots in the aquarium. All of them looked at each other confused.

Toyzamia grimaced. "Sir, you're speaking to them in our language. They don't understand it."

Now Jeejow looked confused. "I thought they had some kind of international translator."

"They do, Sir…in the communication system in their ships," said Toyzamia. "There isn't one…in this setup."

Jeejow nodded. "So I have to speak to them in their language."

Toyzamia nodded with a smile.

Jeejow sighed. "Tolomosh, Undabagen, I need to speak with you."

Undabagen stepped forward. "Then do so in the correct manner, *shooshpuk*! Get down on your knees."

Jeejow turned to Toyzamia looking as if he were sick. "I'm not familiar with…that word…*shooshpuk*. What does it mean?"

Toyzamia flushed and looked straight up. "Sir…it means… uh…raw sewage…I think."

Jeejow sniffed. "I wish I hadn't asked." He looked back at Undabagen. "Okay, Tolomosh…*Shooshpuk*. We need to talk and you need to realize that I am of a greater rank than you, therefore, you will show me the respect due to my rank."

Undabagen looked back at his colleagues and let out the

honking laugh while pointing at Jeejow. "That slave thinks that he can push us around."

"WHO IS THE ONE TRAPPED IN A CELL?" Jeejow stood there fuming. "YOU'RE THE ONES WHO ARE ABOUT TO BE FLUSHED DOWN THE DRAIN! Even though you are prisoners, you still remain insolent…and stupid. We can destroy you and all of your people at our whim…yet you still persist in being stupid." He turned to Zoolkog. "I believe that you were in charge of this prison for a long time."

Zoolkog nodded. "Yes, Sir, I was. Any particular reason that you're asking now?"

Jeejow was still fuming. "Get all the help you need. Dig into their minds. Find every little secret that they have. Find out about that…stupid vow…about a holy compensation. Once you've found out everything that they know…that we can use… take them to the sewage hole…and dump them in. If they somehow survive the trip down…I want them to be sliced open so that they won't survive anything else. Get rid of their shell armor as well. It somehow…can keep them alive…in all kinds of strange conditions. They don't deserve that kind of privilege. Pick their brains for anything you can get. If you turn them into mental deadheads in the process…I don't care." He walked away trying to calm himself down before he made some tragic decision about his own people.

Zoolkog turned to his Team. "Vooskani…go get Officer Leader, Bybisi. I gave her the list of…Teams that wanted to be involved in mass mind control here…when I got promoted to Senior Officer. Have her start calling Teams in…so that we can do some mind control on this *h'oolyach*."

Bybisi showed up with her Team 69. In a very short time, they had twenty other Teams in the viewing area. The mental dissection started taking place and all twenty of the ship Commanders were writhing on the floor in agony as they felt their brains being helplessly cleaned of all information.

Jeejow watched some of the mental torture that was going on at the aquarium. He finally calmed down and called out. "**To all Teams who are not involved in the questioning of the Cookrot Commanders...all Teams from Team 100 through Team 999. All of you, get to the twenty Cookrot space ships. Hop them from Ghost to dimension 45. Start getting all of the information you can from the ships computers and personnel. If any of the Cookrot personnel get in your way...jettison them...without their armor shell. We need to find out if there are any other Cookrot ships responding to that *chokwad* holy compensation that this *doovoft* called for**." He cleared his throat as he thought about the next phase. "**All other Teams...1000 and up...get ready to find the other Cookrot ships that are responding and are coming this way. Find a way...and destroy them at all costs**." He closed his eyes. 'I hope that I haven't caused the deaths of any more Owlamites with that order,' he thought. 'But...we have to stop them from using that horrid torpedo.'

Of the other 934 attack ships, they found out that 220 were currently headed for Hardooth. Jeejow figured that once those ships disappeared the other 714 ships would be headed in for that silly vendetta. If that holy compensation was that important, it appeared they would have to destroy more than just the planet. They would have to destroy every Cookrot in the galaxy.

After eight days of constant bombardment of questions and allowing them no sleep, the twenty Commanders were now all nothing but brain-fried babbling idiots. The Owlamites did find out a few things before the twenty were euthanized.

Undabagen had been the armada commander, however, there were other personnel in the chain of command who did not like or trust him. As a result, those higher ups used their "friends" in the armada to keep an eye on Undabagen.

In the Cookrot hierarchy, there was one Inshondomik. This was the ultimate ruler with absolute authority. Under him there were eight who were given the rank of Superior Dymosh. They ran their own sector with four Major Dymosh under each one of them. Each Major Dymosh had four Dymosh under them. Then came the rank of Tolomosh. When the planet had been destroyed, anyone who was on the planet at the time died. This included the Inshondomik and three of the Superior Dymosh. One of the Superior Dymosh had the planet as his sector and as a result, his entire entourage was obliterated when the planet was split.

Now there were five Superior Dymosh and eight Major Dymosh with no Superior as their leader. The eight Majors could now act independently. Most of these personnel had obtained the services of some of the Tolomosh, the Fethmosh and the Shillmosh under Undabagen's command. Most of them had received the information that the star system Undabagen was in had been responsible for the destruction of the home planet. They did not know or understand how, however, they agreed with the holy compensation and were on their way to Hardooth committed to the genocide of that planet.

Jeejow realized that they were going to have to commit genocide themselves in order to survive. The crazy vow by the Cookrot made the outcome inevitable – kill or be killed – completely.

After getting rid of every single Cookrot that was in the Holgotho system, they hopped the twenty ships back into Home dimension. Immediately all of them started receiving all kinds of calls from the other ships, asking where they were and informing them that reinforcements were on the way.

The information obtained from the other nineteen leaders told them that each one was a spy against Undabagen for one of the Superior Dymosh or the Major Dymosh. Each one of those personnel seemed to be calling in asking for some kind of further updated information on the upstarts who had the audacity (and technology) to split a planet in half. The Owlamites simply listened to the information and found out exactly how many Cookrot ships were headed their way and how soon they would get there.

One of the Cookrot armadas was getting close to the Holgotho system. The Owlamites prepared for their arrival. When it was seen how close they were bunched up together, it was decided to try the proven method of introducing a hand-held bomb into the light speed engine while it was running. All twenty of those ships were fried when the explosion occurred.

After the destruction of the first vowed armada happened, they thought that the Cookrots would become a little more cautious in their manner of attack. They did not. Over the next two years, all Cookrot ships came to the Holgotho system, ready to attack Hardooth and they were all blown away with the same method. The Owlamites continued to listen for any other communications from any other Cookrot out in the cosmos. They never heard another word from any of them. Either the Cookrot had given up or they had all been eliminated.

Either way, the Owlamites still had to remain vigilant by listening to the Cookrot radios for quite some time.

11

One of Jeejow's Team members, Officer Grade 3, Yilla walked up to him after the last of the known Cookrot had been destroyed.

"Sir, did you know that it has been 2,833 years since the Algothon attack?"

Jeejow hung his head. "I'm aware of that…number."

"Did you know that you are now…the third longest serving *Voice of Power* since this mess started?"

"I am?"

"Yes, Sir. Till had the power for 781 years before his death. Wymini had it for 696 years before her death. You're now sitting at 603 years."

He frowned. "What about Hadathoo?"

"Hadathoo had the power for 548 years before his death. After that was Wilfadge with 199 years."

He sighed sadly. "I never thought of it as a contest…to see who could be in this capacity for the…longest duration."

"Sir, considering the fact that the first four – Nagasoom, Plothok, Neenatha and Jahong…total between them was eight years…I think things are improving."

He chuckled. "If we haven't learned any lessons in 2,833 years…we'll never learn. We're constantly learning something… each time we get attacked. I just wish…those deadly lessons would cease."

"Yeah. They sure have been expensive."

"Yup."

94 years later, Jeejow became the second longest one who reigned as the *Voice of Power*. 85 years after that he celebrated his 782nd anniversary and became THE number one longest reigning *Voice of Power*. All Owlamites were hoping that this peace would last forever. 28 years later in the 810th year of Jeejow and 3,040 years after the firestorm attacks that hope was, once again, shattered by another attack.

There were explosions occurring all over the planet simultaneously. There was no warning. There was just more death and chaos.

As soon as Jeejow got word of the mass attack, he immediately called for all Owlamites to hop to Observation. He then asked for anyone to report what they had seen or heard. There were Owlamites scattered all over the world and they all reported that the attacks had all come at the same time, and once again, from out of the sky.

"Whoever is closest to their fighters…get to the skies immediately and…find out who is attacking us," sent Jeejow angrily.

Soolchakan let out a few "choice words" as he and his Team left their fresh hot kwatha on the table in their gorge apartment and headed for their fighters. It did not take long for them to get their suits on, get into the fighters and get launched.

While Team 7016, and a few others, were getting their spacesuits on, Jeejow started a Command Staff roll call. "**Sector 1 Commander, can you hear me?**" He waited a few moments. "**Master Officer, Nantasa...can you hear me?**" He still received nothing. He growled in frustration. "**Sector 2 Commander, Master Officer, Yim, can you hear me?**" He received nothing. A cold chill ran down his back. Zero for two. "**Sector 3 Commander, Master Officer, Xadorm, can you hear me?**"

"**This is Xadorm, Sir. I'm here, awaiting your orders.**"

Jeejow breathed a sigh of relief. He was not alone. "**Thank you, Xadorm. Sector 4 Commander, Master Officer, Marbing, can you hear me?**"

"**This is Marbing, Sir. Awaiting your orders.**"

'Two out of four,' thought Jeejow. 'That's getting better.' "**Sector 1 Vice Commander, Senior Officer, Onga, do you hear me?**" Once again he was tortured by silence. Nantasa, Yim and now Onga. His calls to the last three all had positive results. Zoolkog, Tadesha and Inditam were all still alive. "**All Command Staff personnel who are still alive...Jump to that bell spaceship. We'll convene there and find out**

what's going on."

Every one of them Jumped their entry point in the bell. Jeejow noticed that there were two tearful women who were sitting in the bell. "You look familiar, but I'm not sure who you are."

One of the women stood up. "Sir, I'm Officer Grade 6, Yarbona. My Team member here is Officer Grade 7, Kikika. We're both...were...on Master Officer, Yim's Team 44. We're rather... certain...that the other Team members, Yim and Foosena...are both dead."

Jeejow nodded sadly. "We'll let you know if you're needed. For now...just standby." He headed to the conference table. "Are there any other partial Teams here?"

Everyone shook their heads.

He checked the list of the officers that were present. "Inditam, since neither Nantasa nor Onga are here, I need a Sector 1 Commander. You'll take that post immediately. It may be yours...permanently. I don't know at this time."

Inditam tightened her lips. She got up and moved from her seat as Sector 4 Vice Commander to Sector 1 Commander seat. "Yes, Sir," she said. "Ready to take command."

Jeejow looked out one of the small portholes on the ship. "Do we have any reports yet...on who this is or where they are?"

Xadorm shook his head. "Those spacesuits take a little time to put on. As soon as someone gets up there, I'm sure we'll hear from them."

Jeejow sat down. "What...if anything...did any of you

see?"

Tadesha spoke up. "I saw, in the distance, these bright beams…coming down from out of the sky. They weren't very wide…but…wherever they hit, I saw a lot of clouds of…debris flying around."

Jeejow snarled. "Over 3,000 years of this *h'oolyach* and…we're still getting surprise attacked. Did the beams…look familiar…like from any of the other attacks that we've seen?"

Tadesha just shook her head.

Soolchakan decided that he was not going to wait. The three women seemed to be primping for some reason. The planet was under attack…again…and all they could think about was how they looked in these big baggy spacesuits. He Jumped his ship out of the gorge into a spot about 120 kilotaja above the planet. He had to spin around before he saw one of the intruder vessels that was about 15 kilotaja closer to the planet. "**Supreme Officer, Jeejow, this Officer, Soolchakan. I'm looking at one of the intruders now. I've never seen a ship like this before.**"

"**Thank you, Officer, Soolchakan. Can you stop the thing from firing on the planet before you describe it**?"

"**I'll be glad to do that, Sir.**" He aimed his 459 at the rear of the ship and singed that tailpipe rather badly. He saw a large chunk fall off of the ship. "**Sir, they did not stop shooting at** the planet, they just sent some small fighters after me."

Jeejow snarled to himself. "**Can you avoid them**?"

"**Sir, I can only think of about 200 dimensions to avoid them in. I'm going back to Observation. I'll get closer and…get inside…and then I'll singe the gunners.**"

"**Thank you.**"

Chyning sent out a loud probe. "**WHERE ARE YOU? We've been looking for you and…can't find you!**"

Soolchakan slowed his approach to the enemy vessel. "**Bonarain, landmark on my tailpipe. Kiyalee landmark on Bonarain and Chyning, landmark on Kiyalee.**"

Moments later the three women were in formation with him.

"**I guess we're ready to do our normal chores on that ship**," sent Bonarain.

"**No, this one'll be a little different. Bonarain head for the Main Bridge. Kiyalee, yes, you head for the engine room. Chyning, you and I will each go into one of the side cylinders and stop them from shooting… by whatever means we have to take to stop them from shooting. If we have to kill everything in there in order to stop the shooting…do it!**"

"**Okay**," sent Chyning. "**Which one are you taking and which one do I take?**"

He snarled. "**You take the one closest to us, I'll go**

on the other side of the ship...NOW...let's go!'"

Bonarain watched the enemy fighters coming up. "**What's with this welcoming party**?'"

"**They're looking for me. If you're wondering why, look behind that big ship and you'll see a large part of the exhaust cone floating away. I blew that tail cone off, trying to get their attention away from the planet. It didn't work. They can still shoot and they sent all of those *bimyocks* after me**.'"

Kiyalee snickered. "**Should we do something about them**?'"

Soolchakan groaned. "**No, not yet. Just get to the engine room and...see what you can foul up**." He flew into the starboard cylinder. There were a lot of personnel there... maybe. He took a quick look at them and then decided that exploring them was secondary to stopping the attack. He went up to the front of the cylinder and found that there was a very large machine there that was obviously the cannon that was causing the damage below.

One quick burst with his 459 and there was a very large gaping hole in the mechanism and it was no longer firing. He figured that there would be some panic – wrong. The crew simply started looking at the damage. They assessed the damage and immediately started replacing parts.

While they were busy, he turned his bio-sensor on and set it to send the information to the Command Staff while it was scanning the aliens. He read along as it scanned. [Creature is 5.3

taja in height. Female reproductive organs, however, completely sterile. Skin is bone white and there is no apparent hair anywhere on the body. Biped with three fingers and opposable thumb on hands. Respiratory, circulatory and gastrointestinal system is very similar to Heyyah anatomy.] He turned the sensor to five other creatures and found that they were all female and all sterile. He did a double take on all of the information. He aimed the sensors at six more aliens. All of the crew were female and all of them were sterile. 'What kind of *h'oolyach* is that,' he thought?

He was now very surprised to see that the big cannon was almost completely repaired. He was astonished at the accomplishment. He decided that a quick burst was not going to be successful at stopping them. He aimed his 459 up and blew a hole in the fuselage. The rapid decompression sucked most of the inhabitants out and then he aimed his cannon at their big one. This time he destroyed most of, if not all of, the mechanism.

Chyning called him. **"Have you seen how fast they can repair this *chokwad* thing**?"

"I saw," he sent. **"I decided to have some rapid decompression of the crew and then blew the thing to pieces**."

Chyning giggled. **"That works too. I did it different. I just cut the whole front of the cannon and fuselage off. That took care of both those steps at one time. Of course now I have a bunch of their little fighters going around here looking for me**."

Another call came in. **"This is Officer, Breberton of**

Team 6932. **Which is the best way to stop them from shooting**?"

Soolchakan answered. "**Just destroy the nose cone of the two side cylinders. All of the weaponry is in that part. Once you've blown that away…they don't have any more big cannons…I hope.**"

"**Thank you**," sent Breberton. "**Fee-Aba, Twenda, Safatha…did you get all of that**?"

Three affirmative responses came back.

Soolchakan changed what he was doing. "**Bonarain, what did you find out about these *doovofts***?"

"**I'm still collecting data**," sent Bonarain. "**Come in here…on the Main Bridge and help me…if you've finished with their weaponry.**"

Tadesha was getting a little miffed over lack of information. "**What do the ships look like**?"

Jeejow slammed his fist down on the table. "WHO GIVES A BIG FAT *CHOKWAD* WHAT THEY LOOK LIKE? Until their guns are silenced…I don't care what they look like!

Tadesha flushed and hunkered down in her chair – possibly trying to hide.

Soolchakan chuckled. "**Sir, the one we found is silenced. The ship itself is…a big long cylinder…about four kilotaja in length and two kilotaja in diameter. It has two side cylinders…that appear to house some pretty nasty pulse cannons. Each one of the side cylinders is** up near the front and they're only about half a kilotaja in length. They're also about sixty taja in diameter. They're connected to the main ship with armatures that are about fifty taja in length. Once we demolish their side cylinders...I haven't seen any more shooting from them. They did have a lot of small fighters come out of the bottom of the central cylinder. They haven't been able to find us in Observation so far...so I'm not really worried about any of their fighters."

Jeejow gave Tadesha a dirty look. "**What do the fighters look like**?"

"**They're just a smaller, one seat, version of the big ship**."

"**Thank you**."

Bonarain broke in. "**I still need some help on the Main Bridge with these *bimyocks*!**"

"**I'm on my way**," sent Soolchakan.

Kiyalee was sitting there rather bored. "**What should I do? Should I keep on staring at these engines...or does anyone care**?"

Soolchakan bit his lip to keep from laughing. "**Is there anything special about their engines**?"

"**No, it's just slightly different in the design. Other than that, it's the same old thing. When you got something that works, I guess everybody uses the same thing...even if they invent it in a completely independent** method."

Soolchakan shrugged. "**Either that or…nothing else works. For now…just stay there in engineering. We may need a few acts of sabotage in there**."

'That's entirely possible…and very easy to do,' thought Kiyalee with a big grin.

Jeejow was pondering when he looked at the still embarrassed Tadesha. "**Can you tell me what these *doovofts* look like**?"

Soolchakan grunted. "What's next? Does he want a stool sample?" He took a deep breath. "**Sir, they have skin that is completely bone white…what I can see of it. Their head is…almost completely round. Their eyes are big and…a strange shade of dark green. Their nose is…just a couple of slits. The mouth is the same. The ears… are only two holes in the side of the head. From…facial features…I can't tell one from the other**." He flew into the Main Bridge in Observation. He did not see Bonarain at all. He hopped to Spy and saw her standing behind…what had to be the Chair of Command. He landed his fighter, opened the canopy and got out. "What'd you need?"

"I probably need to get someone else educated on their language," said Bonarain. "Come here…and I'll give it to you."

He tossed his helmet in the seat of his fighter. "Have you found out anything unusual about them?"

"As you pointed out to the Command Staffers…they're all

female and they're all sterile. I haven't found any males among them." She stood back akimbo. "I don't understand how any society can function…with only one sex…and that ONE is sterile."

He got up next to Bonarain. "Possibly…could it be… like those colony insects, that vermin used to be such pests…on Hardooth…a few thousand years ago?"

"What? You mean…where there's one Queen and…she's the only one who mates…with what few males there are…and all of the workers are…sterile females?"

"So far…it sounds right to me."

Bonarain shrugged. "That…is as good an explanation as any…at the moment." She looked around nodding. "That may just be…what they are." She sighed, grabbed hold of Soolchakan, placed her forehead against his and gave him the language.

He stepped back and looked around the Bridge shaking his head.

Jeejow broke in. **"Can anyone tell me what is going on in those ships**?"

Soolchakan rolled his eyes. "Why doesn't he come here himself?" **"Sir, it appears that we've neutralized all of the ships and…we're trying to get their language. They just might be a civilization like those…colonizing insects… that we had on Hardooth before the firestorms. All of the personnel on the ship…are female. They all seem to get the work done…without much supervision. There does not seem to be much, if any, panic on board this** ship. **The Commander is not really giving commands, just receiving information and passing it on. They're all trying to figure out how to reattach and repair all of their disabled cannons...and they are all doing so in a completely calm manner.**"

Jeejow sat down at the conference table. "**Can I communicate with them...and try to reason with them... or are they beyond that?**"

Bonarain sighed. "**Right now, Sir, the only way would be for me to come to you, force the information...and then come back. If you want to communicate with them... what I** *can* **do is relay your words to them...and make it sound like it's coming through their communication devices...by using the address system in my fighter. I'll then relay their response to you.**"

Xadorm broke in. "**Before we start that...are all of their guns silenced...and how many of them are there?**"

Jeejow chuckled in a silly manner. "Good idea."

Bonarain responded. "**From what we've got so far... there are 34 ships here...and they've all been silenced. These people are not upset or panicky, they're just trying to assess and repair the damage...and start shooting again.**"

Jeejow snarled. "**Relay me!**" He shook his fist in anger. "If nothing else it'll buy us some time." "**Are you ready?**"

Soolchakan hung his head. "Why doesn't he listen?" "**At**

your convenience, Sir."

"**This is Supreme Officer, Jeejow. Drey Sssorg of the Owlam Empire.**"

Bonarain looked at Soolchakan and mouthed the word: "Empire?" She then rolled her eyes.

Soolchakan had to fight to keep from laughing as he continued the relay. "**We are wanting to know your intentions. Why did you attack our planet**?"

The Commander (and everyone else on the Bridge) looked around somewhat startled. "This…is Third Seat, Apantosko…of the Hoshchog Gathering. You will surrender your planet at once!" She looked to the communications. "Communicator! Find this *buzzuk*! Triangulate on it and silence it. I don't have time for this."

The Communicator was playing with knobs and switches. "I'm trying to find it, Third Seat. I can't…triangulate…until I've isolated it."

"**We have no intention of surrendering to some third rate species that has no intellect. We have disabled all of your big cannons. We will disable you as well…if you don't stop this stupidity and talk.**"

Apantosko leaned back in her chair. "Communicator…cut them off! I have no time to talk to food!"

"**You have no capability of cutting me off and I have no intention of becoming food…for you or anybody.**"

The Communicator pulled her hands away from her

console as if she had been electrocuted. She sat there shaking for a few moments and then went back to attempting to cut the communications off.

Jeejow scoffed. **"Do NOT attempt to cut me off... Third Rate Upandsoso. You don't have the capability to cut me off. I will talk to you and even harass you as long as I please. I think it best that you leave now...before we execute all of you**."

"That is THIRD SEAT APANTOSKO. You will address me correctly!"

"You will NOT address me as food."

Apantosko turned to the Communicator again. "Shut that thing OFF!"

Communicator turned to Apantosko. "It is...OFF!"

"Then where is it coming from?"

"I have destroyed your capability of shooting at us and I have taken over your communications as well. You WILL listen to us and you will NOT address us as food. Do you understand or do I have to prove our power in another way?"

Apantosko started drumming her knuckles on the armrests of her chair. "You will cease vexing us or we will call 100,000 ships here to annihilate all of you. Serving as our food is a much higher calling...for you."

Jeejow looked incredulously at the Staff. "Is this... *buzzuk*...for real?" He scoffed. **"You are beginning to bother** me."

Bonarain butted in. "**Sir, she is so full of mendacity. According to what I found in her mind...this Hoshchog... Gathering only has 68 ships. 34 of them are here... disabled. Ours is only the third star system that they've found that was inhabited. These *bimyocks* are just getting started in their...reign of terror.**"

Jeejow snickered along with several other Staff members. "**Don't you mean...all 68 ships? That IS all that you have isn't it? Why do you fabricate...when I can find anything in your computers that I want to know...like the fact that this is only the third star system that you've invaded. What other forms of obfuscation are you going to try next? It doesn't matter...I already know the truth.**"

"TURN THIS COMMUNICATION OFF," shrieked Apantosko!

Communicator stood up in front of her console and faced the Commander. "All of it is turned off! I don't know where that noise is coming from!"

Apantosko went to the communications console and started checking things for herself.

Xadorm was curious. "**Officer, Bonarain...how did they get past our electronic guard machines? We received no warning and we saw nothing...HOW**?"

Bonarain sighed. "**Sir, they've been laughing about how archaic our warning beacons are. They simply** sent a false signal to the things...and that's why we saw nothing."

Marbing scoffed. "They're just starting out...and already our system is archaic? What have *they* got?"

"Good question," said Jeejow. "**Officer, Bonarain, we need to keep one of those ships intact...without too much interference from the...original inhabitants...and with computer intact.**"

"**We can do it Sir, all we need to do is get rid of them now. I've already obtained three passwords into their system.**"

Jeejow breathed a sigh of relief. "**All personnel, hop these ships into dimension 45. We'll store them there for the moment...while we get rid of the...fungus...that's inhabiting them.**"

34 ships were hopped into #45. They joined a large collection of ships that were already there just floating around in space waiting to be used at the convenience of the Owlamites. All Hoshchog personnel were jettisoned from their ships and the computer experts were digging into the archives and anything else they could find on the ships.

Yilla and Toyzamia once again started the nasty roll call to find out who was still there and who had been killed in the initial attack. When the roll call was done they found that there were 172 Teams that had been completely wiped out and 71 Teams that had lost one or more members. Total dead was 828, 208 men and 620 women. They reassigned members to other Teams to get as many Teams as possible to full strength. This left them with just over 5,800 Teams and still over 23,300 Owlamites still living. After the reassigning, they found that they were short of males and there were two Teams that were not part of the norm. Team 5378 had four women and Team 5399 had three women. All other Teams had the 3:1 ratio.

Nantasa and her entire Team were gone. Onga and her entire Team were gone. Yim and his Team member Foosena were gone. The other two members of Team 44 were reassigned to Team 297.

Inditam became the permanent Sector 1 Commander. Zoolkog was promoted to Master Officer and became the Sector 2 Commander. Officer Leader, Nasnana was promoted to Senior Officer and Sector 1 Vice Commander. Officer Leader, Chablitha was promoted to Senior Officer and Sector 2 Vice Commander. Officer Leader, Ota was promoted to Senior Officer and Sector 4 Vice Commander.

The computer personnel found how the false signal had been sent to the beacons. They reprogrammed the beacons to ignore the false signal, however, it would appear to any intruder that the signal had worked.

Jeejow called the Staff, and a few special Teams, to a meeting. "What've we got?"

Soolchakan stepped forward. "Sir, according to what the computer people found, they have pictures of all of their spaceships. The only difference with each one is the number on the side. We can use those numbers to landmark on the things and find them wherever they are. We can then destroy them…without allowing them into our system."

"Are you sure that it'll work," asked Inditam?

"Oh, absolutely, Sir," said Soolchakan with a smile. "We've already tried it and done it with one other ship of theirs. That cut them down to a fleet of 33 attack ships."

Jeejow nodded. "What about their home planet?"

Sankiki stepped up. "We sent some of…" She looked at Ota and grinned. "…Senior Officer, Ota's colleagues to the Hoshchog home planet. We found out quite a bit of good information. The original assumption was correct. They are a… colony type civilization, however, they call it a Gathering. They have their Queen of each…Gathering. There are nine major continents on their home planet and ten minor continents or major island chains. Thus they have nineteen Queens on the planet as a result. If we were to destroy one Queen…only that…Gathering would be annihilated. If we kill the Queen and…before the suicide signal goes out, they're able to hatch a new Queen…that Gathering continues. We'd have to kill the Queen…and the Queen hatchery for that Gathering at the same time…in order to assure that we get that Gathering."

Xadorm scoffed. "How many…eggs…are there in the Queen hatchery…at any given time?"

"Depending on which one, there are between ten and thirty immature Queens at any one time."

"How far do the Queens stray from their specific Queen hatchery," asked Zoolkog?

"No more than 20 taja, Sir. They always stay close."

"That's still nineteen firestorm weapons...as far as I'm concerned," said Jeejow. He shook his head. "Why do they need so much food? Why are they going out into space and stealing... sentient species as food?"

"Maybe we should introduce them to the Teltermak and let *them* argue over the menu," said Chablitha bitterly.

"Focus people," said Jeejow. "I still wonder why they need so much food. Why can't they grow enough for themselves?"

"The Queens need the food," said Yoobyool.

Jeejow looked at him. "Who are you?"

Yoobyool smiled. "Since the promotion of Officer Leader, Ota to Senior Officer and her appointment to the Command Staff, I took over her position as primary leader of the spying missions."

"All right," said Jeejow. "We'll have to get used to you now. Back to my original question...why do the Queens need so much food?"

Yoobyool looked a little sick. "They need it...badly. A healthy Queen...she moves around with the help of twenty personal attendants. All of *them* have a normal body. The Queen...she has...a monstrosity of...I guess you'd call it her uterus. She is about 5.3 taja in height and her...uterus is...depending on which Queen...between 33 and 35 taja in length. *It* is carried on several special carts...made just for that purpose. She eats all the time.

She never stops. One does not wonder why when…as I saw…a healthy Queen can…excrete…some 4,600 to 4,800 eggs a day."

Chablitha nearly fell out of her chair. "Four thousand…eight hundred…PER DAY?!"

"Yes," said Yoobyool flatly. "That is why she has to eat so much per day. She has to eat and the…males have to eat."

"So there are males," said Tadesha.

"Yes, there are males. They do three things: Eat, sleep and…breed. When they're awake, they…climb up on the carts and…it appears that this giant uterus has at least twenty…orifices…for breeding purposes. The males deposit their seed in the orifices on the side and the eggs come out of the orifice…at the rear end."

"Enough of the anatomy lesson," said Jeejow looking rather queasy. "They have to eat constantly…in order to produce. I get that." He sighed. "Since they only look at us as food…and no amount of talking to them is going to change their minds…I see no alternative. We have to get rid of them. Set up the nineteen firestorm weapons on their planet and…"

"It's going to take more than that," said Yoobyool. "They have nineteen on the *home* planet. The other two planets they've taken over…there are thirty-three more Queens…and Gatherings."

Jeejow growled. He looked up hopefully. "We have been able to keep them off of this planet…haven't we?"

"Oh, yes, Sir," said Yoobyool. "We have definitely kept them off of our planet."

"That's why they have to conquer," said Xadorm. "They've probably devoured most everything on their home planet that is edible. They branched out…created more colonies and now… they need massive amounts of food…and I thought that this was the third star system that they've invaded."

"That information was accurate…two days ago, Sir," said Yoobyool. "Now, they're invading a fourth."

Jeejow hung his head. "Nineteen on the home planet and thirty-three on other planets…to which they are rapidly expanding. They refuse to reason with anybody…we have to defend ourselves. Destroy their colonies and their ships."

"I wouldn't worry about the ships," said Yoobyool. "Kill the Queens and…there will be no one on the ships…still alive."

Nasnana looked up. "But…if they don't do a self-destruct on the ships…those ships will be floating around out there…for anyone to use…unless we take control of them."

"Good point," said Jeejow. "Do we know if they'll destroy the ship…or just themselves?"

Yoobyool shrugged. "The only way we'll know that is… kill one Queen and watch what happens to any ship that her colony controls."

Marbing groaned. "How do we find out which Queen controls which ship?"

"They have banners," said Bonarain. "The banners are all very similar, but, they do have some small subtle differences. Once you find a ship…let me see their banner and I can figure it out."

Jeejow jumped up. "Do it! Find a ship, get its banner and… tell us which Queen to…" He looked off to the side disgusted. "…dispatch."

Yoobyool nodded. "We have the exact location of five ships right now. I'll get a picture of the banner…and the banners of all fifty-two Queens…and we'll go from there."

Jeejow sat back down. "Do it," he said quietly while nodding.

After four days of looking over and matching the banners for the Queens with the battleships, they finally decided on which one to use. The firestorm weapon was Jumped to the chamber of the Queen (and all of the Owlamites nearly threw up when they saw the Queen and what was being done). Ten Teams Jumped to the battleship to get ready for a hop to #45. The bomb went off and everyone on board the battleship just hung their heads down and sat there waiting to starve to death.

Yoobyool sat there looking rather perturbed. "What… should we wait for? Should we wait…until they're all rotting or…I don't know? I've never been in a situation like this before."

Bonarain called them from the Hoshchog home planet. **"Whoever is on that battleship…where we just cooked their Queen…start jettisoning the inhabitants. Once you've done that…Jump the thing to orbiting Hardooth and then hop it to dimension 45**."

Yoobyool was a little disgusted. "**Who are you to be giving me orders? I'm an Officer Leader while you're just an Officer Grade 6**."

Jeejow came back. "**I'm the one who told *her* to tell *you* that if we can get the ship - GET IT! It seems that another colony, with a living Queen, is going to come to that ship and claim it for their colony. We need to take custody of it before they do. Now…DO WHAT SHE SAID**!"

Yoobyool flushed. "You heard what the boss said. Hop to it! We've got to clean the vermin out…before the other vermin shows up."

Officer Grade 2, Kloob scoffed. "Why don't we just Jump the thing now. We can always dump the garbage anywhere.

Officer Leader, Blana shook her head. "I don't think so. They might have a reason for doing it in that order. Unless you want to argue with Jeejow, I suggest we do it in the order given. We do it now…and ask questions later."

Everyone stopped arguing and started shoving the catatonic Hoshchog out of the ship.

The other 32 ships were all captured in the same manner. After they had all of the undamaged ships floating around in #45, all of the rest of the firestorm weapons were set off and the Hoshchog were never going to be a problem again.

12

Jeejow was talking to all of the Owlamites. "When the firestorm weapons were used, Owlam went from a population of millions...to thousands. We had just over 28,000. Now we have just over 23,300. The attacks come from...everywhere. We sit here on guard for a few years...become complacent...and that's when we get attacked again. I know that it's boring. I had to help with that stuff as well. I know it is dull but we still have to do it. Each enemy...that comes from beyond...has figured out a way to bypass our electronic guardians with...sophisticated technology that what we took...from others...and makes it look like a joke. They laugh at us and kill us. We've won the war every time. But how many battles have we lost? Some of you say, or hope, that the doctors will eventually figure out a way for us to procreate, but... so far they haven't. Even if they do, we still can't afford to lose any more battles.

Vigilance is the key. I know that...because we have to look in every direction, 3 dimensionally, it keeps at least one fourth of us on duty at all times, but, it must be maintained because each battle that we've lost...leaves less people to do that boring job. Keep doing what we were all trained to do watching the borders and warning everyone in advance that an enemy is coming." He walked away from the podium.

Chablitha stood on the side. "Sir, do you think what you said will do that much good?"

"It has to have done something," he said grimly. "If it didn't…we might as well all commit suicide…or surrender to the next batch of *bimyocks* that comes along."

"I've been wondering about that," said Zoolkog. "What would happen if we…did a spectator situation? We allow some off worlder to take over. Then we just live our lives and we don't worry about anyone else. We just live our lives…in Spy or Observation if we have to."

Jeejow shook his head. "Remember the friends who came to help us? The Kalash and the Rahanan-Sar? Remember how we helped the T'Mor? Others that have come along since then to help at the Turgon Wall: The Argaman-Or, the Cowpa, the Towtoo and the Saraff-Or. These are people that I can't forget. They would suffer badly if we were to allow that to happen."

Xadorm chuckled. "There's nothing like hitting someone with guilt to make them see things from a different perspective."

Jeejow nodded. "Sometimes it works…other times it blows up in your face."

"Depending on how hard-headed your audience is," said Ota.

Jeejow looked over his Staff. "Let's get back to the conference room and go over some reports."

Jeejow took his place at the table. "What do we know about

Chokchakchok?"

"The planet has come back completely," said Inditam. "All of the lower life forms are thriving. It'll be a nice planet for someone to…colonize…if you want to do that sort of thing."

"Why don't we go there," said Nasnana? "We wouldn't have to put up with any of the belligerence that we've been put through here."

Jeejow shook his head. "Unfortunately, it is still a useful planet. Other conquerors can still come along and attack it. There's no avoiding space-bound marauders on a different planet. They can hit Chok and Hardooth."

"I didn't think of it that way," said Nasnana sadly.

"You're on the Command Staff now," said Xadorm. "You have to think that way."

Jeejow snickered. "What about the Choks themselves? Aren't there a few of them on other planets…still surviving?"

"Barely," said Inditam. "They were conquerors, now they're the hunted. The inhabitants of those planets have long memories and they now hunt the Choks for sport. I don't see the Choks coming back any time at all."

Jeejow sniffed. "Next! What about the Doolood?"

Zoolkog smiled. "They continue to build more walls and add to the size, and number, of their underwater cities. They haven't tried to build any…spaceships. They're now content to rebuild their lives on their planet."

Jeejow nodded. "Any...*new* technology?"

"They kinda ruined that for themselves," said Zoolkog. "They didn't allow the land slaves to do any fishing and an island can support...just so many people for a finite amount of time...especially when the people who were there were trained in manufacturing and not agriculture. The land slaves all died off and...now the Doolood have no one that can assemble computers... that have to stay dry. It may be a long, long time before they lift off again."

"All right," said Jeejow. "Iyka?"

Tadesha snorted. "Forget that planet. No one could possibly live there...for at least another 300 or 400 years. We poisoned the planet with that residual energy from the firestorm weapons. That...death rocket put a different kind of poison in the atmosphere. If or when either one finally subsides, there is still no life on the planet at all. If you want that planet, you will have to supply your own plants and animals...and even microorganisms... once the toxins have become inert."

Jeejow sighed. "What about the Vagens?"

"They tried to start rebuilding spaceships," said Marbing. "A few well-placed shots with a 459 and a few hand-held bombs and...all of their outer space technology is a thing of the past. They used up all of their metals so...any metal that they still have on the planet has to be regulated and recycled. All of the metals that they took into outer space are now nothing but floating debris."

"They're not building any more space ships then," said Jeejow.

"Wood is a poor substitute for metal. So is ceramics," said Marbing. "They're stuck on their planet...until some other conqueror comes along and hauls them off as slaves."

Jeejow looked at his list. "The Mufayton?"

"The only ones left are living in underground caverns and caves on a different planet," said Tadesha. "They're having a rough time hiding, but, remember they can read minds. They're able to avoid, but they still don't have time to build much. They're still stuck for...quite some time."

Jeejow looked up. "The Zizzikinza?"

"The same thing there," said Chablitha. "They have to live underground on the planet they got stuck on. Since they can crawl into areas that no one else can. They have been able to thrive...but only underground. You need an open shaft somewhere to launch a rocket. If they did...all of them would have to be on that rocket because once the engines fire up, all of their tunnels would fill up with exhaust and anyone left behind would suffocate. I don't think the indigenous people of the planet will allow them to build an open shaft...or rocket."

"And of course the Cookrot have no planet left," said Jeejow. "And there aren't any Hoshchog left to cause us any problem."

190 years later, Jeejow celebrated 1,000 years as the *Voice of Power*. No one had ever anticipated anything like that ever happening. The 781 years of Till and the 696 years of Wymini

had seemed unnaturally long. Now they could talk of Jeejow and a full millennium as the Leader.

32 years later the celebration ended as another attack, seemingly, from nowhere occurred. The thirty ships that suddenly appeared out of thin air (or the void of space) were in formation around Hardooth, firing down on the planet with large deadly pulse beams.

Once again, Jeejow called all Owlamites to go to Observation or Spy. Once again, Jeejow had to perform a very rapid roll call on the Command Staff to see who was or was not still with him.

Once again, they found an enemy that was orbiting around the planet without any warning from the watchers. Just like the Cookrot, they had appeared from nowhere. Just like the Vagens, they had ships that were mostly cylindrical with four large square wings sticking out of the fuselage at three different areas of the ships. Four near the bow, four near the center and four in the stern.

Once again, Team 7016 got to their fighters and headed for the closest ship they could see to investigate who these new marauders were. Someone fired on the four fighters and luckily the rays bounced off of their electromagnetic shields. They had been in Spy dimension at the time. Soolchakan ordered them to go to Observation. As soon as they hopped, the shooting stopped and some kind of probe ray started searching for them.

"**This stinks of the Vagens**," sent Bonarain. "**Look at the shape of the ships and…they saw us in Spy**."

"**These ships are larger**," sent Soolchakan. "**They're**

also made of metal. The Vagens don't have any more metal – or enough metal – on their planet to manufacture one spaceship...let alone an armada. Don't make any decisions until we're inside...and we can see what we've got in front of us."

"**I'm on my way to the engine room**," sent Kiyalee. "**I'll let you know what I find there...as if I'm going to find anything different.**"

"**I *was* going to look for the hangar bay**," sent Chyning. "**But right now, I can see a bunch of small fighters coming out of the center in the bottom. I'll go check that and make sure.**"

Soolchakan sat there muttering to himself. "This is becoming too repetitive. We don't have to guess where we're going anymore. We all know." "**The Main Bridge is ours, Bonarain. Let's find it...and get a few questions answered.**"

Bonarain sighed. "**Lead on, oh semi-great one.**"

'I wish she'd stop that,' Soolchakan thought to himself bitterly.

They flew into the ship and found the Main Bridge almost immediately. Soolchakan was a little surprised – at first – to see two very distinctly different races on the Bridge. He quickly aimed his biosensor at one that looked familiar. It quickly confirmed that the "specimen" was a Vagen. He turned the biosensor to the new strange looking species and turned it on.

Specimen is cone-shaped. 6 taja in height. All internal bodily organs are similar to Heyyah, however, they are in a different arrangement inside the conical body. They are covered, from head to foot, with thick dark hair. Eight optical organs that completely surround the head area allowing them to see in all directions simultaneously. There is no noticeable neck. There are two separate nasal cavities: One is for breathing and one is for smelling. They appear to have no arms, however, the long hair on the upper body is being manipulated to act as arms and hands through some form of kinetic energy. The creature has four legs that are only .7 taja in length. Body is mostly cylindrical, tapering to a conical point at the top and is 2.4 taja in diameter at the center point of the body. This one has male reproductive organs.

Soolchakan snarled at all of the revelations. **"Supreme Officer, Jeejow, this Officer, Soolchakan. Can you hear me**?"

"This is Jeejow. What can you report about these people at this time?"

"An alliance with the Vagens has occurred. Either this new species has…enslaved the Vagens or they've made friends with that bunch of stuck-up *doovofts*."

"They call themselves the Mustooza," sent Bonarain. **"They went to where the Vagens live to conquer them and found technology that intrigued them. They decided to utilize the Vagen technology and the Vagens as well. The Vagens don't like the Mustooza, but they don't have much of a choice at this time. The Vagens are planning on taking over as soon as possible…if they can. The**

Mustooza don't trust the Vagens, but they like the technology. Once again we're dealing with a species that's coming here from dimension 85. They're already in all of the dimensions that the Vagens found and… they're causing all kinds of trouble."

Jeejow stood there with his teeth clenched. "**We go to the Vagen home world…and do the same thing that we did to the Cookrot. We find the Mustooza home world… and do the same thing. We make sure that no one from dimension 85 ever comes at us again. This is why they came from nowhere. We didn't have any of our guardian beacons in dimension 85.**" He sat down in his chair. "The first thing we have to do is find out who is still alive…again." He hung his head with tears going down his face. "I'm getting very tired of counting the dead." He sighed. "Yilla start the roll call."

Master Officer, Inditam of Team 53 did not respond. Officer Grade 6, Kasasinsi and Officer Grade 7, Byshee of Team 53 did. Inditam and Officer Grade 5, Penjetheron were dead. When they called Team 56 for Senior Officer, Tadesha, there was no response from any of the Team members. Once they found this, Senior Officer, Nasnana was promoted to Master Officer and Commander of Sector 1. Officer Leader, Iquanza was promoted to Senior Officer and became the Sector 1 Vice Commander. Officer Leader, Boneech was promoted to Senior Officer and took the place of Tadesha as the Sector 3 Vice Commander.

Another part of the roll call showed that there were only six that still remained who were Officer Leaders. They could only find three Team Leaders that were Officer Grade 1 and seventeen of the rank of Officer Grade 2. The numbers were dwindling badly.

When the roll call was finished they now found that 143 more Teams had been obliterated and 44 Teams lost one or more members. 168 men and 497 women were added to the list of the dead. Once they reorganized all of the partial Teams, they found that they had less than 5,700 Teams. Three Teams were all female and two of those Teams only had three members.

Jeejow shook his head. "We may have to give a few more promotions. I see very few senior officers and a lot of junior officers…among people who have been Grade 5, 6 or 7 for…over 3,200 years."

"We can't promote everybody," said Xadorm. "If we did, all too soon, we'd all be in the top four echelon."

"No," said Jeejow softly. "I'm thinking of just the Team Leaders. We have Officer Grade 5 as…Leaders for several Teams." He frowned. "Plus I'm seeing that there are some Grade 4…who are Leaders of Teams that are above some who have a Grade 3 as their Leader."

"That was the doings of Nagasoom," said Boneech. "He… unfortunately…was a little prone to some favoritism. He did put several Grade 4 personnel above several Grade 3. No other *Voice of Power* ever questioned it before. People have just…kept their Team number…for pride in that specific number."

Jeejow nodded. "I may change a few things around…after we take care of this current…headache."

Boneech looked a little concerned. "Are you going to change our designation numbers?"

"No," said Jeejow looking a little tired. "I'm going to give some of the Team Leaders some promotions. It may make some of the Team members a little...mad or upset, but, I don't like the idea that...someday...may the Great Maker forbid to ever happen...someone going from Officer Grade 3 or 4 to...Supreme Officer...with nothing in between. We need a complete chain of command."

"Can we take care of the Mustooza first," said Marbing?

"Yeah," spat Jeejow angrily! "Just for general principles, I think that maybe we should try talking to them first...before we annihilate them."

Chablitha frowned. "How are we going to talk to them?"

Jeejow smirked. "Fire up the Multifastidigeous Thonlock Communicator."

"That silly thing never existed," said Xadorm looking a little puzzled.

"They don't know that," said Jeejow with a bigger grin.

"I still don't see how that'll help," said Zoolkog.

"It may buy us time while we try to find the Mustooza home planet," said Jeejow flatly.

They received a mental interruption. "**I found a whole bunch of hand-held bombs in their weapons storage area. Thousands of them**," sent Chyning. "**I think I can** hop all of it into the Chok storage ships that we have floating around in dimension 45."

Jeejow chuckled. "I guess it wouldn't hurt to have a few hundred thousand spare hand-helds around. Go ahead. Take all that you can and store them for us." He nodded. "Get a few more personnel working on that mass confiscation. We can always utilize them a lot better than our enemies."

While all of the talking had been going on, eighty Teams of Owlamites had been figuring out ways to silence the Mustooza cannons. There was also a lot of sabotage on the light speed engines as well. The Mustooza were here to stay for a while (whether they liked it or not). Now seemed the time to talk.

"Who is on the flagship," sent Jeejow?

Soolchakan rolled his eyes. "Who else, Sir. Officer, Bonarain is getting a translation of the Mustooza language."

Jeejow shrugged. "Who else?" He sighed. "Who will I be talking to...if I use the Multifastidigeous Thonlock Communicator?"

Xadorm groaned. "You're not seriously going to use that fib on them are you?"

"Hey, we got away with it with the Sodle," said Jeejow merrily. "Why can't we use it again?"

"I'm amazed that anyone even remembers that word," said Ota.

Bonarain shook her head to clear it from all of the information she had been gleaning. "**His rank is Kiydozo. That's equal to an Officer Leader. His name is Bylzhisk. We're ready with our system any time you are, Sir.**"

"**This is going to be tricky, Sir,**" sent Soolchakan. "**We've placed our fighters in the Main Bridge in a circle. We'll use all of our speakers at the same time for quadrophonic sound. If they turn their communicators off we'll let you know...to admonish them. Funny thing, Sir...the Vagens that've been brought here with the Mustooza...are going by Mustooza ranks.**"

"**They *are* the conquered ones. They don't have much choice,**" sent Bonarain.

"**Good to know any information though,**" sent Jeejow. "**By the way, why is Officer, Kiyalee on the Bridge and not in the engine room?**"

"**Sir, I'm getting tired of looking at the same stuff in all of these ships,**" complained Kiyalee. "**Besides... Team 7011 is in the engine room waiting to sabotage it...if needed. It doesn't take much to destroy one of those things.**"

Jeejow nodded. "**I also thought that Officer, Chyning was in the middle of grabbing all of the hand-held devices she could find...and storing them in dimension 45.**"

Chyning huffed. "**Sir, there are about sixty other Teams who're doing that chore right now. I'm with my**

Team…learning the Mustooza language. Plus there are about 1,500 Teams who're currently sabotaging all of the Mustooza fighters…at this time."

"They're getting very good at their jobs," said Marbing.

Xadorm snickered. "And as has been said…by others of your rank, Sir, we need to depend on other Teams for some of this unhappy business."

Jeejow cleared his throat and nodded. He sniffed. "**Let's get on with this communication. I'll send to you and you translate.**"

"**Ready, Sir,**" said all four members of Team 7016.

Jeejow sniffed and prepared himself. "**This is Supreme Officer, Jeejow, Drey Sssorg of the Owlam Empire. Who are you…the people in those strange ships orbiting and desecrating our home planet?**"

Everyone on the Main Bridge jumped at the sound of the very loud communication that echoed around the big room.

One of the Vagens ran up to the Bylzhisk. "I told you that this place was dangerous! They've disabled all of your weaponry and now they contact you when you don't want it!"

Bylzhisk slapped the Vagen with a big clot of long hairs. "Shut up, you Vagehymin underling"

The Vagen looked totally insulted. "I am not a Vagehymin! I am a Gaholvib!"

Bylzhisk slapped him again with an even greater clot of

hairs. "You're an underling *bonsk*! Now shut up!"

Two Mustoozas came up and pushed the Vagen away from Bylzhisk. He protested until each one pulled out a small wand-like apparatus and pointed them at the Vagen. The Vagen hung his head and walked away.

Bylzhisk looked around a little confused. "This is Kiydozo, Bylzhisk of the Mustooza Dominion. We are here to bring this planet into our family in order to unite the universe as one."

"You're not even from this dimension. Who are you to make any attempt at forcing us into your group?"

Bylzhisk snickered. "True, we are not from this dimension. But that is of little consequence. We're going to unite all nineteen known dimensions under our banner. We will unite all of them into one powerful Domain that no one will dare attack. Then we will all have peace."

"Peace with you as the masters and everyone else as slaves. We will NOT be your slaves and we will NOT be in your Domain."

The eyes on the front of Bylzhisk went dull. The eyes on the right side of his head brightened up. "Pabadozo (O-3) Chichit, cut them off for a *skissik*." The eyes facing the Vagen brightened. "Are these the ones that you are so scared of?"

Before the Vagen could respond, Jeejow did. **"We *are* the ones who brought those Vagens or...Gohols...or whatever they call themselves...to their knees. We will do the same to you if you do not leave...IMMEDIATELY**!"

All eight eyes opened wide. "Pabadozo, I thought I told you to mute them!"

The eyes of Chichit that were facing Bylzhisk brightened. "Master Kiydozo, I never turned them on! I don't even know where their communication is coming from."

The eight eyes of Bylzhisk started looking all around the room in confusion.

'Here we go,' thought Soolchakan. **"We're not using your system or your frequencies. We're using our Multifastidigeous Thonlock Communicator to talk to you right now. You may NOT mute us but we can mute you. We can hear anything you say and we can hear anything that those stupid Gaholvib say to each other as well...including the last communication from your pet Gaholvib to one of the Afzylovabi, in which they say that they will betray you and take over your Dominion at the earliest possible opportunity**."

They Vagen started shaking his head. "NO, Master Kiydozo! We...are not making any attempt at betraying you. We...don't have the power! We don't have the numbers!"

Bylzhisk waddled over to the Vagen on his little stubby legs. The eyes facing the Vagen opened wide. "I'm more of an opinion to believe this Drey Sssorg than I am you...even though what you just said is totally correct...about your numbers and power." All eight eyes started looking around again. "What really makes you think that you can stop us? I can have 10,000 ships here...in less than fifteen days."

Bonarain sent out. "**He's full of *h'oolyach*, Sir. They only have 929 attack ships in their entire fleet.**"

"**Don't you mean…929? It seems to me that you only have 929 attack ships. If you're talking 10,000 that would have to be your small fighters as well. If you'll check with your maintenance people…you'll find that not one of them is working…at this time.**"

The two eyes in the back of the head of Bylzhisk widened. "Wiskdozo (O-5), Frop…is this true?"

Frop growled. "Master Kiydozo, I'm afraid that is it true. I've been checking with all of the other personnel on the other ships. It is painfully true. Somehow…all of them have been sabotaged."

Bylzhisk closed all eight of his eyes. All eyes opened again. "We cannot leave. We must bring you into our Dominion…at all costs. We cannot have any renegade star systems anywhere…in any of the known dimensions."

"**If you do not leave…NOW AND FOREVER…wc will destroy your home planet…and the home planet of the Gaholvib.**"

Bylzhisk scoffed. He gave a signal to the communications officer. Chichit hit several switches on his console and a picture of a tall building came up on the main view screen on the Main Bridge.

Bylzhisk scoffed again. "The Holy Temple of the King of the gods, Sonseskoron is still standing tall in all of its glory. Your threat is completely empty."

Kiyalee snickered. **"I'm landmarked on the *chokwad* thing. I'll go take a look and be right back**." She hopped into her fighter and vanished.

Jeejow snarled. He looked at the Command Staff. "I need to buy some time for her…and maybe someone else." **"It is standing at the moment. I guarantee that it will not be there for long…if you continue to disobey me. I guarantee that the home world of the Gaholvib will not be there much longer either.**"

The Vagen went to a console and rapidly hit several keys. A scene of a large ornate building came up on his screen. He looked up at Bylzhisk. "Your capitol building is still standing on Wugavlon. They haven't lived up to their braggadocio."

Chyning scoffed. **"I'm landmarked on that pile of bricks. I'll go find it and be back shortly**." She jumped in her fighter and vanished.

Jeejow snickered. **"Not yet! It does take a little time to go from one planet to another. We will be there shortly. If you have not pulled away from our planet by then…both of your planets will be eradicated**." He looked sternly at the Command Staff. "Get those ships ready to go…NOW! As soon as Kiyalee and Chyning get back, I want our planet killers in place."

All four of the Vice Commanders, and their Teams, vanished.

Jeejow still needed to buy some time. "**Are you still looking at those useless piles of bricks…that will soon be nothing but debris**?"

Bylzhisk laughed. "Nothing that you can do will ever hurt the Holy Temple of Sonseskoron. You are mere mortals. Sonseskoron is the King of the gods. He would never allow you to touch his holy palaces."

Chablitha called back to Jeejow. "**Kiyalee is back. Two of the planet killers, and about 2,000 of our special fighters, will be at the Mustooza home world before you can count to ten**."

Jeejow started counting. He got to eight and another call came in from Ota.

"**Chyning just showed us the way to Wugavlon. We'll be there in a very short time. We'll take another 2,000 fighters with us, so the planetary defenses can't get near the big ships**."

Jeejow started to count to ten again. Before he got to seven, Ota called back and stated that they were all in position. "**Is someone on board one of the Mustooza ships…that is directly above Cifpasica**?"

"**Sir, this Officer Grade 3, Tingatay of Team 1396. We're on board a ship that is definitely looking down on Cifpasica**."

"**Thank you**," sent Jeejow. "**Kiydozo, Bylzhisk…if you don't give the order to pull out of our star system**

immediately, I will start by destroying your ships that are polluting our system."

Bylzhisk laughed. "I won't give that order. As soon as we've repaired the damages to our weapons systems, we will continue the conquest of your planet. I gave you a chance to join us as equals, but…you refuse. You will be slaves! All of you!"

Jeejow snarled. "**Tingatay, get everyone off of that ship and…blow it up**."

"**Yes, Sir**."

Chichit hit a few buttons on his console. "Master Kiydozo! We have reports from two ships…that one of our ships just…blew up!"

Bylzhisk snarled. "WHICH ONE?"

Chichit did a quick roll call of the different Commanders. "Remendozo (O-6), Metheh does not respond, Master Kiydozo. All other ships respond."

"**Still think I can't blow *your* ships to pieces**," sent Jeejow tersely?

Bylzhisk clenched his teeth. "That was just an unfortunate accident!"

"**Really? Keep an eye on your screens. That, so called, Holy Temple of…Sucksuckcarbon goes next**." He sent the mental message to Chablitha. "**Tear that planet apart…starting with that *chokwad* Temple**."

As soon as the Temple disintegrated in front of them on

the view screen, all of the Mustooza people started a high pitched screaming. All of them had all of their eyes wide open and their hair was flailing all over the place.

Jeejow sighed. **"Ota...open fire."**

The Gaholvib that was looking at the structure on his planet started screaming as well. He turned to Bylzhisk. "You... monster! I may not live through this...but I'm glad that I was able to see the destruction of your home planet. I only wish that I could live long enough to see the end of all of you stinking Mustooza!"

At that moment, one of the Mustooza Security personnel shot the Vagen with a pulse weapon and killed him.

Jeejow bit his lip and shook his head. **"All personnel... blow up all of the ships...except the flagship. I want to talk to him some more."**

In less than ten heartbeats, only one Mustooza ship, that was orbiting Hardooth, was still intact. Chichit was making all kinds of summons on the radio and receiving nothing back.

Bylzhisk finally stopped his high-pitched screaming. "YOU...YOU WILL PAY FOR THIS...THIS...THIS BLASPHEMY!"

"How? How are you going to make us suffer any worse than you have already done?"

"The King of the gods, Sonseskoron will have his vengeance on you! I will start it...with a full out attack...with..."

"With WHAT? You have no weaponry on your ship that can harm us anymore. Besides that, if your

god is a real god…he should have no problem doing something to us for himself. We await *his* judgment… while we're yawning."

"HOW DARE YOU DESACRATE HIS NAME!"

"**Again…if the *bimyock* is real…he doesn't need your help. He can act out his own revenge…so where is he and what is he supposed to do**?"

Bylzhisk and his crew started calling on the name of Sonseskoron. The hair on the top of their heads was splayed out in all directions. They spun around screaming his name. After several of them got dizzy and fell down, they all began to realize that they were calling on an entity that was not responding. They all stood in their places panting and puffing.

One of the Mustooza cleared his throat. "Master Kiydozo, should we call upon the name of the Queen of the gods… Quondondinsha?"

All of the hair on the body of Bylzhisk went limp. "If you think it'll do any good…go ahead."

Once again the mad screaming and dancing started up with them spinning around in place. Once again after several of them fell down dizzy, they all stopped and stood there with all hair hanging limp.

Jeejow sighed. "**I think your gods have either abandoned you or…they never existed. Or…with all of that screaming…they're deaf**."

Bylzhisk waddled over to Chichit. "Call the main

Headquarters. Find out the status on the planet. How much damage was done?"

The eyes that were facing Bylzhisk opened wide. "Master Kiydozo, I have already attempted to call them. I only got the outer planetary guard from Pimbim and Kamsosk. They've informed me that...our home planet...has been cut into four pieces by some powerful plasma weapon...they cannot find. The whole planet... is dead."

Jeejow frowned. **"Exactly what are...Pimbim and Kamsosk?"**

Chablitha came back with the answer. **"They had several thousand fighters...of various sizes that were in bases on other planets in their star system. Once we started the attack on their home planet, those fighters launched and headed for us. We finished slicing up the planet before any of them were able to get within range and...we were already in Observation."**

Jeejow hung his head. **"I'm tired of playing with them. Do we have plenty of passwords for their computer system?"**

"Yes, Sir," sent Bonarain.

"Then jettison all of the nonessential beings on that ship and...start getting some landmarks for the... other planets that they're infesting. I want to get rid of the Vagens, the Mustooza...and any other *bimyock* that wants to use their technology."

This quest took six more years and now the Owlamites had 154 more attack ships crowding around in the parking lot in #45 for their use. They were not sure if they had eliminated all of the Mustooza, however, they knew they had depleted the population to almost nothing – if there were any still living – and those would be refugees on planets they had attempted to conquer.

Jeejow looked confused as he was reading some of the latest reports. "We keep on seeing the attackers…and their spaceships. I was wondering…what do all the rest of the races on Hardooth…what do they think of the attacks…when they never see the attackers?"

"Several of them think that it's some kind of strange and horrible weather phenomenon that just happens…every now and then…as a lasting result of the Algothon firestorm weapons," said Iquanza. "Others…think it is some kind of frenzied fit…that some deity is having. The deity is mad and is…taking it out on the planet. They feel that some sacrifices have to be made in order to please…whichever god they happen to be thinking about at the time. So they…sacrifice."

Xadorm shook his head. "What do the Teltermak and Axswain think about the attacks?"

"There aren't any more Axswain," said Ota. "That last attack killed off all of the intelligent ones and the dumb ones starved to death because they were so stupid they didn't know where or how to find anything to eat. *All* of the Axswain are now completely dead…extinct."

"That's no loss," said Jeejow. "How about the Teltermak?"

"They were hurt badly by that last attack," said Boneech. "I'd say that there are about 100,000 of them left."

"That's still 100,000 of those *chokwads* that are still alive," said Marbing bitterly.

Jeejow started working on promotions for Team Leaders and was shocked to find out that the favoritism had not been from Nagasoom. In fact, it had been some Supreme Commanders prior who had bypassed certain individuals on their promotions because of prejudice in rewarding personnel in their specific cliques…a lot of them. He got rid of this favoritism and started promoting all of the Team Leaders – according to the proper protocols. There were many who ended up getting a double promotion, however, once he explained what had happened (prior to Nagasoom) no one questioned it…especially since this ruling had come from the *Voice of Power*.

Soolchakan looked at the notice that he had been promoted to Officer Grade 4. He sat there reading it with no pride or joy at the notification.

Bonarain sat there scratching a spot on her right arm. "Should we…celebrate?"

Kiyalee scoffed. "Maybe he can celebrate. What are we supposed to celebrate? No one person in the bottom two ranks got any promotions."

Chyning propped her feet up on a table. "I don't really think that any of these promotions are worth anything. I checked that big list…of all of our ages and such. It doesn't matter what rank I get promoted to…there are only twenty-four Owlamites who are younger than me. If I ever become the *Voice of Power*… we're in deep trouble…as far as the population is concerned."

"Unless the doctors can figure out a way for us to procreate," sighed Bonarain.

Chyning rubbed her eyes. "There was even a setback there. During one attack…I don't remember which one. I think it was the Cookrot. We lost *all* of Team 225. Two doctors and two nurses dead."

"That still leaves us with seven medical Teams," said Soolchakan.

"So why aren't we inventing anything and why aren't they inventing any new procedures," said Kiyalee angrily?

"None of us have any imagination," said Bonarain. "That's why we're all watchers…and farmers. Inventors have imaginations and that's why they create new ideas and equipment."

"But…the physicists…and the shipwrights…and the computer people," said Chyning. "Aren't they using…some imagination?"

"No," said Soolchakan. "Most of that is just following procedures…that were laid out by someone else. It's just like when you've had to…machine some of the parts to repair the trucks. You are *not* being creative…you are just making a part that was designed by someone else. All you have to do is follow the instructions."

"That's why we have to steal anything…that we get that is new," said Bonarain.

"Congratulations on your new promotion," said Kiyalee dully. "Why don't you use your new found rank…and make us all some hot kwatha."

13

Jeejow was a little upset when he called a meeting of the Command Staff. "Why didn't we know anything about the Vagens being buddies with the Mustooza?"

"The reason behind that, Sir," said Ota. "The Vagens that the Mustooza found…were not on the original home planet of the Vagens. They were a bunch that got stranded somewhere else. They still had some of their technology but…they didn't have any ships. The Mustooza supplied the ships and…then utilized the technology they stole from the Vagens."

Jeejow hung his head. "Why is it…that no matter how hard we try to stop an enemy from…attacking again…?" He trailed off and looked up. "Is there anything new to report? Can anyone tell me why we didn't know that the Vagens had teamed up with the Mustooza? How could they possibly get to the Vagen home world and we still didn't know?"

"We don't keep anyone there all the time," said Ota. "It'd drive them crazy."

Jeejow scowled at her. "Would you rather see a few of us as crazies or all of us dead?" He cleared his throat. "I've been the *Voice of Power* for 1,038 years now. I would like to see all of us stay alive and living in peace. We may just have to establish a network where we rotate a few personnel…every month or so. We may have to find any…Mustooza people that are…stranded on another planet just like the Choks and the Zizzikinzas. We may be stretching ourselves a little thin, but at least we'll be thin and alive."

46 years later an alert came from a ship that the Owlamites had positioned in #85. There were four ships, of the Mustooza type, headed for the position of Hardooth. They reported that the ships did not seem to be in a hurry.

Jeejow was feeling confused. "What did they mean…not in a hurry?"

Xadorm shrugged. "Why don't we take one of those bell ships to dimension 85 and take a look…and contact them?"

"Couldn't hurt," said Chablitha.

"Okay," said Jeejow. "All of the Command Staff and their Teams…to the bell ship and…we'll see what we see…once we hop to dimension 85."

Once they were in Observation and #85 they cast lots. It was Chablitha, of Team 59, who lost. She had to send her Team to the lead ship and try to figure out what the motive was for these four ships to be in this neighborhood.

They were able to see why Team 2178 had reported that the task force seemed reluctant. Two ships were close to the Hardooth position. The other two ships were coming in slowly from different directions. There did not seem to be very much chatter on the radios as the other two approached.

Officer Grade 6, Sormozo of Team 59 Jumped to the Main Bridge of (what he guessed) was the flagship. He found Officer Grade 6, Rips of Team 2178 sitting there with his fighter.

Sormozo walked up with a wan smile. "So what's the story?"

Rips shrugged. "I don't really know. They don't seem to be too eager to attack us, but…I'm only getting about a fourth of what they're saying. I've tried to…translate it but…again…I'm only getting a little of it." He grunted in disgust. "I learned the entire language…a few years ago but…now…it has…changed considerably."

Sormozo tried to get some of the conversations that were going on. After just a few short moments he sighed. **"This is Officer Grade 6, Sormozo. Senior Officer, Chablitha, are you listening**?"

Chablitha came back. **"I'm listening. What seems to be the problem**?"

"Sir, it seems that the Mustooza language has altered dramatically. Officer Rips and myself. We're not getting any of an entire conversation anywhere on this ship. I think that we need that Officer, Bonarain."

Chablitha gave Jeejow a dull look.

Jeejow shook his head. **"Team 7016, and especially Officer, Bonarain, we need you here in dimension 85. It seems that the Mustooza have changed their language**

– somehow - and no one here can decipher it."

Bonarain sat there with her anger rising. "**Sir, I just got in the bathtub. My neck is filthy. Is this an emergency**?"

Jeejow bit his lip to keep from laughing. "**Not at this time. When you're finished bathing…please come to dimension 85…in your fighter…clothed**."

"**Thank you, Sir**." She turned on the hot water and started filling the tub.

Chyning pulled a big tasty lump out of her kwatha. "Does that mean that we have time to finish this before it gets cold?"

"I hope so," said Soolchakan as he spooned through his kwatha.

Kiyalee just sat there chewing while scowling. She dipped her spoon in her kwatha and started looking for another lump.

Chablitha and her entire Team Jumped to the Mustooza ship. None of them were able to decipher the entire language. Ota and her Team joined Chablitha on the enemy ship and all of them were now sitting there confused as to what they were hearing.

Ota scoffed in disgust. "How could a race of intelligent beings…change their language that radically…in only a few decades? If it was four and a half centuries I could understand it." She shook her head again. "We await our expert."

The three Teams started wandering around the Bridge looking for anything they could comprehend (or maybe swipe).

Bonarain finished her bath. She went downstairs and

found her Teammates all dressed in their spacesuits. They were holding her suit up for her to don. She slowly got into it and the four of them went to their fighters. They hopped to #85.

Soolchakan chuckled nervously. **"Which ship do you want us on? There are three that have gathered together and a fourth one on the way here. Gimme a clue which one**?'"

A fighter came slowly up out of the Main Bridge of the ship in the middle. **"Hello Team 7016. I am Officer, Noyee of Team 59. Follow me in this one. We have quite a collection of personnel in here so far."**

Team 7016 aimed their ships at Noyee and followed her in the ship.

As soon as they arrived inside Soolchakan looked around somewhat befuddled. **"Where do we park? You people have taken up...most of the Bridge."**

"There's room up by the view screen," sent Ota. **"Park there and you shouldn't have any problem."**

Chyning shook her head. "Sixteen of our fighters on their Main Bridge. I wonder how many they have in their hangar bay."

Chablitha was a little upset over the parking problem as well. "Officer, Kiyalee, why don't you take Mimihasa, Hooloo and Lebella to the engine room...and show them a few of the finer points of sabotaging them? Officer, Chyning, you can take Noyee, Channa and Taybiya to...other parts of the ship and...start purloining a few things for...our collections."

'One from each Team,' thought Soolchakan. 'That'll make the parking a little easier.'

Bonarain went to the Commander's position. It was more of a location than a chair because the Mustooza did not sit down. Their four stubby little legs did not allow for much of a "sit down" area in their body. Their bodies did not bend very much anywhere so getting up from sleeping was a bit of a chore. There were a few seats in the area for some of the Vagens who were aboard the ship. There were currently only two Vagens on the Main Bridge while there were at least twenty Mustooza at different work stations.

Bonarain started reading the mind of the Commander. She snickered a little as she started picking up the language. "**This new language is a mixture of Mustooza, Vagen and… some language from a planet where they were stranded when we blew their homes to pieces. It seems they found a way to communicate with…the people who became their unfriendly hosts. They made friends with them…because they had no choice. They had nowhere else to go…and the languages merges…radically.**"

"**That's all fine and dandy**," sent Jeejow. "**What are they doing here…now?**"

Bonarain shook her head and sighed. "**It seems that some…high muckity-muck priestess of the goddess Quondondinsha was upset when the temple to that goddess was destroyed…along with the Mustooza home planet. She wants these, and four other ships, to come here and…destroy *our* home planet.**"

Jeejow growled in disgust. "**Patch me in and…I'll talk to them. I think…and hope…that I can talk them out of any…retributions. Meanwhile, somebody, like *you* Boneech, get about ten Teams on each one of those ships and deactivate their weapons systems**."

"**We're ready**," sent Soolchakan.

"**This is Supreme Officer, Jeejow, Drey Sssorg of the Owlam Empire. Why have you come back here**?"

All of the crew of the ship flinched or jumped in fear when they heard the voice.

The one in the Command position stood there shaking. "This…is…Remendozo (O-6) Filshosh…of the…Mustooza Collective. Uh…we…were ordered here…by the High Priestess of…Quondondinsha…to…exact revenge…for the goddess… against your race…for defiling…and destroying…her temple."

Jeejow laughed. He did not try to hide the laughter in his words as he responded. "**That goddess is not much of a deity…if she has to order you here to exact her revenge. If she is real…why didn't *she* stop us? If she is real, why does she need someone else to do the dirty work? If she is real, then why did it take so long for anyone to come here…for this foolish purpose**?" He shook his head. "One thing I've noticed about some of this is that whenever there is someone who worships polytheism, it has always been phony deities. One God that is omnipresent, omniscient and all powerful usually has some basis in fact." He sighed. "**Where is this High Priestess? Does she have the courage to**

lead this idiotic expedition or…is she too cowardly…or is she sitting back somewhere waiting to hear that all of you are dead before she sends another expedition?"

"She…uh…is on the…uh…fourth ship…that is coming in…now. She is…going to be the one…to give the word…uh…to attack."

Jeejow groaned. "Someone get to that fourth ship and see if you can find out which one is this…High *bimyock*. Bring her here…along with a pair of her…escorts."

Xadorm smiled. "I and Team 45 are on our way." Team 45 vanished.

Jeejow cleared his throat. "**Filshosh, we're going to switch our conversation to that High Priestess**."

Ota sent back. "**He doesn't look very relieved. He looks even more apprehensive than before**."

"**So what**," sent Chablitha?

Xadorm called in. "**I spotted her. She's an albino! All of the other Mustooza have dark hair. Her hair is pure white and…her eyes are…uh…reddish. She's on a pedestal that is sitting next to the Command position. She has six Mustooza men who are surrounding her… and they're armed…with…uh *spears*?**"

Jeejow hung his head and groaned. "Spears!" He looked up and sighed. "**Bring the Priestess and two of her flunkies… minus the spears**."

Xadorm nodded with a big grin. "Baynabi…Kiskee…you

Jump two of the flunkies to the bell ship, in the Doolood area…
since we drained all of that water and put in floors, they should be
okay in there…except possibly for the smell. Teechata, make sure
they don't have their spears when they get there. I'll take the high
doovoft myself."

Jeejow looked at the cylindrical Mustooza woman in
front of him. All eight of her eyes were wide open and looking
everywhere around the room. He shook his head. "**Remendozo
Filshosh, we have your Priestess on our ship. We're
now going to talk to her**."

Ota snickered. "**Sir, he's confirming with the
Commander of that other ship to see if the Priestess is
indeed not on that ship anymore**."

Jeejow grunted. "**Let him suffer**." He clasped his hands
together. "So, High Priestess, you're the speaker for this…goddess
that you call…Quon dumb dunce spit?"

All of her eyes narrowed. "That's QUON-DON-DIN-
SHA you defiling sacrilegious *fmirk*!"

He sighed. "The reason that I find it hard to believe in
this…so called goddess…is because…if she were real…how
could she have allowed your home planet to be destroyed? If she
is a deity, in order for her to be worth her divinity, she would
not have allowed her temple and planet to be damaged, let alone
destroyed. The same goes for that other deity…Sonseskoron."

"They will have their vengeance," she spat at him.

"How," he spat back?! "Through you? I have the power of

life and death over you right now. Where is this alleged deity?"

"She is everywhere," said the Priestess. "She will protect me from any harm. She will see you destroyed."

Jeejow hopped to Ghost, walked through the wall, up to the belligerent Priestess and backhanded her as hard as he could, knocking her down. He looked at his hand in a disgusted manner, left the Doolood area and walked over to a sink to wash his hands.

"She didn't protect you from that, did she?"

They all watched as the Priestess used her long hairs to prop herself back upright, along with some assistance from the two flunkies. After the ordeal, she was panting heavily from the effort.

"That was nothing," she snarled. "I am protected from REAL harm."

Jeejow huffed. He looked around at the other personnel in the room. "**Marbing, you have a pulse pistol on you. Shoot that silly *fovok* in one of her feet.**"

Marbing pulled the pistol out, took aim and fired. One of her feet was badly damaged by the shot and blood, which looked dark orange, started coming out of the wound.

One of her imprisoned attendants started screaming. "She'll bleed to death…if you don't do something about that injury!"

Jeejow leaned forward with an angry glare. "Is THAT nothing?"

Her eyes were all looking around rapidly. "I'm *bleeding*! I need the bleeding stopped!"

"So call on your deity," said Jeejow in a patronizing manner.

"I need help," she pleaded.

Jeejow signaled to Xadorm. "Let her aides assist her. See what they can do."

The two surprised attendants were allowed to move. They immediately started pulling some of their own hairs out and made a tourniquet for her injured foot. The flow of blood stopped.

"Your deity didn't help you, I did. I helped you by allowing your friends to take care of your injury. I don't believe in this Quondondinsha. If she were real, I think that she would have done something for herself by now."

One of the aides spoke up. "We need to call on her to help us…in this situation."

All three of them started spinning around screaming with their hair flailing all around. All of the Owlamites looked at the spectacle with trepidation and anxiety – and trying desperately not to laugh. Several of the Owlamites covered their ears. The screaming and spinning went on for quite some time – until one of the Mustooza aides got dizzy and fell down. The other aide fell as well. The Priestess stopped screaming and spinning. She was wobbling a little, however, she was able to remain standing, even though she was limping badly on the injured foot.

Jeejow leaned back in his chair. "Well…did she show up

and…assist you?"

All eight of her eyes closed and her hair went completely limp. "All of my life has been devoted to…something that doesn't respond…when I need it the most." She heaved a sigh. "Is it really true that she doesn't exist?"

Jeejow shrugged. "It has been my experience that whenever someone is dealing with a group of so-called deities, that as a group, each one has some weakness. They depend on each other. That…just doesn't make sense. If a being is supposed to be all-seeing, all-knowing, all-powerful…why do they need other deities to help them out of trouble? Why do they need worshippers… who do all of the fighting and retribution for them? No, I don't believe that she exists. If you really want to make sure of your situation, we'll send you back to your ship…and why don't you see if your weapons systems are working. We have deactivated *all* of your weapon systems. You are the ones who are helpless and cannot hurt us. If you stop this…idiotic vengeance crusade…and promise not to attack us…or anyone else…we will let you go in peace. If you ever come after us again…we will go out of our way to destroy you and every Mustooza that exists…anywhere. Any questions?"

"No," she said in a forlorn manner. "I understand. Can I go back to my ship now?"

Jeejow turned to Xadorm and nodded.

Moments later, the Priestess was getting her injured foot attended to while she was being briefed on how the weapons systems were missing numerous critical components and that they could not even begin to repair them until they got back to some primary base to get the proper parts. She had a fit over the fact that they were so helpless. They would have to find the other ships that were supposed to eventually join up here and use them for their protection and defenses. The four ships departed in peace.

Xadorm shook his head in disbelief. "Negotiations can actually *work*! That is a huge blessing."

"I hope we can get away with it again...sometime," said Iquanza.

"I hope we don't have to use any...negotiations or weapons...ever again," said Jeejow. "Negotiations work...only up to a certain point. She had to see in order to believe and...I don't think she wants to give up the power she has as a *High* Priestess. She might only be going back...for more firepower."

Ota nodded. "So have a Team follow them back to... wherever and landmark it. Once we've got it landmarked, if they come back...we strike."

"Yes," said Jeejow sadly. He sighed. "Let's go home... other than the Team that follows those...*melafathan fovoks*," he said bitterly.

"My Team will put the bell ship away," said Nasnana.

Two years later, Officer Leader, Hrombisk came strutting into a Command Staff meeting looking rather proud of himself. "Sirs, we have done it. We have finally figured it out."

All of the members looked around confused.

Jeejow cleared his throat and smiled. "Uh…what did we ask you to…figure out?"

Hrombisk was now the one looking confused. "Someone asked us to figure out how four 459 cannons could have possibly cut through the entire depth of a planet." He smiled sheepishly. "Didn't that question come from…*here*?"

Jeejow leaned forward a little. "No…but since you went through all of the trouble to figure it out…you have piqued my curiosity. How is it possible to cut a planet in half with our cannons?" He stood up. "And please put it in language that even *we* can understand!"

Hrombisk looked a little affronted. He cleared his throat. "Yes, Sir, I will try. It seems that…once the 459 cannons were rewired with that platinum wiring, it made them more efficient destroying machines."

Jeejow nodded. "I'm with you so far."

"Thank you, Sir. Now, when we had them powered through one of those light speed engines, if it had not been for the platinum wiring, the cannons themselves would have been incinerated… possibly along with the operators. So, the wiring made them more powerful, the engines aided immensely…and then…the idea of combining four of the beams together…that made them even more powerful than we ever imagined."

"I know that," said Jeejow. "Now…how did they cut a planet in half?"

"When the beams were combined, they did not add to the

power of one…they magnified it much more than that. Two beams together became ten times as powerful. A third beam added… made that another ten times as powerful. The fourth…multiplied it by ten…again."

Xadorm looked horrified. "So…four beams…made it… *one thousand times*…more powerful than…just one 459?"

Hrombisk smiled. "Yes, Sir. It sounds as if you do understand what I'm saying."

Chablitha swallowed hard. "Then…does that mean…that the effective range is also…one thousand times as far?"

Hrombisk frowned. "I…didn't look into that. Seeing as how the collectively applied beams cut all the way through to the other side of the planet and still had full destructive force…I would have to say…yes." He shrugged. "Do you want me to attempt finding out the range of the cannons?"

"No, no, no, no, no, no," said Jeejow. "That's quite all right. We know that…they are extremely destructive. How far can they…hit and destroy something? I'm not really sure that I really want to know."

Hrombisk smiled. "Then I bid you good day, Sirs." He turned and departed.

Nasnana had both of her hands over her heart. "We have to make certain…that monstrous thing never falls into the hands of anyone else."

"Don't ever simplify the three stage trigger," said Boneech.

Jeejow rubbed his eyes. "Is there any other business?"

"Yes, Sir," said Ota. "That silly High Priestess has gone back on her word. She's trying to put a very large armada together to come here and take us out."

Xadorm groaned. "Didn't she learn?"

"Apparently not," said Ota. "The dumb Priestess feels that her survival was because the goddess was protecting her. You hurt her foot. You didn't kill her. Therefore, the goddess was protecting the Priestess and her entourage."

Jeejow grunted. "Do we know what her name is?"

Ota grimaced. She picked up her pad. "Her name is…Intipitam…uh…taminaya." She put the pad down. "Intipitaminaya."

Jeejow sat there with his mouth open. "Uh…Priestess is fine."

"So what do we do," said Xadorm?

Jeejow sighed. "If those *bimyock*s do show up…she's the first to die…along with any other of their Priestly group."

Jeejow had sent out a request for all of the Owlamites to attempt at coming up with an idea as to how they were going to watch for the approach of the Mustooza. That Priestess was lying about leaving Hardooth in peace. They knew that the Vagens had explored nineteen different dimensions. That pesky little Priestess could use any of the dimensions to approach Hardooth. Jeejow wanted a plan where they could have some sort of advance warning of the approach.

The Command Staff heard all kinds of strange and radical ideas, however, Hrombisk and several other physicists were able to shoot all of those plans down through some form of hieroglyphic equation that proved their plans were scientifically impossible.

The Teams that had come up with ideas were brought in numerically. Soolchakan had to wait until last (again) in order to give his idea. When he walked in he was looking at some very unenthusiastic faces. They had heard all kinds of idiotic, wild and very time consuming ideas. They did not look like they were ready to hear anything at this time, however, Soolchakan had waited all this time – he was going to voice his idea.

"Good afternoon, Sirs," he said with a smile. None of their expressions changed. "I know that it has been a long…tedious time, but, I think I have the solution."

Several of the Staff rolled their eyes, one covered her eyes and a couple of them just grunted.

"We tether the sensor in place, here on Hardooth while we hop them into the other dimensions," said Soolchakan smiling.

A few of them looked confused, a few of them rolled their eyes again and one of them started studying her fingernails.

Jeejow shook his head. "What do we tether the things to?"

"Hardooth," said Soolchakan. "All we have to do is put them on some kind of pedestal, that we put up above the gorge. We bolt one of the sensors to the pedestal and then we hop the sensor and the pedestal into…whatever dimension we want to put it in. Since the Vagens had found eighteen dimensions, other than Home, we would need eighteen of these things put up there. We can hook them up to our monitors and watch…all of those dimensions…by different Teams on different shifts."

Jeejow all of a sudden looked hopeful. "So…all eighteen… are hooked to this planet. We don't have to worry about them… wandering off in another dimension, because they are hooked…to *this* planet."

"Correct, Sir." Soolchakan let out a little sigh of relief. He was not being treated like the others who had come up with bad ideas. "We don't have to worry about them orbiting anything, we don't have to worry about any strange gravity fluctuations in another dimension…we have them hooked to this planet so that they're guarding this planet alone. When they're in the other dimensions, they won't be seeing this planet, they'll be looking in all directions at the same time. No one will be able to approach without us seeing them from any of the known Vagen dimensions. We need to have them hooked to our planet because we've discovered that…over the years, the Stink planet has moved away from us. It used to occupy the same space, but…now…it is over 40,000 kilotaja away. The sensors will not stray…bolted down."

Hrombisk smiled. "That would be perfect! They're here… watching for just us. No one…outside of the gorge would even see them."

Chablitha frowned. "What about the three dimensions with star systems that are in the same place as ours? Dimensions 13, 79 and 202 all have a star system in our immediate vicinity. As a matter of fact, 202 has an inhabitable planet…right near us. There's nothing on that planet…but small mammals, reptiles and all kinds of things that live in the water. The Vagens…could have a forward base there…couldn't they? Has anyone taken a look at that planet…lately?"

Ota grimaced. "I'll have some of my friends go take look right now. Like you said, the planet is inhabitable and since there is no sentient life form there…no one to argue with as far as who can move in and take the planet over. You just have to be able to fight all of the big reptiles off."

Boneech looked a little skeptical. "What about the other planets in those three systems? What's the possibility of one of those planets…slamming into our sensors and destroying them completely?"

Xadorm grunted in disgust. "Use your head! If someone is diligently, or even lackadaisically, watching, I'm sure that they'll be able to see a *planet* coming towards the sensor. If that happens, all they have to do is get up there, hop the thing to Home and wait until the planet passes by. What's the problem?"

Boneech sucked her lips in, clenched her eyes shut and turned very red.

Jeejow cleared his throat. "I'm sure that there may be a few things that we have to work out, but…this is the best thing that I've heard…in quite some time. Let's get our construction people working on the pedestals and the computer people working on activating the needed sensors. This sounds like it'll work… hopefully very well." He stood up and smiled. "Thank you, Officer, Soolchakan…for ending the meeting with a feasible idea. We've heard so many…" He looked off to the side. "NO! I'm not going to even mention some of those…" He looked back at Soolchakan. "Thank you!"

Soolchakan smiled. "Your quite welcome, Sir."

Hrombisk shook his head. "Such a simple thing to do. I must remember, in the future, to stop trying to complicate things." He shook his head again as he pondered.

Officer Leader, Yoobyool reported to the Command Staff. "Sirs, as you requested we did check on that nearby planet in dimension 202. It appears that a Vagen ship crashed there… uh…we're not sure when. From the condition of the wreckage… meaning how much jungle overgrowth has taken over and hidden the pieces, it has been quite some time. The Vagen survivors haven't been able to repair any of their communication devices so they don't know of any of the actions by…us or the Mustooza. I feel that if they were informed…they would side with their own people and eventually with the Mustooza."

Jeejow closed his eyes. "Are you in communication with anyone who is there now?"

"Yes, Sir, Officer Grade 3, Hoyna with her Team 4241 are there right now waiting for any orders from you."

Jeejow nodded. "How many of them are there?"

"Currently 489 Vagens are living there."

Xadorm scoffed. "Do they still have their prejudicial order intact?"

"Yes, Sir," said Yoobyool. "All of the minority Vagehymin are in charge and the majority Jonlyan are still badly mistreated servants."

"We may have to destroy them…in spite of the fact that they don't know what's going on," said Jeejow sadly. "I hate to do it, but…it may be necessary."

"Destroy their idiotic social order, but not the people," said Nasnana. "Killing the student as a part of the lesson is a lesson not learned…by anyone."

Zoolkog smiled. "How about…we just eradicate those three factions who are in charge? Once the Vagehymin, the Afzylovabi and the Gaholvib are gone…don't you think that the Jonlyan and the Lujetfyvoh will be able to take care of themselves?"

Jeejow looked a little surprised. "I'm amazed that you can even remember all five of those names."

Zoolkog shrugged. "Look at some of the names of the Elf races on this planet. You remember them, don't you?"

Jeejow smiled. "Yoobyool, if we do get rid of the three ruling factions…how many of the 489 will still be left alive?"

Yoobyool did a quick mental communication with Hoyna. "Sir, that would leave 430 of them alive."

Iquanza's jaw dropped. "You mean…that 59 are ruling over 430…and the 430 are doing *nothing* about it?"

Yoobyool shrugged. "It's the way they were raised from birth."

Boneech interjected. "Kill the 59 and let the 430 create their own world, I say."

"I agree," said Marbing emphatically!

Jeejow nodded. "So do I." He sighed. "Tell...Hoyna to get rid of the elite. Let the downtrodden become unshackled."

"That means that we're experimenting with the lives of others," said Chablitha. Doesn't that sound a little hypocritical to you?"

"Considering how much of that nonsense has been done to us," said Jeejow. "I think that it's about time the shoe was on the other foot. Let someone else be the lab rodent. I, for one, am very tired of it being us. Maybe if we do it a little bit, we'll find a way to combat those who are trying to use us."

Chablitha shook her head. "I still don't like it. No matter what we learn from it, it is still disgusting."

Jeejow looked affronted. "I didn't say that we were going to make a habit of it."

"No, Sir," said Chablitha angrily. "But once you cross that line...you can never go back."

Jeejow glared back at her. "I hear your objection! We are going to do it anyway! We will learn...even if it is something disgusting, we will learn."

"At least we won't need a large force keeping an eye on them," said Ota. "I don't see them becoming any kind of a threat any time soon. The followers are still followers and they don't have any...grand ambitions."

The pedestals were finished very quickly. The sensors were put on the pedestals and then hopped to their specific dimension. They figured that it would be a rather long time before there was any activity on any of them.

The next day there was an alert from the sensor in #94. A globe-shaped spaceship of unknown origin came upon the sensor and stopped to investigate. As soon as the ship was spotted, there were five Teams who were ordered into their fighters and hopped to Spy then #94.

Once there, the sensor was then hopped to Spy as well. Some lights came out of the ship and searched the area where the sensor was located. After almost a day of searching for the missing sensor, the ship departed...peacefully.

The Owlamites all let out a sigh of relief. Someone had come along who had not fired a shot and had not shown any form of hostility. They were just curious.

Jeejow watched the monitor as the ship departed. "Whoever that is, they're a long way from home. According to all of our statistics...the closest star, of any type, to our location...is 68 light years away."

"Anyone who searches any galaxy is going to end up a long way from home, no matter where they go," said Xadorm.

Nasnana turned away from the monitor. "Why didn't we send our Team of specialists in there and find out who they are?"

Jeejow smiled. "If they had stayed a little longer...I

would've sent a Team in to investigate."

Sixteen years later it was decided that the Iyka planet was now inhabitable. It could be inhabited if anyone could figure out a way to introduce numerous types of microorganisms along with all of the necessary small land and sea creatures. The Owlamites decided that they did not wish to undertake that experiment. Moving an entire ecosystem to Hardooth had been a big enough headache.

On the planet in #202, the Jonlyan and the Lujetfyvoh were getting along very well. They were even mating between the two tribes (which had been taboo under the rule of the other three tribes). In the sixteen years they had been without the ruling parties, they were surviving and procreating very well, and living in peace.

Other reports showed that the Doolood were coming back, again, after some of the headaches of being attacked by some other persons – which the Owlamites had defeated. They decided to still keep an eye on those crazy talking fish. Others had been there and learned a little too much about the Owlamites from them.

14

Four years later the Mustooza finally had conjured up enough intestinal fortitude (and spaceships) to attempt an attack on Hardooth and the Owlamites. The armada appeared on the sensor and as each ship came into range, it was counted. 77 attack ships and 3 ships that had a rather curious configuration in their design. Jeejow decided he wanted a full report on the three odd ones.

Team 7016 was once again tasked to perform the initial reconnaissance of the strange ships. They headed into the central one of the three ships with their normal targets in mind.

Kiyalee found nothing new. The conventional engines and the light speed engines were the same design that had been in all of the Mustooza ships so far.

Chyning found an incredible plethora of goodies that she could purloin, however, none of them were of any technological value. All of the booty she was finding was of the precious metal and high priced gem area. Many of them were in the shape of some sort of holy symbol for some member of the Mustooza pantheon of deities.

Soolchakan and Bonarain found the Main Bridge of the central ship was more like some kind of temple or shrine. They also discovered that in order to be in the clergy of the Mustooza people you must be an albino. All of the priests on the ship were albinos and all of the attendants (not albinos) were carrying spears.

"That's odd," said Bonarain.

Soolchakan sniffed as he looked around the Bridge. "Which part of this incongruity is *not* odd?"

"We have Mustooza clergy and military ship Commander. But…we only have one faction of the Vagens." She grunted in disgust. "Those two…very bored looking Vagens over there. He's the Tolod and she's the Gyvbufu of the Vagehymin party. Where are the representatives of the other two parties?"

Soolchakan sighed. "You keep reading minds in here. I'll take a quick look at the other two ships…and see who is on them."

Bonarain nodded and went back to reading the thoughts of the Commander.

Soolchakan climbed into his fighter and headed to the odd ship that was starboard of the central one. He entered the Main Bridge and noticed some distinct differences. "**Bonarain, what is the main…deity of that central ship**?"

Bonarain was a little confused by the question. "**It looks like all of this is for that…Sonseskoron…why**?"

"**Because this ship…starboard of your position, is dedicated entirely to Quondondinsha. Plus…I found the Boliluwy and the Jufamy of the Afzylovabi party over here**."

Bonarain laughed. "**I wonder who the big *bimyock* is**

on that third ship."

"**You keep reading minds in there. I'll check the third ship.**" He headed his fighter to the third one. Upon arrival on that Main Bridge he just shook his head as he looked around. "**The Gaholvib are on this third ship. The Vofyhonah and the Byfoli are sitting here looking very bored. I did find a different god though. This ship is dedicated to…I think his name is…Mimboktoom. From what I'm seeing here…he's apparently the god of war.**"

"**That explains that oddity**," sent Bonarain. "**I've been picking up that word – Mimboktoom – from most of the Mustooza on this ship. They're paying homage to Sonseskoron, but, they're also chanting about Mimboktoom. I thought that the word wasn't translating. Now I know why.**"

Jeejow interrupted. "**From what you're saying…all three of the odd ships are…flying temples to different deities. Are all of the clergy on those three ships…or are they scattered on any of the other 77 ships?**"

"**To find that out, Sir, you're going to need a lot more Teams**," sent Soolchakan. "**They're going to have to do the searching. I don't have the time right now to search all seventy-seven ships myself.**"

Jeejow agreed. He looked at the Command Staff. "He's right. We shouldn't expect one Team to search all of those ships. All right people, let's get 77 Teams on those attack ships now. Find the clergy. I did say that their priesthood would be the first ones slaughtered if they ever showed their ugly faces here again. I now have to carry out my threat. Get rid of them first…and then we'll see what happens."

The Command Staff waited while the 77 attack ships were searched for any of the priests of the Mustooza gods. The reports were coming back that they had been on board the attack ships. They had been blessing all of the crews of those ships. They were now all being shuttled back to the three luxury ships that were absolutely flying temples for the gods.

"Perfect!" Jeejow nodded with pride. "Now, we can get rid of all of those pagan priests…and hopefully scare the *piddleeyanks* out of all of the Mustooza and send them back home…in terror." He sighed. "**Please let me know when all of the shuttlecraft have finished moving all of the priests to the three temple ships**."

Soolchakan did some quick thinking. "**Bonarain, let us know when the priests are getting ready to order the beginning of the attack. Kiyalee, get ready to blow that central ship. Chyning, get ready to blow the one that is starboard of the central ship. I'm going to blow the one that is sitting port of the central ship**."

Chyning snorted in disgust. "**How much time do we have before we blow these things up**?"

Bonarain answered. "**It's going to be quite a while. According to these *bimyocks* on the central ship, all three of the gods have to have some long ritual performed before the battle can take place…seeing as** how this is some kind of vengeance war."

Chyning giggled to herself. "**Good! There's all kinds of pretty little goodies on this ship that I want to take home with me.**"

Jeejow was a little shocked. "**Goodies? What kind of *goodies* are you talking about**?"

Chyning looked around with all kinds of lustful greed in her eyes. "**Golden flatware, golden mugs, huge silver platters, gem encrusted candelabras, rings, bracelets and a few gold and silver things that look like symbols of their big high and mighty holy *doovofts*.**"

Jeejow sighed. "**Let's get a few Teams on those ships…and get a few goodies for ourselves. I don't want Chyning to have all of the fun…besides, I like the thought of being able to eat off of a golden plate…with golden flatware.**"

Nasnana huffed. "Shame on you!"

Jeejow snickered. "We should feel ashamed, but I don't. One of the reasons why we should take these things is…if the Mustooza ever come back, we can show them that we not only destroyed those flying temples, we also ransacked them before we destroyed them and their imaginary gods couldn't do a thing about it."

Nasnana stuck her tongue out at him. "I wish you'd said that at the beginning. That makes a lot more sense than just a lot of petty pilfering."

"It does," said Xadorm. "Let's go!" He frowned at Nasnana. "And this is *not* petty pilfering." He grinned. "This is high, grand level, felony larceny on a scale never before attempted or accomplished."

Over 500 Owlamite Teams went to the three temples and grabbed an unimaginable amount of wealth off of the three ships. None of the Mustooza noticed because none of them were currently in their private quarters. All were in the main temple rooms.

Soolchakan was a little surprised that Chyning was not upset over the number of Owlamites that boarded the ships and ransacked the wealth. He was surprised until he found out (later) that she had already swiped a full set of golden plates, platters, some rather large mugs, glasses, cups, saucers, serving spoons, ladles, carving knives, bowls and eight full sets of flatware before reporting all of the wealth that was on board. She had also purloined a rather large cache of some very fancy jewelry.

Still, none of the Mustooza noticed the pilfering. They were much too busy preparing for the big ceremonies that would precede the attack. Nothing that was involved in the ceremonies was taken…yet.

The ceremony on the middle ship started. All of the clergy started their ritualistic spinning, screaming and their hair flailing wildly all over the place. Any Vagen that was on any of the three ships just sat there covering their ears while the noise was going on. As soon as the ceremony ended on the first ship, the second one started.

The Vagens were also rather upset over the fact that no slave was allowed on the Main Bridge (or main temple room) for any reason. Slaves were unfit to be in the presence of the deity. If they wanted to be served by their Lujetfyvoh or Jonlyan slaves, they had to leave the Bridge and go to the slave. The Vagens felt that this was a rather undignified way to handle things. The master never goes to the slave, however, here they had no choice.

Jeejow huffed. "Have we pulled all of the...goodies...off of all three ships that anyone and everyone wants?"

"Everyone is off except for Team 7016," said Marbing. "We haven't pulled any wealth out of the sanctuary rooms. They're just waiting for the order to blow up all three ships."

Jeejow nodded. "**Team 7016, once they start the ceremony for that third one, the one they call their war god, that's when you strike. As soon as they start their...screaming...BOOM! BOOM! BOOM!**"

"**Understood, Sir**," sent Soolchakan. "**Bonarain...go ahead and go home now. I'll let the others know when the...screaming starts on this ship**."

"**Thank you**," sent Bonarain! "**All that screaming! I'm getting a bad headache...and earaches**."

Jeejow frowned. "Does anyone know...which of the 77 attack ships...is the flagship? It might be handy to send them a message...after we get rid of the flying temples."

"I can find out real quick," said Zoolkog.

Jeejow nodded. "Get a Team on that ship and as soon as the

temples have been blown…we'll let them know what happened… and why. It doesn't help to send a lesson without the students knowing that they're being taught something."

Several moments later Zoolkog opened his eyes. "Team 1488 is on board the flagship. Officer Grade 2, Toodooa is the Team leader. They're awaiting orders…as to what you want to tell the students."

Jeejow sent the mental communication to Toodooa. He informed her what he wanted the ship Commander to hear directly after the temples were blown up.

Chyning sent a message to Soolchakan. **"The noisy *bimyocks* are finished over here. Get ready for them to start over there**."

Soolchakan just shook his head. 'It took them long enough,' he thought. 'I'm sure glad I don't have to sit through all that noise on this ship.' He waited for the screaming to start on his ship. As soon as he heard the first high-pitched voices he sent the order.

All three hand-held bombs were attached to the light speed exterior. As soon as they were activated, Team 7016 Jumped back to their apartment in the gorge. They did not have to worry about anything because the explosions were going to take place in #85. The sensor that was spying on #85 had been hopped back to Home so it was in no danger either.

Toodooa had to shield her eyes from the horrible glare that came from the three explosions. She gave the warning and ultimatum to the surviving attack ships and waited to see if there was any response. All 77 ships prepared to engage their light speed engines and head back home in great haste (and with a lot of fear and shock over what had happened to all of their clergy).

Toodooa Jumped back to her home. **"It worked, Sir. For the moment. I hope it left a lasting impression on them**."

"So do I," said Jeejow.

94 years later, Jeejow celebrated 1,200 years as the *Voice of Power*. It was 419 years longer than the second longest reign of Till and 504 years longer than the reign of Wymini. Many were hoping they would not have to have any other new *Voice of Power*, seeing as how Jeejow had been in place so long.

They also looked at the fact that it was now 3,430 years since the Algothons had blasted the planet with their firestorm weapons and none of the Owlamites still had any idea how long they could actually live. In looking around the planet they, once again, found that no other Elf race had their longevity…that they knew of. They had discovered graveyards for the new races all over the territories they lived in. They were not sure of the Teltermak because they had not been keeping track of them, individually, other than to thwart any plan that those pesky Teltermaks had on attempting to duplicate *Tuzine*.

Jeejow decided that it was time to start a new tradition. On each anniversary of the rise to *Voice of Power*, the Owlamites were to recite all of the names that had held that title so far. They must remember the past and learn from mistakes. Remembering the names of the previous *Voice of Power* was part of history. Never forget who came before you. Good or bad, this was a major part of their history.

Nagasoom, Plothok, Neenatha, Jahong, Nakalak, Holla, Wilfadge, Hadathoo, Till, Wymini and now Jeejow.

Jeejow thought about also having them commit to memory how long each one served as Drey Sssorg, however, that seemed a little vain (not to mention the fact that he was still in place) so he just left it as something that was written in the history book with no obligation to memorize those numbers.

100 years later, Jeejow was celebrating 1,300 years as the *Voice of Power*. Once again it was looked upon with happiness that there had been no change, at the top, in a very long time.

They never forgot the ones who had been killed in previous wars, however, there was no memorization required for them – just the Drey Sssorg.

Ten years later another attack occurred…with more deadly results. Another attack from the sky with deadly rays coming down and destroying huge amounts of land. Once again there was a change in the command structure of the Owlamites.

Master Officer, Xadorm waited for some kind of call from Jeejow. He heard nothing. He pulled his list out. He was second on the list just behind Jeejow. If Jeejow was no longer among the living then he, Xadorm, was now the *Voice of Power*. He mentally called out to Jeejow several times more with no results.

He checked the list and called out to Marbing…nothing. He called out to Zoolkog and finally received a positive response. He called out to Nasnana…she did not respond. He called out to Chablitha and again received no response. He received positive responses from the remaining Vice Commanders, Ota, Iquanza and Boneech. That meant that there were at least five of the Command Staff who were still alive. He ordered all of them to the space bell.

Xadorm sent out a general communication: **"This is Master Officer, Xadorm. In case you haven't noticed, we're under attack again. I don't know who it is that's attacking us, but, I think that Jeejow and several others on the Command Staff are dead. All Owlamites go to Observation and let's try to figure out who this new marauder is."**

Team 7016 was currently in their favorite dimension. Originally called Beasties, it was now called dimension #10. They were all doing what they could with one of the gourd eaters, trying to figure out if it was possible to domesticate the thing and use it as some kind of beast of burden.

Soolchakan hung his head. "I wonder who this new *bimyock* is."

Bonarain snarled. "Another one of those conquering fools…that we're going to have to destroy."

Kiyalee looked a little fearful. "Did he say that Jeejow was dead?"

"Yes, he did," said Soolchakan. He sighed. "Let's get in our fighters and go check things out."

"Which dimension," said Chyning?

"Observation seems to be the only one that's still safe… even from the Vagens," said Soolchakan. "Let's go…back into another quagmire of war."

They put their spacesuits on, climbed into their fighters, went into the Observation and hopped back to Home dimension. They were horrified to see over 100 large spaceships orbiting Hardooth and firing down on the planet with pulse beams. They looked very much like the Tashkafa ships, however, these were longer.

"**Pick one and we'll investigate it**," sent Bonarain.

Soolchakan huffed. "**The closest one! Our main problem is…a thorough investigation on a cylindrical ship that's about ten kilotaja long**." He shook his head. "**The sooner we get in there, the sooner we find out who they are**."

"**I'll find the engines**," sent Kiyalee.

"**I'll find us some goodies**," sent Chyning in an overly eager manner.

Soolchakan and Bonarain headed to a raised area near the bow of the ship. It had all of the appearances of being the Main Bridge – from the outside. They flew inside and made two huge discoveries. One: They were not on the Main Bridge, they were in a very large tactical and strategic weapons control area. Two: They found Tashkafa, Mustooza, Vagen, Chokchakchok and Zizzikinza all working together.

"Master Officer, Xadorm, this is Soolchakan! Can you hear me?"

"This is Xadorm. What have you got to report?"

"Sir, we found...the weapons area on this ship instead of the Main Bridge. We also found Choks, Zizzys, Vagens, Tashkafa and Mustooza...all in here. No one seems to be ruling over any other. They're all working in harmony."

Chyning interrupted. "Add Iyka to that list. I found some of them in the hanger bay."

Xadorm sat there with his teeth clenched. "Tashkafa? They were the only ones who knew about our homes in the gorge! Is anyone still in the gorge? Are there any intruders in the gorge?"

"This is Officer Grade 3, Balzoth of Team 2425. We're in the gorge...still getting our spacesuits on. Did you want us to join the fight or search for Tashkafa?"

"Stop the spacesuits and look for Tashkafa...or any other strangers in the gorge," sent Xadorm. "Anyone else who already has their spacesuits on...start checking the list of dimensions that the Vagens were infesting. See if that's how they snuck up on us."

Another voice broke in. "Sir, this is Officer Grade 3, Yaminza of Team 4144. We're in the northern area of North Chilamte. Some of the intruders have landed... and are taking prisoners. Sir...all of the prisoners are being questioned…by the Mufayton. Sir…the primary question that they're asking…any knowledge of the Owlamites!'"

"Good ones for asking the questions," said Ota. "Ask the question and read their minds at the same time. Hopefully…since we've been hiding for so long…no one knows anything and all the enemy will get…is confused."

Zoolkog leaned back and snarled. "Yeah but it's just great! The only ones we haven't heard about are the Doolood and the Jowfoonda."

Ota slammed her fist down on the table. "All of them together. Why can't they leave us alone?"

"Most of them have been humiliated by us…more than once," said Iquanza. "Somehow…they all found each other and have decided to join forces to exact revenge for all of them."

"We need to get some people in those ships up there… and read as many minds as possible," said Boneech. "It's not just the attack. What are they planning…in the aftermath…if they're victorious?"

"Right now, we need to curb the attack," said Xadorm. "We can always ask questions later."

Back on the ship, Soolchakan and Bonarain parted ways. They were searching for the Main Bridge. Soolchakan called Kiyalee and Chyning to assist in the search for the Bridge. Kiyalee could always go back to sabotaging the engines and Chyning could always go pilfering after they found the Bridge. It was finally found in an unusual spot. Usually the Main Bridge was at the top of the ship somewhere near the center. This one was in the middle, just above the fighter hanger bay.

Now Soolchakan and Bonarain could see who was in charge and what the plans were. They found that there were three ship commanders – one Mustooza, one Tashkafa and one Vagen – all working together for two common goals: Take this planet and find that rotten Drey Sssorg.

Back at the bell, Xadorm looked around at who was left on the Command Staff. "What happened? Did any of the personnel on duty see any of this before the attack? How did they sneak up on us?"

"No one saw anything," said Iquanza. "They just… appeared…out of nowhere and started shooting."

"The Vagens have been able to find other dimensions," said Boneech. "Do you think it's possible…they found another one…and came in from there?"

Xadorm shook his head in disagreement. "Not possible… probable. Find a new dimension…approach and attack from there…hoping for surprise. They achieved it."

"**Sir, this is Officer Grade 3, Rafeena from Team 4901. We just found the Doolood on one of the ships. Should we make them spring a leak? There are other… non-swimming races on this ship as well**."

"If someone finds Jowfoonda, I'm gonna scream," said Iquanza. She leaned forward with her hands over her face.

"**We'll worry about leaks later**," sent Xadorm. "**Right now, what we need is information as to where these** *bimyocks* **came from**."

Bonarain broke in. "**Sir, this is Officer, Bonarain. From what I've found, they do have a new dimension… that they didn't have before. The Vagens found it. I don't know which one it is, but the flagship is in that dimension giving orders to the other ships**."

Xadorm was a little surprised. "**Why can't you find that dimension? Can't you landmark something from their minds…and determine which one it is**?"

Bonarain snarled in frustration. "**I don't understand their technology. They hop through technology while we hop through…nature. I need someone on board here…who can understand…some of their technology**."

Xadorm had to do some fast thinking. "Let's get some computer people…and maybe the physicists working on that." He looked up worried. "I hope that they're still alive."

Ota was sitting there with her eyes closed. "I found Tula."

"I've got Sankiki," said Boneech.

"I found Hrombisk," said Iquanza.

"Get all three of them here…NOW," said Xadorm. He leaned back. "**Officer, Bonarain, come to the bell. I need you to take some people, who can help you, to the enemy vessels to find that other dimension**."

"**This is Officer, Chyning. I'll come and get them.**

Bonarain needs to keep on gathering intelligence."

Soolchakan stood there stunned. 'Chyning is going to do it *for* Bonarain,' he thought. 'When did she decide to start doing something useful?'

Chyning Jumped to the space bell. She looked around confused. It was dark and smelled musty…and no one else was there.

"**When are you coming to the bell**," sent Xadorm?

"**I'm at the bell, Sir**," sent Chyning. "**I'm the only one here! Where are you**?"

Xadorm clenched his eyes and shook his head in disgust. "**The OTHER bell ship**," he thought angrily.

Chyning clenched her eyes and mouth shut. 'Oops,' she thought. She quickly Jumped to the *other* bell…with a red face and a guilty smile. "Sorry…Sirs."

Xadorm, tapping his fingers on the table and looking rather displeased, pointed to the trio that Chyning was to Jump to the enemy vessel. Chyning smiled helplessly and went to them. Hrombisk, Tula and Sankiki all got together with Chyning in a huddle and the quartet vanished.

Xadorm shook his head. "I hope the *bimyock* took them to the correct ship."

She did. After delivering the trio to the Main Bridge, she left the Bridge and headed out for her spying and thieving on the rest of the ship…still feeling somewhat embarrassed about her mistake.

Tula and Sankiki went to a console and watched as the Vagen that was working there punched in information and searched for other things.

"They've combined a few of the Mustooza, the Vagen and the Tashkafa stuff into these computers," said Sankiki.

"I can see that," said Tula. "What we need to figure out… how much of each and what do we do with it."

"Just keep reading their minds," said Hrombisk. He looked around the Bridge. "I'll be right back." He vanished.

Sankiki huffed. "Where's he gone?"

"Probably to get a little help," said Soolchakan.

A moment later Hrombisk reappeared on the Bridge with his Team. The three women looked around and then vanished.

Sankiki looked even more perturbed. "Where did they go?"

"They're each going to bring another Team of physicists," said Hrombisk as he continued looking around the Bridge.

Tula shrugged. "Good idea. I think I'll get my entire Team up here." She vanished.

Sankiki sighed…and vanished.

Soolchakan turned to Bonarain. "It's gonna get kinda crowded in this crate."

Bonarain nodded with a half-hearted smile.

In   a   very   short   time,   there   were   four

Teams of physicists on board the enemy ship. Along with the computer Teams, and with the help of Chyning, they found a maintenance terminal that was somewhat isolated. Bonarain had to perform some translations, relayed through Chyning, in order for the Owlamites to understand which words had come from which language. While the computer people found out some interesting things about the allied enemies it did not help in finding the dimension that they were coming from.

Hrombisk and the physicists gave up and Jumped back to the bell ship. He addressed the Command Staff. "Supreme Commander, we have no choice in the matter. We're going to have to search each dimension one at a time. It shouldn't take too long because we only have to check each dimension for just a few heartbeats. If we don't find anything, we just go to the next one."

Xadorm nodded. "Then stop wasting time talking about it and do it."

Hrombisk smiled and bowed slightly and all of the physicists vanished.

"I agree, that it shouldn't take too long," said Iquanza. "Team 85 checks the first four while Team 207 checks the next four and Team 435 checks the third set of four. If they get all of the physicist Teams doing that, we should know rather quickly."

"The sooner the better," said Xadorm. "Meanwhile, we need to get some of those firestorm weapons warmed up…so we can get rid of this pestilence."

Another Owlamite woman appeared on the bell ship.

"Excuse me, Sirs, but I have some troubling information," she said.

"Just what we needed," said Xadorm cynically. "Okay who are you and what is it?"

"Sir, I'm Officer Grade 7, Teeba from Computer Team 254. We found some new intelligence data on all of the allied enemy. The Chokchakchok…our spies have been watching them on seven different planets…they're currently on nineteen different planets and the ones who are involved in this mess are from six of the planets we weren't watching."

Zoolkog groaned. "Does this same information apply to all of them?"

"Yes, Sir, I'm afraid it does," said Teeba.

"Give us the numbers," sighed Xadorm. "One at a time."

"Yes, Sir," said Teeba as she looked down at her notes. "The Doolood were actually able to find another planet where the water alkaline and saline levels were suitable to them."

"That *is* amazing," said Ota. "The alkaline level that they need…would eat the skin off of anything else in existence." She shook her head. "Go ahead…continue."

"Yes, Sir. We've been watching the Iyka on three different planets…they're actually on nine. We watch the Mufayton on four planets while they're on eleven. We watch the Mustooza on three planets, they're on seven. We watch the Tashkafa on one planet… they're on six. We watch the Vagens on one planet…they're on eight different planets…in seven different dimensions. We watch the Zizzikinza on two planets…they're on twenty-two planets."

Xadorm closed his eyes and leaned back. "And all of the planets that we've been watching…are NOT the ones that these attackers came from."

"Correct, Sir," said Teeba timidly.

Boneech was staring at the wall and spoke through her teeth. "Are you gathering all of the information as to where all of the planets are…that we need to…attack?"

"Oh, yes Sir," said Teeba with a smile. "That's the primary information that Tula and Sankiki are gathering at this time."

"From what you're saying…that's eighty-four planets… that all of these *chokwads* are currently infesting," said Ota.

Teeba nodded.

"Eighty-four," repeated Xadorm. "And in all of the time that they've been planning, their populations could be enormous."

"Sankiki and Tula are looking for that information as well," said Teeba.

"Thank you for the report," said Xadorm sadly. "Go ahead and go back…and get all the information that can be…obtained."

Teeba smiled and vanished.

Xadorm turned to his three Teammates. "Teecheta, Baynabi, Kiskee…I know that everyone is…rather busy…but… go ahead and start the…full roll call. The sooner we find out… how many are lost…the sooner we can get things back under control."

The three women all nodded and vanished.

Ota sighed. "Do you think it's going to be another…high number?"

Xadorm stared down at the table. "Four of the nine in the Command Staff are gone. It will not be a low count."

Hrombisk reappeared on the bell ship. "Sirs, we found them. They're in dimension 97. We're going to check all of the rest of them just to make sure, but, that's the only new one…from the previous list of where we found Vagens."

"Is there anything that is interesting there," said Xadorm with a strained smile?

"They do have a ship…that is designed to open a portal for the other ships…to pass from one dimension to another…so that the travelers don't have to use their power for that purpose," said Hrombisk.

Boneech looked up sadly. "What will it take to get rid of that monster?"

Hrombisk smiled. "We still have the quartet of 459 cannons mounted on those two ships. All we have to do is warm one up and Jump it to that location in 97…and open fire."

Zoolkog frowned. "Don't those ships have some kind of electromagnetic shielding…that will prevent pulse beams getting through?"

"Yes, Sir, they do," said Hrombisk. "However…we found out that each shield has a frequency. If we match that frequency with our cannons…when we fire, it'll be as if their shielding doesn't exist at all."

Ota cleared her throat. "Do we have this frequency?"

Hrombisk wiggled his eyebrows with a triumphant smile. "My Teammate, Officer, Xa-Xa has obtained it and is adjusting our quartet of cannons right now."

"What is to prevent them from a counterattack," said Iquanza?

The grin on the face of Hrombisk seemed to get bigger. "Don't forget, when we were firing at the planet, we were about 120 kilotaja away *from* the planet. The combined pulse beam cut all the way *through* that planet…several thousand kilotaja deep. We're going to position our gunships some…oh…ten thousand kilotaja away from that portal ship. By the time they react to the attack and start heading for us, the damage will have been done and we can Jump out of there."

Iquanza nodded. "What happens if…one of their ships decides to be stupidly heroic and jump in the way of the beam?"

"As powerful as the beam is…it'll deplete their shielding very rapidly…if they're on a different frequency. They don't stand a chance against the combined power of four cannons." Hrombisk looked thoughtful. "If you'd like, we could position both of our cannon quartets out there…and hit that portal ship…in a very deadly crossfire."

"I like that plan better," said Xadorm. "It'll keep the enemy occupied…in two different directions…and we still destroy the portal ship." He nodded. "Set it up…as soon as possible."

Iquanza suddenly looked very worried. "How are we going to place them...so that they don't hit each other?"

Hrombisk closed his eyes and groaned. "Sir...you're thinking two dimensionally." He opened his eyes. "We have one fire from above and one fire from the side. That way, their beams do not end up being fired at each other. They will be perpendicular to each other."

Xadorm nodded. "Good point."

Boneech was a little confused. "Why are we putting so much emphasis on this one ship?"

Xadorm gave her a disgusted look. "It is major technology, it is causing us major grief and it will give them a major setback if the thing is demolished in just a few heartbeats. If they have a second one of those things...we'll find out very quickly...and demolish it as well."

Hrombisk smiled. "Xa-Xa is setting up one ship...with the proper frequency and Disdasi is setting up the second. They'll be ready before I leave the bell, Sir. Would you like to pick the Teams that fire the guns or should I?"

Xadorm sighed. "Pick the Teams you want. Just leave Team 7016 out of it because they're busy gathering intelligence on one of the ships that's part of the attack force around our planet."

Hrombisk smiled. "Yes, Sir." He vanished.

Eighteen Teams were on the two deadly ships. All nine of the physicist Teams, all five of the computer operator Teams and all four of the computer repair Teams.

The portal ship was very different from the other ships. It was only four kilotaja in length and looked like the hull of a large sailing vessel minus the mast or sails.

The portal itself looked like a large black swirling pool just sitting there in front of the portal ship.

Hrombisk was watching as a ship was heading for the portal to exit #97 and move to #1. "**I want you to open fire just as that ship enters the portal. I want to see what happens to the portal and the ship**."

Sankiki, who was on the other ship, was a little puzzled. "**What do you expect to see happen**?"

"**I don't know**," sent Hrombisk. "**It might be destroyed by being half way through the portal**."

Sankiki grunted in disgust. "**What if nothing happens**?"

"**Then we'll know…one way or the other**," sent Hrombisk calmly.

Sankiki looked at her Teammates in utter dismay. All they did was laugh. She just rolled her eyes and went back to watching the slow moving ship. "Okay, open fire on the portal ship…when that other one is half way through the portal."

Just as the moving ship reached the portal the nose of another ship was coming through from the other side. The nose of the ship on this side started disappearing through the portal.

"**NOW**," sent Hrombisk!

All eight gunners opened fire. Both super enhanced beams ripped through the portal ship mercilessly. The ship lurched violently in several different directions as the beams sawed through the ship with ease. The sparkling portal vanished while the two ships were in the middle. Now there was the bow of one ship and the stern of the other floating away from the spot that the portal had been located. Both ships had been cut in half by the sudden stop of the portal.

"**Now we know**," sent Hrombisk. "**The sudden shutoff is very destructive to anything in the middle of the portal at the time of disruption**."

"**Hooray for our side**," sent Sankiki apprehensively. "**Can we get out of here before those other attack ships arrive at our positions and start attacking us? They look rather angry**."

Hrombisk nodded as he surveyed the situation. "**All gunners, cease fire and let's hop our gunships back to dimension 45**," he sent calmly.

Both ships were hopped to #45 in order to park them where they belonged. All of the personnel on the ships were eager to review the tapes of the shredding of the portal ship. The slow motion tape would reveal all kinds of things that had occurred that they had not been able to see in real time.

They quickly set up to watch the film. All of the Team leaders were in the front rows and all of the Team members were in the back of the small auditorium on the ship. They started the film in slow motion.

Hrombisk did some narration even though no one needed to hear it. "Our gunship firing from the side from bow to stern and your gunship firing from above from stern to bow. It appears that as soon as we…damaged that large round plate on the front of the portal ship, the portal was eradicated instantly."

Officer Grade 2, Jijinina of Physicist Team 207 nodded. "It appears that we don't need to annihilate the entire ship. Just damage that plate…and we erase the entire reason for the existence of the portal ship."

"We still need to destroy the entire ship…to make sure that they have to start from scratch," said Sankiki.

Several of the Owlamites made comments of agreement.

Hrombisk continued. "Here…is where our two beams crossed and…" He got a startled look on his face. "OH…I didn't see that happen!"

"It happened too fast for us to notice in real time," said Sankiki. "In slow motion, we see…all kinds of things we didn't see before."

"Yes," said Hrombisk. "It appears that…as soon as the two beams joined…they became one beam and…blew the entire port side of the portal ship away. The debris…even in slow motion appears to be flying away very rapidly. No wonder we didn't see that debris. It…is already gone from view…even in slow motion."

Officer Grade 2, Itchami of Physicist Team 435 sniffed. "So we know that we don't have to throw the whole works of our super enhanced 459 cannons at the portal ship. What I'd like to see now…what happened to those two ships that were in the portal at the time it got erased."

"All right," said Hrombisk. "Let's get the other film in."

Xa-Xa switched to the other film. They watched as the portal vanished and both of the ships were sliced cleanly through at their mid sections.

"Just a…clean slicing," said Hrombisk. "No…jagged edges or…any kind of curved cuts, shears, tears…or anything. One clean flat slicing."

"And then the rapid decompression," said Jijinina. "Look at all of the…items flying out of the open ends of those ships."

"A lot of those…items…are personnel," said Itchami looking rather nauseous.

"*Enemy* personnel," said someone in the back.

"Yes," said Hrombisk. "Let's get these films to the Command Staff and let them know of our success and new knowledge."

"Right," said Sankiki. "We still have a war to fight against a powerful alliance."

After watching the films Xadorm sat back looking confused. "They come here as an Alliance…to attack us. They want to conquer us but…they seem to be weakened. What happened to their most powerful assets? The Tashkafa surprised us with that invisibility. The Vagens didn't *need* any special ship to open any portal. The Choks had ships that were incredibly confusing in their design." He shook his head. "Did we hurt all of them so badly that...they lost some of their best technology?"

"I don't think so," said Zoolkog. "Think about it – how many secrets did we hide from the Kalash...and all of the other allies at the Turgon Wall. Maybe each one wants to take over the entire thing...once we've been defeated. Once this star system has been secured, a complete wipeout of the other Commanders and *that* race becomes the dominating species in all of this great empire."

"That makes more sense than any of this other stuff," said Iquanza. "The Tashkafa probably have some hidden program in the computers and their armor suits ready to go...once the takeover is complete. The Vagens probably have an entire fleet of ships just waiting...in another dimension that they haven't revealed to the others. The possibilities are endless."

Ota scoffed. "And the Mufayton are just sitting there patiently reading minds waiting to make their move. They probably have all kinds of other species upper echelon set up for assassination once the command is given."

A Team suddenly appeared in the Jump in point on the bell. They came up to the Command Staff table.

The man on the Team addressed them. "Sirs, I am Officer Grade 2, Xookooz of Team 506. We've just discovered that we have a problem."

Xadorm raised his eyebrows. "*A* problem? You think that

we only have *A* problem?" He glanced around the table. "I wonder what *A* problem is that requires an interruption to this meeting."

Xookooz looked a little perturbed, however, he held his temper. "Sirs, this Alliance has come up with a strategy to stop… one of our most powerful tactics…in getting rid of pests. In the past, we would attach a hand-held bomb to the shell of the light speed engine cylinder and let it go boom. That disrupted the fuel mixture of the light speed engine and destroyed the entire ship. We decided to blow up one of the ships and…well…they have a defense against it." He stopped and sniffed. "You attach the bomb to the cylinder, activate it, count to three, hop it to Home and Jump out. Before I could Jump out…I saw four little blue beams from some kind of pulse weapon…installed in the walls…start firing and…evaporated the bomb before it could go off." He cleared his throat. "We tried it four times…and those wretched things all… reacted instantly. We even tried one that was placed…just under the floor and…they blew a hole through the floor and destroyed the bomb…instantly. By then, there were several Security personnel in there attempting to figure out what was going on."

Xadorm hung his head. "Get Hrombisk…and Sankiki and Tula on this new conundrum immediately. We can't have one of our easiest and most effective tactics taken away from us." He looked up. "Get Officer, Bonarain in here. Let's see if she can enlighten us on any other new developments that these…collective *doovofts* have come up with."

Bonarain stood at the end of the table. "They all hate the living guts of each of the others. Each one is conspiring on how to do a quick and complete surprise take over once this star system has been subdued. The Tashkafa are going to go invisible and surprise everyone, the Vagens have kept six of their known dimensions a complete secret from the others and have a fleet of twenty ships in each one. The Choks are planning on using brute force." She rolled her eyes. "The Mustooza are depending on their deities. Since the Zizzys can hide in some of the smallest places, they have several assassins who will position themselves at the first sign of ultimate victory and once the victory is achieved, they come slithering out of their slits and start killing. The Doolood have some idiotic plan of flooding the ships with water…but where they're going to come up with that much water is beyond me. The Iyka seem to think that they can turn the heat up to a boiling point inside all of the ships…which, apparently, they can survive in extreme heat and cook their enemies to death. Meanwhile the Mufayton are just sitting back, reading minds…and waiting until all of the others strike and kill each other. They're just going to hide and wait until the blood bath is over and come out and kill any upper echelon victors and take over."

"My, aren't they such nice people," said Boneech facetiously?

15

The roll call was finished. 933 more Owlamites were now dead. 232 men and 701 women. 179 Teams gone and 66 others who lost one or more. Once again the funeral pyres burned long and bright (in Spy) and ashes were once again spread over the original city of Owlam.

Xadorm now had to start by naming a new Command Staff. Of course, he, Xadorm became the new Supreme Officer. Iquanza went from Sector 1 Vice to Sector 1 Commander. Zoolkog did not change as Sector 2 Commander. Boneech went from Sector 3 Vice to Sector 3 Commander. Ota went from Sector 4 Vice to Sector 4 Commander.

Officer Leader, Yoganay, Team 74, was promoted to Senior Officer, Sector 1 Vice Commander. Officer Leader, Roobriba, Team 76, was promoted to Senior Officer, Sector 2 Vice Commander. Officer Leader, Yoobyool, Team 79, was promoted to Senior Officer, Sector 3 Vice Commander. Officer Leader, Blana, Team 84, was promoted to Senior Officer, Sector 4 Vice Commander.

Partial Teams were reassigned in order to make complete Teams. They now had 5,429 complete Teams. Less than 22,000 Owlamites from the original 28,064 remained. Anyone moving from one apartment to another, as a result of being placed on a different Team, was postponed until this war was over.

They found out from intelligence data gathered by Bonarain that there were still three of those portal ships in existence. One was on the way and would be here in five days. It was going to be given a huge defense perimeter. Of course now that the Owlamites knew that all they had to do was destroy that large front disc, they did not need to throw two 459 quartets at the ship so the disruption would not take a great deal of time or expose too many Owlamites to any danger.

Three major problems that had to be addressed. One: Get as many intruders off of the planet as possible…by any and all means possible. Two: Keep any other enemy ships from entering the star system and disable the ones that are here. Three: Figure out how to bypass that system that defended the light speed cylinder from the simple hand-held bomb attack. Once those were accomplished, they could start demolition out there on eighty-four other planets.

Another main concern on attacking other planets: Had they set up these defensive pulse guns all over their planets in order to stop any firestorm weapon from being used against them on that planet? If they lost some of the firestorm weapons in that process, this could be a very expensive campaign because they just might have to individually hop every one of the enemy into #45.

Hrombisk and the rest of the physicists started working on the problem of those pesky little defensive pulse guns. One problem was that the reaction time of a computer was so much faster than any physical creature. They could put a dozen bombs on the cylinder and the beams would destroy all of them before any of the explosives could go off. After two or three incidents, the Security personnel were in the area trying to figure out why the guardian beacons kept on going off. None of the Owlamites wanted them to see the bomb suddenly appear on the cylinder. None of the Owlamites wanted to hop the bomb in any sooner because it might go off in their hand. It was causing all kinds of grief to Owlam and all kinds of relief to the Enemy Alliance.

Officer Grade 6, Jaji of Team 4829 tried a partial hop with a pulse gun. She turned her pulse pistol on, aimed the gun at the cylinder and hopped the end of the barrel into Home. Before she could pull the trigger, the defensive beams shot the end of her barrel off, the gun went into overload and she had to hop the gun to dimension #2 and throw it away before it blew her up from catastrophic feedback.

The conclusion reached by the computer research was that these strange new defensive guns were designed to destroy anything that was not normal to the functions of the ship. Any new anomaly was to be eradicated…immediately

The different races in the Enemy Alliance were going all over the planet questioning all citizens of every indigenous race as to the location of the Owlamites. All that any of them could tell the enemy was that they thought the citizens of Owlam were extinct. No one had seen or heard of any Owlamite for centuries. This was extremely frustrating to the Mufayton because they were reading minds as they asked the questions and they found no fabrications in any of those questioned. The people they were questioning actually believed that the Owlamites were all dead and had been for over 2,000 years. They only lived on in legend.

Officer Grade 2, Izzanto of Team 122 reported to the Command Staff that while he was watching the Teltermak, they did not have to be tortured or coerced in any way as to talking about the Owlamites. The Teltermak wanted to find and enslave the Owlamites for their own different reasons. They would not tell why, they could not be coerced as to why and again the Mufayton were frustrated. This time it was because they could not read the minds of the Teltermak either. The Owlamites could only shake their heads in disbelief. What is it that makes the Teltermak skull invulnerable to mind reading?

The Enemy Alliance was originally thinking that the Teltermak wanted the Owlamites because of this wonderful new antibiotic called *Tuzine*. Once the Alliance got hold of *Tuzine* they were ecstatic about it as well, because even with all of their technology, they did not have any antibiotic that worked as well in most of their pharmaceutical inventories. The Alliance found out that the Kalash had the recipe for *Tuzine* and now it was even more confusing to the Alliance because someone other than the Owlamites had this recipe. Why did the Teltermak want to enslave a race that was now supposedly extinct…for a drug that someone else was manufacturing? Why were they completely ignoring the Kalash? Frustration and confusion reigned in these conundrums.

The Alliance knew they had been defeated by Owlamites, however, they could not figure out where the Owlamites were hiding and this made for some even greater aggravation. The Tashkafa had a few notes on the city in the gorge, however, they had not put the puzzle together and come up with the reality that the gorge city was the home of the hunted Owlamites. The gorge was being ignored because they could not find any life signs there at all.

The Alliance knew that the Owlamites did still exist because there were numerous Alliance citizens that were just disappearing into thin air. This was a tactic that was documented in the archives of all of the Alliance races and the Owlamites were the only ones who had manifested the capability of this irritating and mysterious tactic. In reading the minds of other races, no one else knew about the baffling disappearances of anyone…except the sudden annihilation of a fabled city, long ago, called Algothon.

None of the Alliance ships were blowing up in space any more, however, there did seem to be wholesale sabotage of all the weapons that the Alliance was attempting to use against any and all of the races of Hardooth which just led to more annoyance on the part of the Alliance strategists because no amount of torture had given them a clue as to why their citizens were vanishing without a trace and why the sabotage continued.

The Owlamites, for the present time, had to be happy with just sabotaging weapons and shuttlecraft. While they could not add an explosive to blow a ship up, they could remove vital parts without those pesky guardian beams shooting their hands off. The guardian beams were designed to keep someone from adding a device – not subtracting.

In order to torture information out of the Heyyah and all other races, the only thing left for the Alliance was brute force. However, once the citizens realized that these strange enemy forces no longer seemed to have any of their strange weaponry, even the big powerful Chokchakchok could be overwhelmed by the sheer force of superior numbers and the Alliance started losing ground, and personnel, all over the planet.

The Alliance personnel had to withdraw to their orbiting ships in order to discuss tactics and strategy, however, for the most part, all they could do was argue and grudgingly reiterate the strange disappearances.

The Owlamites had withdrawn to live in some of the spaceships they had clustered in #45…temporarily. All of them were still serviceable and had sufficient living quarters for all Owlamites to live between raids on the enemy personnel and equipment. They had to live in these ships until they could completely get rid of the enemy.

The Owlamites were suffering their own frustrating lack of tactics because of those guardian guns that kept foreign objects away from critical devices. The physicists came up with several possibilities, however, each one met the same miserable fate.

The computer repair and programing personnel came up with four different programs they thought they could enter into the Alliance computers. For some reason the computers did not accept the new programs at all. That plan was scrapped quickly.

The second portal ship had arrived and had been destroyed by one quick burst from one of the 459 quartet ships. The Alliance was a little worried about bringing either of the other two portal ships anywhere near this star system. It was finally decided to place both of them in a classified location and bring the Alliance attack ships through there and let them fly in this system on their own. As was the usual, classified data did not remain secret for a very long time from any snooping Owlamite. All it took was one fighter with a 459 mounted on it to destroy the portal creating capability of the portal ships.

One big problem for the Alliance was that all of their shuttles were suddenly incapable of handling their missions. There were all kinds of parts that were suddenly missing and they could not find any spare parts in their cargo or storage bays. They could not cannibalize from other shuttles because they were all missing the exact same parts. Before those parts could be replicated in the work areas and brought to the hangar to be installed, they were disappearing as well.

Every gain that the Alliance had obtained was lost and they could not understand why – other than the fact that the elusive Owlamites were even craftier than had been expected and were behind all of the sabotage. Problem: The Alliance was not really sure what the Owlamites looked like. They could have been torturing Owlamites to try to find out where the Owlamites were hiding and did not even know it. Yes, all of these races had names, however, some of them were a little, or even a lot, xenophobic and the Alliance personnel could not figure out truthfully who was what. There the situation where three Mustooza had been personally in contact with the Owlamites, however, the descriptions given by those three was too generic and therefore mainly useless.

The best information the Alliance received on the Owlamites

came from the T'Mor. Unfortunately it did not give them much more other than the fact that the ancestors of the current T'Mor had been rescued from certain death by the Owlamites. While the T'Mor looked upon the Owlamites, almost, with reverence, they still could not accurately physically describe what the true appearance of the elusive race was.

It was an agonizing stalemate. The Owlamites were stuck on captured ships in #45 and the Alliance was stuck on their 152 ships surrounding Hardooth with no major weaponry and no working shuttlecraft. People on the spacecraft were trapped on the spacecraft. People on the planet were stuck on the planet. This went on for twenty-seven days.

Then one of the Alliance ships blew up. The blast disabled or destroyed seven other adjacent Alliance ships. The Alliance Command was screaming for any information as to how this had happened. The Owlamite Command Staff was sitting in anticipation of getting some information as well.

Soolchakan walked into the Command Staff conference room with a big smile on his face. "Sirs, we've been going about it in the wrong way. I tried a new method…and as you can see, I blew up one of the enemy ships."

The rest of Team 7016 followed him in, all looking a little puzzled.

Xadorm stood up, staring wide-eyed at Soolchakan. "Officer, Soolchakan…if what you're saying is true, you have our undivided attention…for as long as you want it." He looked around the room. "And no one is going to even try to interrupt until he's finished." Xadorm sat down. "Officer, Soolchakan, you have the floor!"

Soolchakan looked very proud of himself. He clasped his hands together in front of his stomach. "As I said, we were going about it in a completely wrong way. We were trying to hide our explosives from the guardian guns. Instead of doing that…I just climbed up there, hopped the barrels of those defensive guns into Ghost dimension…placed the bomb and set it in the normal way. The guns fired their beams *but*…the barrel and the beam…both in Ghost. The beams didn't touch the bomb and it went off…and the ship went off."

Xadorm leaned forward and banged his head on the table… hard…once. He sat back up. "All this time, we've been thinking… of some complicated way to bypass those…exasperating little headaches and…all this time…the solution was…*so* simple." He shook his head. "Zoolkog…send the message out…to all Owlamites. Tell them this *simple*…method of fooling the guardian guns. Let's blow up some Alliance ships and then…start targeting any planet that any of them are infesting."

Zoolkog smiled. "Yes, Sir." He leaned back and sent out a general mental broadcast to all Owlamites.

In no time at all, most of the enemy vessels had blown up. Only fourteen remained and they were running for their lives…at flank speed.

After Soolchakan and his Team departed, Boneech looked a little disgusted. "Team 7016 did it again."

"Yes, they did," said Xadorm. "Do we have any of our

people on those fourteen surviving ships?"

"Absolutely," said Ota with a big smile!

Roobriba looked at her copy of the report. "Since we blew up *all* of the ships with Mufayton on them…do you think that they'll return?"

"I hope they don't," said Xadorm. "If they do then we'll just have to solve that problem when it arrives." He grunted. "Those people make it very difficult for us."

Boneech huffed. "Are we really going to let any of them get away?"

"As soon as we find their home bases…other than the planets where we know they're living, we destroy them completely," said Xadorm. "I'm tired of guessing. I don't want any of them to ever come back."

"Plus…we still have to make sure of where each one of those eighty-four planets…where each one of our enemies is located," said Yoobyool.

"We want to destroy our enemies and not the people who were on those planets originally," said Xadorm. "I don't like killing victims."

"I'm confused," said Yoganay. "Ever since we made peace on our planet…with other factions…we've been plagued by outworlders. Why…didn't these people attack us…before that Algothon attack? Where were they then?"

"They were always there," said Zoolkog. "The difference is peace and war. When we were at war with each other, if some outworlder had come in here to try to conquer, they would've come across several hundred established and organized factions who were well armed with technological weapons and full of highly experienced fighting forces. They would've been faced with battling each and every faction that was armed and ready for any struggle with conventional or technical weapons. Now... we haven't really had any major war...between two of our indigenous factions...for centuries...except for the Teltermak. The outworlders now think that there is no one who can stand up to them."

"Until we start kicking the *piddleeyanks* out of them," said Ota with a big smile.

"And they still don't know who did it," scoffed Blana.

"They *know* who did it," said Xadorm. "They just haven't figured out a way to find or stop us."

"But the Tashkafa did find us," said Iquanza. "They found our city in the gorge. They were clanking around in there, killing some of our people and...yet they didn't show up there this time."

"They're still keeping secrets from others in the Alliance," said Blana. "Each one of them wants to be the ultimate ruler, once they've conquered this planet. They still feel they need all of the others in order to accomplish that mission. Maybe...they're all trying to sacrifice the others in order to do it and they feel that once they've weakened all of the others *and* taken us...then they strike."

Ota scoffed. "That would be an incredible blood bath."

"Let's just make sure that we get them first," said Xadorm.

Much to the disappointment of the Owlamites, the fourteen ships they allowed to escape, went to only two different planets. Eight to one planet and six to the other. Both of the planets were recognized by the Owlamites. Seeing as how the home planets of the Mustooza and the Vagens had been destroyed, these planets had to be conquests.

The first planet was inhabited by a race that Owlam was somewhat unfamiliar with. This race also seemed to be treated as nothing but slaves. The primary "foreign" race appeared to be the Choks. This was one of the seven planets infested by the Choks that Owlam had been originally aware of. Since it was mainly a Chok planet, they knew that they were still in dimension #1.

The other planet was one of the known Zizzikinza planets.

The Owlamites now had to start a campaign of watching the Alliance and see if they contacted any of the planets – of unknown locations – and give away all of their secrets. The only tactic they had on each of these two planets was to start throwing any Alliance personnel into #45 while leaving the original races alone. The hope was that the Alliance would retreat from these planets and go to some other planet for some kind of reinforcements.

Another little bit of information the Owlamites discovered was that Bonarain had been somewhat in error with the information she had obtained. The Vagens did have 120 ships hidden in other dimensions, however, they were not sitting at the back door of Hardooth in those other dimensions. Their locations, in the other dimensions, was classified information. The only ones who knew the precise locations of these task forces were the Vagens…and the Mufaytons. Now the Owlamites were attempting to obtain this information as well.

The disappearances on the two planets started taking their toll. The Chok planet was about to be abandoned because the indigenous species caught wind of the fact that their masters were losing people all over the place and the slaves were fighting back, thus diminishing the capability of fixing all of the problems with the eight ships currently orbiting that planet.

The Zizzikinza planet was a different story. The Zizzys still had numerous underground communities established all over the planet. When it was decided that the six ships would depart to another planet, the Zizzys simply crawled back to their subterranean lairs. The only way that the Owlamites could follow the Zizzys was to stay in Observation and follow them down their horribly narrow winding paths. This was extremely time consuming, mapping out where they were living, so Xadorm kept minimal manpower on that planet and had most of the personnel follow the fleet as it departed.

The Owlamites realized that this could be a very long campaign. It was unfortunately necessary because, again, their very existence was at stake. All of the members of the Alliance, just like the Teltermak, wanted the Owlamites alive. The Alliance wanted them in order to find out how they had been able to elude all kinds of technological scanning. Those wretched Teltermaks wanted the Owlamites for…what?

Boneech sat at the conference table looking very aggravated. "Why don't we just eradicate those *chokwad* Teltermak? Why do we allow them to live at all?"

Xadorm gave her an equally angry glare. "Because we still don't have any clue as to why they want us alive. They slaughtered several races…just to eliminate any competition. The also tried to have other races capture us alive…why? We have all been irritated over trying to obtain the answer to that question for over three and a half millennium. As long as we can keep them contained on Satroco Isle, we allow them to live…until we get the answer to that nagging question." He cleared his throat. "Can we please get back to things that we can take care of now?"

Boneech leaned back. "Yes, Sir. Sorry, Sir."

"What have we got on that Chok planet," said Xadorm?

"We've disrupted things very badly there," said Ota. "We…removed…enough of the Alliance personnel and the planet originals are fighting back for their homeland…very harshly. The eight ships are getting ready to depart that star system and go to… friendlier skies."

Xadorm nodded. "And the gang of six?"

"They've already left that Zizzy star system," said Yoganay. "The Zizzys that were left behind…to attempt to reconquer and rebuild…we're harassing them every decitaja of the way. It's possible that we can eliminate all of the Zizzys that are there… within a few months."

Xadorm sighed. "Elimination of the Zizzys on that planet

is fine. Finding the exact location of all of the strongholds of the Alliance is more important." He clenched his teeth. "Leave minimal personnel on that Zizzy planet…to eradicate the… invaders. Keep most of our attention on the ships and where they go." He frowned. "Why are we having such a hard time finding all of the planets where they are all located?"

"Same reason as always," said Ota with a shrug. "We always let them lead us there and then…we landmark a spot…and lead other Owlamites to that landmark. We don't know how they find those places."

Xadorm groaned, closed his eyes and shook his head. "They find them through navigation." He looked up. "Hasn't anyone…here…ever tried to…navigate anywhere?"

All of the Staff shook their heads.

Xadorm looked up at the ceiling. "In over 3,500 years, none of our people have learned how to navigate?" He looked back down and glared at the Staff.

"We *JUMP*," said Zoolkog! "Why should we learn how to navigate?"

Xadorm leaned forward. "We are going to learn," he said in a sinister manner. "I'm tired of having to wait for them to lead us. We're going to take the fight to them…by finding them first."

"How are we supposed to learn how to navigate…when we don't even know where a navigation school is," said Yoobyool impatiently?

"And who do we decide to send to this school, once we've

found it," said Blana?

"How did some of our people learn certain specialties before," said Xadorm?

"Usually by being commanded to learn, by the *Voice of Power*, whether they wanted to learn or not," said Iquanza. "The only ones that were commanded to do something because of aptitude were the physicists. All others were just…commanded to do it…by whoever the *Voice of Power* was at the time."

Xadorm sighed. "So the physicists had the aptitude…they just didn't have the intestinal fortitude to…apply themselves and learn…until they got a swift kick in the cerebellum…by the *Voice of Power*."

"That sums it up pretty good," said Boneech.

"Then it is about time I started kicking," said Xadorm. "I was pretty confident that what you've said is the correct procedure…now I have some confirmation."

"So…who do we start with…as far as this education," said Yoganay?

Xadorm leaned back doing some soul searching and pondering over that question. He looked around at all of the apprehensive faces at the conference table and sniffed. "We have to start somewhere…don't we?"

"Maybe we can start it with a request," said Iquanza. "Someone who volunteers will always do a better job than someone who has been ordered to do it."

"I know," said Xadorm. "But…I have to start somewhere."

Team 7016 all looked at the computer screen in a rather glum manner. They all saw the "request" that was sent to them – as a Team.

Chyning glared at Bonarain. "I hate you," she said flatly.

Bonarain smiled. "At least that is something where Kiyalee won't be handling a weapon."

Kiyalee looked back affronted. "I hate you."

Bonarain huffed. "Come on! We're still the bottom of the barrel. You knew that they'd do this to US."

"I hate you," said Soolchakan. He walked away snarling. "Let's take that shuttlecraft with us."

"Why should we do that," said Chyning?

Soolchakan looked back. "Because we can put more kwatha on the shuttlecraft than we can on all four fighters."

"Good point," said Kiyalee. She glared back at Bonarain. "You get to pack the food on the shuttle." She walked away scratching her derriere.

Bonarain went limp in her chair. "I don't even know… where to start…looking for a…navigational school."

"Where *ever* the enemy is. They have to have someone who can navigate," said Soolchakan. "Let's load up a shuttlecraft…a couple of fighters…and…Jump."

Bonarain looked up confused. "Where?"

"Wherever the *bimyocks* are," he said with a shrug.

Bonarain got up from her seat. "It'll keep us out of the fighting for a while…I guess."

"I'd rather fight," said Chyning. "It gives me a little satisfaction…causing the enemy no end to grief."

"You get a great deal of satisfaction from stealing them blind," said Kiyalee.

Chyning stuck her tongue out at Kiyalee. "I know you're right…but I still like destroying their plans. If we're in some class…I won't see any of that destruction…for quite a while."

"You can still steal from them," said Bonarain.

Chyning huffed. "And do what with it? That shuttlecraft doesn't hold that much."

Soolchakan chuckled disdainfully. "Once we're at the school…you can landmark it and…between class sessions, you can always Jump from there to here…and back, carrying all kinds of goodies when you do Jump."

Chyning got a big bright grin on her face. "You're right! This might be…just a little bit more fun, and profitable, than I originally thought."

Soolchakan smiled back. "Then help pack the kwatha on the shuttle."

Bonarain sighed as she got up to start packing. "Which one do we start with?"

"The one that's in charge," said Soolchakan. "The Mustooza seem to be the dominant ones who are using all of the others to aid in their quest for total domination. I guess we start with them."

Kiyalee looked at the other three. "Who starts learning in the classes?"

"You and Bonarain," said Soolchakan.

Now Kiyalee looked a little miffed. "What are you two going to be doing?"

He smiled. "Watching for Mufayton."

Kiyalee pursed her lips as she thought about the last statement. "Sounds good."

The four of them went to their rooms thinking of what they might take with them in the search for the navigation school.

After almost two months of searching for a planet, Soolchakan got the idea of finding a Mustooza ship. There had to be at least one navigator on that ship. That person had to have been taught somewhere. All they would need to do was search the memory of that individual, find out if there was any form of keepsake from the school and use that as a landmark. It worked.

Four days later they were at a college where the Mustooza were learning to be crewmembers and warriors on spaceships. Administration, supply, security, engine maintenance, hull maintenance, facilities maintenance, food preparation, weapons, tactics, strategy, medical, astronomy…and navigation.

Soolchakan decided to be the lone lookout for any Mufayton

while the three women took the classes on outer space navigation using the stars, nebulas, space clouds and certain anomalous items that had been spotted but not fully explored or studied yet.

Chyning was baffled by most of what was being said because she did not do very much studying in the books. She was more interested in looking around for anything that she could "obtain" for some of her collections back home. After failing the course miserably, she was informed by Soolchakan that she was going to take the course again – with him – while Bonarain and Kiyalee watched out for the Mufayton. She grudgingly applied herself in the next class and this time came out with a moderate understanding of navigation among the stars.

Two years had gone by since Xadorm took over. Team 7016 was one of 48 Teams that had attended a navigation school. The Owlamites were ready to take the offensive. All they had to do now was figure out which of those trillions of stars, in 19 different dimensions, had a planet orbiting it that had an enemy force inhabiting that planet. Since they could Jump to the different stars, now that they knew how to map them, they saved immensely on power usage on their attack ships. They figured that the search was still going to take some time to accomplish.

Soolchakan and Bonarain did not have much trouble navigating one of the big Jowfoonda ships that had been taken out of #45. Using some of the information they had obtained during down times from the class they started looking for the enemy. They quickly found, landmarked and mapped, all nine of the planets that had an Iyka population on them. They reported their findings back to Ota, their Sector Commander.

Now they had the unenviable position of forcing Chyning to use her knowledge (what little there was) of navigation to attempt to find any planet that was inhabited by any of the other Alliance enemies. It did not go well. She still did not apply herself as a navigator.

Ota reported the findings of the Iyka planets to the Command Staff.

Xadorm looked at the report and shook his head. "Why do we even bother sending anyone else out there? Team 7016 found all 9 of the Iyka planets and…only five other planets have been found and mapped by 47 other Teams. How do they do it?"

"They do have some talents," said Ota. "I just wish I could get others motivated in the same way that they are."

Boneech looked at the report. "Why don't we put them on the task of finding the Zizzikinza planets? There's supposed to be 22 of them and we only know the location of 4 of them."

"We only know the location of three…navigationally speaking," said Zoolkog. "One of the planets we can Jump to but…as far as navigating a ship to that planet…we don't have a clue to that information."

"I think that it's best to just leave them alone and let them find the stuff on their own," said Iquanza. "If we tell them to do something…well…they just do better if they're left alone…I think."

"We'll give it a few more months before we do any

commanding," said Xadorm. "Let's see what they find. Right now, we have to concentrate on any attacks coming our way. Those *doovoft* Mustooza are listening to the Priests and those vindictive *bimyocks* are saying that their gods are angry at *us* for defiling and destroying temples and clergy."

"Tough," snarled Yoobyool!

"You'd think that by now, they've learned that those gods have no power over us," said Boneech. "What keeps them coming after us…using those gods?"

Zoolkog grunted. "Because the higher ups, who keep on sending all of the lower level ones, keep on telling *them* that they're failing because their faith is weak. All they need to do is apply themselves more to their faith and the results will be more positive in their favor."

"What we're getting from a lot of our spies is that the other races are all getting a little tired of the Mustooza deities," said Ota. "They had their own faith and the Mustooza are not allowing any defilement of their pantheon of gods. They do seem to have the upper hand, however there is a lot of divine dissention among their…*allies*."

"Maybe we can keep using that to our advantage," said Xadorm. "Keep them all off balance and…other than the continued sabotage of their ships, we can make them fight amongst each other."

"They're already doing that," said Iquanza. "Trouble is… it's only in the planning stages in their minds."

Team 7016 continued on their way, mapping the stars. They had to do considerable hopping around the different dimensions, however, they finally mapped out the seven planets inhabited by the Mustooza. These seven planets did not have any of the other members of the Alliance living or working on them.

The Mustooza were content in controlling the seven planets they had taken over, up to and including sacrificing the young of the indigenous sentient creatures to their gods.

Team 7016 interrupted one of those ceremonies by dissecting all of the attending clergy with a 459 cannon. After several bursts with the cannon, all of the Mustooza clergy were in bits and pieces while no one else had been injured. The parents of the children that had been tied down on the altars went to rescue their children. Any Mustooza guards who tried to stop those parents were drilled with pulse pistols. Soon enough all of the Mustooza were running from the temple…as fast as they could on their short stubby legs, in fear of *their* existence.

After 7016 reported back to the Command Staff on their shenanigan, the Command Staff gave all Teams permission to do the same thing any time they came across the vulgar ritual of sacrificing the children of any sentient race to any deity. The Mustooza attempted to continue the unholy horror underground. The Mustooza clergy were becoming an even smaller population than they had been before. Many other Mustooza were losing their faith in the pantheon of gods when they noticed that the other races of the Alliance were not getting slaughtered while practicing their rituals. Even the High Priests were beginning to lose their faith in the Mustooza deities.

After Team 7016 mapped out the exact locations of all seven of the Mustooza planets, there were 2,000 Owlamite Teams that were sent to the planets, one at a time, and soon the Mustooza population was decreased dramatically.

After another two years, the Mustooza were reduced in their power among the leaders of the Alliance and now the Vagens and Tashkafa took over…without any counsel from the Mustooza… especially where religious faith was concerned.

While the Mustooza were licking their wounds, the other races in the Alliance tried to keep their focus on finding those Owlamite headaches. The Tashkafa and the Vagens were quickly losing faith in the Mufaytons because all of the reports coming back said that the Owlamites were extinct. No one, on Hardooth, knew where they were. All the stories came back that said that Owlam was no longer there. The Alliance knew better, however, the only proof that they had was that their citizens, and a lot of their spaceships, kept disappearing without a trace.

Xadorm decided to put the priority on finding all of the Mufayton hideouts. The Tashkafa and Vagen people could wait. They Mufayton people could read minds and that made them the most dangerous…just as dangerous as the Owlamites. There could only be one mind-reading race in the cosmos, as far as he was concerned, so the Teams that were the most successful at finding hideouts were ordered to stop looking for the other races and concentrate on the Mufayton.

Fifteen other planets, inhabited by different Alliance races, had been found while only two had been mapped.

Six of the Mufayton planets had been found, however only two were mapped. Eight Teams (including 7016) were given the task of finding and mapping all of the eleven planets that the Mufayton were dominant on. There were Mufayton on many of the Alliance planets, however, Xadorm wanted the Mufayton to start becoming an even smaller, if not extinct, race.

Once a planet was found and mapped, Bonarain had figured out a way to find the Mufayton mentally. Once this system of tracking was spread through several other Owlam Teams, it only took three years and the Owlamites were rather certain that the Mufayton were now added to the list of extinct.

Xadorm looked at his report. "We finally have all of the Vagen planets located and mapped. We also have the locations of their…six secret task forces…that are patiently waiting to swoop in and take over."

Zoolkog smiled. "Are you saying that it is time to start doing to the Vagens…what we already did to the Mufayton?"

Xadorm nodded. "It appears that we're still going to keep the Mustooza on hold until we eradicate someone that's more important."

Blana scoffed. "You'd think that…with all of their setbacks, some of those people in that Alliance would have learned by now. We keep hurting them and making them weaker, but they keep on coming."

"And they still haven't found *us*," said Roobriba.

Iquanza shook her head with a big smile. "Those task forces are waiting to find out what our location is...before coming in and trying to take us out...or enslave us." She leaned forward with a bigger grin. "When are you going to give the word to... make all 120 of those ships disappear?"

Xadorm hung his head. He sat there silently contemplating for a few moments. He looked up. "Get ten Teams on each ship... knock out all communications...remove the vermin inside...and park all 120 ships in dimension #45."

This task did not take long, due to the amount of practice that the Owlamites had at purloining ships and making enemy personnel vanish. All went very well because the task forces were supposed to maintain radio silence.

The Vagens were completely unaware of the mass theft for over a month. They did not find out until a resupply ship arrived at one of the rendezvous points and found nothing. The supply ship sent the message that they could not find anything. The Vagen High Command started a search for all 120 ships and found that their backup plan was mysteriously absent.

The Vagens now became suspicious of everyone. They had found that all of the Mufayton were missing and now their ships were missing. Were the Mufaytons behind the disappearance of their ships or...was it someone else in the Alliance...or was it those super crafty Owlamites? They had a lot of questions but few provable answers.

The Choks noticed that the Mufayton were all missing and that the Vagens were now having some secret meetings. The Choks started having a few secret meetings of their own.

The Doolood noticed that they were being left out of some meetings, so they started having a few secret meetings of their own.

The Iyka noticed that they were being left out of some meetings, so they started having a few secret meetings of their own.

The Zizzikinza noticed that they were being left out of some meetings, so they started having a few secret meetings of their own.

The Mustooza noticed that no one was paying very much attention to their pantheon of deities any more, no matter how hard the clergy (what was left of them) pushed the issue. The Mustooza started having a few secret meetings of their own.

The Tashkafa noticed that they were being left out of some meetings, so they started having a few secret meetings of their own.

Iquanza looked up from her report. "It appears that all of our efforts are bearing all kinds of fruits of suspicion among that Alliance."

Yoobyool sat there snickering. "What a shame?"

"They're all turning on each other," said Xadorm. "I still wish that we could figure out all of the possibilities and tricks…in regards to the Tashkafa."

So far, the Tashkafa had been the most elusive. Of the six planets they had privatized, the Owlamites had found only five. Only two of those planets were mapped out. The sixth planet was still a mystery as to location or purpose. For some reason they were very adept at keeping that planet secret.

16

Xadorm sat there looking rather sullen. "I want…Team 7016 on the task. Find that last Tashkafa planet…and map all six of their planets. Everyone else is found and mapped. While…7016 is looking for that last planet…let's start feeding the other members of the Alliance all of the *h'oolyach* that we can muster."

Ota chuckled nervously. "I finally found out why…Team 7016 has been so successful in…mapping…while others are not."

Xadorm looked up. "And?"

"All of the others, who were mapping, were looking for enemy strongholds and then mapping just that." Ota flushed a little. "Team 7016…found a star…and they mapped it…using the process of elimination to mark that star or star system as… currently devoid of any of the Alliance personnel."

Xadorm sighed. "How quaint? They've mapped all kinds of other systems and now we know a lot more about the universe… several of them, than what we knew before. Get that information out to all of our…mappers. Use that process of elimination and we just may get a little further than we expected."

Zoolkog nodded slightly. "Map everything…that way we know all of it and not just a smidgeon. That does sound a lot more promising…for future endeavors."

Xadorm nodded in agreement. "Do we have anything else on the Alliance?"

"Yes, Sir," said Iquanza. "It seems that some of the discord is coming out. The Doolood struck early. Their plan was to flood the spacecraft with water. We had no idea where they were going to get that much water…however…we now know…what they had in mind…because they took three ships…in a rather revolting manner."

Xadorm frowned. "Revolting or not…what happened?"

Iquanza looked as if she were fighting off nausea. "They… mixed…the potable water with…the sewage. They then released this…throughout the ship. They turned off any filters that were in the ship that would…filter and cleanse that water in any way. Now…all other personnel on those ships…who are not Doolood… are having some severe problems with the smell, dehydration, as well as starvation and filth diseases associated with raw sewage. There is absolutely no clean water for them to…bathe…wash their hands before eating…or drink. They can't eat until they can get to someplace where they can clean the ship out and…the Doolood are preventing that very act from occurring."

Xadorm now looked as if he might lose his lunch.

Yoganay was the first to find her voice. "Have the… Mustooza and Vagens heard about this…mutiny?"

"So far, there isn't any reaction from the Mustooza, Vagens or Tashkafa." Iquanza shrugged. "According to our contact on the first ship that this happened…Officer Grade 3, Chasta of Team 3674…only the Doolood are able to send or receive messages from those ships."

"Then I have a different report," said Boneech.

Xadorm gave her a side look. "About what?"

"Almost the same thing…except it involves the Choks instead of the Doolood," said Boneech with a smile. She turned to Iquanza. "This one might not be…quite so disgusting – brutal but not disgusting."

Xadorm leaned forward looking a little upset. "WHAT?"

Boneech was a little taken aback. "According to Officer Grade 3, Nixa of Team 3898, the Choks have taken over two ships…by force. They brutally pounded everyone else on the ships into submission. They also have complete control of all communications from those ships."

Roobriba scoffed. "With the Mufayton out of the way… none of them fear having their minds being read…without their permission. The discord is becoming infectious."

"Which could be very helpful for us," said Xadorm as he leaned back. He licked his lips. "Let's try to…leak the information about the mutinous acts…to the Vagens, Tashkafa… and Mustooza."

Boneech smirked at the thought. She cocked her head. "Just how leaky do you want us to become?"

Xadorm looked thoughtful. "Might as well leak it to the Iyka and Zizzikinza as well." He grinned. "The more problems that we can cause them…the better for us."

Yoobyool was now grinning as well. "So we burst every dam that we can find. Open every floodgate…and lock them in the wide open position."

"We still don't have that last Tashkafa planet located," said Ota. "How much time are we going to allow 7016 to look for it… alone?"

"We're going to have our hands full…informing all of the Alliance personnel," said Xadorm. "Since we're only missing one planet…I think we can spare one Team to continue the search… no matter how long it takes. Possibly they'll give something away during the leaks. Then maybe we'll just find out by accident."

Five months later, Team 7016 was sitting in the spaceship they had been allowed to utilize for their search performing their explorations.

During their explorations, they had discovered fourteen star systems that had inhabitable planets with sentient creatures on the planet. There had been no sign of any of the Alliance interference so those planets were recorded and left to live their lives unhindered. They were all curious as to why these systems had been left alone by the Alliance, however, the only thing they could come up with was that none of the Alliance knew of them - yet. This seemed odd because of all of the thousands of years of exploration, these were still not conquered. The only other reason was that the Alliance was too busy trying to tame the Owlamites before they could perform any more conquering. They did not have time to dwell on the subject.

Kiyalee had learned more about the ship than she had ever cared to know, in keeping up with the preventive maintenance. No matter which system it was, she was able to keep it running. Since the ship was rather large, they decided to temporarily shut down certain areas so the maintenance would not overwhelm her. She kept a bedroom – with a bathtub – working for each of the Team. That was probably her most important task. Or was it the light speed engine? Or was it the arboretum…where they were growing fresh kwatha? They even had a large aquarium for their favorite fish dishes. She was usually very busy.

Bonarain was learning more about the ship functions as well. She could scan all kinds of anomalies at great distances because of the sensors on the ship. Unlike the small fighters, they did not have to be in close proximity to scan something. She also found out that the light speed engines, in this ship, had seven different speeds and each one seemed more incredible than the last one she looked at. It was mind-boggling trying to figure out, in terms that others could understand, exactly how fast they were going.

Chyning, for the most part, was bored to tears. There was just nothing on this ship to steal, anymore. She would work with Kiyalee on some of the maintenance functions just to have something to do. She would also work with Bonarain on figuring out all of the functions of all of the strange devices on the Main Bridge, just to have something to do. She also did a lot of the cultivating of plants in the arboretum, just to have something to do.

Soolchakan was reading through some of the logs that had

been kept by the previous inhabitants of the ship…when he was not assisting Bonarain or Kiyalee. The day to day life of each of the Vagens, that had written the logs, was very boring. He found that the two slave groups did not keep any logs other than keeping track of how this one wanted her feet massaged and this one did not like the bath water to be too hot or cold. The three ruling class groups were all about personal gain and power. He was beginning to hate the Vagens even more each time he read some of the logs because each one seemed to be the same boring rhetoric about personal desire for massive gains with minimal effort by taking from the other two leader factions. He got so bored with reading some of them that he actually fell asleep during the process of reading one of them.

"Soolchakan! WHERE ARE YOU…you *doovoft*?"

He woke up with a start. Bonarain was mentally calling him…for some reason and it sounded urgent.

"I was resting! What's your problem?"

"We just happened to find a stray Tashkafa ship… and it is going somewhere…in a big hurry. We're trying to keep up with it. For the most part, all we can do though…is follow the trail."

Soolchakan was bewildered. 'Trail,' he thought? 'In space? How does a spacecraft leave a…trail?' He decided that he needed to get to the Bridge and learn a few of the little things that Bonarain had so diligently been teaching herself. He made the Jump. "What are we following…and how?"

Bonarain pointed up to the main view screen. "That

Tashkafa ship there. We've been following it for quite a while… and…it's not going anywhere close to a trajectory that would take it near the other five planets. Maybe it'll lead us to that last planet."

He cleared his throat and sat down. "All I see…is a bright dot…in the center of the screen. Where's the ship?"

Bonarain looked at him angrily. "That dot! That's the ship!"

Soolchakan frowned. "It's got…quite a lead on us."

"That's why we're following it with the sensors," said Bonarain. "We're following the trail it leaves behind."

Soolchakan put his fingers to his forehead trying to grasp the concept. "How does…a spaceship…leave a trail…of any kind in a void?"

Chyning grunted in disgust. "It leaves some kind of energized particle in the wake as it moves along. We can follow that trail of particles."

Soolchakan was a little surprised that Chyning had responded to the question, until he realized that Bonarain was doing some mental communications with Kiyalee in the engine room. Apparently the engines had not been given this kind of test for quite some time and they required a great deal of attention while being pushed to their limits. He was feeling a little stupid, in that Chyning knew more about the ship then he did.

He shook his head. "If we're in Observation…how can we follow this…energy trail…in Home?"

Chyning gave him a dirty look. "The sensor is in Home!"

He grimaced at the stupid question. Of course the sensor would be in Home. Why not? He was the one who had come up with the tethered sensors in the different dimensions and it had worked rather well…for a while.

Chyning looked down at her console. "Oh…*H'OOLYACH*! It disappeared completely."

Bonarain opened her eyes and looked at the screen in shock. "It must have…gone to another dimension."

"But it's the Vagens that have that technology," said Chyning angrily. "How could these mongrels have it as well?"

"Espionage," said Soolchakan. "They haven't been sleeping. They somehow obtained it…through espionage or… theft. Now they use it for their benefit."

"All right," said Bonarain. "Let's get up to where it hopped and…we'll stop there and check the other dimensions for the trail."

"Slowing down," said Chyning. "We don't wanna overshoot the location."

"Right," said Bonarain.

Soolchakan was now feeling a little silly. He had been reading all of those logs when maybe he should have been doing a little reading on how to run the ship. He decided he had better watch and learn while the women performed the tasks and get a better feel for the ship.

Bonarain left the command seat and took a chair next to Chyning. "We need to make sure that they didn't deviate before they disappeared."

Chyning shook her head. "I've already checked for any yaw, pitch or roll. I didn't find any...yet."

Soolchakan raised his eyebrows. 'Pitch...yaw... roll? Huh?' He discreetly moved to a console and checked the dictionary to figure out what they were talking about. He was definitely going to have to pay closer attention to the ship itself if he was going to familiarize himself with this strange new jargon. He found he had forgotten a lot of information about the ship and navigation.

"Okay," said Chyning. "We're at dead stop. The trail ends about 25 taja ahead of us." She shook her head. "A complete end of the trail. I can't believe that they went to another dimension... at that speed."

"Believe it," said Bonarain. "They just did it...right in front of us."

"I've got the list here," said Chyning. "Let's hop to 13."

They hopped the ship and found no trail. Next was dimension #19 – no trail. #22 – no trail. #51 – no trail. #53 – no trail. #73 – no trail. #79 – no trail. #85, #94, #97, #99, #128, #136, #145, #156, #160, #184, #202, #205 – no trail.

Bonarain was looking mystified and horrified. "But... that's all 20 dimensions on the list. How...?" She flopped back in her seat. "They couldn't possibly make their trail just...

disappear…as well." She leaned forward. "Did we miss any of the dimensions on the list?"

"No!" Chyning was sitting there with her teeth clenched. "We hit all of them."

"This is bad," said Bonarain desperately. "We have to check all of them…again."

"No, we don't," said Soolchakan.

Bonarain stood up and glared at him. "So what are you going to do to help us, you, who don't know any of the workings of the ship?"

Soolchakan remained calm. "First of all, I'm not going to panic or get mad."

She got up in his face. "How wonderful," she said in a sinister manner. "Now what do you suggest?"

He smiled. "The Tashkafa stole the dimension hopping technology from the Vagens. They used it…right in front of us. If they now know how to technologically hop to a different dimension, then it is a very high possibility that they have discovered a *new* dimension of their own…independent of anything that the Vagens found."

Bonarain scoffed. "That is the most…!" She stopped herself and her expression went completely blank. "…possible thing that…," she whispered. She went limp and flopped down in the seat. "Now…we have to…hop this huge ship…into all 219 other dimensions…to find the trail. It's gonna wear us out."

"No we don't," said Soolchakan calmly. "All we have to

do is hop the sensor into the different dimensions."

Chyning gave him a dirty look. "Someone has got to go out there…and physically touch the *chokwad* sensor head…in order to hop it," she said snarling.

Soolchakan smiled at her while Bonarain sat there snickering.

Chyning stuck her tongue out at Bonarain. She got up and walked over to where her spacesuit was draped over another seat. She sighed. "I need some help getting this headache on."

While Soolchakan and Bonarain were assisting Chyning, Kiyalee walked onto the Bridge.

Kiyalee frowned as she saw Chyning getting dressed. "What's going on?"

Bonarain finished a long zip up on the suit. "Chyning is going out there to hop the sensor head into the different dimensions so that we can find out where those Tashkafa went."

Now Kiyalee looked confused. "But the Vagens only found 20 dimensions. We know all 20 of them, why do we need to do this?"

"It seems," said Bonarain, "the Tashkafa probably stole the technology from the Vagens and now have found their own dimension. So…either the four of us hop this big ship into all of the other 219 dimensions…or Chyning just hops the sensor head."

Kiyalee's expression did not change. She simply moved her eyes to look at Chyning. "Be safe," she said and then smiled.

Chyning scowled back as she picked up her helmet. Then she dropped her arms, looked up and growled. "Why does it always have to happen like this?"

Bonarain frowned. "What's the matter now?"

"I just finished getting all trussed up in this cocoon…and now I gotta go pee!"

Kiyalee turned away laughing.

Soolchakan tried to keep from laughing as well. "Let's hope that it's not one of the dimensions in the 200's. That way we can find it and you can get out of that suit sooner."

Bonarain looked at Soolchakan incredulously. "You're going to send her out there like that?"

"It'll teach her to pee before getting dressed up," he said nonchalantly.

Chyning stood there silently muttering something as she put the helmet on and headed for the nose of the ship to get to the main sensor array. "**I hope we find it in the first forty**," she sent angrily.

Bonarain sat down at a console and pulled up the sensor readings. "**Just make sure that you give me a few heartbeats in each dimension before moving on. I still have to look for those particles**."

"**Just tell me when to switch. I'll wait…as long as you need it there**." Chyning sighed. 'It's not as if I got much of a choice now,' she thought.

Dimensions #1 through #12 went rather quickly. #13 was already one of the dimensions that the Vagens had found. #14 through #18 were checked. #19 was another one of the Vagen finds. #20, #21 showed nothing. #22 another Vagen find. #23 through #50 droned on. They kept on bypassing all of the Vagen finds and kept checking all of them. Finally at #107, they found a trail. Bonarain did a triple check to make sure that it was the correct trail.

"It's starting to dissipate so we have to get to following it…quickly," said Bonarain.

Soolchakan nodded. "**You can come back in Chyning**," he sent. "**We found it in 107**."

"**How thrilling**," sent Chyning sarcastically.

She Jumped back inside the ship. Kiyalee walked over to assist Chyning in getting out of the cumbersome spacesuit. Suddenly the entire spacesuit just fell to the floor as Chyning had hopped to Ghost, without taking the suit with her, and she headed for the latrine without saying a word.

Kiyalee looked at Bonarain with a small grin. "That's one way to do it."

Bonarain simply nodded and started getting everything ready to follow the trail again.

Soolchakan sat down at one of the navigation stations. "Kiyalee we need you back in the engine room."

"Right," said Kiyalee. Then she vanished.

A little while later Chyning came back. "Does anyone

mind if I take a bath right now? My neck is…gooey."

"All we're doing is following a trail right now," said Soolchakan. "Go ahead and bathe. We'll call you if we need you."

"Thanks," said Chyning as she departed the Bridge.

"I'm not picking up her spacesuit," said Bonarain flatly.

"No one is asking or telling you to," said Soolchakan. "Right now, I'm going to inform Xadorm of our current situation." He closed his eyes. "**Supreme Officer, Xadorm, this Officer, Soolchakan. Can you hear me**?"

"**This is Xadorm! We've been waiting for something from you. What've you got**?"

"**The reason that no one could find that last Tashkafa planet is because _they_ found another dimension – 107. We're tracking their progress now and hopefully they'll lead us to that last planet**."

"**Thanks for the update. Any new information is always helpful**."

"Here we go," said Bonarain as she engaged the engines to maximum speed.

Soolchakan looked at the results from the sensor. "I see the trail but…where are we going…specifically?"

"It's one of three stars," said Bonarain. "I can't tell which one of them because…at this distance…they're all in a bit of a line. The first is seven light years away. The second one is nine light years beyond the first. The third one is twelve light years beyond the second."

"So we just keep following their trail till we get to the one we want."

"Mm-hm," said Bonarain as she put the ship on automatic and then leaned back in her chair. "Now it's just a waiting game… finding out what our destination is."

Xadorm was thinking about what else could be done in order to cause more dissention among the Alliance members. "Maybe we should inform the Vagens that the Tashkafa found a new dimension…and didn't tell anybody."

"I don't think that's a good idea," said Iquanza. "All that'll do is inform the Vagens that there is at least one more dimension that they haven't found yet. Bad enough that they're infesting twenty dimensions. We don't need to give them another one."

Xadorm sighed. "You're right. We can put that one on hold…for now…until we really want to use it…against somebody."

"Like whom," said Ota?

"We'll know when we get to that point," said Boneech.

"IF we get to that point," said Zoolkog.

Xadorm looked a little distressed. "Are you planning on us failing?"

"No," said Zoolkog. "We just might defeat them all… before we have to use it. If we completely defeat them before using it…" He shrugged. "All the better."

Xadorm just nodded.

Ota sniffed as her pad beeped. "I just got another report here," she said. "It seems that the Zizzikinza have made some preemptive strikes on four ships. They…came out of their small little slits and got rid of…all of the opponents on those ships."

"Good," said Xadorm. "That'll make a few more problems for the ruling class."

Blana was going through her information. "Has anybody heard anything about the possibility of the Jowfoonda ending up in this mess?"

Yoobyool laughed. "I've seen several messages between most of the factions. They're looking for the Jowfoonda but are rather confused as to how no one can find any of those bug-headed people anywhere."

"I've seen the same messages," said Roobriba.

Xadorm nodded. "We may have to do the same thing to all of these headaches…in order to have some peace on our home planet…and the rest of the universe."

"Here's a new report," said Boneech. "Team 4412 just blew up another one of the Mustooza Temple ships. Officer Grade 3, Yinseea says that it was larger than the other ships we've blown up and had sanctuaries for ten different Mustooza deities."

"That should give the Mustooza some pause," said Xadorm.

"One hopes," said Iquanza.

"It is definitely giving the Vagens some pause," said Ota. "The Vagens are demanding that they are not required to be aboard any of the Temple ships." She looked up from her report. "They are asking in a rather rude manner."

Xadorm shook his head with a smile. "Anything that helps cause dissension among those *bimyocks* is welcome."

Bonarain sighed as she watched the monitor. They had passed the first star with no results from the sensor scan. They were now passing the second with the same results. They were now headed for the third star and she could see a fourth star that had been hidden from view at their starting point. The fourth one was twenty-five light years beyond the third so it could be a long ride.

Soolchakan walked onto the Bridge drying the back of his neck. His hair was still a little damp from the bath he had just taken. "So we still don't know?"

She shook her head. "We may have to slow down as well. According to Kiyalee, the light speed engine is getting rather hot and…we don't want it to go into overload…or possibly something much worse."

He flopped down in a seat. "We've been spoiled rotten by Jump."

Chyning wandered in. "This ship is no fun. We've already picked it clean of anything of value. There's nothing new here to explore. I'm bored."

Bonarain smiled. "Why don't you catch up on some of the messages that have been coming in?"

Chyning snarled at her. She sat down at a console and pulled her messages up. She sighed as she started reading. She leaned back with a shocked look on her face. "Our people have been a little busy! They've annihilated the Choks on…thirteen planets. The Choks are only living on…six planets now."

"The ones that haven't been blown away in space," said Soolchakan.

Chyning looked closer at the screen. "We've…removed the Zizzys…from twelve planets." She angrily folded her arms across her chest. "We're sitting here…following some vapor trail of a Tashkafa ship…and everyone else is having fun…eradicating the enemy…and grabbing spoils."

"We're not in any danger out here," said Bonarain.

"We're not profiting either," said Chyning. "Look at this! Teams 5345 and 5346 are making some profits…selling Chok pelts." She leaned back looking a little perturbed. "You can either use them…as a rug…or a big winter coat."

Soolchakan looked disgusted. "Would you really want to wear a Chok skin…as a coat?"

Chyning smiled. "Why not? It looks warm. Memtoy of Team 5346 says that it's even big enough to use as a sleeping bag as well."

"That's still revolting," said Soolchakan.

Chyning went back to reading. "Did you see this one?

There was an outer space collision…between two of the Alliance ships. One that was controlled by the Choks and one controlled by the Iyka…just crashed into each other…no survivors."

"Keep reading," said Soolchakan glibly.

Chyning frowned and went back to reading. "Oh! Team 5403 orchestrated it. They did it just to see if they could…control two ships…with just four people."

Soolchakan smiled. "Worked…didn't it?" He went back to his monitor. "Keep reading."

Chyning shook her head. "The Iyka have been removed… completely…from four planets. The Mustooza are now extinct… on two planets." She huffed. "Everyone else is having all of the fun."

Bonarain now looked a little sick. "You call…killing… fun?"

Chyning smiled. "No! It's the looting afterwards that I'm interested in."

Soolchakan sighed. "Once we find this last stronghold…of the Tashkafa…I guess we'll give you first crack at…obtaining… *items*."

"Don't we have to report it…immediately…once we find it," said Chyning?

"Yes," said Soolchakan dryly.

"So we don't have time for any of that," said Chyning.

"It all depends on what we find there," said Bonarain.

"Look at the new message," said Soolchakan. "We just knocked the Vagens off of one of their captured planets."

"That leaves the Tashkafa," said Bonarain. "They're the only ones that we haven't hurt…yet."

Soolchakan looked up. "What's that…on the monitor?"

Bonarain looked up. "The trail has changed. That means… they slowed down here. We're about to enter that star system. Maybe the planet is here!"

"I hope so," said Chyning. "Chasing is boring. Throwing them off by sabotaging their goodies is fun."

"Slowing and switching the sensors…to analyze the system," said Bonarain.

Kiyalee called mentally from the engine room. "**Are we slowing down for a reason**?"

"**The trail is finally leading INTO a star system**," sent Soolchakan.

"**Good! I'm going crazy down here! I'm ready to kill something**," sent Kiyalee.

Bonarain looked at Soolchakan in a dull manner. "Her too?"

Soolchakan just shrugged. He looked back at his monitor. "It looks like there's eleven planets here…and the fourth one…is inhabitable."

"It also looks as if…there's some activity…in outer space…around that planet," said Bonarain. "I'm putting it on the main view screen." She hit a few keys on her console and the big view screen changed to a magnification of the planet.

Chyning's jaw dropped. "*Some* activity? It's everywhere. They're building all kinds of ships...in all kinds of space stations... all around the planet."

Soolchakan adjusted his monitor. "It looks like...there are two moons orbiting that planet and...they have other stuff...either being built...or parked on them."

Bonarain looked a little sick with surprise. "How do we... go about...*this*?"

Soolchakan cleared his throat. "We park somewhere...in the middle...between the two moons and the main planet. Kiyalee and Chyning will take their fighters and each one will explore a moon." He looked at Bonarain. "You and I will...explore the planet." He sighed. "We have some serious counting to do here. Population...ships...space stations and any other paraphernalia that we can think of...or not think of but see it."

Chyning looked a little concerned. "Do we call...the Command Staff...now?"

Soolchakan shook his head. "Let's get...some kind of preliminary count done first. That'll give them some kind of idea of the magnitude of what we found."

"Meanwhile," said Chyning, "the last Tashkafa planet is found and mapped...as far as the location is concerned."

Soolchakan grunted. "Right! Mapping what is on the planet is going to be something altogether different."

"Let's start counting," said Bonarain.

Chyning frowned. "Counting…what?"

"Everything," said Soolchakan! "Count personnel, count the attack ships that are mission ready…and ones under construction. Count the manufacturing plants and what they're putting out. We count the cities, towns and villages…along with any crops that are being raised." He took a deep breath. "First… we count whatever we find on the moons. Then we count all of the stuff on the planet."

The ship was centrally parked in an area that gave them quick access to the two moons and the planet. Soolchakan and Bonarain headed for the planet. He went west, she went east. Kiyalee headed for the larger moon. Chyning headed for the other moon. Once the quick inventory of the moons is accomplished, Kiyalee and Chyning will head to the planet and assist in the inventory on the planet and orbiting space stations.

They spent two days circling the moons and the planet looking and counting. They all got together on their mother ship and compared notes.

Soolchakan sighed as he got ready for the call. "**Supreme Officer, Xadorm, this is Officer, Soolchakan. Can you hear me**?"

"**This is Xadorm. I hear you. Have you got something informative to report…I hope**?"

"**Sir, we found that last Tashkafa planet…and we have a *big* problem. The Tashkafa are preparing for a big** strike. This planet is located in Dimension 107. Even the Vagens don't know about it. The Tashkafa found an uninhabited planet...and they're getting their war machines built, staffed and ready for a very massive act of conquering."

Xadorm felt a little indignant. "I'll be the one to decide if we need to worry or not. Just give me the numbers."

Soolchakan looked at his Team and shrugged. "We stopped counting the population of Tashkafans on the planet when we hit five billion. The entire planet is nothing but weapon and space ship manufacturing plants as well as food processing plants. There are two moons that orbit this planet. They're using the large moon as a parking spot for the attack ships...of which they have 461 assembled, staffed and ready to go. The small moon is a survival training area. They're being trained to survive on planets with hostile or no environment."

Xadorm interrupted. "Did you say...NO environment?"

"Yes, Sir. I'm not on the committee that made that decision. I can only report what we found."

Xadorm scratched his head. "Right! Continue the report."

"Yes, Sir. They have sixteen space stations that are orbiting the planet. Each one of the stations is an assembly plant for more attack ships. It takes 1,200 technicians approximately 70 days to assemble a new attack ship. **The single seat fighters and shuttle craft are assembled on the planet and flown to the attack ship they'll be stationed on. There are also numerous plants where they're manufacturing different size pulse weapons. There are eight continents on this planet. They are utilizing every piece of dirt that they can find. Cities, towns, villages, livestock and crops**." He paused and shook his head. "**The primary crop that they're growing here, on this planet, a planet where the entire population is Tashkafa, the primary crop is…kwatha**."

The entire Command Staff sat there dumbfounded. The Tashkafa were growing a crop that was indigenous to Hardooth. They could not have known about it until they had someone land on Hardooth and discover it for themselves.

Xadorm smacked himself in the forehead. "**Why are they growing kwatha? Have they obtained a taste for it**?"

Soolchakan smirked as he looked at his Team. "**No, Sir. They found out, when they were questioning people on Hardooth, that Owlamites have a strange craving for kwatha. Of all the things that the people of Hardooth could remember about Owlamites, the main thing that they remember is that we love kwatha…almost to being an addiction. So…the Tashkafa are growing trillions of the plants…in order to use it as…believe it or not… bait! They have some twenty billion cans of prepared kwatha…ready to use as bait**!"

Xadorm sat there with his teeth clenched. "**They think…

that we're so stupid…that they could lay out a pest trap for us…bait it with kwatha…and they think that we'll helplessly go in like some low-life rodent and…get trapped?"

Soolchakan sighed. "**They don't seem to have much respect for our intelligence.**"

"**I've heard of arrogance to the extreme,**" sent Iquanza. "**This brings a new definition to haughtiness combined with stupidity…and bigotry.**"

Xadorm had his face in his hands. "**Keep finding out what you can, Officer, Soolchakan. We'll make some decisions here…and let you know what to do…as soon as we make a decision.**"

Boneech groaned. "FIVE BILLION?! If we were to go there…all of us…and start throwing all of them into dimension 45…that's well over 215,000 that each one of us would have to toss. I don't think they'll stand still and wait for that."

"We have to do something," said Xadorm. "461 ships already to go. A population of over five billion that are preparing for an all-out attack against…anyone who would question their… superiority." He chuckled. "It'd be a shame to waste all of that kwatha. I'd like to get it…but I don't want to risk any lives getting it."

"Which means that we can't attack with firestorm weapons," said Zoolkog. "That'd destroy all of that kwatha…real quick."

"They did say that the 461 ships that are ready…are on the large moon," said Blana. "We can…blast anything and everything on the two moons and it won't do anything to the kwatha on the planet."

Xadorm smiled. "That is very true."

Yoganay smiled back. "Plus, they said that the ones who are trained and are staffing those ships are probably also on the ships or are in some kind of special building on that moon. We could get rid of all of their ready forces…and leave them wondering what happened."

Boneech looked at her suspiciously. "How?"

"They're on a zero atmosphere moon!" Yoganay smiled. "If the building that they're living in…were suddenly to experience rapid decompression…what would happen to anyone in that building?"

Yoobyool was now looking suspicious. "How do you make a building experience rapid decompression…and make it a mystery?"

Yoganay looked at her fingernails. "You hop an entire wall into Ghost. After all of the catastrophic things have ended, you hop the wall back. Now…they see debris all over the place… and no hole in the wall that explains what happened." She looked up and grinned. "And they can't blame us…because we're not there."

"That would get rid of a lot of trained personnel," said Ota. "It could give us time to do all kinds of detrimental things to the planet while they're investigating the mystery on the moon."

Xadorm leaned back and looked up at the ceiling. "All kinds of interesting possibilities." He sniffed. "We need to start thinking of any way that we can cause them grief."

17

The bell ship was now orbiting the stronghold planet of the Tashkafa in dimension #107. The Command Staff was able to find out, for themselves, everything occurring on the planet. The planet was nothing but one huge processing area for the military machines the Tashkafa were building and growing kwatha. The moons were used for storage and training.

A full count had been accomplished once the Command Staff had arrived. Team 7016 had stopped counting population when they hit five billion. The closer number was approximately 5.8 billion…and climbing. Individually hopping all of the Tashkafa into #45 was an impossible task. They could not imagine each Owlamite hopping almost 265,000 Tashkafa into another dimension.

Stealing all of the enemy vessels would be a daunting task as well. The Owlamites had obtained a gargantuan armada of enemy ships (parked in #45) and it was getting a little crowded (in their parking area). True, these newer ships had more new technology and would be a wonderful addition to their inventory. The main problem was how crowded #45 was becoming with all of those captured enemy ships (even though there was nothing else in that dimension except for one tremendously large star). Maybe the solution was to allow a lot of the older ships to just float away in the gravitational pull of that one and only star. That way, no one would have to worry about them being used by anybody else.

Ota looked at all of the figures and shook her head. "Maybe we should step up with the bad blood between the factions. Let each one know a little more than what they know now."

"It can't get much more damaging than it is right now," said Zoolkog. "None of those *bimyocks* trust any of the others at all now."

"Maybe we could invent some new things," said Boneech.

Yoganay snickered as she pondered that thought. "The truth has been so completely damaging already. If we start making things up…it might get…"

"More chaotic…than it already is," said Yoobyool with a big grin.

"Rumors, however, may *not* help," said Iquanza. "In many cases a rumor can be squelched with accurate information. The truth has hurt them more than any fabrication that we could come up with. If they find out that some of the information is mythical, they might start questioning whether or not the true items are really true."

Xadorm looked around suspiciously. "Have any of you been swiping any of the kwatha plants they have here?"

Roobriba looked up from her copies of the reports. "Why would you even ask something like that?"

Xadorm looked indignant. "Because I'm seeing reports,

that we've intercepted from the planetary Tashkafa headquarters, that there are over 400 kwatha plants that are suddenly unaccounted for."

"Where are our on-scene spies," asked Ota?

"They're in the lower section...having some...kwatha... for lunch," said Blana.

Xadorm gave Blana a rather disgusted look. "Kwatha? Go get them."

Blana took the stairs to the lower level. She could smell the strong, pleasant aroma of the kwatha that was still bubbling on the stove. She walked over to the table and picked up one of the raw tuber plants. "Is this thing...real?"

Bonarain looked confused. "Of course it's real. It's a kwatha plant."

Blana held it out at arm's length. "But...I've never seen one this *big*."

"They really know how to grow them big on this planet," said Chyning with a grin.

Blana cleared her throat. "Yes, apparently they do. Right now...Supreme Officer, Xadorm would like to talk to you about..." She pointed the tuber at Bonarain. "...this."

Team 7016 all put their mugs on the table and headed for the stairs.

"No," said Blana. "You can take the mugs with you."

They went back and each retrieved their mugs. They then

went to the stairs with Blana following.

As soon as they walked into the conference room, all of the personnel present started sniffing as the aroma hit them.

"Smells real good," said Xadorm with a pleasant smile.

"It is good, Sir," said Kiyalee.

"I'll bet," said Xadorm still grinning. He looked around the conference table then back at Team 7016. His grin disappeared. "Where'd you get the kwatha plants?"

Soolchakan, Bonarain and Kiyalee all turned to Chyning. Chyning looked a little surprised (and somewhat guilty).

"I got them from the planet below, Sir," said Chyning. "They grow them big and tasty…Sir."

Blana held up the big tuber that she had picked up from below. "It is rather large."

"It is at that," said Xadorm as his gaze turned to shock at the size of the kwatha plant. "I…don't remember ever seeing one that big." He leaned back in his chair. "Who authorized you to steal kwatha plants from this planet?"

Chyning looked a little shocked and then smiled helplessly as her face flushed. "Sir…it wasn't…really theft. It was…more…like…reconnaissance."

Xadorm raised his eyebrows. "Reconnaissance? Really? How so?"

"Well…Sir…" She cleared her throat nervously. "We… had to find out if…they were really…quality…plants…Sir."

Xadorm frowned slightly. "And?"

Chyning cleared her throat again. "I had to...uproot... over 400 plants...before I found...10...that were edible."

Now Xadorm, and the entire Command Staff, were sitting there looking shocked with frowns on their faces.

Xadorm leaned forward. "What do you mean by...edible? Uh...not enough information. What made the other 390 plants... inedible?"

Now Chyning looked a little more confident. "Worms... Sir. There are worms here that...are indigenous to the planet. Those worms like the kwatha plants. They bore into the tuber and...they just start eating it. The plant, when you pull it up, stinks. It stinks like it's already rotten."

Iquanza leaned forward as well. "Are the Tashkafa, who are harvesting the kwatha, separating the...*stinky* from the good... before they process the kwatha?"

"No, Sir," said Chyning. "They take all of them in the processing plant, kill the worms, process all of the plants and can them...including dead worms."

Xadorm closed his eyes. "That means that...they've got over twenty-two billion cans...of *rotten* kwatha! Kwatha that we wouldn't touch...under any circumstances." He opened his eyes. "They want to bait us...with ROTTEN kwatha."

"Worm infested...rotten kwatha," said Ota.

Zoolkog sat there calculating. "You found ten good plants out of four hundred. That means that less than three percent of the kwatha is good."

Chyning looked up at the ceiling. "Actually it was 416 plants total…that I uprooted."

Zoolkog gave her a dull, nasty glance. "That's still less than 3%."

Boneech looked a little worried. "What did you do with the…rotten ones?"

"They're floating around in dimension 2," said Chyning calmly.

Blana laughed. "The whole lot that's been canned…is rotten. They package at least five plants per can. If they don't separate any of the good ones…ALL of the canned stuff IS completely useless and rotten."

Xadorm sighed. "So much for their bait! Obviously they can't use it against us." He gave Chyning a nasty look. "So… you accidentally found out that their stuff is no good because they don't do anything about that worms. You still did a reconnaissance without letting us know."

Chyning swallowed hard. "It…won't happen again…Sir."

Xadorm looked at the mug. "You said…that it is very good…didn't you?"

Chyning looked at her Teammates.

Soolchakan chimed in. "Yes, Sir, it *is* very good."

Xadorm produced a spoon from somewhere in his jacket. He signaled Chyning to come closer. She walked up and handed him her mug. He spooned through the thick broth and found a big lump. He popped it in his mouth and crushed the lump against the top of his mouth with his tongue. He rolled the mashed stuff around his mouth with his tongue and nodded.

"It is! It is very good," said Xadorm as he nodded and looked around the table. "And less than 3% is edible. Too bad." He handed the mug back to Chyning. "It seems that this theft has given us some valuable data…even though it is disheartening to come across…*twenty-two billion cans* of…rotten kwatha."

"They can't bait us," said Yoobyool with a smile. "Is there something that we can bait them with?"

Soolchakan shrugged. "Why don't we damage some of their crops? We don't need the stuff. If we mess up…a big portion of their crops…it'll make them forget about the theft."

"Wonderful idea," said Xadorm. He smiled at Soolchakan. "Why don't you go ahead and come up with some ideas on how to do exactly that?"

Kiyalee scowled at Soolchakan. "Big mouth! Why couldn't you have submitted something to Ota and have her make the suggestion?"

"It would probably still have come back to us…through Ota," said Bonarain. "What would you say then?"

"Big mouth!" Kiyalee turned away and folded her arms across her chest pouting. "So…big mouth…have you come up with anything?"

"Yes," said Soolchakan. "That southern continent…has a manufacturing plant for fighters…right near some huge fields of…rotten kwatha."

Chyning scoffed. "There's a manufacturing plant on all of the continents for those things. So what?"

"So…when the next fighter takes off out of there…to head to the mother ship that it is assigned to…we make it crash…and blow up…and ruin an entire field." Soolchakan looked off to the side. "We may not be able to do that…very often…but…it is a start."

Kiyalee nodded. "A crash like that…would contaminate the ground…for quite some time…especially if it has a full load of that…Type 7 fuel that they're using."

"Good idea," said Bonarain with a smile. "Good start."

Soolchakan decided to take the first ride of devastation. The Tashkafa pilot climbed into the cockpit of the fighter…with Soolchakan. As soon as the Tashkafa was ready for takeoff, Soolchakan hopped the pilot's arms into Ghost. Now Soolchakan had full control of the ship. He mentally paralyzed the pilot, took off and started flying the fighter, at full speed, in a completely erratic way. He watched for the big fields of kwatha. Once he saw them he headed the ship in a central location where the blast shrapnel would fly into all of the surrounding fields as well. He nose-dived the fighter straight down in the middle of the field… and at the last possible moment…Jumped to his bedroom on the big spy ship where Team 7016 was currently living.

The Command Staff was watching the flight path of the fighter. They heard some of the control personnel from a watchtower screaming at the pilot to alter his course...or at least report what the malfunction was. Then impact. Then...disaster.

The explosion was not just spectacular, it was so much more totally devastating than any of them would have imagined. The fire from the small ship spread out through the entire field faster than any of them could comprehend. The fire then spread to all of the surrounding fields as everything went up in flames. The fire was spreading so rapidly that many of the Tashkafa farmers were being caught in the flames and being incinerated before they had any chance to get out of the fields.

The fire spread, without any form of slowing, from one field to another as if they were covered with a sheet of some kind of petroleum. Any structure that was in the way was going up in flames. Any farm vehicles that were in the way were burning.

The fields that were further away had not caught fire yet and the Owlamites could see all of the Tashkafa in those fields running for their lives...using anything that they could to speed up their escape.

The fire spread to a small village where there was one rather large structure. As soon as the fire got to that large structure, it blew up with a massive explosion. The explosion leveled every other structure in the immediate vicinity. The explosion threw burning debris everywhere and helped the fire cross a main highway into another set of kwatha fields.

Faster than what any of the Owlamites could comprehend,

all of the kwatha fields in that area of the continent were burning out of control. Almost 10% of an entire continent was in flames and burning completely so rapidly that no one could respond with any firefighting equipment.

The fire reached a second and a third large structure and the devastating blast from those buildings was equal to the first.

Xadorm was the first to find his mental faculties...even though it took him a few heartbeats to form a sentence. "What... how...what was...did that...?" He pounded his fist on the table. "How could that have happened? Kwatha isn't...flammable... especially to that degree!"

Ota came out of her fog. "I think another primary question...what was in those *buildings* that...blew up?"

Yoobyool was looking through the reports. "According to...what I've found...the first one that blew up was...fertilizer storage." He looked through a few other reports. "Uh...so was the second. Uh...All three buildings were for fertilizer storage."

There was another massive explosion on the surface of the planet.

Xadorm looked from the monitor to Yoobyool. "How about that building?"

Yoobyool checked the geography and locations. "That one...was for processing the fertilizer...so that they could use it in the fields."

Iquanza started looking through her reports. "What, in the name of sanity, are those people using for fertilizer?"

"VERY good question," said Xadorm as he continued looking at the devastation in horror. "Somebody find out...now!"

Meanwhile the Tashkafa on the planet were doing everything that they could do to investigate how something like this could have happened. They started an investigation on any of the personnel who worked on that fighter as well as the steps for construction. They also started an investigation on the psychological evaluation of the pilot.

The doctors were immediately tasked with finding out what was in that fertilizer. They were the ones who were the most experienced at chemistry. Nine days later, when they had finished testing the fertilizer (and some other captured kwatha plants) the doctors reported to the Command Staff.

Xadorm stood up. "Welcome doctors. What have you got to report on this...very weird turn of events?"

Doctor Kazkim shook his head as he looked at his report. "They have developed some kind of super powerful fertilizer. It'll make plants grow much faster than normal, it will make them larger and...it seems tastier. This fertilizer...as we have seen... is extremely explosive and flammable." He looked up from his report. "It will also make the food grown with this fertilizer... flammable and...toxic!"

Xadorm swallowed hard. "How bad is this...toxin?"

Kazkim looked at one of his colleagues. "Doctor Voolatha...would you like to take this part?"

Voolatha smiled as she walked up to the table. "You don't need to worry about what you've consumed. The toxin only works if it has a chance to build up in your system. The amount that you got from one meal…is so minute that…if you don't consume any more, your system will clear it out without anything detrimental happening to you. Before you could consume any amount that could possibly make you sick…or die…you'd have to eat at least ten of those very large kwatha tubers per day, every day, for a period of over two years."

Boneech let out a sigh of relief. "No one could possibly pack down that much kwatha…in a month…let alone two years."

"Exactly," said Voolatha. "No one could possibly consume that much, so as long as we discontinue devouring any of the Tashkafa grown kwatha…I don't foresee any problems for any of us."

Soolchakan was standing off to the side listening as the report had been given. "Sirs…may I make a suggestion?"

Xadorm sighed. "I did order you to come up with some way of sabotaging this planet…so…yes…I'll listen to your suggestion."

Soolchakan smiled. "Thank you, Sir. If this fertilizer…and the toxin are still in the tuber…even after it has been processed… and canned. I wonder…what would happen if we set off a hand-held bomb…in that one-and-only storage facility where they have over twenty-two billion cans of processed kwatha?"

Xadorm smiled back. "Why don't you go and find out?"

Soolchakan, still smiling, showed a hand-held bomb, saluted and vanished.

Bonarain, Kiyalee and Chyning all looked at each other with different degrees of disgust – then they vanished.

Xadorm leaned back in his chair and clasped his hands across his stomach. He turned to one of his Teammates. "Teecheta, turn the monitors on. Specifically…I want to see that giant storage facility…for the canned kwatha."

Teecheta sat there quietly snickering as she aimed the cameras at the storage facility and turned the monitor on.

Team 7016 placed themselves at four main spots in the massive storage facility.

Kiyalee looked over at Soolchakan's position. "YOU *H'OOLYACH* SUCKING BIG MOUTH! Why can't you just keep that yapping hole SHUT?"

Soolchakan looked back at her. "**I could have told them in this manner**."

Chyning responded. "**Why don't you just shut your brain down for a while? Maybe someone else would have to do the dirty work**."

Bonarain huffed. "**Shut up! Mind and mouth! Let's set these things to go off and get out of here**."

Soolchakan shook his head. "**Now…activate them, place them and Jump out**."

All four bombs were put in place and activated. All four of

Team 7016 Jumped to their favorite chair in their spy ship.

Bonarain quickly activated the monitor. "We should have done this before we left."

Soolchakan looked at the monitor. "Well…nothing so far that…"

At that moment four plumes of fire blew holes in the roof of the storage facility. Cascade explosions added more and more to the devastation as each one of the twenty-two billion (plus) cans exploded from the extreme heat of the fire.

Kiyalee clicked her tongue. "I think we just made another *big* mess."

Xadorm watched from the monitor on the bell ship. "Can you imagine…how bad it must be for the Tashkafa? Twenty-two billion cans…of processed toxins…going up in flames."

Ota leaned back and clasped her hands behind her head while smiling. "It doesn't hurt my feelings."

Iquanza leaned on the table. "It is still…only one part of their plan. All of their military equipment is still in good condition. The only thing we did was destroy their…bait!"

"I think maybe we did more than that," said Roobriba. "There are secondary alarms going off…all over the planet. That one continent…that's in flames. Now this plant going up in flames on a different continent. There are planet wide alarms going off… because of sensors that are reading all kinds of toxins…in the atmosphere."

Zoolkog looked at his private monitor. "Almost everyone

on the planet…they're putting gasmasks on. We've polluted the whole planet…with toxic gases."

Xadorm nodded. "We've hurt the planet. We've hurt the crops. We still have all of the technological and mechanical stuff to worry about."

Ota turned to Xadorm. "Do you want to keep Team 7016 working on that?"

"No," said Xadorm as he stared at the monitor. "Let them take a break. They found this planet, they've hurt the Tashkafa crop and bait plans…immeasurably." He frowned as he looked up at the main monitor and leaned back. "How long does it take for all of those cans to blow up?"

"Remember how many cans there are in that place," said Yoganay with a grin.

"I remember," said Xadorm. "It's just that…oh turn that monitor off." He looked off to the side. "We know that the devastation is…or is going to be…total."

Boneech looked up a little distraught. "Should we bring our planet killers here and finish them off?"

"No," said Xadorm. "They took the planet and made it into what they wanted. I don't blame the planet and I see no reason to hurt the planet…any further. Just…get them off of it and defeat them. That is what I want."

"THEY destroyed the planet," said Yoganay. "Look at their landscaping! There had to have been some tall mountains. No more! All of the mountain tops are the same height. They shaved them all off at a specific level and started growing crops on them…or put a factory up there. The mountain slopes are no longer slopes. They look like some kind of odd staircase with more crops or more factories…or apartment complexes. All of the other land has been leveled off and is now farm or factory. Find one piece of dirt that hasn't been disturbed."

"They're even gutting the fish supply on the planet," said Roobriba. "Along the coastlines…look at the fishing industry. They're scooping in billions of…aquatic life daily. Whatever plant life was here initially…is gone."

"I don't see or detect any animal or avian life as well," said Blana. "And as Roobriba pointed out, pretty soon, there won't be many…or maybe any indigenous sea creatures remaining."

Zoolkog huffed. "It also looks like they're overfishing the rivers as well."

Xadorm sighed. "What you're saying is…they've already killed the planet. What was here when they first got here…is no more."

Yoobyool shrugged. "No telling how many different species were on this planet that…don't exist anymore."

"Okay," said Xadorm. "Let's start with the ships that are ready. They parked them on the larger moon. We take them first. How many are there…461?"

Ota looked down at her monitor. "When we first got here there were 461. Now there appears to be 473…and maybe in two or three days there'll be four more…if they continue manufacturing…through all of the devastation."

Xadorm nodded. "Get the necessary number of Teams here…and start getting them into our parking lot in 45. Once we start those thefts, the Tashkafa will realize that we're here and… hopefully we'll be able to *chase* them out."

Zoolkog looked down at his monitor when he heard it beep. "I just got a message here from Officer Grade 3, Nyantay of Team 3742. She found a new Temple ship. According to what her Team found, this ship has THE number one big high holy *doovoft* on it. He's the Supreme Officer of their clergy. He's telling all of his… subjects…that their faith is weak and that's why they keep losing battles…to us." He looked up. "According to this…the Mustooza think that this guy is never wrong…and can do no wrong. He is totally perfect in every way." He huffed. "Talk about conceit!"

Xadorm snarled. "Tell Nyantay to get a hand-held and blow his high holy butt off of that ship."

Zoolkog nodded. "Uh…Sir…they want to know when."

Xadorm looked a little angry. "NOW!"

Zoolkog closed his eyes and relayed the message. He suddenly opened his eyes in surprise. "Uh…she just informed me that…Officer Grade 6, Zhadow…shoved the hand –held…into his high holy mouth…and it blew him in half."

Xadorm frowned. He then raised his eyebrows. "Now they don't have any high holy, infallible hypocrite…do they?"

Zoolkog huffed. "They're already planning on assigning a new replacement. Nyantay says that their ceremonies will take sixty-six days to…make the new one *holy* enough to take this new position."

Xadorm shook his head. "Then tell Nyantay to make sure that she's there to shove a hand-held in the holy orifice of that one as well…about the sixty-fifth day."

The monitor in front of Boneech beeped. She looked down. "We now have confirmation that the Choks have just been totally eliminated from a fourteenth planet. That gives them only five more havens."

Xadorm nodded. "That's five too many." He got up and walked over to one of the small portholes. "I want those…outer space assembly factories done away with as well. I want that done as soon as possible. The ships that are assembled will make a good addition to our fleet."

"And maybe convince the Tashkafa that they should stop trying to get us," said Iquanza.

"If it doesn't…" said Xadorm sadly. "Eradicate them!" He shook his head. "I'm tired of killing…but I have no plans of surrendering and becoming a slave…to anybody."

"We haven't been able to convince anyone yet," said Iquanza.

"I know," said Xadorm. "But I can still hope."

Iquanza pursed her lips. "Should we go ahead with that plan to…hop a wall into Ghost and…then put it back after the disaster…as a diversion?"

Xadorm nodded. "Absolutely," he said flatly.

Teams 7013 and 7015 headed for their appointed position on the large moon. There were eight buildings that were being used as barracks for the crews of the Tashkafa ships parked on the moon. The diversion was set up where four of the buildings were going to get their east and west walls hopped into Ghost and the buildings would suffer complete decompression. After the dust settled the walls were to be put back into #107 to give the appearance that nothing had happened.

The two Team Leaders, Zhanzhee and Oonzeel were going to be on barracks number 2.

"**I don't like this**," sent Oonzeel.

Zhanzhee frowned. "**What's wrong? Don't you think it will work**?"

"**It's not a question of whether it'll work or not…once they find that the buildings are intact, after suffering rapid decompression…they'll know that it was us**."

Zhanzhee snickered. "**That's not up to us. We're both just Officer Grade 4. This escapade came from the top so…they're the ones who have to worry about the consequences. We just do it and…get out of here**."

Oonzeel just grunted.

Xadorm had been covertly listening in on the mental conversation. He just rolled his eyes and grunted himself. He turned to Iquanza. "How many are still getting into position?"

Iquanza looked at her checklist. "There are still five ships that have to be manned. We also had to pull some extra personnel because there are nineteen of the ships that have Tashkafa personnel on board."

Boneech looked up worried. "Are we going to end up with a running gun battle on some of the ships?"

"No," said Iquanza. "The Tashkafa are just doing some practices on preventive maintenance. Once we've hopped the ships to dimension 45, we just jettison any Tashkafa that came with us. They might not even know that they're in dimension 45."

Blana looked over her checklists. "How many of those workers have we found?"

"210," said Iquanza.

"A lot more than that are going to be scattered all over that moon pretty soon," said Roobriba. "If the decompression of those four buildings causes enough ruckus, they might not even notice…at first…that all of their ships are gone."

"Okay, we're good," said Iquanza. "All personnel are in place and ready to start the Tashkafa disaster."

Xadorm just sat there watching a monitor.

After hearing nothing from Xadorm, Yoobyool felt a little uneasy. "Sir, what are we waiting for?"

Xadorm pointed at the main monitor. "That flight of twenty-one fighter ships that're headed for their mother ship on the moon. I'm waiting for them to report to their ship and then… hey, guess what…we have some more brand new fighters."

"That's gonna be a few extra personnel that we have to jettison," said Yoganay.

"That's why Team 6975 is riding along with that group," said Xadorm. "As soon as we find out which of…possibly four… ships gets those fighters, Officer Grade 4, Koosasa and her Team will add to the personnel on that ship…and assist in getting rid of…what we don't need on our new ships."

"This is Officer Grade 3, Tyzoth of Team 3677. It looks like that flight of fighters is headed for the ship that I'm on. The hangar doors are open and there are 21 vacant parking slots where the lights are blinking. All of the maintenance personnel on this ship are in the hangar bay waiting for them to land and do their normal routine of looking them over."

"Good," said Xadorm with a smile. "It affects only one ship. Koosasa and her Team will assist in the jettisoning on one ship…after the hop and then we'll have everything under control."

"While we're watching the Tashkafa have another major catastrophe on their hands," said Zoolkog.

"More than one catastrophe, Sir," said Ota. "We just got a report from Officer Grade 2, Sleea that the Tashkafa have just been completely eradicated on one of the six planets that they're infesting."

"If that doesn't add more mayhem to their confusion, I don't know what will," said Yoganay.

Xadorm sighed. **"Officer, Tyzoth. As soon as the**

hangar doors close, that'll be the moment that this entire plan starts. Keep us informed as to what is going on in that hangar bay. All personnel, listen in on the report from Tyzoth."

Tyzoth stood there in the hangar getting a little twinge of ego. He was going to be the one who gave the command of execution for this mission to start. One of the Team members of 3677 walked up to Tyzoth looking at the big haughty smile on his face.

"Your head his swelling," said Officer Grade 6, Yabita.

He looked at his Teammate and gave her a nasty snarl. "I'm not the one who made that decision. Xadorm gave me an order. I'm going to do it."

She wrinkled her nose. "Your head is still swelling."

Another member of 3677, Officer Grade 7, Sositski, walked up. "Why are we gonna toss these *bimyocks* into dimension 2? Why don't we just kick them off of the ships into 45?"

Yabita scoffed. "Because if we push them into 45, we'd have to fight with them to get them off of the ship. If we hop them to dimension 2, they are out of here before they even realize that they've been attacked."

"Stop distracting me," said Tyzoth. "**The first fighter had entered the hangar and is heading for his parking spot. There's the second**."

Xadorm yawned as Tyzoth continued with his oratory, counting each fighter as it landed. When the oration got to fighter number twenty, all of the Owlamites mentally geared up for the dirty tricks that each one had been assigned. Fighter number twenty-one was now in the hangar and Tyzoth turned his attention to the big hangar bay doors.

"**They've started the door closing**," sent Tyzoth. "**Twenty taja to go…eighteen taja…sixteen taja… fourteen taja….**"

Yabita stood there a little disgusted. 'Drag it out you egotistical *doovoft*,' she thought.

Tyzoth continued. "**Ten taja…eight taja…six taja… four taja…two taja…NOW**!"

Four buildings on the moon had two of their walls hopped to Ghost. All of the victims inside the buildings were instantly killed as the air was sucked out of their lungs and they were thrown around and out of the building as the atmosphere was sucked out of the buildings.

475 brand new Tashkafa attack ships were hopped to #45 and before any of the personnel who were on board those ships could figure out, or knew, what had happened, they were all thrown into the void of outer space.

On the planet, the ranking Tashkafa, Third Mishasak (0-10), Kiychichik was standing on a balcony at the main headquarters. It was early evening, at his location, and he was getting a breath of fresh air before going back to his duties of attempting to turn the kwatha field catastrophe back into a group of working manufacturing plants. He saw and heard several hundred alarm bells and lights go off. He turned and saw on his monitor, from his vantage point, that something was happening on the large moon. He looked up at the moon and his vision was obscured as four of the outer space assembly stations, in that immediate vicinity, blew up. He had to avert his attention and close his eyes from the four huge fireballs in the sky. He staggered back inside rubbing his eyes. "I WANT SOME REPORTS…NOW! WHAT IS HAPPENING?"

Everyone in the headquarters control center was running to their assigned monitor to try to find out what had happened. Over 130 personnel were all talking at the same time on their communication links attempting to get in touch with somebody on the other end and find out what was going on.

Kiychichik got to his seat still rubbing the tears (and pain) out of his eyes. He was having trouble focusing on anything. He tried looking at his communication panel, however, he could not see anything clearly. He was desperately hoping that his vision was not permanently marred by what had just happened. He was also terrified at what would happen to his career, considering the fact that he had just observed four of those outer space assembly plants blow up right in front of him…after numerous other warning lights and bells had given rise to something bad happening.

He turned on his microphone. "Can anyone give me some kind of report yet?

Even through the haze of his dimmed vision he could see that all of the controllers were turning on the blue light at their station. Blue meant that they were still gathering information and could not give a full report. He pulled out a tissue and wiped more tears from his aching eyes.

Some of the lights started turning yellow. There were some runners headed up to the command seat. The first runner arrived at the command seat and held a message out for Kiychichik. He sighed as he realized that he could not focus on the writing. "Read it for me!"

The man looked shocked. "But…Sir…I'm only a Vandin 5 (E-5).

Kiychichik glared at him through his red eyes. "Does that mean that you're too stupid to know how to read?"

"Uh…no…Sir...I…uh…"

"I just got my eyes singed looking up at those big fireballs. Read the thing for me…NOW!"

"Yes, Sir." The Vandin 5 saluted and looked at the paper. "Sir, according to this, all of the outer space assembly stations have…blown up." He looked up terrified. "All sixteen of them… are gone…Sir." He looked as if he was expecting to be executed.

Kiychichik snarled. "I figured that one out on my own… seeing as how I saw four of them blow up simultaneously." He sniffed. "Dismissed," he said calmly.

The Vandin 5 let out a sigh of relief and made some hasty tracks back to his station.

Another runner reported and Kiychichik had to give the same story about his eyes.

The runner looked at the paper and stood there for a moment looking shocked. "Uh…Sir, it seems that…four of the barracks… on the moon…all suffered catastrophic decompression…at the same time. All personnel…in those four buildings are dead. The other personnel, from the other buildings, went to inspect the damaged buildings. They say that…they can find no structural failure…but…none of the four buildings have any atmosphere in them and…some of the dead were…blown out of the building… by means they cannot ascertain…Sir."

Kiychichik sat there baffled. He was going to order more inspection of those buildings because what he was hearing was impossible. "Put the message down." He cleared his throat. "Dismissed."

Another runner came up and heard about the eyes. "Sir, according to this…all four of the Dimensional Transfer Stations have…blown up. The reports are coming in from fighters that were performing normal patrols. They're the only survivors of the explosions. They were far enough from each of the blasts. They're requesting rescue, Sir."

Kiychichik closed his eyes. "Why do they need to be rescued? If their fighters are intact…what's the problem?"

The runner swallowed hard. "I don't know, Sir. I got this message from Stipkonik (O-4), Habanjook. You'll have to find out from him…Sir."

Kiychichik growled. He picked up his microphone. "Stipkonik, Habanjook! Not enough information!"

Habanjook left his station and ran to the command seat. "What kind of information do you require, Sir?"

"Why do intact fighters need to be rescued?"

"Sir, the fighters all have limited range and oxygen. It would take them at least six days to get here, at their maximum speed, from their current location. They only have enough oxygen for six *kassik*. Even if they had enough oxygen…they have no food or drink aboard a fighter. They'd starve to death before they got here."

"How long would it take for a mother ship to get to where they are?"

"About four *kassik*…at maximum speed."

Kiychichik nodded. "All right, let's dispatch one of the attack ships to…wherever those fighters are…two if necessary."

The next runner had arrived at the command seat. "Sir… we can't send any attack ship!"

Kiychichik looked up bleary eyed. "And why not?"

"Sir, according to the report I have here from Lelkonik (O-3), Kiship…all of the attack ships…that were on the large moon… have vanished…without a trace…Sir."

Kiychichik stood up. "Lelkonik, Kiship! What happened to my fleet of attack ships?"

A controller stood up at his station. "That's the report I got from the Sub-Planet Base 1. The ships…have been…somehow… stolen…Sir."

Kiychichik flopped down in his chair. "Do we…have any…shuttlecraft?"

Kiship shook his head. "None that could rescue those

fighter pilots in time, Sir."

Xadorm had been listening intently to all of the information. He turned to the Command Staff. "Do you think that we could claim those fighters? I mean if they're going to die from oxygen starvation anyway…why don't we claim them?"

Ota nodded. "I'll get a couple of Teams on it right away." She closed her eyes and started sending a few mental communications.

Xadorm nodded. "Thank you." He went back to listening in on the Tashkafa bad news.

Kiychichik hung his head. "Somebody contact our Primary Headquarters…back in the primary dimension."

A woman stood up. "We can't contact them, Sir."

Kiychichik looked up. "WHY NOT…And who are you?"

"Sir, I am Stipkonik, Whetwheth. When the transfer stations were blown up, we lost all contact with the home base. All of the multi-dimensional radios were located on the transfer stations. We have no way of contacting them…until the transfer stations are…rebuilt…or someone comes here…from the primary dimension."

Kiychichik felt his shoulders sag even lower. "How long would it take to…rebuild one of the transfer stations?"

Another man stood up. "Yohdkonik (O-5), Kondoktok here, Sir. We can't build them. All of our technicians…who have the knowledge of…putting one of those stations together… or any of the dimensional transfer technology…were on the four stations. When those stations blew up…we lost ALL of *our* multi-dimensional knowledge and capability. We'd have to contact those…Quintrouble people to get back any multi-dimensional capability…Sir."

Xadorm frowned. "What is a…Quintrouble?"

"Sir, that's what the Tashkafa call the Vagens…behind their backs," said Roobriba.

Xadorm raised his eyebrows. "Behind their backs? How disrespectfully bigoted of them?" He shook his head. "Shameful!"

Kiychichik wanted to go hide under his bed. "So…until someone comes here from the primary dimension…we're… isolated…and stuck!"

"And, unfortunately…we're pretty much disarmed," said Kondoktok.

Kiychichik sighed. "Those *hoofquat* Owlams!"

Kondoktok frowned. "Sir, how can you even think that the Owlams are behind this? They're not here."

Kiychichik looked up angrily. "Ten *kassee* ago, we had four functioning dimensional transfer stations, sixteen outer space ship assembly stations, 475 attack ships and no problems of any type on the large sub-planet. SEVERAL days ago, we had a massive crop of that stupid kwatha plant…all over the planet. We had almost twenty-three billion cans of the stuff ready for shipment. NOW… we have no dimensional transfer stations…or any capability of reestablishing it. We have no assembly stations. We have several thousand of our highly trained personnel laying dead on the large sub-planet. We have absolutely no attack ships and therefore no way of rescuing several fighter pilots who are going to die from oxygen starvation before they die of malnutrition. We have one continent where almost 15% of the land is scorched and ALL of that nasty processed kwatha is destroyed. The fires that are coming from these catastrophes are giving off highly toxic fumes that are poisoning the entire planet. Historically, of all the enemies that we have encountered in our past and present…who else has displayed the capability of creating this much chaos…without ever being seen by us…or any of our allies?"

Kondoktok turned away and slumped down in his seat.

Xadorm sat there looking thoughtful. "They're totally isolated. They can't do a thing…because…we inadvertently destroyed their dimensional transfer capabilities. They have no technicians who can repair it. They're going to have to start from scratch…on building any type of attack force. They can't even get out of this system…or dimension…without help. I doubt that the Vagens will help them." He sat there stroking his chin. "I think that it is possible…that we can leave this bunch alone…for a while. They're stranded…and therefore totally impotent…as far as attacking us. Not to mention the fact that they've polluted the entire planet with…blown up kwatha."

Blana shrugged. "So we leave them alone other than keeping an eye on them. If they're able to make some noise… then we blast them."

Zoolkog snickered. "Meanwhile we can get back to all of the headaches in Home dimension and focus our attention on them."

Boneech laughed. "Nearly six billion Tashkafa that we've killed or completely cut off from causing us any harm. Why couldn't we do that with all of them?"

"That'd be nice," said Xadorm. "However…those we haven't cut off completely…need to be reckoned with. Let's get back to Home and take care of business."

"I got an uneasy feeling about this," said Yoobyool. "I think…that once we stop the others in Home dimension…we should come back…and wipe these *bimyocks* out."

"That option is still open," said Xadorm. "Fortunately, we can discuss it at a later time."

18

Two years later, after looking over all of the captured Tashkafa ships, the Owlamites finally broke their special code and were able to get into the security logs of the ship that Team 7016 had been chasing.

Xadorm called the Command Staff, as well as Team 7016, together to hear the reading and find out exactly what had happened. Many were curious because of a few unanswered questions.

Officer Grade 2, Sankiki was there to unravel the entire mystery. She smiled as she pulled out her pad. "Sirs, it is rather a remarkable thing that happened. To begin with, when Team 7016 discovered that Tashkafa ship, it was going at full power to their secret location in #107. Team 7016 started following using their forward sensor array. Somehow…the Tashkafa ship sensors were able to pick up the sensor on the ship that 7016 was flying. They were now running *to* their secret and *from* the puzzling thing that was following."

Bonarain was baffled. "How could they possibly see the sensor head at that distance? That thing is so small…it'd fit inside my mug. That's the only portion on our ship that was in Home."

Sankiki smiled. "It's also a sophisticated technological device. That is why they were seeing it. It was a tiny object that was chasing them, they didn't recognize the configuration of it and that was what worried them. Now, when their engine overheated and they were forced to slow down, the Tashkafa turned their dimensional transfer mechanism on and hopped to #107. They had been wanting to shift over, however, because that tiny little object was trailing them, they didn't do it until they absolutely had to. In the process of hopping, while flying at maximum speed, they burned the machine out. Once they were in #107 they figured that they were safe so they didn't worry about the damage. They continued on to their destination. Once they were there, the device, which was a prototype, was then taken to the technicians on their outer space dimensional transfer space stations. We didn't know that the contraption was there, we just figured that the technicians were working on a part of the ship, so we ignored it. The time it took Team 7016 to find the power trail in #107, that was the time used to transfer the device to the stations for repair. They had tested it, it had worked…with a major malfunction to itself and they figured that they had escaped from the anomalous little item that was chasing them."

Xadorm chuckled. "Then, when we attacked their four transfer stations…we took out all of their dimension hopping technicians and equipment."

"Yes, Sir," said Sankiki.

Ota snickered. "According to all of our spies, the Tashkafa that are trapped there are still not in communication with any of their comrades. They're still totally isolated and the ones here in Home dimension are terrified of going to the Vagens to ask for help getting to a dimension they discovered once they purloined the dimension hopping equipment and technology."

"Right," said Zoolkog. "The Vagens still don't know about #107, so the secret is safe and the Tashkafa are still stranded until they can come up with the dimension hopping technology for themselves. All that they had, they stole...and all that they had, we destroyed."

Xadorm leaned back. "Are they still growing their toxic kwatha on that planet?"

"No, Sir," said Roobriba. "They knew that the fertilizer was toxic and highly flammable. Once they were trapped there, they got rid of all of that fertilizer and the kwatha. Now, they're trying to grow crops they can eat. Their main problem, of course, is that pesky worm that virtually destroyed the kwatha crops. They've found that if they put a lot of underground high voltage wires...and shock the *h'oolyach* out of the worms, they can then grow a crop without having to worry about the worms. Funny thing is that they electric shock supplies more ground nutrients for the plants when it kills the worms."

Xadorm nodded. "Are they attempting any outer space technology?"

Yoobyool laughed. "Once we blasted all of the assembly stations, they had nothing in outer space. They had to quickly construct four shuttle craft in order to rescue their personnel that were stuck on the two moons. They're starting from scratch in building a new space station, in order to build on and build more. They have a problem in that it is slow going because of all of the debris that is still orbiting the planet from the stations that we blew up. They have to build while cleaning at the same time."

Xadorm frowned. "Do you think that we should stop them from achieving space travel again?"

Yoobyool laughed again. "We're slowing them dramatically. They would have been finished with the first space station quite some time ago…if we hadn't been…changing a few settings on some of the machinery."

Xadorm smiled. "It seems that we're getting pretty good at sabotage."

Most of them got a good hearty laugh over the comment.

Xadorm sighed. "All right, thank you for the report. Officer, Sankiki, you and your Team 254 are dismissed. Team 7016, thank you for what you've done…and you are dismissed as well." After both Teams vanished, Xadorm turned to the Staff. "All right now…what do we know about our rotten enemies in this dimension?"

"They've been slowed in any form of conquest because of all their bickering among themselves," said Zoolkog. "What more could we possibly do to hinder that?"

"Destroy a few of their ships…and attack some of the planets that they're located on," said Xadorm. "The less that any of them have to build with and the more bickering there is…gives us more time to destroy even more of what they have and prevent them from doing anything else to us. We still have almost forty planets that they're all located on…where they don't have any business being there because none of them are on their original planets. They're all borrowed or enslaved planets. They have no right to be on those planets, I want them off and if it calls for the complete extinction of a race...so be it. I'm tired of being attacked from this or another planet...or dimension."

Yoobyool sighed. "So we're still going on the offensive against all of them."

Xadorm nodded. "I want all Owlamites to be safe from any on world or outworlder exploitation."

Because of all of the fighting between the factions the Alliance was dissolved and each one was once again fighting for themselves.

The Chokchakchok were hunted down on the planets they were infesting. Their skins became a great prize for anyone who could bring them down. The last few planets they had conquered were won back by the indigenous races (aided immensely by the Owlamites). The Choks were finally eliminated as a threat to Owlam, Hardooth or anyone else.

Defeating the Doolood in the space ships was rather simple. The water they were living in was reduced to below freezing or diluted with fresh water. Due to the high alkali and saline content of their natural habitat they were quickly eradicated on the ships that they did not have control of.

The Doolood planets were once again deprived of the barrier walls that kept the predators out. Now the Doolood were exterminated on one planet, hopefully, and forced back into hiding from indigenous predators on their original planet. It would, once again, take them a long time to recover from this setback. The Owlamites were going to keep a close watch on them to make sure that they did not come back again.

The Iyka were not able to get back to their home planet in any form of complete safety. The planets they were on did not have the right kind of environment for them to bury their eggs in mud. Parasites that were on the conquered planets soon destroyed all of their young and as a result the planets where they were not captured and killed, they simply died off because of no new generations.

The Mustooza were constantly calling on their pantheon of gods for help. Finally after about fifty years of humiliating defeats the ones that were left lost all faith in those gods. This started a lot of infighting among the different factions of Mustooza who wanted to control the new order. Over half of their fatalities were self-inflicted. The rest were taken care of by Owlamites, the indigenous races of the planets they were on and the other factions of the former Alliance took care of the a lot.

The Tashkafa were finally subdued by the same kind of bickering between the former Alliance races – and the Owlamites. The only place that was left for the Tashkafa was that one lone planet in dimension #107. They were prosperous in that dimension. They never did recapture any of the technology to hop from one dimension to another. The Owlamites still kept a close eye on that one planet to make sure that they never caused any more grief to Hardooth.

It took nearly eighty years, however, due diligence finally

brought down the last of the Vagens on six planets they had initially conquered. The only planet where there were any surviving Vagens was the planet where the Owlamites had "removed" all three of the ruling classes and left the two serving classes to fend for themselves. Those Vagens remembered that things like electricity and space travel existed. Since they had never been educated in regards to manufacturing these mysterious things, the survivors were now living very different lives. Their most dangerous weapons were the bow and arrow. They could make wooden carts and they were able to domesticate some of the local wildlife as beasts of burden. It would be several hundred years before they were able to finally obtain any of the technology of their oppressors. Space travel was probably a few thousand years away.

The Zizzikinza were probably the biggest headache of all. Due to the fact that they could slither away through the smallest of holes, it was extremely difficult to follow them. Since the Vagens had found the Spy dimension, the Owlamites could not risk using that dimension to follow them. They had to use Observation and unfortunately they could not hear the Zizzikinza in that dimension. They had to use sight only. It was incredibly difficult, however, in the one hundred eleventh year of the reign of Xadorm as the *Voice of Power*, the Zizzikinza people were finally eliminated on all twenty-two planets they had infested.

The Owlamites were satisfied at the moment. One Doolood planet, one Tashkafa planet and one Vagen planet. All of them were being closely watched and sabotaged where it was necessary to keep them from obtaining any new technology, especially dimension hopping capabilities.

Xadorm and the Command Staff were walking through one of the captured Tashkafa ships. They were reading through some of the maintenance guides as they went through each section.

Ota scoffed. "All of these wonderful things…all of this incredible technology and…why can't we come up with anything like this?"

Zoolkog sighed. "Because we were all placed in the positions we were in because of our lack of imagination. The only ones who survived that blast from the Algothon firestorm weapon…were the ones without any skills for inventing or creating. We have a few doctors, nurses and some farmers…but none of us were ever among the elite inventors. That's why we were placed as watchers in the wall offices. No imagination is required. Just watch the screen and report what you see. Someone else made the rules and regulations. Someone else designed and built the computers and all of the paraphernalia that went with them. Someone else planned all of the tactics and strategy."

Blana frowned. "But after that attack from Galsino…we were able to rebuild that big hole in the wall. Doesn't that take some imagination to build?"

Zoolkog shook his head sadly. "No. We were following guidelines laid out by those before us who had already made the designs. We didn't invent anything new we just followed the instructions. You don't need an imagination to follow instructions. All you need is the capability to follow the recipe that is in front of you."

"That is why all of this new technology that we have in front of us is stolen from others," said Xadorm. "All of our imaginative and creative minds were killed in the blast. The ones that we stole all of this technology from were never handicapped by that limitation. It has been over 3,600 years since that Algothon attack and we still haven't aged a bit. Maybe that's why we haven't done any procreation because we don't need children. We have lived… for so long…and it appears that none of us has aged.

Roobriba was a little miffed. "If we have no imagination, how did those architects come up with the designs on the apartments in the gorge?"

Xadorm shook his head. "Most of that was following the design of a building that already existed. They just followed the floor plan…over and over and over. The idea of moving stone and strengthening it…was not that great of an invention. It was minor compared to designing and building a spacecraft from scratch."

"What about the physicists," said Yoganay? "Isn't there some creativity there?"

"Again," said Xadorm, "they're following set procedures. They haven't really invented anything new. They have figured out a few things by using set standards. What have they invented? Nothing…just like everyone else."

"That kinda ruined my idea about that Officer, Kiyalee," said Boneech. "I was thinking about how she had kept…that big 161 running…for over three and a half millennium. She has had to machine parts for it and redo the upholstery several times but…all she's been doing is remaking and re-machining parts that someone else designed."

Iquanza looked up from her pad. "Why haven't some of the other races on Hardooth start making new inventions? Why are they so…stagnant in their thought processes?"

Yoobyool scoffed. "Because each one of the outworld attacks that occurred…they did not just haphazardly shoot down at the planet. They targeted technology and personnel who were building and designing that technology. We Owlamites are not the only ones who have lost a lot of imaginative minds…virtually every other race on the planet has suffered the same losses that we did. It's just that none of them had the capability to purloin any of the enemy technology the way we did. This puts us way ahead of them and…keeps us having all of this to ourselves."

Yoganay snickered. "As long as no one else finds dimension 45."

"That definitely helps," said Xadorm smiling.

Soolchakan was walking through apartment 12-563. Chyning had gone back to that one Tashkafa planet and had done some mass plundering. The apartment was full of all kinds of treasures and trinkets. He marveled at how much was there, however, he knew her capability of Jumping a shuttlecraft to the planet, filling the thing up and then Jumping back and filling the empty apartments with her loot.

Chyning had been upstairs. She came down the stairs, saw Soolchakan, gave him a dirty look and just stood there akimbo.

"What did you want?"

He glanced around the room. "Do you really need all of this…stuff?"

She wandered over to a very fancy table and started caressing an ornate candelabra that was near the edge. "None of the Command Staff has said that we can't have any treasures. A lot of our people have…," she cocked her head to the side. "… plundered!" She grinned as she looked around the room. "The Mufayton don't need it…now that they're all dead. Neither do the Zizzys or the Choks or the Mustooza. Someone is gonna own it." She gave him a stern look. "What's wrong with me owning some of it?"

He scoffed. "SOME? SOME? Some of it okay! Not ALL of it! You can barely walk through this room. Why didn't you… scatter it around in some of the other rooms in this apartment?"

She giggled. "I did. The whole place is full…of my goodies."

His jaw dropped. "ALL FOUR FLOORS?"

She picked up a gem studded chalice. "Yup! All four floors." Her grin got bigger. "You should see what's in Spy dimension and Observation dimension as well. If you want to see all of that…I suggest that you go outside the door before hopping. You might just accidentally…join…with some…trinket."

He shook his head. "Have you had any spats with Bonarain or Kiyalee…about filling an entire apartment with just…YOUR stuff?"

She stood there laughing for a few moments. "Bonarain has a lot of her goodies in 564, Kiyalee has most of her things in 565 and all three of us have one floor in 566."

He sputtered. "What? You haven't crammed apartment 567 full of things as well," he said facetiously?

She put her arms behind her back and looked around the ceiling with a big grin. "We put some things in 567…things that we thought that…*you*…might like." She looked back down at him with the same impish grin. "We did think of you. We shared." She gave him a big toothy grin.

He felt a little sick. "Does Xadorm know about any…or all of this?"

She scoffed. "He's the *Voice of Power*. What…in this gorge full of apartments…is he *not* aware of?"

Soolchakan stood there thinking for several moments. "I guess…if you tried to hide something from him…it wouldn't be hidden for long."

"Either that or he wouldn't care."

He sighed and left the apartment. He decided to go check on 12-564 and see what Bonarain had plundered. He was beginning to get a little worried about how the bad habits of Chyning were rubbing off on the rest of the Team. He wondered if he should knock. He did not wonder for long, he just scoffed in disgust and opened the door.

Bonarain looked up a little surprised. She was polishing a very large silver platter that could probably hold an entire cooked ovine or porcine. She stood up looking rather disgusted. "Haven't you ever heard of knocking?"

He gave her an equally disgusted look. "Haven't you ever heard of keeping your Team Leader aware of what you're doing?"

"We're off duty right now. What difference does it make?"

"I should be informed."

"All of us are only one little mental communication away." She smiled.

He sighed and nodded. He looked around the room and was somewhat awed at how much he had seen in the nest that Chyning had filled and yet this room was crammed full as well. It was more organized, however, it still looked like a little too much.

She sniffed. "Would you like a tour…or something?"

"I'm not sure what I want at this time." He frowned. "What…is that over there? Is that just…a pile of…ingots?"

She followed his gaze. "Yes. That used to be…a bunch of idols that the Mustooza worshipped. I couldn't stand the sight of the ugly things staring back at me…but I wanted the gold. So…I melted them down and poured the liquid gold into molds." She gave a triumphant smile. "Now, I have the gold but I don't have to worry about looking at hose weird, pagan atrocities."

He tried to think of something to say, however, any comment seemed anticlimactic about melting the idols down. He simply nodded and looked around. He noticed that there were five very large cabinets that were full of ceramic and crystal figurines of animals and people. He walked over and started looking at some of the animals. "Do you have any idea what any of those beasts are called?"

She shrugged. "We demolished the home planets of those enemies. It probably doesn't matter what they are er…were. They don't exist now. They only exist in myth…or history now."

He snickered. "You could check the archives of some of those extinct enemies. You might find some names for those creatures."

Her face lit up. "That's a good idea. I'll try it. I'll even label them, if I can find a name for them."

He nodded. "I remember…a long time ago…Kiyalee destroyed your truck. Has she ever…found a way to…replace it?"

Bonarain grinned. She got up and headed for the garage. She beckoned him to follow. He followed suspiciously wondering what could possibly be in this garage. She opened the door and had a loving look as she stared into the garage. He approached slowly wondering what could possibly have her so enraptured with pride. He got to the door and peered in.

Parked in the garage was a massive golden carriage that covered with all kinds of red wood and markings. He estimated that it would take at least ten very strong equines to pull the monstrous thing. It could seat at least eight people comfortably in the big plush padded seats.

He swallowed hard. "Are you…ever going to get some equestrian team…to pull that…highly ostentatious thing?"

She looked it over lovingly. "Right now…all I can think

of is…It is *mine!*" She walked along the sides, lovingly caressing some of the ornate lines of the carriage. "It used to belong to one of the High Priests on Mustooza." She giggled. "He doesn't have any more use for it…so it is now mine."

"Usually they displayed their…god. Where's the…main idol that he worshipped?"

She gave him an evil grin. "Where do you think some of those ingots came from?"

He then felt confused. "Those…Mustooza…they couldn't sit down. Where did those seats come from?"

She looked in at the seats. "Kiyalee and I…we built them ourselves. We looked at some of the overstuffed chairs that we have in our bedrooms. We followed that design when we put the seats in."

"Looks like…you did a good job."

"Thanks! It took a while…but it was worth the effort."

He nodded "Have you…like Chyning…filled…all four floors?"

She looked affronted. "Of course! Why waste the space?"

He simply smiled. "I think I'll go see what Kiyalee has."

She chuckled and headed back to continue polishing her gargantuan silver platter.

He left and walked slowly down the hallway to the door of apartment 12-565. He closed his eyes and shook his head wondering how they had obtained all of these treasures and he had been totally unaware. Either they did not tell him or…he was not paying attention when they did.

He decided to be less intrusive. Call her first. "**Kiyalee, this is Soolchakan. Are you in your…treasure apartment**?"

The response came back. "**Yes…why**?"

"**I thought I'd come for a visit. Check and ogle your goodies.**"

"**Sure…come on in. I'm in the garage.**"

He took a deep breath to prepare himself for another apartment full of plunder. He opened the door and walked in. The main room was full of colorful tapestries and paintings. There were a few tables that had smaller paintings set up on them. He looked around even more awed at how they had been able to get away with all of this stuff and still managed to do their assigned duties. He slowly walked to the garage as he glanced at all of the plunder. He looked down at, what he thought was, a rather thick rug. Then he realized that most of the floor was covered with Chok pelts. He rolled his eyes and grunted in disgust.

He walked into the garage and was taken aback. Kiyalee was standing next to a fighter (the configuration of which he had never seen before) and had her finger in some kind of technical manual.

Kiyalee turned to him and smiled. "Hello."

He frowned. "Where…did this come from? What is it? It's too small for a shuttle…but too big for a fighter."

She giggled. "It's a new fighter that the Tashkafa, in 107, had just came up with. As soon as Xadorm found out about it, he had a few dozen…obtained…for us."

He cleared his throat. "Is there…anything special about it?"

She looked up with a big smile. "It flies faster, further, longer…and it has three times the firepower of any of the previous fighters that we've come across…from anybody." She giggled. "Other than our 459 specials."

He nodded as he started walking around the craft. "Are we…going to install any of the 459 cannons on this one…as well?"

"Nope! Don't need it. It has four different kinds of armaments on it. In the nose of the ship…there's a cannon that is…," she looked up thinking. "…according to the physicists… about 80% as effective as our first 459 cannons. There are three other types in the…I guess you'd call them wings…that have different kinds of nasty ways to shoot at your enemy. It all depends on how much power you want to use…when confronting an enemy."

He stared wide-eyes. "Effective? Don't you mean… dangerous?"

She nodded. "You could say that."

He cleared his throat again. "Is there…one of these monsters…for each of us…on Team 7016?"

"Sure!" She went back to her technical manual. "This one

is mine. Chyning has one in 563. Bonarain has one in 564." She looked up. "Yours is in 567."

He smiled helplessly. "Oh…thank you. Why wasn't I… told about these things before?"

She had a confused look on her face. "I thought…you *were* told. Maybe check some of your messages."

"I've kept up to date on my messages. I don't remember… anything about some…new Tashkafa prototype."

She frowned. "Well…you know now."

"Yes…I guess I do." He nervously cleared his throat again. "I think…I'll go check on…my fighter. See how it fits…to sit inside it."

She smiled. "You'll like 567. We decorated it for you. We got some things…that we thought you might like."

"Thank…you. That was…very thoughtful." He sniffed and gave her a wan smile. "I'll see you later."

She smiled and went back to the technical manual.

He left her apartment and continued down the hall. Apartment 567 was the very last one in the hallway. The hall ended at the door. He stopped at the door and stood there for several moments attempting to conjure up some intestinal fortitude in order to prepare himself for…their idea of what he might like. He closed his eyes and opened the door. He took two steps forward and opened his eyes.

The first thing he saw were some marble statues. Twelve

statues of male figures (of different species) in different poses. There were several armoires in the room as well. He walked up to the first one and opened the doors. Inside he found several different types of pulse weapons that had been confiscated from the different enemies. He nodded and went to the next one. More of the same.

The third armoire had antique weapons in it. They were in the shape of weapons, however, no one would ever have used them *as* weapons. A longsword with a golden blade would never be able to stand up to an enemy that had a sword made of steel or iron. It was just a high-priced ceremonial showpiece for some snobbish aristocrat.

The rest of the armoires all had antique, show-piece (rather deadly looking) weaponry as well. Battle-axe, longsword, short sword, dagger, and mace were all well represented and displayed.

He backed away from all of the armoires and then noticed a large table with at least five Chok pelts. He shook his head as he was not really sure how to take that offering.

He looked up, wondering what could possibly be on the second floor…where the bedrooms were located. He headed for the stairs, trying to NOT anticipate what might be there.

The common room had been arranged with a very nice set of furnishings. The three bedrooms (that would have been guest rooms in this case) had some very nice furnishings as well. The master bedroom was fit for a king. There was a huge four poster bed with a plush canopy. He estimated that six people (or forty Zizzikinza) could sleep on that bed comfortably without disturbing anyone else who was sleeping there.

There were four ornate chests of drawers, made of wood that came from who-knows-where, which could hold more clothing than he could possibly wear in a year.

The private bathroom had all gold in it – no porcelain. Bathtub (with shower), toilet, sink and a clothes hamper. All of the towel racks were gold as well. He shook his head and chuckled. The bathtub was large enough for all four of his Team to bathe at the same time – without being crowded.

After staring in awe at all of HIS furnishings he looked up and then headed for the third floor. What could they possibly put in the gymnasium? When he walked in the room, he stood there dumbfounded. Three long banquet tables arranged in a horseshoe. There were twenty-eight chairs along the three tables. He gave each chair a good looking at. Chairs? They were thrones. Each one was very ornate and looked extremely expensive. Some of them did not look comfortable, however, there were others that appeared very comfortable. He could have a very nice party in this room…if he wanted to have one.

He looked up at the ceiling and now was really curious about the fourth floor. He almost ran up there to find out what was there. He looked around and almost wanted to cry. He could remember getting that order, from a *Voice of Power*, where he was commanded to stop drinking alcoholic beverages. Very neatly arranged in this large room were hundreds of cases of all kinds of spirits.

This included his collection of fifty-nine cases of *Golden Age Liquor*…that was now over 3,650 years old. He remembered how mellow it tasted. He remembered how it burned going all the way down. He also remembered that until another *Voice of Power* rescinded the order, he would never be able to touch any of it.

He wondered how long it would be before some of the other Teams got jealous of all of the material possessions of Team 7016 and might start trying to claim some of this wealth for themselves. He wondered if his next enemy was going to be another Owlamite. All of this material possession and now he was wondering if it might get stolen from him. Greed is a vulgar vice.

He just hoped that from now on, he and the rest of the Owlamites could live in peace. He hoped, however, as long as the Teltermak were still alive, peace was a dream. They still had that infuriating and puzzling mystery to try to figure out: Why were the Teltermak so eager to kill everyone else, but want the Owlamites alive?

He sighed wondering when the next war would hit…and what kind of enemy would they be fighting. Maybe, just maybe they had finally put all of the arrogant conquerors out of their misery. So many races here on Hardooth and an unknown number of alien races out there in the cosmos. How long would this peace last?

He went to the third floor and tested each of the thrones for comfort. When he found the one that he considered to be the most comfortable, he sighed, looked up at the ceiling and started contemplating possibilities of and for the future.

Peace and freedom are things that you have to work for constantly. How much more would they have to work for these luxuries?